SUMMER OF SEDUCTION

AUDREY SMOKE—A broken heart sent her seeking solace on the rocky cliffs . . . where her destiny lay in the embrace of a captivating stranger.

BAY LOCKHOLM—He was the richest of the rich, scion of a family steeped in scandal . . . and none more titillating than the mysterious death of his first wife.

ALABASTER McGREGOR—Managing editor of *The Newport Daily Whirl*, his sly eye and wicked pen could make or break any of Newport's elite.

DOVE PEERCE—Reigning queen of Newport society, she wore the best clothes, threw the best parties and kept the best secrets.

THORNE COCKBURN—He jilted Audrey for a Newport debutante on the rebound. He was handsome—and calculating. Was he also capable of murder?

TORY VANVOORST—Beautiful and exotic, she had married the richest man in Newport—but her shady past was a favorite topic of gossip. She saw an ally in Audrey—and decided to show her just what friends were for.

EDMUNDA LOCKHOLM—She roamed the halls of Whale's Turning calling out in vain for her dead daughter-in-law—and vowed to get rid of her son's new wife.

Turning Point

Coming soon from Shannon OCork and Worldwide Library
ICE FALL

Shannon OCork

Turning Point

WORLDWIDE®

TORONTO · NEW YORK · LONDON · PARIS
AMSTERDAM · STOCKHOLM · HAMBURG
ATHENS · MILAN · TOKYO · SYDNEY

TURNING POINT

A Worldwide Library Book/March 1988

ISBN 0-373-97062-5

For the Hill I love to climb

1

AUDREY SMOKE, IN PANTALETS and camisole, lifted her wedding dress. It was like a bouquet in her arms; long, light folds of shiny cotton, camellia white. Her heart beating fast, she tucked her head under the modest flounce at the hem. And suddenly, in a rush of softness, the dress was upon her and whispering down her body.

She spun and faced the cheval glass.

The mirror was good glass, long and oval, set into a pine stand stained the color of hickory wood. Twenty-five years ago, it had been built by her father, Lawrence Smoke, as a wedding gift for his bride, Josephine, who died of pneumonia in the winter of '89–'90. The day in February they buried Audrey's mother in the harbor cemetery, her father carried the mirror into Audrey's room. He was steaming sweat from hours breaking the frozen ground. "From her to you," her father said. "You're the lady of the house now."

Audrey had been fourteen and heartbroken. Josephine Smoke had died just when Audrey realized how much she needed her. Audrey got into the habit, then, of sitting at the foot of her little muslin-sheeted bunk with its faded peony quilt and thinking over her troubles in front of the mirror. With school to go to and rooms to keep and meals to get and clothes to wash and dreams to dream, Audrey would sit before the mirror and talk to her mother, and then listen quietly inside herself for her mother's guidance.

Now, five years later, she still thought of the mirror as her mother's eyes, and she still talked to it.

Afternoon summer sun slanted through the single window. The room was small and the mirror in its corner faced the light. Looking into it, for a moment all Audrey saw was a shimmering of white, as dazzling as the wings of gulls. She was almost beautiful. Tawny hair drifted around eyes so darkly blue they seemed black. Cheeks and full lips were peach-warm in the flush of her face, and her throat was gilded by the pendant Thorne had given her last year, worn only in secret alone in her room. And then the whiteness of a bride began. The thin, white slip of a dress stroked plump breasts, tight waist, lean hips and washed around muscular legs curved from swimming.

The dress should have been satin but cotton was good enough. She had bought the cloth and copied the pattern from a book and sewn it in the nights, inch by inch. In the warmth of June, she shivered at her reflection, her lips mouthing "Mama." She was happy. Yes, of course I am happy, she thought. But she was lonely, too, and very much afraid.

Her reflection shivered back.

And then from below she heard a rapping at the back door. A strong three-beat rapping.

She knew the signal: it was Thorne.

But he couldn't see her now; not in her wedding dress! That would be bad luck. Thorne was not to see her like this until next Saturday in Reverend Camplin's parlor. She would be on her father's arm and her hair would be a tumble of curls, and she would wear a wreath of red roses and white stephanotises and pink-and-white ribbon streamers. And for the first time, as Mrs. Thorne Cockburn, she would wear in public the golden rectangle pendant etched with fine silver lines and embedded with a tiny ruby heart....

And anyway, Thorne was supposed to be working today, schooling the young ladies of Gilt Hill in seamanship, teaching them how to sail in his dark red boat. Whatever was he doing here?

The Smoke house was a simple two-story clapboard on Bridge Street, not far from the harbor. The door in front opened to the first floor and Lawrence Smoke's carpentry shop. The door at the back led to a narrow flight of stairs and the three rooms Audrey and her father shared. A knock at the back door meant a personal call.

Rap, rap, rap.

Audrey pulled the sheet from her bed and threw it over her shoulders, leaned out the window and called down, "Hello!"

He stepped into her view, his head tilted up to her, his face shadowed by the brim of a Panama hat.

She did not understand. He was beautifully dressed, like a gentleman from the hill, when he should have been in painter's pants and a striped swimming shirt. He should have been out in Narragansett Bay being splashed by the slap of whitecaps as he swung *The Rose* around, across the wind. His black Irish curls should have been blowing, misted by the sea, and his naked arms tense with muscles as he steadied a sail. He should have been laughing with the daughters of the rich as they sat before him in cool Indian cotton under ruffled parasols and learned how to daintily duck in a jibe....

But no.

His dark hair was combed and dry and curled around a starched high collar. His sea-bronzed shoulders were subdued in a jacket of yachtsman blue. His long legs were elegant in white linen. There were gold buttons on the jacket breast and a deep gloss on oxblood shoes, and something gold flashed in the silk of a foulard tie. No, she thought, it was not a Wetmore or an Oelrichs he reminded her of. He must be in his wedding clothes. He was dressed as a bridegroom! But it was next week, next Saturday they were to be married—not today....

"Hello," he called up. "I have to see you."

She pulled away from the window. For no reason she could think, her knees were weak. She wrapped the muslin top sheet around her to hide the dress and hurried down the steps in bare feet. She unbolted the door and threw it open. He stepped inside. A hundred words filled her mouth, but when she looked him in the face she stared at him, silent, her eyes wide, and hugged the sheet to her throat.

His eyes were dark. Under dark brows in a golden face they shone beautiful and hot. "Audrey," he said and laid his hands upon her shoulders.

She could not breathe. She opened her mouth to ease the constriction in her chest. "Yes," she said.

"We have to talk. I have something important to tell you."

It was strange; she thought she knew what he was going to say. She thought her mother had whispered it to her as she'd stood before the mirror just a moment ago. But she could not recall what it was. It had something to do with...other women.... Yes, that was it. Brigit Norris, the harness tanner's girl. She'd threatened suicide two years ago when Thorne broke off and began to court Audrey instead. She had gone to Connecticut and married a dairy farmer there. Had Brigit come back...?

"You mustn't look at my dress," she said. "You mustn't see it till next Saturday, it's bad luck if you do. I'll change first, shall I? Then we'll talk."

"I can't stop long," he said. He leaned against the wall. "I won't look at the dress."

"What is it, Thorne? What's the matter? What's happened?" He was so solemn, so formal...so different from usual.

"I feel rotten, you must believe that, Aud." His eyes searched above her face, glanced up the bare wood stairs, rested on a patch of brown wall. "It's so dark here," he said. "So little and so mean."

"'Mean,'" she repeated like a lesson to be learned. "Oh, Thorne, tell me. Whatever's happened, it can't be that bad. We'll fix it.... Oh, has *The Rose* sunk?" And then another thought struck her; drained her of hope. Had a girl gone overboard? Had Thorne drowned a daughter of Ochre Point? She sank onto one of the steps, but kept the sheet pulled around her dress, close, close. "Oh, Thorne, what *is* it?"

"I can't marry you," he said. "I'm marrying someone else, instead. A girl I teach sailing to. A rich girl, immensely rich. Extremely beautiful. I love her very much."

She heard what he said, heard it the way she had heard Sunday sermons when she used to go to the Congregational church with her mother. It is a speech he is giving, she thought, a rehearsed speech. He memorized it on the way over here; thought it up while he dressed so fine, repeated it going down Thames Street.

"How can it be?" she said from the dim of the stairs. "We've been promised to each other for more than a year."

He leaned against the wall with his arms crossed, a foot cocked, his eyes focused on the top stair landing.

"It was sudden," he said. "These things happen. We're marrying quickly, too. In three weeks. You'll find someone else, Aud, someone better for you than I am. You'll be happy, too, someday. I know it's a shock."

She hated the way he was speaking to her, the way a teacher speaks to a child. It is power makes him able to talk that way, she thought. He has the power because he doesn't love me anymore. Perhaps he never did....

He seemed very tall standing over her hunched on the step. In her stomach she could feel the tears, a whirlpool churning, but they couldn't find a way to her eyes. Her hands and feet were winter cold.

She stood. On the first step she was as tall as he was. She extended her hand. "Goodbye then," she said. "Good luck, Thorne."

He took her hand and held it. "I'll miss you, Aud," he said. And then he turned and opened the timbered door and he was gone. And all there was was the door swinging.

She wiped the sweat from his palm on the door as she closed it and reclimbed the stairs. "It's so dark here," he had said. "So little and so mean." She'd never noticed it before....

In her room the sun's rays had fallen below the window. There was no more brilliant beam, no heavenly light.

Audrey dropped the sheet on her bunk and glanced into the mirror. She saw a pretty girl in a new dress, a simple summer dress with a round neck and cap sleeves and a little ruffle around the hem. There was an incongruously beautiful bauble adorning the girl's neck, a glistening rectangle with fine silver lines and a heart-shaped ruby embedded on the left-hand side. She took off the pendant with stiff fingers and wrapped it in a bit of leftover cloth from her almost wedding dress. She held it for a moment, heavy in her hand. And then she put it away, deep in the back of a drawer in the chest Lawrence Smoke had made for her.

"I'll have to tell Father," she said. She put on her sandals and brushed her hair. "I'll have to tell Father I'm staying on awhile."

THE GROUND FLOOR that was Lawrence Smoke's shop was dark; a gas lamp always burned while he worked. The two windows in the front, either side of the door, faced south but slumped too low to ever catch the sun.

Audrey, in the dress she would not be married in, pushed open the stout shop door.

Her father was planing a table leg at his lathe, turning the piece against a belt that cut and sparked. It was a cabriole leg of hard mahogany, dull now in his hands. But by the time it was affixed to its frame, it would shine with a luster famous in Newport: Lawrence Smoke's boiled neat's-foot-and-linseed oil and hand rubbings were the trademarks of his carpentry.

The smell of new sawdust was good in Audrey's nostrils. Warm and fresh. In the doorway she smelled it and paused to watch it drift and spill upon the earthen floor, soft as feathers, warm as sand, a gold-speckled cone of powder at her father's feet. The sawdust reminded her of the father she had known as a child. The artisan she admired, the gentle man she loved. Sometimes that man was with her still.

But in the years since his wife, Josephine, had died, Lawrence Smoke had changed. Once he had worked with joy all day and half the night, worked hour after hour in the dust and low light. After supper, Audrey, a little girl in a hand-me-down frock, would wander down to "Daddy's room." He would talk to her then while he cut and carved and oiled; tell her stories of Newport town, the poor and the rich. She would sit and watch in a little rocker he had made for her, watch his hands move and listen, content to stay forever.... Audrey's chair. It was only simple knotted pine, but Lawrence Smoke had made it well and painted it an airy pink and lacquered it with birds of all colors. Fantasy birds in crimson and purple and yellow, silver beaked, ebony winged. The rocker sat now in Audrey's room, in the corner where the chimney turned, still magical....

But her father was a lesser man. Whatever his wife had given him, without it he had coarsened and toughened. Lawrence Smoke was a fine craftsman, but now he worked silently, without laughter, his mouth pulled down. And now he didn't scrub the oil stains from his hands as he used to do or change his overalls unless he was reminded. Now he stopped his labor at odd hours and visited Grimsby's Tavern on the Long Wharf. Sometimes he stayed away all night, in a room above the tavern with Dolly Dowd who wore her russet hair loose and her bodice low, and pierced her ears with imitation diamonds.

Audrey and her father did not confide as they used to do. She had been going to be married. And Lawrence Smoke had been relieved.

"Father," she said to the strong, gray-haired figure bent over his work.

Lawrence Smoke did not look up. The belt of the lathe spun and spat. "Yes, girl," he said.

"He isn't going to marry me, Father, after all. He's found another. She's very beautiful, he said, very beautiful and very rich...." She would not break. The tears had found the way to her eyes, but she would not let them out. She would dam them, push them back where they had come from, back to the whirlpool in her belly.

The lathe slowed and stopped. Her father turned to her from the depths of the shop. The gas lamp threw his face into deep shadow. "Stay there in the doorway, girl. You look like an angel, surrounded with light."

Don't be kind, she thought. It's kindness hurts the most. Kindness will tear me open....

"I'm sorry, Father," she said.

Lawrence Smoke cleared his throat of wood dust. "I'm happy to have you with me, Audrey girl. An' you'll find another an' a better, soon enough. But I have to tell you—" He started forward. Stopped.

"I been meanin' to tell you..." he said. "I wanted to tell you tonight once I got myself clean." He rubbed his hands on the bib of his jumper. "Don't come in the shop now, you'll get your dress dirty. I'll come out. You wait for me on the street."

She backed out of the doorway and stood on the brick sidewalk of Bridge Street. Westerly in a yellow sky the sun hung huge and orange. The street was tarred gravel. A black-and-white horse in blinkers and a sea captain's hat pulled an empty vegetable truck past the shop.

"Evenin', Audrey," said the man in the seat.

"Evenin'," she said. She watched them go. Mr. Kirchner and Sal. She'd known them all her life.

Lawrence Smoke came out of the shop, oil stained and grimy. "Don't touch me now, Audrey. An' let me say my piece."

She watched the back of Mr. Kirchner's wagon. She was miserable and proud. She didn't want speeches. She wanted embraces. She wanted to lay her head in her mother's lap and howl. She wanted her mother's hands on her forehead, stroking her hair, and her mother's lullaby voice telling her things would be all right. She wanted her father to carve her a toy and her mother to tie a ribbon around it. She wanted her mother to bake strawberry cobbler and her father to laugh and straighten his shoulders and tell her a story about Gilt Hill....

"Yes, Father," she said.

"I was figurin' to tell you, girl, or maybe just have you see for yourself after you got settled. But seein' as you ain't goin' to be goin', I better tell you now."

She waited, wanting to be away, anxious to be alone. She'd walk along the shore to Cliff Walk, climb up to

WaterWalk and see if there were whales far out in the bay. They came, sometimes now, to the mouth of the sound, lured by the schools of sand lances. One or two of them, once in a while. In the old days the whales had kept far away, beyond Nantucket, beyond Cape Cod, because of the boats that hunted them....

Her father was speaking again. "I'm fixin' to bring a woman in to live with me, Audrey. Not to marry—sort of a housekeeper." He stopped and tucked in his chin. "Don't you go thinkin' there's anything wrong, now."

"A housekeeper," she said, not taking it in. "But I won't be going, Father. Thorne won't have me, I just told you. I'll stay and clean and cook. I'll take back my job at the flower shop."

"Nevertheless..." said Lawrence Smoke, and there was an edge in his voice.

"Father—"

"Let me speak, Audrey Alice!" His eyes smoldered, blue eyes like hers, but flecked with gold, the gold sparking like the belt on the lathe. He was still handsome, she realized. He was still virile. At forty-five, he was not an old man. His hair was gray, yes, but it had always been gray, hadn't it? It was still full and wavy, and when he smiled, as long as he smiled, the aching inside her eased.

He was smiling now, but not for her. "I'm bringin' in a woman, girl. You be nice to her."

"Father!"

"So now you know. Be careful what you say."

"Who, Father? What woman?" Her father didn't know, hadn't courted, any woman she knew— "Oh, not that tavern creature!"

He was in control of himself again, he was calm again. Calm and stubborn. "You been listenin' to gossip, Audrey Alice. Dolly ain't no tavern woman. She ain't the lady your mother was, that's so, but she's a good woman who's had a hard life, is all. An' she's a good-lookin' woman an' she suits me."

Whatever did he mean...Dolly Dowd? Dolly Dowd was a whore.

"When will she come, Father?"

Lawrence Smoke swiped at his nose. "As you was gettin' married Saturday next, I told Dolly she could come on in on your wedding night."

"And where will she stay, Father? Where will she sleep?"

He was nervous again. He folded his hands, flexed them back and forth. They were dirty hands, large and splayed and calloused, but Audrey liked them. There was healing in her father's hands, and artistry.

"That wasn't to be none of your business. I was fixin' to put her in your room for a bit. But as you're stayin' on, maybe she'll have to bunk in my room."

"You mean Mother's room, Father? You mean sleep in your bed?"

"Maybe I do mean that."

"Oh, Father, you can't." He didn't, he couldn't, mean that.

"Don't you go tellin' me—"

"Father, it would be a sin! If Mother knew . . ."

Audrey's tears were gone. Now there was a raging in her breast. How dare her father shame her mother and her like this. Now it was her eyes, midnight blue, that smoked and flamed. "We may not be fine and grand like the Belmonts and the Peerces of Gilt Hill, but the Smoke family is a decent, respectable, God-fearing family here in Newport, and I'm not going to let my father, my poor, wayward, lost, woman-missing father shame the memory—"

"All right!" he shouted in her face. "All right! I won't have the sin. I'll marry her on Wednesday. How does that fix your wagon, missy?" He slapped his hands in the air like cymbals, spun on his heel and went back into his shop. Slammed the door.

Audrey, out on the sidewalk, heard the lathe turn and begin to tool the wood.

2

MRS. PERCIVAL PEERCE—Suzanna Reed Peerce, whom everyone called Dove—as the reigning queen of Newport society, had commandeered the crimson silk Louis XIV chaise that looked out, from the lower loggia, upon the east lawn of Whale's Turning. Bayard Lockholm's garden party was in full flower, and from her position she could see, among the assembled guests, her daughter Nicola hand in hand with her betrothed.

Dove shook her head slightly, still in wonderment at it all. To think that her Nicola, Nicola of the uncorseted waist and horse-hardened thighs, Nicola who smelled more of the stable than of Shalimar, Nicola of the unruly frizz of orange hair—good heavens, just *think* of it—had made the catch of the season before it had truly begun. Not only made the catch, but stolen it; snatched Rolf, Lord Pomeroy, the marquess of Denton, right out of the soft arms of Celeste Lockholm, languorous Celeste Lockholm of the wasp waist, elegant head and superb Worth gowns. Wonders would never cease!

Alabaster McGregor lounged beside Dove, sipping a pink gin. He was managing editor of the *Newport Daily Whirl*. More than that, Alabaster McGregor was Newport's society arbiter, it's history maker and scorecard keeper. Lean and tall and bald with white skin and liver spots—and not yet forty—Alabaster McGregor was an old-Newport-family bachelor of imposing demeanor and questionable sexual preference. He was incessantly courted by the nouveau riche and the social climbers, to his delight. Even the established tried to stay on his good side. For Alabaster McGregor could be cruel as well as kindly, and cruel on a whim.

"Power is a mental muscle" was one of his guiding
principles, and he used that muscle from time to time to
keep it toned. He was a dedicated diarist and an energetic
mole into the undergrounds of other people's private lives.
As a monarchy of two, he and Dove were friends. Determined friends. They were of great use to each other.

"Well, it was a scandal, my dear," said Alabaster, following Dove's glance with his own. "Your Nicola took
everyone by surprise. Even you. Admit it."

Dove Peerce stretched nails lacquered in the new red
upon her companion's gray jacket sleeve. Not clawing;
stroking. "I tell you, Ally," she said, "I can't stop singing
for joy. I feel so guilty, though. Poor Percy is in constant,
terrible pain with his insides. Has been ever since Christmas.... Remember the pheasant pâté? 'Unpleasant pheasant,' I think you called it in your column. Well, I know I
should be worrying about my husband, but I can't keep my
feet from dancing. I'm so uplifted. Nicola a bride! Nicola,
my problem Nicola, an English marchioness! And Rolf's
so decidedly nice, don't you think so, too? I'm bewitched.
I'm just in heaven."

"So suddenly. So unexpectedly," Alabaster purred.
"Why the way she did it was almost criminal." He lifted
Dove's talons from his arm and smoothed his trouser crease
with a veiny, liver-spotted hand.

Criminal indeed, thought Dove. Nicola had done it in a
night, in one evening's dinner, and the dinner right here, in
the dining room of Whale's Turning, gilded over with stags'
heads. In May, before season. The first dinner ever in the
great house, two nights after John Bayard Lockholm settled in with his mother and sister...and Rolf Pomeroy. For
Celeste Lockholm had brought Lord Pomeroy with her,
straight from London by way of Saint Moritz; virtually
engaged but not announced.... My God, what a night that
had been.

Celeste's brother, Bay, was just returned from a year
away, traipsing around the world like a gypsy while Whale's
Turning was being completed. Trying to get over the death
of Virginia. He had gone to Africa first and then to Egypt

and then into the East. Alone. His mother, Edmunda, had packed herself and Celeste off to Paris and then to Rome and then to Switzerland. Husband hunting. Title shopping.

And hadn't they found a beauty. Gentle Rolf, Lord Pomeroy, recently bereft of both mother and father and just acceded to his title. He was a wholesome, sporty boy: sunshine and carrot juice, polo and grouse shoots, fox and bush. And skiing, which was where Celeste had found him. He had an angelic face, a bit long in the English manner, blue eyed and full cheeked and red-blond hair as gorgeous as any actress's.

Celeste had fallen for him—snap! like that, and coaxed his interest. He had been shy at first, but he was genuinely fond of Celeste soon enough. And by the time the Lockholm women sailed for England, Lord Pomeroy sailed with them, having invited them to guest at his ancestral home in the English midlands.

In Denton and then in London he squired mother and daughter everywhere. Introduced them to British society. Rolf was in Edward, the Prince of Wales's set; second player on the prince's polo team. The Lockholm women had been presented at court. They'd played croquet with the queen at Balmoral. Dove Peerce envied them that. She would like to be one of the rare who had whacked a ball of Victoria Regina's into the rough.

All the new year into spring the matriarch Lockholm and her daughter, Celeste, stayed at Rolf's London town house. And when they sailed for America on the *Cliffs of Dover*, later than they planned, they brought Lord Pomeroy with them, all but matrimonially declared. Rolf had still not committed himself, Edmunda Lockholm admitted that. And he should have done; it was high time. That was why the Lockholms had come so early into Newport this season: to get settled into Whale's Turning, a year late being finished; to introduce Lord Pomeroy to their friends; and to make the nuptial announcement—once the proposal came—official right away.

To get the thing done, for heaven's sake.

It wouldn't have dragged so if Celeste's father had been alive. He'd have gotten to the crux of it before setting foot in England. Oh, yes. But Edmunda Lockholm was in her sixties and alone. Her husband—"sweet William," she always called him—had died ten years ago last January, slogging up Fifth Avenue in a snowstorm. He had been pulling Edmunda on a sled and singing "It Came upon a Midnight Clear" into the wind. Dove had heard the story many times; it still touched her heart. He had stopped to catch his breath, turned to his wife and collapsed, dead before he hit the snow. Edmunda had never gotten over it. Never would....

But Edmunda—as she should have, Dove decreed—rallied for her children's sake. She wanted Celeste, at twenty-five, fixed in life so she could concentrate on the son. Bayard had been difficult since Virginia died; reclusive and withdrawn. He'd ignored his mother and sister entirely in Europe. Had insisted on being by himself: a dangerous tendency in an only son. Poor Edmunda. She had seen Bay married to a lovely girl, and then the tragedy after only a year. He was a widower now of thirty-six with a fortune of forty million and growing, and he was not yet settled and had not produced a child.

So Edmunda Lockholm, Dove thought, had had her troubles....

And then the next thunderbolt had struck in the person of Dove's Nicola. Of all the girls! Headstrong, unpresentable Nicola. A twenty-four-year-old spinster "out" for six years and nary a beau to show for it.

How many times had Nicola sent her mother to the aspirin with a migraine? Dove smiled, remembering her former despair. Dove herself had been a model of a debutante and all her life a beauty. Though never more so than now. She was, at forty-five, the quintessential lady. Silver-haired—her hair was her exceptional feature, her fashion signature—blue-eyed and flawless of skin and figure, she was always fastidiously groomed, fashionably coiffed and beautifully dressed. And that, as she'd often lectured Nicola, was the least of it. The hard part came with nurturing her charm, ripening her sense of humor and learning the right touch with a party. Now Dove Peerce's parties were the best in Newport; original and witty and fun. Never terrifyingly stodgy like Mrs. Astor's. Never the-same-old-thing like the Benson-Wards'. Never overweeningly ambitious like Tripp and Clarissa Railses'.... Dove had earned fair her "queenship." She had married the right man in Percival Peerce. Affable Percy, with his banking and railroad bonds. She had made the right friends, lived a good life. The only imperfection she hadn't been able to correct had been Nicola, her only child, her ugly-duckling daughter.

And now it seemed that that little cloud had passed...at long last.

Nicola had not meant to do it. All were agreed on that. A husband was never in Nicola's thoughts. She lived and breathed horses and hunting: deep-chested, heavy-haunched Thoroughbreds and keen-nosed hounds. She had no interest in feminine finery or feminine wiles. As an heiress-to-be of upward of seventy million dollars, Nicola might one day be the single richest woman in America. Perhaps the world. Certainly she was rich enough to never marry, and she knew it. Nicola lived her life exactly as she chose, uncorseted and unberibboned. And if men didn't like it, well, said Nicola, to hell with them.

Nor had Rolf meant to be a cad. He and Nicola were as dumbfounded as the rest by what had happened to them. Only happier, of course. Deliriously happier.

There was one shadow.

Alabaster McGregor had been invited that evening, too. Edmunda, as mother triumphant, knew the value of letting Alabaster feel he was in on the start of the news while all was still a guarded secret. She had expected him to break, in an exclusive scoop, the news of the engagement of her daughter, Celeste, and the marquess. The reason for the dinner had been to introduce Rolf to Dove, Newport's unofficial queen. Edmunda Lockholm wanted Dove to be the first, outside the family, to bestow congratulations.

Dove had brought Nicola along that night almost as an afterthought. Anything to get the girl into a dress! Her

husband, Percival, was ill with his colon again and not up
to gallivanting around, he said. Percy's bowels were becoming a serious social problem; Dove had needed a dinner partner. She could have gone in on Alabaster's arm, but
she never did that. That would have broadcast too publicly her and Alabaster's alliance.

Better Edmunda Lockholm with him, even though Mrs.
Lockholm hadn't paired herself off with anybody, really,
since sweet William died and probably never would again,
not having the imagination or the inclination for a second
marriage. Edmunda preferred her status as professional
widow. But for that night, Dove thought, Edmunda Lockholm could sit with Alabaster at table and gossip to her
heart's content; Edmunda was straightlaced—tight as a
corset, to Dove's mind—but she was not above a good
gossip.

Who was?

So Dove had gone to Whale's Turning with Nicola. Nicola pouting and protesting, stomping into a gown of forest green with a deep collar of seed pearls. The dress paled
the freckles on her bosom and emphasized the ivory bloom.
It threw her hair, curled by Dove's own maid, Rosalind,
into flame. Her hands were lotioned and perfumed, the
nails shaped and painted. Dove insisted Nicola wear her
emeralds—a heavy lavaliere necklace and teardrop earrings. So dressed and adorned, Nicola had looked lusty and
pampered and pink. Almost pretty.

But Nicola hadn't noticed or cared. Nicola was simply
Nicola, there was no getting away from that. Her hands
were rough from reining in blooded hunters and as hard as
a working man's. Her figure was robust. Her walk was the
march of a soldier going into battle. And her voice... It was
either full and enthusiastic, when engaged in heated dis-
cussion on how to build wind in a racer or how to prevent
hoof disease, or flat and disinterested, almost grunts, when
asked about something that did not please her, such as a
chat about hats or talk of the landscape painters of the
Hudson River Valley.... No, not for Nicola the niceties of
the drawing room.

But they were in the drawing room when it happened;
their wraps off barely fifteen minutes, one sip of champagne partaken.

Lord Pomeroy, introduced to Nicola, said "How do you
do?"

Nicola, who despised small talk, said, "Well, sir, I'm not
so well. My mare wouldn't cool down after our gallop today. I must have walked her an hour under her sheet before she did. And after her rubdown she sneezed twice. I'm
so mad I could kick."

Lord Pomeroy stared at the girl, buxom and strapping,
orange haired like his mother, so lately ascended to heaven.
He had never known a woman to start a conversation so,
talking his kind of talk. He led Nicola to a love seat of
coral-embossed brocade, already oblivious to anyone else.
Sitting her down, he sat close beside her and held her hand.
He looked into her great brown eyes. "Croup," he said and
inched closer. "It could be croup."

"Oh, poop on croup," said Nicola.

Dove almost fainted there and then. But Alabaster was
watching like a cat, so she swung her attention to Celeste;
Celeste left standing where Lord Pomeroy had been.

Celeste was saying, inanely, to the air, "Oh, Nicola, what
a pretty, pretty dress. I think you're a dream in green. Is it
new?" She went unanswered. Unheard.

Edmunda Lockholm, the matriarch, from her gold-
armed side chair, said, "Do you cool down your own
horses then, my dear?" And was also ignored.

Lord Pomeroy maneuvered even nearer to Nicola. His
knee was brushing the silk of her dress, he was snuggling so
tightly against her. "Well, what is it then?" he said.

"Grass fat," said Nicola.

Celeste paled to white, then flushed pink all over, darker
than the bows on her gray crepe gown.

"Grass fat," said Nicola. "She's gone out of shape over
the winter. Lost her wind doing nothing but grazing. Well,
never again. Once I get her whipped into shape this time, I
won't let her get so far out of condition. It's all my own

fault, you see. That's why I'm so mad. I neglected her for another last fall. For my fine black stallion...."

"You ride stallions, then," breathed Lord Pomeroy, his eyes stars.

"Astride," said Nicola. "Don't you?"

"Astride!" cried Celeste.

"Astride," whispered Rolf, captured for good and all....

And just like that it was done. The whole night no other woman existed for Rolf, Lord Pomeroy, the marquess of Denton. Not his hostess, Mrs. Edmunda Lockholm, not his almost declared Celeste, not the famous Newport beauty, Dove Peerce, in a filmy slip of burgundy.

Dinner had been a horror of four silent guests listening to two fall in love. Just remembering, Dove shuddered: the most incredible conversation! All about horses on lounging ropes, uphill sprints, cross-country trots. Dreary, dreary, stuff. But the lovers so rapt, so thrilled with each other—with every word the other dropped—their tongues galloping together, their eyes locked, both unconscious of anyone else in their newfound happiness.

And Celeste, pale as lettuce, quaffing claret like a club man, unable to eat a thing. And Alabaster, a never-ending pit for wine and roast beef, eyes glittering, filing the news flash—better than he'd hoped, oh yes, *much* better—as he plowed through asparagus soufflé and Yorkshire pudding and silently totted up the column inches.

And Edmunda, poor Edmunda, at the head of the table, at a loss, eyes as wounded as a goat's being led to the slaughterhouse. Eyes fixed like plaster on Rolf at the other end, winged by Celeste to his right, Nicola to his left, turned always to Dove's daughter. Actually showing Celeste the better part of his back! Edmunda, not knowing whatever in the world to do. Trying to keep up the brave front. Apologizing for Bayard not being able to join them. Asking about Percival's "condition." Going on about Nicola's dress—as though that had anything to do with it—over and over. Had it come from the Paris collections, she wanted to know. Certainly it had. Didn't everything? Not waiting for a reply. Rambling on about how she and Celeste had been to the showings, too, in the spring, but they'd been with Rolf, of course. Rolf this, Rolf that. How it had been such a whirlwind.... Such a pity...she was all confused.

And Dove, sitting at Edmunda's right, across from Alabaster, thinking how Edmunda had forgotten, in the panic, her promise to tour Dove through the rooms, the brilliant rooms of Whale's Turning. Dove, lusting to see it all before anyone else. But not asking. Not now, not with her Nicola deep in prime rib and eros....

Dove, conscious throughout the ordeal of the magnificent dining room. Forty-five soaring feet to a curved, vaulted ceiling painted in Renaissance pastels into a mural of the seasons depicted as mythological gods and goddesses. The ceiling itself wreathed in raised gilt ribbon, which looped life-size golden statue-heads of antlered stag and horned boar. The ceiling held up, like Olympus, by towering columns—she counted thirty—of pink Numidian marble; their tops forests of leaves of gold....

Dove, aware of the footmen behind each Venetian-blue chair, the damask dyed to match the heavenly tint of that ceiling. The footmen silent—but later, would they tell? You never knew about other people's servants—each man solicitous of physical needs, unheeding of emotional ones....

No, not Dove's finest hour. Honed all her life to perfection as hostess or guest, she sat in her place as helpless as the rest. Rent in two. Torn to the heart. For once, bewitched by Nicola. For once, a wallflower to her daughter's charms.

And when finally it was over and they rose to take their dessert and coffee in the music room, Celeste took Rolf's arm and smiled at him. A little tipsy, but correct and good-humored. "Rolf, dear, you have captivated my friend Nicola long enough. Will you captivate me a little now?"

Rolf might not have heard. "We've got to go," he said. He meant himself and Nicola! Celeste, aghast, released his arm. Stepped back. Almost stumbled on the hem of her gown. "We've got to check on Rapunzel. If I'm right, we have to get veterinary help right away and quarantine her

from the rest of the horses. It can't wait, I'm afraid....
Fisher, Miss Peerce's wrap...and mine.''

Celeste stared, stunned to immobility.

Edmunda Lockholm stared.

Dove stared.

Alabaster, quicker than they, said, "And mine, too,
Fisher, please. I must see this Rapunzel for myself.''

Rolf shook a fist in solidarity. "Good man," he said.

Alabaster smiled his self-congratulatory smile. "Rolf, my
boy, I'm with you all the way.''

"And I," said Dove, finding her voice, realizing this was
the way out of an impossible situation. She turned to her
hostess. "Edmunda, oh my dear, tomorrow. Tomorrow
we'll have a long tea and talk—''

"I'm coming, too," said Celeste, not giving up without
a fight. Possessively, she took Rolf's arm again. "Whither
thou goest, my darling, you know that.''

Rolf patted Celeste's soft hand. "Righto," he said like a
brother, Cupid's arrow almost visible in his heart.

And then Edmunda was rallying. How proud Dove had
been of her friend, down in the bucket but all grace in
stress. "We'll all go," cried the matriarch. "Fisher, the
horses!''

And go they had. In two coaches. Dove with Nicola and
Rolf. Celeste and Mrs. Lockholm with Alabaster. Rolf ex-
pounding at tiresome length about a boar hunt in the Scot-
tish wildlands, Nicola in blissful, quiet attention.

Dove astonished...stupified....

And then, at Peerce House, the traipsing to the stable.
Dove lifting her gown off the packed-clay floor to save it;
mentally writing off her silken pumps. All of them standing like stable hands around the box stall of a sleepy, thoroughly healthy, handsome bay mare.

Nicola went to change into her jodhpurs. When she returned her father was with her, in pajamas and smoking
jacket and slippers, his face abeam with excitement.

"What's all this, what's all this?" said Percy. "Lord
Pomeroy? Good evening to you, sir. Edmunda. And Celeste, my dear. And Ally McGregor, too. Well, well, what

a party. Come in to the house after. I've got Nevvers up and making toddies."

And then the mare was trotted out, and Rolf looked up her nostrils and into her mouth, examined her gums and tongue, ran his hands along her windpipe. She was clear-eyed and clean nosed and snorting by the time he was done, head up, tail plumed and ready for a midnight canter.

"Want to see her go, Rolf?" said Nicola, already slipping a bit into the animal's mouth.

"Oh no, Nicola," said Dove.

But Rolf said, "You bet."

And Nicola led the mare outside to the mounting steps, stripped her of her blanket and slid onto the glistening naked back. "Come on," she dared him. Then Rolf was up and behind, holding Nicola snugly around the waist.

And they were gone over wet night grass like some great ghost, their laughter flowing behind.

"I've lost him, Mother," said Celeste with only a catch in her voice to mark what it meant to her. "He's found his own."

No one denied the obvious. They stood there in a pool of stable light and looked into the darkness where Nicola and Rolf had disappeared. All knew the couple would have to marry. Riding off like that, unchaperoned, they were both completely compromised. In the silence Dove thought, Yes, that boy has found his own, and Nicola's come into hers. From somewhere deep inside, long buried, she felt a prick of pride....

They waited an hour at Peerce House for Nicola and Rolf to return. The whole damp party. Celeste was quiet and sobered. Edmunda Lockholm was blank eyed. Alabaster was too serene. Percy drank toddies and held a hot water bottle disguised as a pillow on his lap. Dove counted the peach roses in the Aubusson carpet, and then she counted the scarlet ones....

The couple came back engaged. A sixteen-carat square-cut diamond—which must have been intended, that morning, for Celeste—winked on the little finger of Nicola's larger hand.

And so now the happiness.

But then the shadow. For hadn't Celeste, taken home that evening shattered like glass, hadn't Celeste gone out the next noon, the very next noon, onto the waters of Rhode Island Sound with her boating instructor, a harbor Casanova if ever there was one?

She had....

For hours and hours out of the sight of land she had sailed with him alone, twixt heaven and earth suspended.

And then, without a word to her mother or brother, she had caught the last day train to New York, accompanied by the fellow. He was a penniless, no-social-standing-whatever beach boy; less than a house servant. Handsome. A little too much sun and salt for Dove's taste, but handsome.... Celeste had checked them both into the Waldorf—separate suites, but never mind!—and *spent the night incommunicado.*

Shocking.

Then the next morning at Tiffany's she'd bought herself a ring. Worse and worse! She hadn't chintzed about it, either. It was a twenty-carat diamond marquise, mounted in platinum and flanked by two-carat baguettes. A gem for an empress's hand.

And all the while her poor mother, Edmunda, was flat in her bed with the vapors, and her brother, Bayard, was combing Newport high and low with a pistol. The police were alerted, though sworn to secrecy; they suspected she'd been kidnapped and waited for a ransom note. Edmunda was certain it was suicide....

Again....

After Virginia, just last year....

Oh, it was terrible, Dove thought, carefully screening any expression from her face.

And then the next day—just in time for cocktails!—Celeste had sauntered into the grand hall of Whale's Turning, as innocent as applesauce, with the strange man in tow. She waltzed herself up the marble staircase to her mother's bedroom and announced herself engaged! His name was

Thorne Cockburn, pronounced Coburn for decency's sake, but still as Irish and common as peat moss and potatoes.

And there was Alabaster, tarantula Alabaster, watchful in his corner, his liver-spotted fingers dangling in the pages of a book. He'd begged to leave, he said, but had lazed back fast enough, horns and tail hidden, when told by Celeste he could stay. Celeste insisted she wanted him to be among the first to share her happiness. She asked him to bruit the news in his tell-all column, to lead her engagement before Nicola's, if he would be so kind. And Alabaster—anything for the inside story—promised her not only the lead but the headline, a picture and two paragraphs....

Dove sighed. Well, it had gone all right, after all. After Edmunda's tantrum and weeping. After Bayard Lockholm's quiet acceptance of the inevitable. After Dove's pledge to hold all word of Nicola and Rolf until after Celeste's engagement was announced, and her further promise to instantly "take up" Thorne Cockburn as one of society's own.

It had gone all right, so far....

But not without whisperings behind double-hung mahogany doors. Not without murmurings in the Casino over tea.

Dove would be glad when this season, barely begun, was over. Safely over. Percy well. Nicola married. Then all of them, she and Percy and Rolf and Nicola, would be off on an ocean liner bound for London and Victoria Regina's croquet green....

"I wouldn't say it was criminal at all," Dove, who was known for her wit, finally answered Alabaster's gibe. "I'd say it was just the luck of the Irish.... Shall we mix?"

3

IT WAS EARLY EVENING now in Newport, the sun getting ready to set. Gas lamps flamed warm in narrow wooden houses. Martha Whittaker sat crocheting on her porch, waiting for her husband, Wallace, to bring home a bit of his catch. At the corner of Marsh and Third, Mrs. Olsson, working late in her bakery shop, swept crumbs from a worn linoleum floor. Two laughing boys carried a canvas canoe along Thames Street.

And Audrey Smoke, her heart burning, struck out for Cliff Walk, a footpath beaten into the side of the cliffs that soared up from the sound. At the water's edge, Cliff Walk wound around and below the sweeping green lawns of the very rich, but was a free way for every man. Where the bulge of land known as Gilt Hill cut a crescent deep into the sea, Cliff Walk became WaterWalk; higher, more steep, more treacherous, less traveled. Audrey wanted to sit on the rocks of WaterWalk, suspended above the world. There was the best vantage point to overlook the ocean beyond the bay. From WaterWalk she would be able to see the whales far out, blowing and basking in the warmth of a settling sun.

For she had to think what she was going to do. Thorne Cockburn did not want her; her father did not want her. She had left her job at Gardenflowers to become a wife. She had seventy dollars saved. She had graduated high school— she could go away. But no. She wouldn't run like Brigit Norris. And she didn't want to leave. She wanted to stay where she was.

She'd ask for her job back. And she would leave her father's house. Maybe take the second floor flat Mrs. Burrough's had rented to her and Thorne. It was freshly painted and a new stove sat in the sitting room, ready for winter. After all, Thorne was marrying a rich woman, or so he said. He and his bride wouldn't want the chintz curtains Audrey had hung; factory made, cheap cotton. They wouldn't want the low pine bed with its fat straw mattress that seemed so fine to Audrey...so enticing. She had wondered, making up that bed, thinking it her bridal-bed-to-be, what sex would be like. Physical love.

Her mother had told her only that, for women, it took some getting used to, but men liked it more than was seemly. Audrey had been too young when Josephine Smoke died to learn more. Her girlfriend, Katya, though, before she left for California, had told Audrey it was awful; hurtful and humiliating but, mercifully...quick.

Audrey had read in books of melting from a fire inside. Sometimes when Thorne kissed her, she had felt a stirring. She had had wild hopes of much, much more....

It was cooler by the sea.

She shivered in her light, white dress, but her blood was hot from her emotions and the climb; she did not really notice the cold. She felt she could, if she wanted to, plunge from where she stood, high, steep; plunge down into the blue, blue carpet of the sea. She could leap out in a spectacular arcing dive beyond the splash and froth of the whitecaps. She could swim to the hull of that three-sailed sloop anchored down there, wide of the rocks. A yacht, with sides of amber, softly golden, the sails a brilliant yellow. It burned, exotic, in the lowering sun. Audrey strained to read the boat name: *Catbird Seat*.

The air was full of sea salt. She sat on a limestone boulder and breathed deep and sought the whales.

At first all she saw was the lemon-yellow sloop swaying in sapphire waters, which changed, as she looked, into running ribbons of many colors, green and purple and spangled gray. Then she saw other boats and other sails, white sails tinted by the sun into pinks and shadow blues. The boats skimmed with the wind, heading into Newport harbor at the end of day. There were skiffs, too, as close to the water as logs, the color of wave-washed rock. Rowed by poor fishermen, they made their slower way to shore. Beyond them all, far out on the horizon, an ocean liner's funnels bellowed steam as white as clouds.

And then Audrey saw what she was seeking, closer than she had thought to find them. Four humpback whales lazed in the bay. Three floated on the water's surface; a family. They played gracefully in the fading light, flashing the white of underflipper in long, curvaceous slaps. In turns they threw their tails high, flukes like tandem scythes, and sliced the deep without a ripple to show where they'd been. And then they breached, long, black shapes swelling up from calmest underwater, bursting into the air, hanging free-borne, and flinging, as they sky climbed, bubble nets to catch the sand lances.

The fourth logged on the water's edge almost below her feet, a hundred paces down sheer rock face.

Behind Newport Island, the sun was setting, spreading its weight on the rim of the world, throwing long shadows down the cliff side. The lone whale in darkening ocean was great and black and blowing a fine mist that rainbowed round its head. Silent, motionless, it lay. And then it dropped, rippleless, and was gone...though the rainbow lingered.

Audrey sighed. Somewhere inside she felt a kinship with the whales. She knew they were oblivious to all her world but still, just being in her sight, they comforted her.

She turned away and gazed at the great house behind her, tall and arcaded, seaside and wide, of almond-colored stone. It was in the midst of a garden fete. Behind a sea-wall, the minipalace sat like a jewel on green velvet, a jewel built of marble and gold.

On the spreading lawn ladies in diaphanous dresses drifted on the arms of pastel-jacketed men. Couples lounged at white tea tables under lacy umbrellas. Candles under glass burned in candelabrum as tall as Audrey, and colored balloons blossomed in the weeping beech at the porte cochere side of the house. Beneath a lemon-and-gold striped awning, liveried servants served food and drink.

The voices of the rich washed over Audrey in the dusk. There was the laughter of women, little waterfalls. And strong in the laughter, like trout surging, leaped the murmurings of men. There was the tinkle of crystal—of course there would be champagne!—and the quivering trills of a solitary harp.

Audrey stood like an orphan, woebegone and uninvited, and beheld the splendor.

Was this what Thorne had left her for?

Had he really wooed a rich girl in his boat on the breast of the sea; won a rich girl who offered him this paradise as a dowry? While Audrey had worked day and night for pennies, snipping flowers and arranging them in vases for the tables of the rich.... Perhaps her flowers, Audrey's flowers, had graced the place where he proposed, down on one knee, the scent of tea rose in his mouth. Or had he sent a bouquet of camellias, say, the day after their first kiss, and signed on a pale white card, "from a secret admirer"? Even a rich girl would have been thrilled by this, and then one thing had led to another... while Audrey's back was turned.

There was a man on the rocks not far from her. He was in a white suit and polished black shoes. He had light brown hair, and a glass of champagne in his hand, and he was strolling toward her.

Close, she realized he was many years older than she was.

When his eyes met hers, she saw they were gray, blue gray and brooding. His nose was aristocratic, sharp and thin. His hair was tousled by the sea breeze; it fell over his forehead like a boy's. He sauntered down WaterWalk, obviously familiar with it, and sat on the stone where she sat. As she had, he faced away from the house, out to sea.

"I came away for a bit of quiet," he said. His voice was light and dark together. He fiddled in his jacket pocket, brought out a cigar. "Do you mind if I smoke?"

He watched her. He was not smiling and not sullen. He seemed almost indifferent to her reply and yet he waited for it, as though it would sway him.

She stood before him, shivering in her dress.

"I didn't mean to intrude," she said. "I came to see the whales. I live in town, you see. I come here often." She gestured to the party behind the sea wall. "I didn't know there was a party. If I'd known, I wouldn't have come."

"If I could have avoided it, I wouldn't have come, either," he said, bending his head, setting flame to his cigar. He exhaled a few first puffs of smoke. Like lifting fog, they flew away. "But as it's my house and my party, I had to put in an appearance."

She did not know what to say in reply. She knew who he was now. She had heard of him and his family from her childhood; so many tales. He was John Bayard Lockholm, great-grandson of old Captain Lockholm, and the house was called "Whale's Turning."

Whale's Turning was a scandal already in Newport, a legend before it was lived in. John Bayard Lockholm's new wife had died there while the mansion was under construction. Died there, with a baby in her womb. Last June; a suicide. Only married a year, not long back from their honeymoon. She had leaped to her death from a third-floor servants' window. He, a father-to-be, had been in his sailboat, tied in *there*, to the left of them now, at the private dock.

Smoking a cigar, it was said....

Maybe watching the moon....

Helpless, he had seen his wife falling. Too late, he had sprinted across the expanse of lawn, moss black in the night, to her side. Hopeless, he had carried her body to the carriage that waited for her in the curve of the uncompleted driveway. Unknowing of the tragedy seaside, the coachman had been asleep. He said his mistress had told him she would be hours inside, inspecting new furniture stored out of construction's way on the servants' floor.

John Bayard Lockholm had, of course, been desolate. He ordered the great house completed as his wife had planned it. And then he had gone away. Around the world he went, they said. For almost a year he was gone. Now he was back and the summer house was finished, a perfection in Newport. Newly finished . . . and already haunted. Or so it was whispered.

For what, everyone wanted to know, had made Virginia Lockholm, rich, beautiful, *beloved* Virginia Lockholm, who had every reason to live, decide suddenly to die . . . ?

Unconsciously, Audrey had been shivering.

He was shrugging out of his jacket. "Here," he said, "put this on." His shirt was beautiful linen.

Blushing, she slipped her arms into silk-lined sleeves, too long, warm with his body heat. She closed the jacket around her, too large, and hugged herself.

"Thank you," she said. She wondered if she should leave, excuse herself, turn back to town and go . . . where? Instead she said, "My name is Audrey Smoke. My father is the carpenter, Lawrence Smoke. He worked on your house, inside. On the cabinets, I think it was."

John Bayard Lockholm, hair ruffled, shirt trembling with wind like a luffing sail, still looked out to sea. "I know your father's work," he said. "He makes fine daughters, too."

She leaned against the boulder on which he sat and remembered another tale, a story about his great-grandfather, founder of the Lockholm clan and fortune.

Her father had told her, down in the shop, while he oil-swabbed a chest of fine wood.

Old Captain Lockholm had made a prodigious fortune, first in hunting whales and then trading in rum and slaves. He was a pirate and a brigand and a privateer, Lawrence Smoke had said, and he came to a bad end.

For his sins he had been killed at sea.

No one knew for sure who murdered him. Some said it was Abel Larcher, who skippered the *Quicksilver*. Some said it was Margaret, Captain Lockholm's own wife, along, that trip, for the ride; Margaret, heartbroken at her husband's many infidelities. But most said it was a wild black buck whose woman had been stolen away and sold, who hid himself aboard the *Quicksilver*. The black man hung from a spar the next day. The doomed man laid a curse on

Captain Lockholm as he died, or so the story went: cursed the fortune and the progeny. Cursed the name....

"Who was the black man?" Audrey said, and then realized she had spoken her thought out loud. She covered her mouth and stammered to apologize.

John Bayard Lockholm tossed away his cigar, spinning it down the cliff side with a snap of his fingers. "Phineas," he said evenly, as though he had been expecting the question. "Phineas Brown. Although he didn't really have a last name that they knew of. It was given him when he died, for the death record. August 19, 1808, that was, in the year the United States forbade further importation of slaves from Africa. Phineas caught up with the captain in the last black rush."

"I didn't mean to pry," she said, rushing her words in a hurry to explain. "But in town we hear stories about the rich, you up here, and when you told me who you are, I remembered about..." her voice faltered, "about your great-grandfather, the captain...."

"Great-grandfather, yes," he said. "The legend of the Lockholms. Everybody asks about it sooner or later." He gave Audrey a quick half smile. "Some I tell, and some I don't."

He handed her his glass of champagne. It was yellow-white and silver-bubbled. "Drink up, Audrey Smoke. You've just been invited to my party."

She took the glass, trembling, and drank a swallow, then handed it back. "You're not cold and distant as I would have thought," she said.

He chuckled darkly. "Oh, yes, I am," he said. "In general I am not a friendly man. I'm serious and preoccupied and not at all interested in most other people. But you were standing alone and I couldn't resist the lure of you."

The wine was tingly in her throat, warm in her stomach. "You mean you came down here because of me?"

"For you and you alone."

"Not to get away from the party, then?" she persisted. "You wouldn't have come if I hadn't been here?" It was unlike her. Usually she was shy, unsure of herself.

He sipped from the glass and handed it again to her. "Well, not as quickly," he said.

"But there are so many beautiful women over there." She gestured toward the party aglow behind the seawall. "Beautifully dressed and highborn and cultured and very rich. Your sort." She stared at him, at his sea-colored eyes. "You're teasing me."

He was almost, but not quite, smiling.

He is not handsome, she thought. Not exquisitely handsome like Thorne. He is good-looking, and he was sad. He had been hurt, too. . . .

He was saying, "Ah, but I have known those ladies all so long, and you are new and fresh and very mysterious. How old are you, anyway?"

"Nineteen," she said. "And you?" She felt so *bold*.

"Thirty-six," he said. "Too old for you."

She stood away from the rock. She had been impertinent; she had forgotten herself. She sipped again at the champagne. It was flatter now. . . .

"I'm a very old nineteen," she said with a stab at dignity.

"And what do you mean by that?"

And then she was telling him. Babbling how she was wearing now the dress she had planned to be married in. Telling him how Thorne had come an hour ago, or two—a lifetime ago—and told her he was marrying another. A girl he had fallen for while pledged to *her*. A girl immensely rich and very beautiful. They were to be married right away, so she wasn't to hope it wouldn't happen. She wasn't to pray and wait and see. And her father wanted her gone, too, to make room for a woman he could sleep with. A loathsome woman of the night who kissed any man who asked her for the price of a whiskey in her lipstick-stained glass. She had climbed up here to WaterWalk, she said, to clear her head, to see the whales. The whales gave her a measure of peace. They were so grand, so independent, such islands unto themselves. . . .

She told him in a burst, told him everything, recklessly flinging champagne down her throat as she talked, sputtering sometimes in her haste to get the words out.

When she was finished and breathless, John Bayard Lockholm said, "Do you know who's the girl he left you for?"

His face was gray now in the failing light. Alien and faintly threatening. She realized, again too late, what she had done. She had exposed her innermost misery to a stranger, to one of *them*. Of course he, John Bayard Lockholm of the staggering fortune, knew all about it. Knew more than she did. Of course! It must be the talk of Gilt Hill: the heiress and the beach boy. They would be gossiping about it right now, at *his* house, at *his* party, behind the seawall. All Bellevue Avenue and Ocean Drive. And they would be snickering about her, the spurned one. They would be making sport of the town girl in a rag of a wedding dress, dreaming of love on a straw mattress made private by curtains of cheap cotton chintz....

Him, too.

The rich boys did it all the time in season. They called it "slumming." They came into town and flirted with poor girls and raised their hopes—raised their *skirts*, her mother told her—and then they went away. Savage little wolves marauding gullible little lambs....

"No," Audrey said, very small. "Do you?"

He had been turned to her instead of out to sea for some time. But the growing darkness must have veiled her features to him as it did his to her. She would be ghostlike now, vague in outline, indistinct in expression. He could not see the quivering of her mouth, the great lump in her throat, the mist in her eyes.

Please, God, let him not see....

With a wave of a white-shirted arm he signaled to someone behind the wall. "Yes, I do," he said. "The woman Thorne Cockburn is marrying on the thirtieth of June is Celeste Maxwell Lockholm, my sister. This party is more Celeste's announcement than my housewarming.... I've ordered more champagne."

Audrey sank against the rock. There was no stopping her tears now. They flowed down her cheeks, ran into her mouth, spattered the lapels of his jacket, made her nose run. She had never been so humiliated. Never so ashamed.

"Now, now, none of that," he said. "Let's not have any of that. Your former fiancé is an opportunist and my sister is a fool. Let's just hope they are happy together. You'll survive this, little one, and lots more. Come on now, there's a good girl." He thrust a handkerchief into her lap. "The footman's coming. Blow your nose, please. It's the champagne that did it. You're not used to it. Sentimental old champagne, it'll get you every time."

"I shouldn't have told you," she mumbled, smothered in the cambric cloth.

"Well, never mind, you have told me. There's no undoing that. And as I don't care a damn, why should you? Now don't be childish. Buck up. We'll find a way out of this."

She looked up. *We.* He had said *we.*

A footman in a yellow jacket presented a green bottle, silver-labeled, and two glasses on a silver tray.

"Thanks," said John Bayard Lockholm. "Just set it down here on this rock. We'll serve ourselves."

The man lumbered away up the stones.

"Here," he said. A tall, thin glass was in her hand and fizzing under her nose, as obediently she drank. This champagne was very cold. It chilled where she was hot. It stopped her tears. She wiped at her eyes and coughed and sniffled.

"You see," he said. "Hair of the dog. Works wonders."

"Do you think I'm drunk?" And what if I am? she thought.

"Well on your way," he said. "Would you like something to eat? There's lobster up there. Stuffed crab. Cheese, all kinds of cheese. Some kind of spinach pastry. Shall we sit on the seawall?"

She would not sit on the seawall. Behind that wall was a woman in a Paris gown. She would be tall and willow-slender and aristocratic like her brother. Her hair would be

smooth around her head, held in place by an invisible net
that flashed and twinkled as she moved. Behind that wall
was a woman who had written in her diary, "I think he
loves me," as Audrey had. And she had written, "Tonight
he proposed and I accepted him," as Audrey had. And then
she had added, as a postscript, "We plan to be married
right away." Not, as Audrey had put down last year, her
heart racing, "We will both work a year and save, and
when we have enough, Thorne will start up his ferry service, and we will be wed. Thorne is keen for a business of
his own, and he's sure Sea Trains will be a success. We'll
work together for it, very hard, for the business and our
family. How I wish Mother could be here...." The woman
behind the seawall had no need to wait and work and
scrimp. She would be on Thorne's proud arm tonight, in
satin. And she would be shining like the moon....

"Let's stay here," Audrey said. "And let's have some of
everything. Especially the lobster."

"Done," he said. He made a sign, and a man who must
have been watching scuttled over the wall.

"Your mother and your sister are looking for you, sir."

"Don't tell anyone where I am, Fisher. Just bring two
plates for the lady and myself. Two full plates, mostly lobster."

Audrey hugged herself. He wasn't going away. He was
staying with her, he wasn't going to *them*.... He had said
we!

"How wonderful it must be," she said, "to be rich. It's
better than magic, isn't it? It goes with you everywhere."

"Well, in the worldly sense it's better to be rich than
poor, but if you've got enough to do whatever it is you want
to, then you're as well off as anyone can be, I'd say. What
do you want to do, Audrey Smoke?"

Out in the bay the whales were in shadow, or gone away.
The boats were all in port, too dark to see. The men would
be at their suppers, their women content. Far to the right
below, in the harbor, she could see outlines of riggings and
spars because of the tavern lights. Her father would be in a
tavern now, his arm around Dolly Dowd, his mouth wet

and red from her lip rouge. He would be buying two whis-kies, one for him, one for her, his right foot keeping time to a tune....

"I thought I would grow up," she said. "Only that. Be married, raise a family. Work. Try to be good. Now I'm not sure what to do. I could go back to the flower shop. I'm not fit for too much else."

"How would you like to work for me?" he asked. He had his hands in his trouser pockets. He was striding back and forth on the path, his polished shoes scuffing the dirt.

"Work for you? Work as a maid in your house?" She would not do that. Not after standing here with him as a friend. Spilling out her heart. Almost as an equal....

"I own the newspaper in town," he said. "Perhaps I could find you a position there. Nothing big. Assistant to one of the editors—that kind of thing."

The *Daily Whirl*. She, Audrey Smoke, working on the *Newport Daily Whirl*. "It's more than I would dream," she said.

"Can you type?"

"No," she said. "But I can write and do figures. I can plane a board, and I know good wood from bad. I can lis-ten and follow instructions, and I can walk to the ends of the earth and not get tired. I have a lot of energy. Like a workhorse, I go and go and go—"

"Whoa, workhorse," he said.

The plates of food had come. The man, Fisher, brought them in white-gloved hands, maneuvering down the gravel in the dark. He was lighted by two footmen, one before and one behind, carrying tribranched candelabras. The last footman set down his candle holder, spread a cloth on the great rock, and two napkins starched to stand. He set the candelabra on the cloth in the center. Fisher laid the two plates. The footman placed the glasses, refilled them with champagne. Fisher bowed. And then, silently, illuminated by a single candelabra, the butler and the footmen climbed away.

They were alone again. Alone together again in an out-door palace with an ocean at their feet.

"I shall never forget tonight," she said.

The candlelight was reflected in his eyes. "Let's eat," he said. "I'm starved."

So was she.

They stood, leaning against the boulder. Her plate was heaped with lobster under cream, hot and sweet and better, she thought, than anything she'd ever had. She ate with big mouthfuls and a solid silver fork.

He watched her, amused. "You have been deprived," he said.

Her cheeks packed, she wondered, Are the rich, then, never hungry? But she was too happy to care if her table manners were rough, and the food was too good. It was heavenly food.

He ate, too, but his bites were almost impersonal, while she hove to like a dockhand, smiling all the while.

Halfway done, she paused to drink a great draft of champagne. She glanced up WaterWalk, along to the left where the wall broke into steps down to the dock and the sea.

Coming toward them was a vision of billowing white, a drift of pale organza over apricot satin and velvet bows. Yes, she was tall and delicate, very white of skin, very dark of hair. Yes, the hair was lifted in a soft sweep like a halo. And there were flashes in it, a ribbon of diamonds across her forehead, and diamonds in tiers upon her breast. She was floating toward them, with eyes like jet and a face like gauze in the night.

She stood at the edge of the candles' light, and yes, the satin *glowed*.

"Bay," she said. "We want you. Everyone's wondering where you are."

He had seen her coming, too. He extended a hand and said, as though it was the most natural of moments, "Celeste, come and meet Miss Audrey Smoke. She's a native Newporter. Audrey, here is my sister, Celeste."

Audrey did not know what to do, whether to curtsy or run.

She set down the champagne she was holding, thankful her mouth was empty. "Good evening, Miss Lockholm," she said. And then she just stared; words gone, cheeks aflame. She was conscious of how she must look, lost in John Bayard Lockholm's white jacket, the sleeves pushed up in bunches. In a simple handmade frock with no decoration except a little ruffle around the hem. With her blond hair wild and loose and tangled, without a pin in it or a jewel. With simple sandals on bare feet dirty with dust from the cliff side. With no silk stockings, no arched satin shoes....

Celeste Lockholm inclined her head. "Good evening, Miss Smoke." And then to her brother, "Won't you come now, Bay?"

He set his fork down. "Yes, I'll come straightaway. I'll be up in just a moment, I promise."

And Celeste was gone, a glittering cloud floating over the stones, away.

"I must go," he said.

Audrey nodded. Yes, he must go. He must leave her and go back to *them* forever and ever. She would hold this evening in her heart as long as she lived. He had been so kind, so impossibly kind....

It's kindness hurts the most....

"This—this has meant so much to me," she stammered. She was out of his jacket, handing it back. The wind was cool. It rippled through her dress. The candles, which just an instant before had burned calm and straight, smoked in their silver pockets and dripped their wax. Her eyes bored into his face. She wanted to carve his face deep in her memory so she could reproduce it precisely in her dreams....

"I'm sorry to leave you," he said. "But the rest of my party—"

"Oh, please go," she said. "I've monopolized you beyond justice. Please go back. I'm ashamed enough already. I can't hold you more."

He was in the jacket, folding down the collar she'd mussed, shaking out the sleeves she'd wrinkled, buttoning

the lapels she'd tear stained. "I'll send someone down to
escort you home."

"Oh no, don't," she pleaded. "Please don't, no, no. I
know the way. I don't want to leave while you're here with
me. Someone might be watching and it would look so bad.
But once you're beyond the wall I'll be gone. And I want
to be alone. To hold all this inside. To stretch it out, to keep
it while I'm walking home."

"You're a funny little thing," he said. He lifted a lock of
her hair, brushed it behind her shoulder, smoothed it
around the nape of her neck. "Come to the paper on
Monday. If I'm not there, ask for Mr. McGregor."

"Goodbye," she said. "Thank you for this. Thank
you—"

He found a cigar in the jacket breast pocket. He bent and
lighted it from a candle, blew away smoke. "Smoke," he
said, and laughed. "Well, good night, Audrey Smoke." His
heels ground against pebbles as he left her, leaning forward a little in his haste.

She was alone on the clifftop. She snuffed the candles to
hide herself. In the dark she drank off the champagne and
bolted the rest of her food like a thief.

There were spinning lights behind the seawall now. A
pole with long wires of colored lights, the new electricity,
turned like a carousel in the middle of the lawn. There was
an orchestra, playing a waltz. Couples swept around the
giant spinning top, aflutter, aflame in the lights. The skirts
of the women swung back and forth like bells.

Audrey turned and went down, down, down.... From
WaterWalk to Cliff Walk to Bellevue Avenue into town.
Left on Church Street and then right on Thames and so on
to Bridge Street and her father's house. She let herself in
through the timbered door and climbed the stairs.

The rooms were empty, her father somewhere else.

She went into her room and sat on the foot of her bunk
and faced the cheval glass. From the gas lamp outside on
the street there was enough light to see to undress, enough
light to see herself dimly in the mirror.

"Mama," she said in a whisper. "I met the most wonderful man. And he said 'we,' Mama. Once in my lifetime, he said 'we.'"

The mirror was dark, dark. Her never-to-be wedding dress was gray and dark in its depths.

She got up and undressed; hung the frock away. She washed her hands and face and feet in the basin. In the dark she brushed out her hair. In camisole and pantalets, she lay down on the bed.

And then the tears came, wrenching up from her soul. She had lost so much today, a fiancé and a father. But what hurt the worst and made her absolutely wretched was that she had fallen in love with a man on WaterWalk, and in her heart her mother was saying, "Forget him, Audrey, darling, forget him, let it go. His kind is not for you. He won't remember your name tomorrow. He will only break your heart...."

She could still hear his heels grinding against pebbles as he climbed away. And to the sound of that, finally, she fell into a dreamless sleep.

4

AUDREY AWOKE to the sounds of laughter, a strange woman's laughter, low and contralto, husky and mischievous. The sounds were coming from her father's room beyond the partition of her own.

Dolly Dowd.

One of the whores who worked out of Grimsby's Tavern. The fishermen used them, it was said, and during the summer season, the young heirs of Ochre Point and Gilt Hill, inexperienced and hot and desperate to learn. Dolly Dowd, Newport whore, already in the house, already in her mother's bed with her father. Already at home, at her ease. She would be slovenly, of course, ill kempt and lazy at cleaning. She would lie around in gauzy, too-bright petticoats, cheaply laced and brazenly cut away. She would paint her mouth and cheeks, even in the light of day, and she would expect to be waited on. She would carry tales to Lawrence Smoke about Audrey's insolence. She would lick her fingers at table and tell racy stories to make a man laugh....

And in the night she would pant with Audrey's father, do his pleasure, and so own him. She would be in command, and Audrey would have no ally, no home, here which had always been her home. And none of the women on Bridge Street, respectable women all, would acknowledge Audrey ever again while she remained with a fallen Lawrence Smoke and his tavern doxy.

Audrey got up, dressed in the sturdy, yellow-flowered, dark blue cotton frock that was her everyday wear, even on Sundays; that and another brown-and-cream striped dress.

She did not look in the mirror, sure it would be dark and silent.

Her father murmured behind the wall. The bedsprings creaked. Audrey flushed at her thoughts. Could what her father was doing be so important, after all, that he would ruin his name and his daughter's for the pleasure of that used woman's buttocks curved into his belly?

Well, she would not stay. She would make the oatmeal as she always did, leave it on the stove with the lid on to keep in the heat, and she would go straight to Mrs. Burroughs's and ask to take immediate possession of the flat meant, just yesterday, for Mr. and Mrs. Thorne Cockburn, newlyweds, moving in June 15, but the rent paid, just a few days ago, from the first.

The rent was sixteen dollars a month. Audrey earned two dollars a day at Mrs. Maddley's Gardenflowers at the corner of Thames Street and Mill; noon to six, Monday through Saturday. If she worked late she doubled her day's pay. But only in those two golden months of July and August when the rich were summering en masse was there much need for that. More likely, through ten months of the year, Audrey would be sent home for the day or asked to work a half day only and her pay cut accordingly. For in the winter there was rarely a party that required extra hours devoted to handwork. Most days there was no need to trim unsightly leaves from the flower blossoms or to make bouquets, no call for flowers prettily arranged in colored vases, no long-stemmed roses to dethorn, no order for an orchid from Mrs. Maddley's hothouse. In summer, when the rich families were in residence, there were more parties than hydrangeas in Newport, and Newport was famous for its fulsome blue hydrangea heads. But in the winter the flower shop existed mainly for funerals.

Audrey remembered Virginia Lockholm's funeral last June. Virginia Lockholm, bride of John Bayard Lockholm III, widower now, who had stood over Newport on WaterWalk with Audrey last night, given her champagne and lobster and climbed away, heels grinding, over the stones. Virginia Stotesbury Lockholm, twenty-three years old, a year a bride and newly blessed with child. She had flung herself from a third-floor window of Whale's Turn-

ing, while her husband, smoking in the night, stood and
watched from a docked boat. Virginia Lockholm, the suicide.

Audrey had worked on the funeral flowers for five days,
from six in the morning till long after the sun went down.
She had worn red grooves in her fingers twisting thin green
wire around stems of glorious gladioli and masses of lavender wisteria, under leaves of roses in a palette of colors,
white and yellow and pink and crimson and some so deep
a purple they were black, for sorrow, in shadow. Audrey
had plunged flowers into scratchy wicker baskets as big as
tubs, sewn them into gigantic wreaths, woven them into
tall, black-banded crosses. Her fingers bled and throbbed.
She wrapped her hands in flannel—gloves were too coarse
for the fine work—and still the fingers bled and hurt. But
finally Mr. and Mrs. Maddley and she had stood back,
done; proud of their finished handiwork.

Mr. Kirchner, the vegetable man, and Sal, his painted
mare, had carted the flowers, a wagonful piled high, to
Trinity Church on Spring Street. May the Lockholms never
know they had not used a black barouche and a brace of
black Morgans, Mrs. Maddley prayed! It was not far, just
around a corner or two, and Audrey, thrilled, rode on the
wagon seat beside Mr. Kirchner; she in her cotton stripe of
brown-and-cream, he dressed for the occasion in what was
probably his only suit, a once dark blue serge, too shiny.
Mrs. Maddley had put Audrey in charge of setting up the
flowers for the funeral service, and Audrey had been numb
with the honor and frightened at the responsibility.

Until the last possible minute—Mrs. Maddley almost
went "true madly," she said, not knowing—it had been a
delicate question whether Virginia Lockholm's body would
be permitted within the church. But the doctor in the case
at length wrote "accidental" on the death certificate and
not "suicide"—a sin for which the guilty were punished
ever after; not allowed to break a hallowed circle, no min-
istered service held, no consecrated grave—and Virginia
Lockholm's body was freed from open scandal and the
service proceeded as planned.

Once in the church, forsaken by Mr. Kirchner, Audrey had had an attack of nerves. The names on the flower cards, all scripted in flowing black by a calligrapher hired by the Lockholms, stopped Audrey's mind. There were Astors, Belmonts, Berwinds, Oelrichses, Vanderbilts and more, names that ran the nation. To displease one of those with "bad placement" of their floral tribute...! Mrs. Maddley had warned her: keep the flow circular and all to the front.

Audrey stood in the center of Newport's grandest church, alone, under the famous wineglass pulpit. Before her, a bed for eternity: a closed casket of such mahogany brilliance that Lawrence Smoke's oil rubbings could not equal. The Lockholm crest was cut into the casket lid: three waves in chips of tourmaline, blue as the bay, and a platinum sailing ship, the *Quicksilver*.

The casket was borne by a castered table draped in folds of purple velvet that just missed the church floor and made the burial box seem to float on air, like a magician's trick. Surprised to see the coffin in solitude, already in place in the empty church, Audrey had reached out a hand and touched the Lockholm crest with still-wounded fingers, and stroked the velvet, deep as cat's hair, soft as mink.

For one long moment she had stood, petrified, knee-deep in a field of flowers of her own making, surrounded by two heights of the boxed, numbered, cabinet-doored pews of the mighty. And then she went to work, ignoring the name cards, hanging flower baskets from the second-story balcony and flower crosses on the pillars, two tiers of pillars. She stood the shafts of flowers on the flight of steps up to the pulpit, setting their frames back on the stair tread so as not to worry the Reverend Elliott when he ascended to speak. She laid the roses, so many roses, upon the casket's face, roses three bouquet-blankets deep, but kept the platinum-and-tourmaline crest of the Lockholms uncovered, free and visible.

And still there were flowers. Audrey set them on the pew seats, banked them on the church floor around the casket dolly, spread sprays in every corner, dropped baskets from the lights. When she was finished the church was a bower, and the fragrance of the flowers, warmed by the lights, was a perfume.

Two hours she worked in the church, and no one came. No one checked on the girl from the flower shop alone with the body of a woman from Gilt Hill. At the time Audrey thought it was strange, and then went away and forgot Virginia Lockholm.

Later Gardenflowers was complimented on the job they had done by several important families in the town. Even by the elder Mrs. Lockholm herself and the Reverend Elliott. John Bayard Lockholm, new widower, wrote Mr. and Mrs. Maddley a note of appreciation. Mrs. Maddley had been very pleased. She framed the note and nailed it to a wall as an endorsement, and gave Audrey a fifty-dollar bonus.

Now Audrey stood in her father's kitchen and remembered Virginia Lockholm. She wondered what she had been like, the woman Bayard Lockholm had chosen to marry. Had she been very beautiful and full of natural charm but doomed by a melancholy in the soul? Had she tried, night after night, to lose her sadness in his arms, and had he, in embrace after embrace, promised her the world wrapped in gold foil just to see her smile . . . ?

The Smoke kitchen-sitting room was long and narrow. Not a beautiful room. "Little and mean," Thorne had said of Audrey's father's house. "So little and so mean." But there was an east window to let in the morning light, and the furniture and cabinets were well made and handsome, of old pine long scoured white but oil rubbed, oil rubbed time after time for years and years after the scrubbings. Lawrence Smoke's simpler, for-his-own-use carpentry work glowed with a porcelain-vanilla patina that Dove Peerce would have envied. Audrey's father may have used cheap lumber in his home, but he measured with the same care and cut with the same skill and fitted the joints with the same pride, and hand rubbed his own with just as many coats of his Newport-famous oil as dressed the splendid mahoganies and fruit woods of the rich. And Audrey, as her mother had before her, kept the wood well oiled, well polished.

Would Dolly Dowd, in her time, buff Lawrence Smoke's simple pine with the same pleasure, turning the rag, always, in little circles, moving with the grain, applying good pressure to work the oil deep where the heart of the wood was thirsting?

She hated Dolly Dowd.

The small cookstove stood on a floor plate of black tin, wood kindling in a basket beside it. The long table, ringed with six matching armless chairs in the Windsor style, dominated the room; a few black pots hung from nails in nature-weathered beams. The kitchen was undecorated except for a canning jar filled with daisies that Audrey had pulled from the backyard days ago. There was an old horsehair-stuffed armchair in the corner, squeezed against a table that held a gas lamp, where Lawrence Smoke read his newspaper after supper. The kitchen was clean, its pinewood glowed, but it was stark and spare. No curtains at the window. No cat to enliven it; Lawrence Smoke said cats were emissaries of the devil on earth. No bright towels, no pretty tea set. No pictures or samplers on the wall.

What would any woman want with this? Audrey thought. Surely Dolly Dowd had better in her rooms above Grimsby's Tavern. Surely there would be curtains in the window of Dolly Dowd's kitchen, curtains full of flowers, the folds swagged back to catch the sun, which would linger all day long. She would have, charming to behold, tiny clay pots of thyme and chives on the windowsill, or hanging cleverly from the wall above by wire invisible to the eye. She would have room enough for a rocker with ruffled pillows in bright colors. It would be drawn close to a big coal stove, and in her cabinets there would be china plates that matched the cups and saucers. There would be a long-haired cat—its hair redder than Dolly's—to keep mice away, and a braided basket for the cat to sleep in and a blue-rimmed bowl for its cream. Dolly Dowd might even have an ice chest—how Audrey longed for an ice chest—to

keep her milk and butter fresh almost forever if she
wanted. . . .

Audrey made the oatmeal in a hurry, not caring if she
scorched the bottom of the pan. The noises from the bedroom never stopped; the careless, lascivious noises. The
woman's laughter was low and coaxing. Her father's grunts
were disgusting and loud.

Audrey took an apple from a bag and ran down the long
flight of stairs to the timbered door and the street. Shaken.
She had lain in her bed for fourteen years next to her parents' bedroom. She had heard the bed, before, bouncing
sometimes in the night, but she had never heard her mother
make a sound of pleasure or of pain. . . .

Had Virginia Lockholm laughed with pleasure while
John Bayard Lockholm made love to her?

MRS. BURROUGHS WAS shaking her head. She stood in the
doorway of her two-story wooden house, gray blue with
white trim, and said, "But didn't he tell you, dear? He
came on Wednesday and took back the deposit, and on
Friday I gave the rooms over to Mr. Smythe, a gentleman
from Providence. He's up there now, I expect, havin' a cup
o' coffee, settling in. Oh no, dear, ya canna have the rooms
now. Mr. Smythe has rented for the season."

Audrey stood on the porch—she had not been asked in—
and stared at Mrs. Burroughs, soft-bodied Mrs. Burroughs, her dark hair graying around her face. Thorne had
told Mrs. Burroughs Wednesday? But it was just on Saturday, just yesterday morning, when Thorne had come to
her.

He had known then, long before. . . .

Days before. A week? Always? He had known long before. . . . And so had the new one, the beautiful, rich new
one. Even Mrs. Burroughs had known. But Thorne had not
told Audrey, the one he was leaving behind. He had let her
finish the wedding dress and buy the silk stockings, so dear.
He'd let her . . .

While everyone else had known, *long before*, while
everyone else, behind her back, was pitying her. . . .

Thorne had known Friday night when he came to dinner, the deposit taken back and in his pocket. Knowing, he had held her hand under the table and kissed her while they washed the dishes after. Knowing, not telling. The rich one had known—Celeste, named for the heavens. She had known Friday night that Thorne was going one last time to see the one he would be breaking his promise to. Bayard Lockholm had known, and all Gilt Hill.... And Reverend Camplin? Had he known, too, before the rejected bride, that there would be no wedding this Saturday to come, no troth sanctified between Thorne Cockburn and Audrey Smoke, for Thorne Cockburn had found a better? Only Audrey Smoke, finishing the flounce on her wedding dress, happily humming a tune, glancing from time to time into the cheval glass to wink at her mother, only Audrey hadn't known she'd been . . . supplanted.

"But we signed a lease, Mrs. Burroughs. Both of us, we signed the lease. He can't take away my signature, can he? I want to take the apartment myself. I—"

"I'm sure I don' know, dear, but your man, he came and said you wouldn't be needing the rooms, after all. He went up and packed away the things you'd brought by—" Mrs. Burroughs jerked her head "—the box stands there now in the hall. 'Tain't much. He said you'd be by for't, dearie, I'm sure I don' know, had no idea. Were you left in the dark, then? I never figured all that out, how could I? I thought you'd prob'ly found better than mine, and chosen that instead. I could have kept the deposit, you know, I'm legally entitled, but as I can rent the upstairs anytime I want, to nice folk, and as I knew you was gettin' married with not much to spare, I give the money back. Cash money in his hand I put it, and wished him good day."

Audrey straightened her shoulders, willed a smile on her face. She had forgotten this was June and the season was upon Newport; she would not find rooms now. Rents would be exorbitant until October. Tourist rents: full payment required in advance. She and Thorne had been lucky Mrs. Burroughs was willing to rent for the year at a reasonable rate beginning in June. Mrs. Burroughs had hoped they would stay for a couple of years, she'd said, so she wouldn't be bothered with renting again and again, never sure what the tenant would be like....

"The man from Providence," Audrey said. "He's in for the season, you're sure?"

Guile gleamed in Mrs. Burroughs's eyes.

"Well, he paid me for three months and a deposit, too, and even spoke of the possibility of stayin' into autumn. 'I might be here with you a long time, Mrs. Burroughs, it all depends,' he says, very sober, very straight. And then he paid me with a business check from the State Attorney's office. Well, when I saw that I dinna ask him what it all depended on, me not bein' nosy like some, though I have a natural curiosity as much as the next one. But them government checks don' never bounce, I'm here to tell ya, so I pressed no questions that were not strictly business of my own. Tourist rates he paid, flat out, and not a hem or a haw about it. No, you can't have the upstairs. Even if it weren't for him up there, I wouldn't rent to you now, bein' as how you're by yourself. Young girls like you are too unstable. I don' approve of young girls livin' alone. No tellin' what they do from day to day or how they get the rent up, come every first."

She kept shaking her head, twisting her soft fists in her apron pockets. "You come on in here now and take these things away. I don' want them clutterin' up and botherin' in the hall. I done held them for you four days. Try to be kind, people take advantage. My husband tells me that every day. 'No good deed goes unpunished, Marcella. You gotta watch 'em cause people take advantage.' And do you know, Phillip's right as rain on that, though Lord knows I do forget it. Like he voted for Mr. Cleveland the second time. Phillip told me he shouldn'ta. Once they been in and out of ⸺ White House, they'll know what opportunity was lost ⸺he first time. And if they go back to the candy store, they gonna eat one for every three they sell. And weren't he right? Just look what Mr. Cleveland done soon as he got back to Washington, shut the door and unpacked his suitcase. Repealed Sherman's Silver Act. Ha, that was a good

one. Then he shot at the Pullman strikers and stirred up
that Eugene Debs. He'll be the ruination of the country,
you wait and see. Phillip told me. 'Di'nt I tell you so, Marcella,' he says.''

Mrs. Burroughs came out on the porch then and held the
screen door wide. She had little feet and black, polished
high-laced shoes. ''You take your things off with ya now,
and good luck to you. You look a nice-enough young
woman, no reason for you to make trouble for me like
this.''

Audrey went into the hall and picked up the box. It was
a white pasteboard box advertising Jack Daniel's whiskey.
She knew what would be inside: the cabbage-rose kitchen
curtains, two sets of bed linen, the bright blue china, two
towels. And a white satin nightgown, almost see-through,
with a neckline that plunged.

The box was bulky but not very heavy. She walked away
from Mrs. Burroughs toward the Congregational church
and Reverend Camplin.

Along Thames Street and Spring Street, Newport was
going to church. It was a sunny, cool Sunday and the horse-
drawn carriages, black and brass, shone against blue sky
and green water. The horses pranced in their traces. The
dresses of the ladies from Bellevue Avenue spilled from the
broughams like treasure from a sultan's coffers. Audrey
always liked Sundays, liked to walk on the sidewalks admiring the splendid displays of the rich. She knew she
would not be noticed, her admiration no different from all
the others who lived in Newport town year-round and
worked for their living.

But now, suddenly, she was self-conscious and ashamed.
Thorne Cockburn could be in one of those fine buggies,
snug in a corner upholstered in glove leather the color of
sun-bleached bone. He would be watching the passing view
through a pane of etched oval glass. Audrey would not be
able to identify him; he would be only a pair of storm-dark
eyes framed like a stranger's portrait. But he would see her,
miserable in her two-year-old cotton dress, tramping the
main streets of Newport like a transient, toting away her

marriage dowry, "so little and so mean," in the box he had dumped their future in.

Beside Thorne would be The New One, resplendent in sweeping taffeta, her skirt intimately overflowing his lap like a golden caress. They would be holding hands beneath the stiff folds of what was one of a hundred gowns. And Thorne, so happy, would see Audrey sweating and struggling, awkward with the box, trying to cross the street, her hair limp, her frock less than ordinary, a sullen expression on her face. He would point and say, "Look, Celeste, my angel, there she is now—the woman, but for you, I would have had to marry."

And Celeste Lockholm would stretch a little from perfect shoulders and look through the glass where Thorne pointed, and behold a wretched girl of no distinction. She would laugh a little and sigh and snuggle against Thorne's now-well-clad chest. Her brother would be in the carriage seat opposite. She would tilt her head prettily at him and say, "Why, Bay, isn't that the town girl you were talking with last night on WaterWalk? The one who ate so much and so fast and became quite drunken on champagne?"

Without interest, John Bayard Lockholm would glance through his own oval window at the stumbling, head-down girl. Then he would look away quickly and flick a bit of road dust from his sleeve. He would murmur, "If so, I don't remember," displeased at Celeste's reminding him. His mother, having taken her own long look, would sit back in her place with a whoosh and fan herself archly with ostrich feathers, and exclaim, "Well, I should hope not!" And then the Lockholm barouche would have passed Audrey by, and they would, all together, talk of other, more pleasant things. Thorne would be careful never to allude to Audrey Smoke again; the subject, with the turn of a carriage wheel, now a dead one....

THE REVEREND CAMPLIN, assistant minister, stood outside on the church steps after service, talking to his flock. Audrey waited under a hickory tree, the box at her feet. She wanted the sweat off her face and her heart quiet before she approached him. But he spied her and came, cheerful, across the lawn, trailing womenfolk, and caught her hands.

"Ah, the bride!" Reverend Camplin said in his flat, deep voice. The women of the Congregational church surrounded him and her, and tittered. Someone behind Audrey squeezed the back of her arm. "And where's your fine young man?"

The Reverend Camplin was young, too, only a semester out of the seminary and off the farm, and still stout from plowing fields. He had not gone soft yet from sitting in the rectory composing sermons; his complexion had not yet sallowed from its years of darkening under an unshaded sun. His cheeks were plump but hard; they sat on either side of his nose like muscles, and flexed when he smiled. His mustache was small and brown and shiny with pomade to make it lie flat on his lip instead of bristling out. The mustache, he thought, gave a bit of deliberation to his face. But it was his eyes that were his best feature. They were sad and serious, older than they should have been and wiser than his exuberant manner. The Congregationalist women of Newport liked him. His voice was a comforting baritone, he came into their kitchens and ate with gusto, he took in all their chatter with a benevolent silence and smiled at the end rather than preached. The men liked him, too; he was essentially one of them, a simple man of no grace or social pretensions, a practical man used to hard labor. He was a man who knew what it was like to be, after a day's work, too exhausted to eat and then again too hungry to go to bed.

Audrey liked him as much as the rest, but right now she hated him because he did not know that she was no bride-to-be but a woman who had been spurned, and she would have to tell him now, before a gaggle of women if she could not draw him off.

"Could I speak with you, sir, in private?"

Mrs. Olsson, who owned the bake shop, said, "Her cake will have swans, egg-white and sugar swans with white ribbons round their necks. She designed it herself."

The women oohed, and whoever it was behind Audrey's back pinched her again in excitement.

"It's taking me hours," said Mrs. Olsson, "but it'll be worth it."

"Sir—" said Audrey. She heard the pleading in her voice and despised herself.

"Yes, yes," said Reverend Camplin, agreeable as virtue. "Excuse us, ladies."

He walked Audrey a little distance away on the green grass, but not far enough to suit her; she could still hear Mrs. Olsson describing the once-upon-a-time wedding cake. Only two tiers, she was saying, but set on blue glass to simulate the waters of Newport....

"There's not to be a wedding, Reverend, after all. My man has decided against me. He—he's found another, you see...." She could feel her eyes swimming in tears and stamped her foot to give herself backbone. It helped. She forced herself on, raised her chin and met his eyes. "I'll send a donation to the church for the inconvenience. I'm sorry to be so late telling you, but today was my first opportunity."

Reverend Camplin was quiet. He took one of her trembling hands between his two and rubbed it. His hands were large and warm and steady as rocks. "When did you find out, Audrey dear?"

"Yesterday, Reverend."

A woman was coming toward them, coming purposefully, a woman Audrey didn't know. The woman was dressed in blue-and-gold stripes, very loud, with a great flopping blue bonnet, the brim dipping under the weight of artificial fruit. The woman was tall and buxom, and her gold-fringed earrings swayed as she came. She was handsome, with high color and hair the shade of sun-dappled autumn, thick and curling. Her shawl was mottled watersilk, deep blue, which flashed and glittered as she moved.

"But all day yesterday I was in such a shock—"

The woman was pulling a man behind her by the hand, a man almost lost behind the woman's hips. The man was tall and thin, and stooped a little from a lifetime of bending over his work. His hair was gray, full and wavy. He was wearing his good gray suit and a new shirt and a tie Audrey had never seen before. A red tie, bright as passion. And he was smiling in the old way, in a way Audrey hadn't seen him smile since her mother had died. She recognized her father and saw, with a start, that Lawrence Smoke was again a proud and happy man.

"Yes, of course," Reverend Camplin was saying. "I'm in shock myself. I can't imagine a better girl in Newport nor a prettier. Which of our town lasses does your young man prefer to you?"

Audrey shook her head. Thorne had not told her the name of Celeste Lockholm. She would not pass on what she did not know for certain. "It doesn't matter to me who, Reverend, it's just that I have to tell you there won't be the wedding next Saturday, after all—"

That woman with her father, that overdressed, overbearing woman, must be Dolly Dowd!

Audrey had not thought of her father's whore as being majestic, as this woman was, for all her vulgar finery. Audrey had envisioned Dolly Dowd as small and mewling, an old cat still kittenish and devious; an aging sexpot, with bleached hair thinning at the crown and wrinkles between her breasts. This woman was plump enough to be firm skinned at fifty, and though she would not see thirty again, she was not yet the other side of forty. This woman was still able to bear children; in the prime of her life. This woman looked as though she knew how to get a day's work done and how to laugh while she did it. This woman could get a man to scrub the wood oil out from under his fingernails and make him like it.... This woman was dangerous.

"Ah, then," said Reverend Camplin, but Audrey hardly heard. She was watching the great ship Dolly Dowd as she breasted upon them, Lawrence Smoke in her wake.

The Reverend Camplin was oblivious to the coming collision, all concern for his charge. He took Audrey's other hand and briskly rubbed it between his stone-broad palms. "You've had a tiff, that's all," said the reverend. "Your man has a little bit of cold feet, you got your feelings hurt—''

"No, Reverend, no."

Dolly Dowd and Lawrence Smoke were almost upon them. They had been spotted by the good women of Newport's First Congregational Church and, led by Mrs. Olsson, the women were closing in on Audrey and the reverend from the other side.

Do they mean to protect me, Audrey wondered, or to spread my shame? Must she tell, then, under a midday turquoise sky not only the Reverend Camplin, but everyone she knew in Newport and some she didn't, and even her father's tavern woman?

There was a thick lump in her throat, but she got around it. She forced it down with a hard swallow and then sent it plummeting with a great inhale of air. "Thorne's marrying the other one, sir, in three weeks," she said. Her voice was steady. "It's absolutely settled. I'd hoped he'd tell you we'd changed our plans to save me this embarrassment, but he probably didn't think of it. It's me, after all, who's responsible, I guess: I'm the one who made the church arrangements."

"Yes, yes," said Reverend Camplin, "so much falls on the woman. It's God's way." He blinked, serious and sad. He still held one of Audrey's hands quiet within his own.

And then Audrey's father took Reverend Camplin by the arm. "Revern," said Lawrence Smoke. "I'd like you to meet my intended. An' you, too, Daughter."

The woman was behind him, panting slightly from her march. Close, she was even more handsome, more flashy. Despite the makeup, her skin was good. Despite the flamboyant colors, her dress was of good make. Despite her occupation, her carriage was proud. Her perfume was expensive, but too strong. It filled Audrey's nose like incense and made her, for a moment, dizzy and unsure.

The woman towered over her, and Audrey swayed in her shadow.

The Reverend Camplin was confused.

He glanced up from Audrey; took in, with surprise, the bevy of women suddenly surrounding him, Audrey's sheet-white face and Lawrence Smoke's vicelike grip on his forearm. But the Reverend Camplin was a careful man of no undue haste. He waited for enlightenment.

"I'm this one's father," said Lawrence Smoke with that edge in his voice Audrey had heard more and more often in the years since Josephine died.

Reverend Camplin cleared his throat, took his hands from Audrey's and his arm from Lawrence Smoke. "I know you, Lawrence," he began benignly. "I miss you at services now. Have you changed your religious affiliation or have I— "

Lawrence Smoke interrupted. "Revern, without a missus I ain't much of a churchgoin' man, but I'm aimin' to marry again, an' here she is."

He edged the woman ahead of him. She gave a little curtsy and the fringe on her earrings danced. She stood eye to eye with the reverend, as tall as he was, and seeing her, handsome, openmouthed and panting slightly, involuntarily the Reverend Camplin smiled.

"Her name's Dolores Dowd," said Lawrence Smoke, "but everbody just calls her Dolly, an' you can do the same. She lives on the Long Wharf, over Grimsby's Tavern, for now."

"Mornin', Revern," said the woman in blue and gold. "Sure is a nice day, ain't it? Soon be warm enough for swimmin'."

The churchgoing women murmured; everyone in Newport knew about the women who roomed over Grimsby's Tavern. Mildred Falk, who had never married despite three engagements, sounded a startled exclamation, but covered herself by pulling loose her bonnet bow and then retying it with flustered fingers.

Audrey stood obstinately silent.

"Hello, Audrey," the woman said to her. "My, you're even prettier than your daddy claimed. It's good to meet you at last. I been a-wantin' to." She was smiling. Her voice was friendly. She seemed unconscious that she was a living scandal and that it was inappropriate for her to be on church ground at all, much less greeting a young woman who was ignorant of the ways of sin in which she specialized.

"Miss Dowd," Audrey mumbled to her toes.

Lawrence Smoke sensed the hostility around him. He felt hostile in return.

"This one makin' trouble for me, Revern, is that it? Talkin' against Dolly? Well, pay her no mind. It's her mother she's protectin'."

Reverend Camplin said, "Your daughter's no trouble, Lawrence, nor ever gave any, I should think. We were simply talking over her wedding plans."

"But she ain't gettin' married, didn't she tell you? He is, but she ain't. He lassoed himself a fine filly from the hill and he's gone, kickin' up his heels."

A loud gasp from Mrs. Olsson. A flutter of indignation from the crowd.

Reverend Camplin tried for calm, but lost.

Mrs. Olsson swung herself toward Audrey. "But I've started the cake already. I'll have to be paid...."

"I'll take the weddin' cake," said Dolly Dowd.

"An' we'll take her weddin' hour, Revern," said Lawrence Smoke.

Mildred Falk who, it was whispered, had been left virtually at the altar three times by different men, collapsed in a billow of starched brown gabardine.

Someone behind Audrey wailed. Out in the street a dog bayed in answer.

Audrey pushed out of the circle of women, hoisted the box advertising Jack Daniel's whiskey with a heave, and ran, as best she could, she knew not where.

She pushed through the families coming or going to church, shined and pressed. Stormed past little girls, skipping and coy, in wide-skirted dresses over tiered eyelet petticoats. Hurled herself around father-restrained boys scuffing their shoe tops, wanting to run. Waiting for nothing and no one, she dodged carriages and horses in the streets. Let anyone see her who did, she didn't care a *damn*

anymore. On fire, she surged into the heart of the town.
Aimless, she thought. But she came at last, as though by
design, to Gardenflowers and the Maddley flat above.

Mrs. Maddley was in the shop alone. She often was, on
Sunday mornings. Herman liked to sleep late then and sales
were generally small and light, a few tulips to grace a dining table to a woman with guests unexpectedly coming for
the day or a hand bouquet to an embarrassed male to be
presented, in splendor, to the lady of his choice before
walking her to church.

Audrey opened the glass-paned door with a rush. Set
down the burdensome box. Ran her hands over her gone-
wild hair to smooth it.

"Mrs. Maddley, it's me."

Rosemary Maddley was watering ivy pots hung high. Her
long, full sleeves, navy-dotted swiss, draped daintily from
gathered cuffs. She looked at Audrey through black-
rimmed glasses; seemed startled to see her.

"Audrey, dear, you look a sight. Well, I don't wonder."

Mrs. Maddley was older than she cared to be by fifteen
years, but she was very pretty and chic for a shop woman,
more stylish than most of the matrons of Newport who
worked with their husbands at trade. Nearly all the other
female proprietors Audrey knew—husbanded or widowed, prosperous, hardworking, mature—neglected their
feminine charm of person for the beatitudes of motherli-
ness, good cooking and hard common sense. Either their
waists spread and their hips pillowed, or their bodies
shriveled to crepey skin and bone.

Audrey admired Mrs. Maddley for her fashion sense and
her social acumen: she knew all the grand ladies of Bellevue Avenue and Ochre Point; knew their winter addresses
in New York City, the names of their children and what
their husbands did—or didn't do—to merit their fortunes.
Audrey had once aspired to be like Mrs. Maddley when she,
in her turn, would work in business with Thorne. Rosemary Maddley was not richly gowned, her clothes were
durable wools and cottons and she cared for them herself.
She was quick with a needle, had her own dry-cleaning

chemicals, and did not begrudge a few nickels more a yard for a better cut of cloth. Her dresses were smart, well fitting, of good fabric and long-lived. Her body was trim and her grooming absolute. She had, through familiarity with their ways and likes, taken on some of the airs of her better clientele, but she was not arch or pretentious in Audrey's eyes, though she had been called so by some of her less-modish compatriots. Rosemary Maddley was, rather, simply and keenly aware of the values of the rich and attuned to those values for herself, her shop and her produce.

In the three years that Gardenflowers had been in Newport, the Maddleys had taken for their portion nearly ninety percent of the "bought flower" business of the rich, though the year-round, working Newporter continued to prefer Wicke's Wreaths and Flowers for Every Occasion, which specialized in reasonable, if unimaginative, funeral baskets and dried-flower bouquets, which, Wicke's exclaimed from a sign in their window, Last Forever... They Never Die.

"Mrs. Maddley, I'd like my job back if it's still open. Is it?" What had Mrs. Maddley said just a moment before?

Rosemary Maddley put down the watering can. She removed her gardening gloves as though they were doe skin. She patted the fingers together and laid the gloves on her desk.

"Mrs. Maddley. The job's been taken, then?" Her former employer seemed distant and unwelcoming. Well, I did give in my notice a month ago, Audrey thought. I've been replaced, that's all, and there's the end of it.

Mrs. Maddley leaned against her desk, folded her hands in her lap. She sighed and reformed the dark curl over her right ear. "Your job is still open to you, Audrey, if you're sure you want it."

"Whatever do you mean, Mrs. Maddley? Of course I want it. I've run all the way to you on Sunday."

"Yes, I can see that, dear, but you don't know yet what the job entails now."

"Am I to be punished for giving notice?" Audrey didn't understand. "Will you put me to swabbing the floor and carrying out the refuse? Well, so be it, Mrs. Maddley. I need my job again."

"No, Audrey, no. Of course not. Don't be silly."

Mrs. Maddley picked up a sheet of paper from her desk, one of the pink order sheets. She began to read from it.

"For the wedding of Miss Celeste Maxwell Lockholm to Thorne Larcher Cockburn, taking place at Trinity Church on Sunday, June 30, at 4:00 p.m., one thousand white roses, dethorned, with hand-gilded stems. Five hundred pink roses, the same. Three hundred white satin baskets, small, with two tea roses each, bow tied with pink-and-white satin ribbon, to be hung from the trees of the reception lawn at Whale's Turning, Gilt Hill—"

Audrey sank onto one of Mrs. Maddley's two white wrought-iron chairs. "I see," she said.

"I'm sorry, darling. I know how it would hurt you, and I can't tell you how truly sorry I am, but if you come back, and God knows Herman and I can use you—overuse you, this is going to be such a season!—you'll be working on his wedding to her. I welcome you back with open arms, but I can't think how you'd bring your best attitude to this work. I've hired two girls already and one divine young man, but I can use you, too, all the time you can give me. First tell me what you say, and then tell me what happened. You must be devastated, of course, that goes without saying. He is such a handsome man, and so enterprising, I could tell that from the—"

Audrey stood, picked up the pasteboard box, and walked out the open door.

Rosemary Maddley spiked the pink sheet with its expensive, large-profit order on a iron spindle. "I knew she'd do that," she said to her ivy plants. "And good for her."

After that Audrey walked. Unconsciously she headed toward the wharves, her mind blank, her arms tired, but her feet feeling ready to walk forever. She stopped only when the land did; she ended where the waters of Narragansett

Bay tossed and sighed and strew foaming bubbles on the shore.

And still she walked. The piers were crowded with boat-owning Newporters, working men taking their children for a row, young men taking their ladies for a sail. And far-ther out, the rich, sipping champagne on their yachts, pre-paring to lunch.

Finally she came to a deserted stretch of beach at the water's edge. She set down her burden. She opened the box that advertised whiskey and pulled out the little things of which she had been, in an age long past, so fiercely proud. She rolled the cabbage-rose curtains and the flatwear in one towel, the satin nightdress in the other.

And then, stooping, she smashed the blue willow china, piece by piece, upon the rocks and loosed the fragments, like seashells, to the sea.

5

OUTWARDLY AS PEACEFUL as her namesake, Dove Peerce sat in silk in ascending shades of lemon yellow through cream, in the family pew of Trinity Church, Percy on her left, Nicola and Rolf on her right; impatient for luncheon.

Not for the food. Long ago Dove had sentenced herself to a life of vegetables, thin soups and white meat; though occasionally hungry, she rarely had an appetite.

No, not for the food. For the gossip.

She wondered if Graf Elliott had chosen his sermon this Sunday to please her. He was not above it—he had a male's weakness of wanting to be admired, and under his surplice was the devil's own mischief.

Whichever, she wished he would hurry and finish.

Oh, it was all right, his talk of miracles and weddings, and decidedly timely. But the Reverend Elliott was prone, even on happy topics, to dwell on life's darker aspects.

Now, for instance, he was warning those shortly to be wed, "cleaved in HOLY matrimony," of what a "MIRACLE a happy marriage was beyond the conjugal BED." As though all marriages were happy there at least, Dove thought, and smiled, and patted Percy's knee. Percy had never been a thrill in the bedroom, and these days Percy was a total bust. Well, it didn't matter. Not now. Not anymore. And it never would again.... The reverend went on, warning of the need for patience with each other. And compromise. And "a CHRIST-like forgiveness."

The Reverend Elliott had a booming voice that he flung carelessly around the rafters like bunting and rolled along the church aisles like a careering croquet ball. And yet while he exhorted his congregation to virtue, he lingered, as though talking to Dove alone, on the pleasures of the flesh.

He was tremendously admired among Newporters for his knowledge of church doctrine, but Dove, who kept her own counsel and knew a thing or two, thought him the worst kind of hypocrite. Not that she objected to that. Better a beloved pastor than a defrocked one. But hearing him thump so solidly for goodness was a little odd, he who yesterday afternoon had lain naked on her belly, afire.

Still it was a lovely story: Christ as guest at a wedding in Cana and his first public miracle a wedding gift. An original idea entirely, transforming that well water into wine. Perhaps Dove could do the same....

Why yes, it would be stunning. Full of the most perfect religious symbolism and so very, very pretty. And she wouldn't have to worry about the punch bowls then, which, no matter how big they were, were never big enough. And they were heavy and clumsy for the servants to manage, and they always *slopped*. And all those cups hanging from the rims by their handles was just boring. Yes, she would change the water in the marble fountain at the head of the driveway. It would only mean disconnecting and rerunning a pipe or two. No trouble at all.

She meant no disrespect, but it was too bad Christ couldn't have managed champagne. She could. A pink champagne, New York domestic, would do since she'd be ordering buckets, cascading it unendingly from the Greek god's mouth. Up in the hall where the guests would start, moving through the house on their way outside, she would serve the fine stock. In crystal shafts as delicate as new ice. A yellow French brut kept teeth-tingling cold....

A champagne waterfall would keep the guests moving, too. Keep them from huddling like frogs on the rear lawn that opened upon the ocean side. She'd festoon the fountain in an umbrella of pink and silver lights. In the afternoon they would wink like silent firecrackers, and when the sun went down they would flash like dazzle from a magic wand.

Of course, to give Christ his due, he couldn't have done the fizzy. It would have been too mischievous—champagne wasn't invented until the seventeenth century; a monk discovered the proper how-to in a little monastery in France. The Catholics should make Dom Perignon a saint.

To hurry the time Dove tried to think of the bridesmaids' gowns, but it was no use. Graf was booming now about infidelity....

"There's a serpent in EVERY MAN'S paradise, and the serpent in wedlock's garden is sinuous and black indeed. The unholy fruit it proffers are EVER UNEXPECTED and always new. It slithers from under its rock-bed of human frailty toward sudden sin, noon or midnight. It coils and dances, mesmerizing. To ALL this serpent comes, to all, sometime, it lures and beckons. Be warned, you about to wed, all bliss, of this GRAND MONSTER. His temptations seem delectable but they are only detestation. Once taken, they are ruinous...."

Her left eye twitched. Dove put a gloved finger on the lid to stop the muscle jumping and glanced over at Bay Lockholm to see how he was taking the shaking of a finger in the face.

No reaction. Nothing.

But then there never was with Bay. Yet whispers about him and Tory VanVoorst, before she *was* Tory VanVoorst, while she was still clever Miss Tory June, show girl—a stripper is what she was, dead set on marrying cream— whispers about Bay and Tory were drifting through the drawing rooms of better Newport. It was being said that Bay and Virginia had had a ghastly quarrel the night she died; that he had stormed from her in anger and sailed himself to some shoreside spot where torrid little Tory was *performing*, and dined with her, all laughter and smiles.

Under her finger the eye twitched again.

With a lift of her chin Dove could see the VanVoorsts, in an upper tier box pew. The woman was a beauty. A spectacular beauty. Gorgeous black hair, that enviable Spanish complexion of almond tint that glowed, inner oiled, even in winter and never ever wrinkled, a perfect high-boned face. And she dressed herself like a dream; she really had exquisite taste in clothes. But her body was all courtesan: the breasts too round, the waist too fragile, the hips too perfectly scythelike, the legs too...developed. Exercise did it, Dove supposed. Pliés and barre exercises an hour a day with not even Christmas off, and practicing the shimmy while she took off her clothes night after night for years.

Dove turned her head away.

Well, she was Victoria VanVoorst now, married to Burton, who rivaled Percy in riches. Dove thought back. Yes, Burton married the minx not long after Bay went off for his year abroad after burying Virginia. Of course, Dove didn't remember exactly when Burton succumbed to the woman. The VanVoorts were new-rich; not in Dove's set.

The Reverend Elliott had moved now from marital sinning to the blessings of parenthood. A safer ground.

Dove thought again of bridesmaids' gowns. She and Nicola had been having a tiff about them. Dove thought the young women to accompany Nicola down the aisle should be like tropical birds, in brilliant turquoise under flowing coral-and-white chiffons, with head feathers that plumed on bands of bugle beads.

Nicola wanted butterflies.

Monarch butterflies, appropriate, Nicola said, to Newport. "I am not, after all, Mother, getting married in a jungle."

Dove said to her maid Rosalind, who was brushing Nicola's untamable hair, "Did you ever hear of bridesmaids in black and brown? Ever? In your whole life?"

Rosalind gave a little dip to approximate a curtsy and said, "No, ma'am, I never did. Black is bad luck at a wedding. Even the guests can't wear it."

"There, you see, Nicola," Dove said, as though Rosalind was the final authority. "Even guests can't wear it."

"Rain is good luck," said Nicola. "Edmunda Lockholm told me so. She says she wishes almost every day of her life that it had rained the day Bay married Virginia Stotesbury."

"We are not talking rain, Nicola, we're talking brown and black."

"Oh, plop," said Nicola. *Plop*, with a diamond as big as an eye upon her heartline finger! "Monarch butterflies are heaven, and I'm going to have them. A dozen butterflies. And Rolf is having rabbits.''

"Rabbits."

"Yes, Rolfie's having his escorts in white satin tails with vests and pocket watches, like the rabbit in *Alice*. You know, the one who's always late...."

And there they had stood, mother and daughter, battled to impasse. But this Dove knew: Nicola's attendants would *not* be in black and brown, though Dove could live with the white satin tails and pocket watches.

Nicola—sweet this Sunday in white linen appliquéd with pink silk fleurs-de-lis, her waist clinched by a tricolor cummerbund, mauve and pink and white—was squirming in her seat, making her crinolines cry with abuse, and whispering to Rolf.

With her burning-bush hair, Dove had told her daughter this morning, she would be a beautiful bride thirty pounds lighter and her freckles faded. But Nicola only stuck out her tongue. Rolf, still wretchedly intoxicated with his fiery betrothed, laughed good-naturedly at whatever Nicola did and shook his head at Dove for not seeing what a goddess Nicola was. It amazed Dove sometimes to see lust in Lord Pomeroy's eyes when he gazed on Nicola.

Now Nicola was drawing the Blueblood Steeplechase in a black notebook hidden inside her hymnal. Actually setting down each jump, and the course, with extensive side notes to Rolf who, on Nicola's right, looked the picture of a studious nobleman—or the prime minister he might someday be—motionless, hands folded on lap, head bowed in meditation. But Lord Pomeroy's big blue eyes were wide open and intent upon Nicola's notebook, and he nudged Nicola's thigh from time to time in response to something she had written out.

It reflects on me, Dove thought, these improprieties of Nicola's. How strange she is, this woman formed half of myself. Where does it all come from? Percy can't be entirely blamed. Dove prayed, Forgive me, Lord, I did my best. And what I did to deserve Nicola I shall never ever know....

The sermon was over *at last* and the Reverend Elliott was preparing for the communion. Indiscernibly, Dove relaxed. It would not be long now....

Alabaster McGregor was coming for luncheon. And Edmunda. And Celeste Lockholm and her beach boy, though they didn't count; Celeste knowing nothing of interest except perhaps the size of that sunburned man's organ of love, which must play a sweet tune, indeed....

For Dove had it in the strictest confidence from Alabaster—"this is really off-the-record, you understand, Dove, darling...I mean really!"—that the day Celeste had gone "over the horizon" in that crimson sailboat with Thorne Cockburn, she had given herself to him like a wanton and now was terrified she was enceinte.

Pregnant before the wedding vows.

Dove could scarcely credit it, Celeste was a lady and an aristocrat; and before Rolf had tumbled for Nicola, Celeste had surely been virgin. But Ally had sworn Edmunda had told him all, in tears, explaining why she had given permission for the match.

And, according to Ally, they had sinned not only in the boat at high noon, but also that night in the Waldorf again and again.

My God, was it possible she *liked* it from the start? It had taken Dove years to work up an appreciation.

And then the next morning *in the shower chute*, after breakfast in bed! Eggs Benedict, Alabaster had confided in that smirking way he had when he knew he was dropping bombs, and champagne cocktails with strawberries in them shaped like hearts, and Viennese coffee, dark roast. He claimed to have seen the very bill. Celeste brought it back with her and shoved it under her mother's nose to force a capitulation....

Mr. and Mrs. Burton VanVoorst did not take communion.

Neither did Dove...though Percy did, and Nicola and Rolf.

Well, Celeste wouldn't tell about that messy little experience; not today, over the shrimp and watercress and pine

nuts. Ah, no. And as for The Opportunist himself, Thorne
Cockburn knew nothing of interest absolutely. And never
would, as far as Dove was concerned.

Zack was coming; Zachary Punt Pink, architect for
Newport's rich.

Zack was the one Dove was looking forward to talking
to. She was desperate to know how the VanVoorst "cottage" was coming. It was being built on a magnificent slope
of land, high on Gilt Hill. They were calling it Godsend.

Dove had seen Zack's talents early on; it was she who
had given him his first great commission, the design and
construction of Peerce House. Others, larger, more carved
and gilded had come Zack's way since then in 1882, but he
had promised Dove that no other mansion in Newport for
which he was responsible would ever have the perfect unity
of design and materials that Peerce House boasted.

He had kept his promise. Indeed, he told Dove often, it
was easy. Every multimillionaire who sought him out was
richer than the one before, or at least willing to budget
more for the summer home. And each wanted bigger and
grander than those who had come before. Zachary Punt
Pink always gave exactly that and then some. He did not
design, had never designed, only a handsome house. He did
not build, had never built, merely a splendid mansion.
Zachary Punt Pink created a castle, a cathedral, a palace,
all in one magnificent massive edifice worthy of an em-
peror, a pope, a czar.

He told Dove he would have liked to create again the
beautiful proportions of Peerce House, but no one had
thought as Dove did, except perhaps Bay and Virginia
Lockholm with Whale's Turning. And Virginia Lockholm
had insisted, as did all the wives, that Whale's Turning be
the grandest showplace in Newport.

And so it was, so far.

But Zachary Punt Pink was now putting the finishing
touches on the VanVoorst mansion, said to have been ordered expressly to outdo Whale's Turning after Burty and
Tory had seen Zack's plans for Bay Lockholm's estate.

Well, Burty VanVoorst may have even exceeded Percy's multimillions by now, his success had been that cosmic. The man's investments—ocean liners, railroads, even the new motorcars—were doubling almost monthly, Percy said. But he would not yet have, of course, the Peerce taste. How could he? Polish didn't come with mighty new numbers on your asset sheet.

Dove particularly wanted to know what garish vulgarities Tory VanVoorst was forcing down her poor husband's throat and what wretched excesses of style Newport's nouveauest nouveau, richeest riche, were insisting upon to Zack's despair.

The congregation was rising now. Percy stifled a groan, shifted a little but remained in his seat. Dove held his hand a moment and then stood without him. Dear Percy. He wasn't jealous of Burton VanVoorst; didn't care a whit. She loved Percy for that. He'd done splendidly in this world and now was his time to play. Only he was tired now. And ill. That distressed her.

And inconvenienced her. Now, when they had an invitation Percy would insist that of course she should accept, of course they would go, he was looking forward to the fun intensely. And then, come the afternoon or evening, usually while she was dishabille, in only corselet and perfume, Percy would call her on the house telephone from the library and ask her to come to him.

He almost lived in the library now, spending his days and his nights on a leather sofa with his pillows and hot water bottles and brandy-and-milk and telephones and stock receipts and his advertisements for the new motorcars. He would sit in the dark library for hours, sit like a stone, and conduct all his business by telephone. Once the library had been a handsome room; oak wainscoting, green damask walls, hunting prints, green-veined marble around the fireplace. It had smelled always of the fresh flowers Dove arranged every day. But Percy didn't want the flowers now, and wouldn't let Bethany in to clean, and now the library was unpresentable to company and smelled only of medicine and liquor and Percy's pain.

And he had commandeered the telephones from Nevvers.

During the week, day and night, Percy from the library answered every ring. When a call was for Dove, she never knew who was on the other end of the line because Percy hadn't asked or, if he knew, hadn't told Nevvers. Dove would have to say hello without knowing who she was talking to; without being able to decide whether she wished to talk to that person at that time.

So, he would call Dove into the library and she would go, knowing what was coming but pretending she didn't. She would cover herself in her peach peignoir, afloat in marabou, and let the shoulder slide.

"Yes, darling," she would say and give him a kiss and make some silly remark. The kind he used to love from her, like "Do you think I should go out without my panties tonight, Percy? It's supposed to be so warm."

"Hell, no," he used to shout, and then, "Well, let's just see how you look without them."

But these days he was serious and apologetic, and she hated a serious, apologetic Percy. "Dove, my love, I'm afraid to go *wherever*. I can't seem to make my bowels behave. You go, princess, you go and have a jolly time. Shall I ask Reverend Elliott to escort you for me? I know he's not your favorite man, but it's short notice, and if he'll come out, he'll have the most beautiful woman in Newport on his arm."

And Graf Elliott always came out.

Which is how she and Graf had begun. Not at first. Not till long after. Not till one intoxicating night last month, weekending in Kentucky at the Courtland's after their Derby ball....

Percy, seeking the safest of men, had found the most *deceitful*....

At first she had protested and sulked and pouted. What was a husband for but to come along and have fun with his wife? They were a couple, a terribly exciting couple. Their friends didn't want Graf Elliott, they wanted to see Percy. And how boring about his bowels!

But the only thing that excited Percy this entire year was the idea of a motorcar. He pored over the advertisements as over gold. To Dove a conveyance without a horse was just another pair of shoes, smoky and dirty shoes, of no style or interest. Why, the Benz Patent-Motorwagen that Percy was favoring at the moment didn't even have a top to keep off the rain. And Tripp Rails, who had one, was always having trouble with it and needing someone's carriage to give him a pull. Still, there was no talking to Tripp, he was so puff proud. All he sputtered was how gasoline and motorcars were the investments of a lifetime and how many miles an hour he was able to achieve. Ha! Dove's blacks passed Tripp and Clarissa all the time in town, just trotting.

But, "whatever my darling wants," Dove purred. Anything to get him well again.

But Percy wasn't well and he seemed satisfied, satisfied even with his pain. To Dove, he seemed more at peace than she had ever known him, and Percy had always been a peaceable man, for all his drive in business.

And though he pored over the motorcars, he didn't buy. Dove thought, and prayed it wasn't so, that Percy was getting ready to die....

He'd had a happy marriage. He had the fortune of a pharaoh, and his only child was marrying very well: his daughter would be a marchioness.

She was surprised at how pleased Percy had been at the engagement. Perhaps she shouldn't have been. Percy had said from the day Nicola was born that she was wonderful, simply wonderful just as she was. Not once had he frowned at Nicola's ways in twenty-four years, while Dove died nearly every day. Percy never objected to Nicola helping herself, for the second time, to whatever Nevvers brought round the table again, even those sliced fried potatoes that used to bring Dove to breakdown almost, the way Nicola piled them and piled them and the way they made her skin *erupt* in acne. Finally Dove banished them entirely from the Peerce households, except for Sunday breakfast when Percy loved them so. If she hadn't, Nicola would have been a horse. A Clydesdale.

And Nicola's midnight raids on the kitchen! Cook fussed and Dove nagged, but Percy only smiled and said that his daughter, in his opinion, was a miracle of grace. And her perpetual grimy jodhpurs too tight over tree-trunk thighs. Percy said she was a glory of a woman, worthy of the brushes of Rubens. And he never concerned himself with her lack of interest in eligible young men. Or, more to the point, their lack of interest in her. He never agreed Nicola was headed for a miserable spinsterhood.

And Percy had been right. Nicola had proven him magnificently right.

How had the changeling done it . . . ?

The service, swelling now, was almost through. Dove was conscious of Percy beside her, pale and heroic for coming, pressing his hand, inside his trouser pocket, against his liver to hold in the pain. Poor Percy. . . .

And now that things were settled—almost settled: Dove wouldn't breathe easy until after the ceremony was not only performed but recorded in Newport's City Hall—Percy was so pleased, quietly pleased. And proud.

But no I-told-you-so's from Percy.

He doted on Rolf. Well, so did she. Lord Pomeroy was a true British treasure. Dove, of course, was sky-high. For the first time since Nicola was seven or eight, Dove could hold her head up in the Casino during tea, when talk turned to her daughter. It was astonishing—that is what she must call it—but Nicola was coming through astoundingly well.

Dove realized, as her eye twitched, that she had always been jealous of her daughter. . . .

The service was over.

Lord Pomeroy and the Peerces moved into the center aisle, a portrait unto themselves on Trinity Church's living mural of exiting privilege.

Out on the church steps, for just a moment, Dove's lover held her in his glance. Her heart warmed as it always did when she knew she'd won the prize, but she swept toward her carriage arm in arm with Percy, without a blink, without a flaw.

On Monday, Percy had an appointment with Dr. Lake. And Monday would be soon enough to gaze, with favor, upon the Reverend Elliott. Monday would be soon enough for her—and his—little afternoon's skinny-dipping into sin.... Dove thought of Monday, and her left eye twitched.

By an early-blooming hydrangea bush Alabaster Mc-Gregor smiled with thin lips upon Tory and Burty Van-Voorst, but his eyes were on Graf Elliott and Dove Peerce, and he was calculating, calculating....

6

IT WOULD be a long day. She would not go back to her father's house until evening when that woman would be gone, back to whatever lair she called her own.

And Lawrence Smoke would stay at home. He always did on Sunday evening, planning his work for the week to come. During supper Audrey would try to explain—what would she try to explain?—that maybe he didn't know the kind of woman Dolly Dowd was; didn't know about the women of Grimsby's Tavern.... No, that wouldn't do. That was why he had gone, in the first place, to the Long Wharf in the nights after Josephine died. To find a woman. Find just such a woman....

Why else?

Lawrence Smoke had never been a social man. Never been a drinking man. He had worked in his shop and stayed at home with his family. He had no hobbies, no close male friends. He was a solitary man who did not swim or sail or hunt, a man who even worked alone, a man who had never worked for anyone except himself. He had been, as Audrey knew him, always self-reliant, self-contained and self-content.

Had been, in the time of Josephine....

Audrey made her way to the public beach, her bed linen, two towels rolled around curtains and nightgown under one arm, kicking through the sand as she went. She rented a bathing dress from the attendant for twenty-five cents, a two-piece dress of black wool, its skirt rimmed in bands of yellow and red. An ordinary, ugly bathing dress, the kind spinsters wore...and women who were no longer betrothed....

"Oh, ain't you the brave one," the attendant said. She was reading a Friday *Newport Daily Whirl*, turned to the gossip column, "Ally's Oops" by Alabaster McGregor. "But I seen you before. You're always out there, ain'tcha? You like the water. I know. I used to like it, too, years and years ago, when I first come here with Jeoff."

She had a finger on the gossip column to keep her place. Her hand was arthritic, yellow and crooked and dry on the fingertips, with tiny splits in the skin. Her uniform was an unbecoming green, wrinkled, a button gone, a safety pin inserted to hold the bodice closed.

Audrey wanted to say something nice. The attendant was a poor woman as Audrey was, a lonely woman as Audrey was. And probably she was an unloved woman, as Audrey was....

"I remember you, too. What's your name?"

"Esmeralda Diego. Ain't I got a pretty name?"

"It's beautiful," said Audrey and started to pass on to the changing room.

"My daughter's name is Daphne. Jeoff chose that. We was Eckkles while Jeoff was with us, but once he left us I took back my first husband's name. It's more comforting to such as I, I say. And Daphne Diego sounds better than Daphne Dawn Eckkles, don't it, even if Jeoff did leave me some stocks and bonds. They was all worthless, anyways, far as I know."

Audrey moved on without reply.

"It's really a sin, what some men do," the woman said behind her. "And ain' it a shame about that Virginia Lockholm?"

Audrey caught her breath. She was past the woman. She did not have to turn back, did not have to ask. She could leave yesternight on WaterWalk as dead as her mother in the cheval glass had told her....

But she turned. "What do you mean?" she said.

The woman was just making conversation. Audrey had been nice and she was only being nice in return. Business was slow, the woman wanted to talk a moment to ease her boredom....

"Right here in the paper," Esmeralda Diego said, stabbing at the paragraph with a twisted first finger. "Virginia Stotesbury she was, before she married him. Don't you remember last year? It was in all the papers. She killed herself, they said. Just married to that Bayard Lockholm who rides so high and mighty on the hill, and she jumps out of the house he was building for her. I thought it was strange at the time. Don'tcha remember?" The woman looked up from her chair at Audrey with oddly piercing black eyes, eyes whitening with cataracts at the corners.

Why wouldn't her breath come? Why was her heart clutching, fist tight, in her chest? Audrey nodded and dropped her eyes from the ones becoming blind—what would Esmeralda do then, poor thing?—and stared down at the twisted finger, the knuckle too large, turned at a strange angle.

"What about her?" said Audrey. "What does the paper say?"

The fingernail was curved and yellow. It tapped like a bird's beak. "The maid come back," Esmeralda said, bending her head to get close to the newspaper print. "She's French, name of Fanni St. Flour. That's a pretty name, too, huh? She come back from France to take a job again. Says here she's been taken by Mrs. VanVoorst—you know, them new rich ones building on the top of Gilt Hill?"

Audrey didn't know. Audrey didn't know anything. But she nodded, impatient, her throat dry. "Yes," she said.

"Well," said the beach-house attendant, "the maid, this Fanni St. Flour, she went to the Providence police and told a story on this Bayard Lockholm. Said she had to clear her conscience. Said Mr. and Mrs. Lockholm had a big fight the night the lady jumped, and he said he was going to kill her, and now they're going to have another investigation. Opening old wounds, I guess you'd call it. But what if he did? Murder her, I mean. I know them Lockholms. I wouldn't put anything past the likes of them."

Esmeralda Diego looked up from the paper. "Why, honey, you're gone all white."

"What does it say exactly? Could I see it?" Audrey bent over the newspaper, too.

"Take a look. God knows, trouble never ends." The woman was pleased. She had caught the young one's attention; brought a bit of excitement into a quiet Sunday afternoon.

Audrey read:

After all the pain of last year it seems a crime that the new joy of the Lockholm family this season with their summer cottage, Whale's Turning, finally finished—magnificently so, by that genius of the building blocks Zachary Punt Pink—and the impending marriage of Miss Celeste Lockholm to young entrepreneur Thorne Cockburn, should be marred by wicked insinuations of a dismissed servant girl.

But such is the sorry case.

A Mlle Fanni St. Flour served in the Lockholm household for a short time as personal maid to Virginia Stotesbury Lockholm, beloved bride of John Bayard Lockholm III, prior to her tragic death last year. Well, this Mlle St. Flour has returned from her homeland of France after a year away, telling tales. I have it that she couldn't wait to run to the Providence police to spread rumors of a fight between the happy couple only hours before Mrs. Lockholm fell from a window of the then partially completed Whale's Turning.

Bayard Lockholm is the owner of this newspaper and my employer. And, I am proud to add, my dear friend. He is a gentleman of the highest reputation; one of Newport's most popular summer citizens. After a year of mourning, a year in which he traveled the world in search of peace, his heart is still not completely healed. And now, just when he is beginning to put his life together, now this.

Mlle St. Flour was given a very generous severance by Mr. Lockholm in the aftermath of the tragedy, but she has the nerve to return to *his* town—*our town*—

and, metaphorically, yank a poor woman from her
grave and rake her poor widower over the coals.

So who would listen to the lies of a spiteful, ungrateful French coquette? A Mr. Jeremy Smythe of the
Providence, Rhode Island, homicide unit, it seems—
that's right, I said homicide!—and Mrs. Victoria
VanVoorst, wife of the oil and motorcar magnate,
Burton VanVoorst, known to her friends as Tory, if
she has any. She has just employed the French chit for
the season...

"Oh, the poor man," said Audrey.

"Maybe he ain't so poor. Maybe he murdered her. Did'ja
think a that? You may not think it to look at me today,
honey, but I know them Lockholms, ha, do I know them,
and they're a mangy bunch."

Audrey wanted to run to him. She wanted to race, right
now, to the top of WaterWalk and call his name and then
tell him how sorry she was, how she knew he was being pil-
loried by jealous, evil tongues. She wanted to hold him, kiss
his sad mouth—

"No," she said. "I'm sure he didn't. Of course he adored
her. He built the house for her. She was having their baby.
They were only just wed."

Esmeralda Diego was ready to be convinced either way.
"I did hear he was bent at the funeral, bent with grief. And
folks do argue, that's a universal failing, seems to me. I
used to fight with Jeoff, never real bad, but we had our
times, we did."

Audrey left the woman then and changed into the long
bathing dress. She was alone in the room and glad of it.
Then she crossed the beach with long strides, eager for the
rush the water always gave her, and flung herself into the
sea.

There were only a few hardy children playing in the waves
where they breasted on the shore and one other swimmer,
far out, a man; he wore no bathing cap. The beach would
not be crowded with swimmers until July; the waters of the

Atlantic were still cold from northern currents, blue-lip cold.

But Audrey liked the hit of the frigid water, liked the toughness of waves lifted by June winds. She liked the struggle of propelling herself toward the breakers, half a mile out. She was a good swimmer, strong and easy in the waves. And out from shore a little the ocean calmed and warmed, and she swam, swam beyond where she was supposed to, swam far and then up, along the coast, past Bailey's Beach where the rich had colorful striped-silk cabanas and bathing wagons and tables under white eaves.

She swam to the hull of a golden yacht with yellow sails. The *Catbird Seat*. She held on to the chain that moored it and caught her breath. I should not be here, she thought, but she hung on to the chain, lifted herself, and looked.

The rock where last night she had supped with a stranger and drank too much champagne was clean and cold and only a part of the rocky landscape now; deserted, not even a gull on its nose using it as a sentinel's rest. On Water-Walk there was no one, though a man and a woman strolled on Cliff Walk; wider, safer, farther away. Audrey could not see from where she was, low in the water, over the wall of Whale's Turning. But where the wall broke and stone-stepped down to the pier and a small rowboat, she could see a thin lane of lawn. There was no one. No one beyond the wall and no one visible on the lawn where last night a carousel of lights had spun and beautiful people waltzed, and a woman named for the heavens with a dress like the moon had floated toward Audrey in the night and taken her brother back where he belonged....

I must go, she thought, go back....

Still, she stayed, telling herself she was catching her breath from the long swim, telling herself it was only that that held her, quiet in the water, against the high, golden side of John Bayard Lockholm's yacht—John Bayard Lockholm III, Esmeralda Diego had said.

If Thorne is there and sees me out here, he will think me a fool, Audrey thought. Worse than a fool, a pest. And worse than a pest, a scorned woman with no shame who moons at his heels while he worships another....

But I haven't come for Thorne, she thought, I've come for the other one. The one who walks alone on Water-Walk, his breast torn with passions he cannot sweat away. The one who, like a stag, is great and vulnerable together, his power subtle and hidden, but flashing when he moves. Last night the wind whipped his shirt, flattened it against his body, showed me his clean, hard chest. I wanted to caress him there. I'm still longing...

He had given off such a heat. Even now, in cold water, she was warmed remembering. Last night, jacketless, he had enflamed the very air....

And his face, his highborn face, boyish the way his hair fell, reckless, on his forehead; boyish when he half smiled. She ached to see that face again, and his haunted, sea-storm eyes. Elegant he was, too good for her, all right. But still, the draw of him... She had swam all this way, and he wasn't even there.

He would never be there for her again.

Last night, at the end, he had come close to her, had touched a lock of her wayward hair. She had been thrilled; she had wished with all her heart that he would take her in his arms and kiss her. Kiss her deep and long, and wake to roaring what had only so far been stirred.... He had thought of it. She had *felt* him thinking of it. Or had that, too, been only her desire, so strong the sea air whirled it all around her, made her dizzy, and made her think it was what he had wanted, too?

Yes, of course, that was it. Because he hadn't kissed her. Hadn't tried. And if he'd wanted to, he could have. He must have known that, mustn't he? He was, after all, a man who had been married, a man of experience, a man of the world....

There was a figure on the lower loggia, a tall, feminine figure in royal blue and loops of pearls, so many pearls, so white and lustrous against the wide bosom. Her hair was gray, her face was pale, her stance mature. She leaned upon a cane. She was standing between two white pillars staring where the water broke upon the rocks.

And then she was walking down veined-marble steps onto the lawn. She turned and straightened her back and stared up at a high window. It was a closed window, dull and blank. It was the one unwashed, unattended-to window of Whale's Turning.

No one lived behind that window. It was curtainless and it revealed nothing. It was the window where Virginia Lockholm fell. Fell to her death last June. It must be....

Seallike, Audrey dived.

And the woman in pearls would be Mrs. Lockholm; matriarch of Whale's Turning, John Bayard Lockholm's mother. Thorne's soon-to-be mother-in-law....

Audrey left then, swimming slowly, kicking dreamily. The heat in her heart was gone, dissolved by her exertion. There was only a dull lump where the coal of passion had fired and flamed. It was time to go home. If only she had a home....

She lazed in the water, pleasantly tired now. The current carried her back and she drifted, wondering, What was it made a man love a woman? She was not in love with Thorne. She had been. Only yesterday she had been. Happily, blissfully, in love....

Hadn't she?

Hadn't she leaped to the sound of his three-beat rap at her door? Hadn't she waited for it, dreamed of it many nights, many days, like a siren song, when they were first courting and she did not know if or when she would ever hear it again? Yes, yes she had. And loved it. Loved, too, his face in moonlight, handsome and tender, his black pirate's eyes lost in shadow, but burning, burning. She'd loved his kisses and the almost trembling they engendered in her secret places. She'd loved him half naked in his red, red boat, his chest broad and tight and muscular and bronze, the dark hair on it like the mane of a lion, proclaiming a fierce masculinity. She'd loved his white trousers, damp with sea spray, limning the muscles of his thighs....

And did all this love stop with the single shutting of a timbered door, with the words "I cannot marry you, I love another"? With the explanation of the *new one* so "beautiful and rich" and she, Audrey, "so little and mean"?

Yes.

Strange, surprising, Audrey thought, but yes, the love had stopped. Stopped because she had seen behind the glamour of Thorne Cockburn and seen what was unlovable. She had seen greed and falseness, and a love that could be coaxed away, like a dog, at the lure of a bigger bone. Seen it all of a sudden. Seen it with pain. But seen it, and the love had stopped....

Thank God.

But was she different from Thorne? She had swooned like a silly girl at a rich man she did not know, would never know, because he had flirted with her, harmlessly, while her heart was down.

The rich did what John Bayard Lockholm had done last night all the time; it was what the rich did. They did it in early evening over their champagne cocktails, in between hors d'oeuvres of caviar and French cheese. They did it at the dining table, too, across platters of pheasant and English sole and strawberries out of season. They even did it before they went to bed, playing whist or dancing, without even thinking. It was called "drawing room manners," and it didn't mean a thing.

She who, now, knew what love was, though she would never know the lover, how was she different from Thorne? They both had fallen suddenly in love with someone rich.

She floated awhile on her back under a rampaging orange sun, and thought she knew.

She had fallen in love with Bayard Lockholm last night not because he was handsome—he was handsome, but not in the mesmerizing way of Thorne; not because he was rich—inconceivably fabled rich is what he was; not because she was hurt and looking to salve her pride—she was hurt, still hurt, but not shattered. It would take more than Thorne Cockburn to turn Audrey Smoke into a Brigit Norris. No, she had fallen in love with the man on the rocks because he had been kind and gracious and generous and, most important, hurt, too. There had been an invisible wire between them last night, tying soul to soul. Like an angel's lyre, it had sounded such a sweet note she could still feel it, was still stirred. She had heard it so keenly!

He hadn't.

She realized that, too. Her mother in the mirror had told her, and, really, Audrey had known it even as she'd asked. Men were different. They were not attuned to cosmic wires the way a woman was. Bayard Lockholm would find a woman to love him, and she would be his kind of woman, of his world. She would know "drawing room manners" for what they were. She would know how to furnish a Newport summer palace, and how to address the cook and how to dismiss an impertinent maid. She would know how to travel the world; how to cross an ocean on a cruise ship or a yacht. She would know how to pack so as not to crush her velvets. She would know how to joke with royalty and how to tip in Paris, and what to talk about to strangers in hotels. She would know how to choose her dresses from a couturier, and how to wear the jewels her husband would give her. She would know how to give a dinner party, whom to invite this time, whom the next, what to serve, what entertainment would please. She would know how to ease his life, enflame his nights, and always grace his life. She would fill his heart, still cleft by the death of his first wife—

Mr. Smythe. . . .

The newspaper had said a Mr. Smythe of Providence homicide would be investigating. Wasn't a Mr. Smythe the man who had rented Mrs. Burroughs's rooms away from her?

Audrey rolled over onto her stomach and began to stroke for shore. It was true, then. John Bayard Lockholm was being investigated for the possible—no, the impossible— murder of his wife. . . .

She would go. She would not have had the courage for herself, she was too afraid, too unqualified, too ignorant. But she wanted to know about John Bayard Lockholm. She wanted to help. She would go then, tomorrow, at dawn, to

the *Newport Daily Whirl* and ask Mr. McGregor of the
gossip column, ask him for the job promised her by Bayard Lockholm last night in wind, under stars, over the sea.

And she would not take no for an answer. . . .

THERE WAS A YOUNG GIRL in Esmeralda's place, a beautiful young woman about Audrey's age. They said nothing
to each other.

Audrey changed, returned the bathing dress, and began
a slow walk home, carrying the bed linen and the two
rolled-up towels under one arm. She was very hungry from
the swim, but her feet dragged. She did not want to go
home to Lawrence Smoke and Dolly Dowd.

The harbor area was busy as it usually was on Sunday
evening. Townsfolk strolled with their children, eating fried
fish bought for pennies from a waterfront booth. Men from
the yacht club were bringing in their catches from the deep;
dockside, hired men sliced the fillets from the sides of fish
still thrashing, still pumping scarlet gills, trying to breathe.
The ladies of Bellevue Avenue, Ochre Point and Gilt Hill
paraded their carriages and showed their clothes. Alongside them, older children preened on ponies, beautifully
dressed boys on sleek Welshes and Shetlands with rib-
boned manes and tails grown full and long that swept the
ground. Haughty and proud the young rich were as they
pranced, like lords, past the town folk, and even among
themselves there was already an air of appraisal of one another. The smaller children and girls too young to ride with
their mothers, rode in pony carts driven by coachmen. The
little ones sat quiet in their seats, like great, gorgeous dolls.

Audrey, hair stringy, dress damp, skirted the main thoroughfares, stayed with the crowds on Washington Street as
far as Elm, and so walked roundabout, avoiding the carriage parade as well as she could, to Bridge Street and her
home.

Would Dolly Dowd be there after all, installed already as
queen of the house while Audrey had been away? Would
she be in the kitchen now, Josephine's kitchen, *Audrey's
kitchen*, with an apron over her blue-and-gold gown, smil-

ing maternally and stirring a chicken stew, the table already laid for three, a cosy three, as it used to be...? Or would her father and the woman be together in his room, closeted behind a bolted door, the bed *thumping and thumping*, and Dolly Dowd's laughter their orgiastic music...?

Audrey was at the door of her father's house, the timbered door. She opened it and saw that the door at the head of the stairs was open, which meant that her father was upstairs. There was light in the kitchen, the light from her father's lamp by the side of his chair. She recognized the oval pool of amber it made in the paler glow of the overhead gaslight. There was no noise.

She climbed the steps, holding her breath, wondering what she would see. She stood in the doorway.

The kitchen table was bare, except for the canning jar of daisies that Audrey had left that morning on the counter beside the sink. The stove was unfired, the pots hung as always. And as usual, Lawrence Smoke sat in the horsehair armchair, a Sunday paper on his lap.

There was one change. Instead of a cup of cooling coffee, a water tumbler of whiskey sat on the side table at his elbow.

"Daughter, I've been waiting for you," was his greeting.

"I went for a swim," she said. "I'll start supper right away, as soon as I brush out my hair."

She stood before him, uncertain. She set down the towels on the kitchen table and stared at this man she seemed no longer to know. His chin was set, he who had been so gentle. That was new. And his eyes were focused intently on her, the way an osprey sights a flounder; focused long, through depths of distance, focused tight. That was new, too. And the squaring of his shoulders and the muscle taut in his leg crossed on a knee. And whiskey in his home. All new....

It's true, Audrey thought; he loves her. No matter what she was or is, he loves her and he's going to have her, and there is nothing I can do....

Lawrence Smoke had been drinking, off and on, all day. He and Dolly had drunk red wine with Sunday dinner. They had emptied a tall glass of whiskey in his bedroom with their dalliance. It was exciting for him there, in his bed, in the bed he had lain only with Josephine...and then lain in alone for years, twisting his pillow around fantasies of women; soft, naked women, eager and hot and yielding.

And then, nervous, he had had more whiskey in her rooms where he had gone with her and carried back three valises of her belongings. There was more to come, but this was a start, Dolly said, and three valises were all she owned. And then he'd had another glass, roaming his house, first down into his workroom, then up into the living quarters, trying to distract himself and not *think*, not *interfere*, while Dolly packed away Josephine's little bottles of toilet water and Josephine's brush and comb, and Josephine's few dresses and undergarments and her single pair of shoes.

"It has to be done, Lawrence," Dolly said with a sweet upturn of her mouth and a madonna light in her eyes.

He had only nodded.

He knew it had to be done, but he felt bad doing it. He was so used to seeing Josephine's things as soon as he got up in the morning—he avoided them in the night—so used to remembering Josephine. So used to regret....

He knew it was no good. He would pause in the morning, almost without thinking, to stroke the top of the jewel box he had built her. Give it a dust. It was a delicate box of balsam wood, but its joints were pinned, not glued, and it was painted deep emerald and bright gold, and lacquered to a Chinese shine. He had constructed it like one of the mansions of the rich, three floors, and behind every window and every door there was a little drawer for a pair of earrings, a string of pearls, a sapphire bracelet. Of course, Josephine had had none of those things. She used the box for pins and buttons. But she had loved her jewel box and it had stood—until this afternoon—unaged, where it had always stood when Jo was alive, in the middle of her bureau.

Dolly made the transition as easy as she could. "This has to be done, pet, so our future can begin. You know that, and I know how hard it is for you. So just let me. Turn your back for an hour, and it'll all be done. This should have been taken care of when she left, you know. It's past time."

He had nodded, too full to speak.

"Lawrence," Dolly said. "You don't need these things to remember her, she'll be in your heart always. I'm not dispelling her or her place. Your heart and your house can take us both in, have us both. You realize that, don't you?"

He had nodded, and poured more whiskey.

And finally it was done. Now Dolly's silver-backed brushes and combs sat on Josephine's bureau in his room. And camisoles and nightgowns and shawls and black undergarments lay abundant in the bureau drawers. And Dolly's toiletries, so many, flashed upon the bureau top. And her dresses. They almost filled his closet, and they were only a few of all she had. Dolly, tired from her work, lounged on the bed while he examined her things, exotic in their new place. They pleased him. They were colorful and frilly. They were new and sensual. Josephine had never worn orange or blue-and-gold or vivid red. Jo had never had deep necklines cut like hearts or tight waists like these. Or the hats that would come, or the shoes. Dolly's personal things looked like mischief, man-woman mischief, and life was beginning again. And suddenly he wasn't sad or nostalgic for the past and what used to be. He was excited and very happy. Life was beginning again! And Lawrence thought it would be good. He looked around his room and saw a shared room again, a true bedroom again. It was his room and it had a woman in it, a woman who belonged. There she was, right now, on his bed. She was a voluptuous, openmouthed woman, and she was moving in to stay. In less than a week her name would be Mrs. Lawrence Smoke, and he would never be lonely or woman-longing again....

They'd had a final whiskey to celebrate.

And then he had stored the two cartons of Josephine's things down in a corner of his workroom, difficult to get to, impossible to see. He'd walked Dolly home and returned. He'd gotten out his newspaper, after looking in his—their—bedroom one more time. He'd poured himself another whiskey.

Last, he sat down in the kitchen to wait for the only trouble in his life that he could see; he sat down to wait for his daughter who would not be leaving, after all....

Lawrence Smoke watched Audrey now, as she stood uncertain before him. She was not at her best. Her dress, dark blue, yellow flowered, was dirty and wrinkled and damp. Her hair was matted with sea salt and drying into frizz. Her face was blotchy with early summer sun. There were long dirt streaks on her arms and shins.

He loved his daughter, loved her very much, had always loved her. But looking at Audrey these days recalled only old, deep sorrows he wanted, these days, to forget.

Looking at his daughter, Lawrence Smoke remembered his son. And he did not want that....

Joseph Arthur Smoke was born in January of 1872, eleven months after Lawrence and Josephine wed.

He died four months later.

In an accident, the worst kind of accident.

A little one.

One that should never have happened. One for which Lawrence had only himself to blame.

He had been playing with his son, tossing him high, proud the boy was bold, while little Joseph shrieked in bolts of joy and tried to climb in his flight ever higher in the air.

It was a little accident....

It should not have happened.

Lawrence Smoke missed.

Joseph Arthur broke his neck, falling on the kitchen floor. Not far. But he broke his neck and died some hours later. He'd never known what hit him. Never known what happened. Never known that Dada missed and killed him....

Lawrence made the coffin himself. Made it that night and the next day until noon, working without stopping. Josephine, upstairs, sat alone and keened without women to help her. All that night and next day she sat in the horsehair armchair and listened, while beneath her, the dirge of saw and plane and hammer sounded and re-sounded, sadder than bells. Her lap was her baby's bier.... Lawrence and Josephine, they grieved alone, the two of them, separate even from each other.

They never spoke of it.

He tried once, in their bed, but she covered his mouth with hers and stroked his head and whispered, "No, no, just love me, Lawrence, make love to me. Let's not look back into the dark. Not now. Not ever. Let's not look back...."

But for a long time, he didn't remember how long—it seemed all his young manhood—he was impotent. Hard, he would soften as soon as he found his way into her open-ing flesh. Soften inexplicably.

He would lie upon her then, both of them in silence. She to wherever she retreated at those times. She told him it was a garden where all flowers bloomed in an always season, but he did not believe that. He in a masculine rage. He imagined her as a chest of gold, her womb the sacred cleft to an unknown treasure mine, he the key. And he would push and rub, and push and rub, and try to think of the magic word and rock and rock...and not gain entrance.

She never protested, never discouraged. Never said a word to break his action. And then after, her hand on his back, they would sleep.

That time passed finally, and Josephine was pregnant again. And Audrey came, a little girl baby to whom Law-rence was reverentially gentle. A little girl baby whom Lawrence dearly loved. She was golden haired and mid-night-blue eyed.

She was his treasure. Found.

But she was not Joseph Arthur....

Lawrence buried Josephine in the ground where their first child lay. Baby Smoke's pine box, one-fifth the size of his wife's—though it had taken him as long to make—was brought up and set upon Josephine's coffin at Lawrence's request. Both names were set into the stone. "He lies now upon his mother's breast," Lawrence thought then, "as he should. And I, in my time, will lie beside her and feel, once again in my sleep, her hand upon my spine...."

Audrey learned of Joseph Arthur's existence at her mother's grave side. She asked her father to tell her about him, but Lawrence only shook his head and brought her, after Josephine's grave was filled back, her mother's cheval glass and told her she was once the lady of the house.

Audrey, as she had grown these past five years, reminded Lawrence more and more of Josephine. Try as he would to forget, when he saw Audrey standing at the kitchen sink, with the way her hair caught the gaslight, the way she laid her body against the sink wall, arm-deep in dish water, it was Josephine. A younger Josephine, a more golden Josephine, a slighter Josephine. But Josephine, for sure.

It would take him by surprise and cut his heart.

And the way she had of smoothing the crown of her hair with two hands, the palms cupped, the face so endearingly serious.... And the way her eyes questioned, looking up from thick brown lashes, innocent and daring together. And the way she had of lifting her chin when she meant to have her way. And her laughter, rare like Josephine's, rippling like Josephine's.... Even the timbre of her voice. And the perfect toes, straight and flat: ballerina feet. All Josephine. And Jo had told him not to look back into the dark. Not ever. But how could he not when her living replica was with him daily?

He had not known what to do. He had taken to drinking after his workday, in Grimsby's. Not too much. Not nearly enough.... And he had found a new woman. A woman entirely different from the sensitive, stoic Josephine. A bubbly woman with a head on her shoulders and a sense of fun. A voluptuous woman who knew how to show herself off. And a woman who knew how to help a man in bed

when he needed it . . . and how to enjoy herself when he
didn't.

A good woman, forget her past. A good woman for him.

He had thought he would make it. Audrey had been engaged to that Thorne Cockburn. Well mannered, a hard
worker, with a head for business. Lawrence had built his
daughter an oak armoire. It stood now in his workshop,
under sheets, and what could he do with it, except sell it off.
It took too much room. He had hoped to walk her down
the aisle, kiss her goodbye and send her on her way. . . .

From the armchair, with whiskey-narrowed eyes, Lawrence Smoke confronted his daughter. He wished Thorne
Cockburn had taken her; he wished it heartily. Oh, she
would find another. She was beautiful, more beautiful than
she knew, and sweet tempered and she had a good spirit.
She had, too, though she was unaware, a great appeal to
men. But finding another prospective husband would take
time, and Lawrence wanted her gone now, out of the house
and out of his and Dolly's new life. . . .

He loved his daughter . . . and he hated her. It was too bad,
but that was the way it was.

"No thanks on supper, Jo," he said. "I've already et.
Dolly fed me. I'll just say good night. I'll move into my
room so's I don't disturb you none."

Tomorrow night, after a good day's work, after supper,
he would start Dolly's mirror. He had already ordered the
glass. It was to be his wedding gift; she would look ripping
in it. . . .

He rose, tall, stooping a little. The newspapers fell from
his lap to the floor. Heavy of step, he left his daughter
looking after him in wonderment.

He's drunk, she thought. He must be drunk—there is
strange fire in his eyes and he called me by Mama's
name. . . .

7

THE FACADE of the *Newport Daily Whirl* was unprepossessing. Unwelcoming. The windows were unwashed, the interior was dim. Behind the windows there was nothing but a printing press thundering and several men in green trousers and shirtsleeves. The building itself was narrow; two humble stories of flaking green-painted wood at the corner of Thames Street and Howard. A well-worn staircase to the right of the building's face led to the public door; an arrow at street level said Enter Here and pointed up the stairs. Audrey stood before the dirty glass and felt the street tremble from the printing press and watched the rickety stairway quiver. It was not at all what she had imagined.

But it made her feel a little better, a little more equal to the challenge, a little more acceptable. After all, she thought, standing before it, what had I supposed—another palace? Errand boys in uniforms like footmen carrying silver trays, and reporters in morning suits like gentlemen? She was wearing her brown-and-cream striped cotton. Her long hair was twisted, businesslike, into a coil at the nape of her neck. She had had to choose between a pair of black winter walking shoes and her scuffed brown sandals; she chose the sandals, polishing them three times to get a shine. Over the dress she wore a brown cardigan sweater, edged in darker braid. She had knitted it in high school and never worn it since. It made her look old, she thought, and spinsterish. But now it seemed appropriate. She was seeking a professional position in the world; looking older could only help her cause.

She ascended the steps, repeating to herself, "May I speak to Mr. McGregor, please? I believe I am expected."

There was a bell on the door, but when she entered, no one looked up. There were only three people in a large room of gray steel desks shoved together in groups of four, the groups divided by cheap, desk-high partitions of pasteboard painted brown that gave no privacy.

Three men.

One of them was Bayard Lockholm. He was in the rear, his back turned to her, behind a partition as high as his shoulders. He was listening, intent, hunched in his chair, to another man maybe fifteen years older with a wrinkled face and a swag of double chin. She could see the stranger clearly, but she could see Bayard Lockholm only as she could see a waning moon, his profile a pale sliver of nose and cheekbone and chin, and the back of his head with brown hair neat around a white collar and an ivory jacket.

The third man was closer to her. The third man was sitting in a tipped-back chair, a mug of coffee in graceful, womanlike fingers, though unjeweled and liver spotted; a pile of photographs in his lap. His legs, long and thin, stretched out on his desk. His trousers were the soft gray of a pigeon's wing. They were perfectly creased above glowing black shoes. He was bald, completely bald, ears close to his head and a high, straight forehead. He was clean shaven; he looked as though he had never shaved; had never had to. His face was lean almost to gauntness, with large, ash-colored eyes and pink spots high on flat cheeks. His suit jacket was buttoned over a vest, threaded with a gold watch chain. There was something feminine about him and something very masculine.

"Hello," he had said, a long time ago. "What do you want?"

"Mr. McGregor. Are you Mr. McGregor?" Whatever she had planned to say, she had forgotten. Her eyes crossed the room to Bayard Lockholm. He took no notice of her.

The thin man shrugged. "Yes," he said, "I am that famous man. What can I do for you, I'm busy."

"Mr—Mr. Lockholm said—"

"Yes, yes. Get on with it. Do you wish to make a complaint? I'm not your man, I only take compliments and gifts at Christmas.... What *do* you want, child?"

Audrey sank into the chair opposite him. "A job," she said.

Alabaster McGregor snorted and dropped his legs from the desk and righted the tip of his chair. Photographs scattered.

Audrey slid down on her knees to chase them.

McGregor let her, saving his coffee from spilling. "A job," he said. "Whatever for? Do you have a journalism degree? Then go to Providence, to New Haven, where real newspapers are. Go to New York. We don't hire women here except to sweep the floor, at which you seem qualified enough, but Mrs. Gottschalk has held that position for years and isn't about to quit. So thank you for my photographs...." He took them, straightened the stack and laid them facedown on his desk. "Thank you very much, and good day to you. I'm really in a rush—on deadline, you see."

His nod indicated the door.

Audrey sat back in her chair. "Mr. Lockholm promised me a job," she said. "I'll wait to speak with him, then." She folded her hands over her purse and stared at the man. "I'll wait right here."

McGregor heaved an elaborate sigh. He spread his elbows on his desk and leaned his body over them. "Mr. Lockholm promised you—what exactly?" His eyes glittered; ice-colored eyes.

"A job. An—an assistant job. Assistant to you, I think he said." She mumbled the last; she wasn't about to get that.

Mr. McGregor appeared to be enjoying himself. "Assistant to me. How nice of Bayard. God knows I've been needing one for years. Had a few in my time, but they never seemed to stick.... Why do you suppose that is, Miss... Miss..."

On her side of his desk, she inched her chair closer.

"Audrey Alice Smoke," she said. "I'm nineteen, twenty in October. I graduated Newport High, and English was my best subject. I've lived in Newport all my life, summers and winters. My father is the carpenter and cabinetmaker Lawrence Smoke. My mother was Josephine Nally, her father was a fisherman, very good with lobster traps. Grandfather Nally taught me a lot about the waters of Rhode Island. I know where all the good fishing is around Newport, and why the whales come. I know how to sail and how to swim—I was on the swimming team, fourth position, the first girl they ever invited in and the only one all four years I was there—this is an unusual skill in a woman, but much, I think, to your advantage. I can report to you on currents and wind positions and tell the readers in advance where the fish are going to be—"

Mr. McGregor held up his index fingers, as stiff as flag-poles. "One moment, please. The first thing a newspaper person must know is how to pay attention. Do you understand that?"

Audrey nodded, still eager to get all the words out she had inside her mouth. "Yes, sir," she said.

"Then," Mr. McGregor said with a lift of an eyebrow, "answer the question." He sat back in his chair, no longer intense over his desk.

"You mean why you have no assistant now, Mr. McGregor?"

"Yes," he said, and made a tent of his fingers. "That is precisely what I mean."

Audrey sat as straight as she could. "The answer is obvious, sir. You haven't wanted one."

"Yes, Miss Smoke, I see. Pray continue." And he continued eyeing her over the steeple of his hands.

"I know all the tradespeople in Newport, and they know me. I know the town area, the back alleys as well as the main thoroughfares. I know the history of Newport and what the townsfolk gossip about. I know which of the rich they respect and which they don't. I know who pays their bills on time, and who argues too much over a price. I am energetic and able to take direction and correction. I will work hard for little money and I ask only to learn. I will work late whenever you say and go wherever you tell me. I need this job very badly, Mr. McGregor, and it was promised to me by Mr. Lockholm and I won't take no for an answer."

"You amaze me," he said.

She had amazed herself. It must have been Bayard Lockholm, far back in the room, who had given her courage. It must have been the quietness of his back as he listened to the man—Mr. Smythe of the Providence homicide unit, it had to be—explaining in long-winded legal terms that John Bayard Lockholm III was under suspicion of murder, the murder of his bride.... Virginia Stotesbury Lockholm within a sealed casket in Trinity Church, a crest of tourmaline and silver set into the lid. And no one else in that holy space except a flower girl, a stranger. No one in the church at all but *them*, Audrey and Virginia, alone together, each unable to see the other's face.... And would Bayard Lockholm, if she asked, have anything to say for himself...?

"Yes, sir," she said.

"Well." Heel of hands together, fingers curved, tips patting, he said, "I give you fair warning, Miss Smoke. I am not an easy man to work for. I'm a perfectionist and a demon for work. I drive myself, drive others. If you were to work for me you would be working virtually all the time. I am not kind or understanding, and I have no patience with incompetence. We do not pay well here out of the starting gate nor, truth to tell, up the straight. You're into the stretch in this game before you can expect any kind of decent return for your industry and time, and I predict you will not be at the *Daily Whirl* long enough for that.... So. All having been said, when are you prepared to start?"

"R-r-right now, sir."

"Fine. Then just let me get my hat and we'll go to lunch."

There was a clock high on the west wall. The time was 10:20 a.m.

"Yes, sir," she said.

"*Very* good. Yours is not to question why, yours is but to do or die. That's the first lesson." He seemed delighted with himself, delighted with her, his new toy.

"And please, Mr. McGregor, won't you call me Audrey. I'm not used to anything else."

"Well," he said, "whatever I call you, 'goddess' or 'idiot,' remember to call me always Mr. McGregor. I like the sound of it, thank you very much." He was out of his chair to a coatrack and back, a straw boater on his head. "Now. Do you have a notepad and a sharp pencil, quite a few sharp pencils?"

"No, sir."

"Do you have any clothes better than the rag you're wearing?"

"No, sir."

"Who does your hair?"

"I do."

"Ah, the liabilities mount."

He reached inside his jacket, withdrew a burgundy suede wallet, soft as lamb. He riffled through greenbacks, found the bill he wanted, eased it from its fellows, folded it and handed it to her. "Do you know a dressmaker? If you don't, find one. Not the best, you can't afford the best. But someone decent. Order yourself two dresses, three if there's money enough. And tomorrow morning at seven, when you step beyond that door, be more appropriately dressed as assistant to Alabaster McGregor, managing editor and gossip columnist extraordinaire. Now. Go. Meet me at the Casino in an hour and we'll continue on with the day's work. And remember, my precocious little English student, a reporter is always working, whatever he's doing, to whomever he's talking—even at his own ablutions, a good reporter is always on the beat. And we do want to be good, don't we, dear?"

She did not know how to refuse and dared not look at the money—Bayard Lockholm was coming toward them, trailed by the man Audrey assumed was Mr. Smythe, a towering man of bulk and muscle. Audrey slipped the bill, loose, into her purse. And as for the dressmaker, she would ask Rosemary Maddley; Mrs. Maddley would know.

Bayard was with them. He was smiling at her, but his eyes were dark, shadowed by worry or sorrow or lack of sleep. "Hullo," he said. "You came after all. I'm glad. Has Ally been treating you well?"

"How could I not?" said Alabaster McGregor. "English was her best subject in high school and she knows where all the little fishes are."

"I told you she had a lot to offer. Welcome, Miss Smoke, welcome to the team. I hope you're happy here."

"Oh, yes," she said, stumbling over her tongue. "I love it very much already. Thank you so very much, Mr. Lockholm, I'll work very hard to prove myself...."

He was older in daytime. Paler, more drawn. And she did not know him anymore. It had all been a dream, after all. There was no invisible wire between him and her; there had only been his kindness, his pity at her situation. He had, probably, laughed at himself afterward and apologized to his sister. "Celeste, what do you think? I've offered Thorne's old flame a job with the newspaper. She was so bereft, you know, without him. Abject, really. She cried all over me out by the rocks...."

His sister would be kind about it, too; kind but not interested. "Oh, did you, Bay," she'd say, looking up from a woman's magazine. "How sweet. Well, tell me now, do you like this green silk frock? And what do you think of Venice as a place to honeymoon?"

"That's a possibility," he'd respond, his hands casual in his trouser pockets. "You've been to Paris too often for it to thrill...." He would forget, that quickly, what he'd been talking of; he would be reminded then of his honeymoon with Virginia, and he would sink into a chaise on the lower loggia in the night and listen to the ocean crash and remember Venice or Naples or Bali and the two of them....

He was walking out.

He was gone, the stranger at his heels.

Alabaster McGregor was on the telephone to the Casino, ordering luncheon for two: snails in garlic over escarole...

Audrey watched him, transfixed.

There was a telephone in Mrs. Maddley's flower shop, but it rarely rang. And Audrey, forbidden to touch it, had never seen it used to place a call. Mr. McGregor's telephone was tall and black and thick, a heavy, blunt instrument that could be used to kill; yes, she thought so. But for more than that was it mysterious and sinister...it could take you anywhere. Walls wouldn't stop it, or bodyguards or threats. Disembodied, you could invade anyone's house, slip the bolts of all the doors. Ghostly, you could whisper in anybody's bedroom, and disturb a sleeper from his dreams....

BAY LOCKHOLM WAS all the talk in the Casino during lunch. Not only was the reopening of the investigation into the death of his wife a scandal, and the coming of Mr. Jeremy Smythe, detective from Providence, a sensation, but the return of Fanni St. Flour, Virginia's maid, and the tales she was telling had Newport reeling with excitement and speculation.

At the table for two by the first window, Nicola Peerce, magnificent in a black riding habit, her hair wild and uncombed from a gallop, sat across from Rolf, handsome in summer tweed.

"They're *exhuming*," she said around a raw clam. "Actually digging the body up! Isn't it rotten?"

"I'd think it must be," agreed Rolf, grimacing at the thought. "But it has to be done, they say, to satisfy—"

"No, dum-dum," said Nicola. "I don't mean the body! I mean what they're doing to Bay!"

"Oh, yes, Nick. Decidedly barbaric."

Rolf sipped at his preluncheon cocktail—raw egg and brewer's yeast beaten to a brown paste in honey and orange juice. "Poor Bayard is being crucified. Even if nothing comes of this, he'll be tarnished by it. Suspicion, I find, is a funny thing. Once it gets on you, it soaks in and clings, won't go away no matter how hard you wash.''

"Look," said Nicola, conspiratorially. "There's that Tory VanVoorst, coming in with Zack Pink. She's taken Virginia's maid for the summer, and I'll bet she knows everything about Bay and Virginia's private life. Probably made that a condition for employment. But we can't ask her. Let her go by—don't even nod.... Good afternoon, Zack.... Mum hasn't taken her up yet, never will now, in spite of Zack yesterday championing her cause. Mum hates nouveaus, especially the proud ones who try to climb too fast. But the men are mad for her, Mum says, because she was fast and loose before she married Burton VanVoorst. Edmunda said Mrs. VanVoorst used to do a striptease at men's stag parties, and let the men stuff money into her costume, which was just three little triangles."

"Oh, I don't know I believe that," said Rolf, unperturbed at the idea.

"Well, she is wonderful looking, isn't she?"

"Quite. But nothing beside you." Rolf started on the oyster crackers, ready now for crab salad, already anticipating his carrot cake. "I say, Nick, when we're married we must be very careful of the servants. Do our arguing alone, above stairs. It doesn't do to let the help see behind closed doors. They're awful tattlers."

"I agree," said Nicola, tossing her hair. "And we'll only argue when it's fun, never when it means anything. And then we'll make love after, each time in a new place. Sometimes in the hayloft, sometimes in the ballroom. And I won't be frigid or Victorian, will I? I'll enjoy myself as much as you. You'll teach me."

Rolf grinned and grasped her hand. "That's the ticket.... You know, Nick, I thank my stars I met you. I don't think the Lockholms are a good family to marry into. Not just because of what's happening now to Bayard. I thought it before, with Celeste. Why I never really proposed to her when I should have. I just never felt right about her, the way I feel perfectly right with you. There was something dark, something hidden, under wraps.... And that fellow she's marrying.'' He dropped his voice so other tables wouldn't overhear. "He's not really the right sort, though he may turn out all right, of course, seems a decent chap. But the whole family is, I don't know, unlucky some-how.... Ah, here are your croquettes and my crab.''

"They're under a spell, Rolf," said Nicola, eyeing her salmon under cream sauce and peas. "Didn't Celeste ever tell you? They've been cursed by Phineas Brown.''

Rolf sank his teeth into a hot buttered roll. "You tell me, Nick. I love to listen to the sound of your voice.''

She told him; their ankles, under the table, intertwined.

ALABASTER MCGREGOR USED his table at the Newport Casino as an extension of his desk. It was always held only for him, and he passed many hours at it, talking of this and that with those in whom he was interested. His table was behind the main clutch of best tables in the center and near the front windows. It sat back before a curved banquette beneath a large bay window that afforded Alabaster a sweeping view of Thames Street and the harbor. Inside, the table was partly shielded by a short divider of green mosaic draped in ivy and dressed, daily, with fresh flowers from Wicke's. In this way he could watch and not be watched; a satisfactory arrangement.

Free of Bayard Lockholm's new chit for at least one happy hour, Alabaster took a turn or two up and down Thames, seeing what he could see. He saw Percival Peerce go by on his way to Dr. Lake, deep in one of his carriages, driven by Percival's best man, Nevvers. Alabaster waved and was acknowledged, but the barouche didn't stop. He's a very sick man, Alabaster thought. So why isn't Dove with him? It's not like her to neglect him. What—or who—could be more important to her today? Graf Elliott? Or a new gown for Celeste Lockholm's nuptials?

Probably neither one.

But Graf Elliott was having an affair. Alabaster McGregor would bet on it. All that talk of marital sinning yesterday was the dead giveaway, because Alabaster knew from two years of listening to the bishop's sermons and studying him in public and in private, that Graf Elliott always preached against his own sins.

Alabaster found it fascinating; fascinating and highly informative. When Graf Elliott first came to Newport, all they'd heard on Sunday for six weeks was greed, greed, greed. Alabaster had picked up on the Reverend Elliott right then, for the cleric had refused the post of Trinity Church until the salary and perks were commensurate with the "standard of living of the populace"; Graf Elliott's exact wording—Alabaster still had a copy of the correspondence in the G. Elliott file in his home—and the reverend had not meant by "the populace" the Newport townies, ah no....

And after greed it had been gluttony, all while Graf Elliott was on a diet, one whole summer. And then it had been charity. Soon the reverend would be perfect, and have nothing at all to say....

And so this past Sunday, when Graf boomed so powerfully upon the temptations of the boudoir, Alabaster from his high forward pew—the better to see you with, my dears!—had swept the faces of the beauteous looking for a blush, a snigger, a secret smile. And whom had he found...

But Dove, the ne plus ultra lady of Newport, holding a finger to her eye—to catch a tear?—and gazing around, like Alabaster, as though she knew what he did, and was looking for the woman in the case...as the guilty so often seek themselves among the innocent! Oh, clever Dove Peerce. Alabaster admired her enormously. If she had been a man, what would she not have accomplished! Luckily for him she was a woman, and therefore subject to a woman's limited ambition. But maybe, just maybe, at long last she thought she could have her cake and eat it, and he had found her out.

Alabaster hoped so. There was nothing in his Dove Peerce file to give him what he wanted, what he wanted over them all, a secret—maybe-never-to-be-used, but a secret—hold.

Still, wanting did not make it so....

He recognized her black Morgans, high headed, glittering of coat, smart of tack, trotting smartly down Thames toward him, for all the world to see.

Rats.

He had been wrong, then. She had been late dressing, he supposed, and now was hurrying after Percy to be with him at Dr. Lake's.... Well, all right. Graf Elliott was not the man Alabaster would have chosen for Dove, anyway. Dove deserved a lover better than a hypocritical preacher; she would never succumb to the likes of Graf Elliott, thank-you very much!

There she was, running after Percy like a perfect wife and Alabaster had been wrong. Rats, rats. Inwardly he apologized to her. If he could have loved a woman, she would be the one. She was magnificent; his equal in every way....

Except in deception.

He saluted her carriage.

She was dressed in white and gray, ostrich and crepe de chine, gorgeous to behold. She blew him a kiss and swept on, a finger at the corner of her left eye where it pulsed, to hold the twitch.

IN THE HOUR Audrey had she didn't go to Rosemary Maddley. She went to Darling's Drapers and Dry Goods on Spring Street. On the way she snuck a look at the money Mr. McGregor had given her: a fifty-dollar bill, a fortune!

She would buy yards and yards of stout cotton in different colors, and find a pattern for a working girl. She would stay up all night sewing a new dress and then, after work tomorrow, the same, and then, on the weekend, another. She would have three dresses by the first of next week, strong handsome dresses that could take the strain of long workdays and still retain their lines. She wouldn't know herself she'd be so sophisticated, and Mr. McGregor would be pleased. And Bayard Lockholm? Would he approve her new dignity, her new maturity?

She hugged herself hurrying. She'd gotten the job! Got the job, got the job: her feet marched to it. She would find one of her mother's friends to room with. Mildred Falk, midwife, was alone; maybe she would welcome the extra income and the company. And Audrey would be independent. She would work very hard to learn. She would be nice to Mr. McGregor when he was snide or cutting. And she would do all that she could do to help Mr. Lockholm—yes, he was "Mr. Lockholm" in her mind already; much more sensible.... She would do all she could to help him.

Audrey had to wait a moment for a horseless carriage to chug by. It was bright black and topless, and the man and woman in it were indifferent to the dust it threw up in bursts from the street. The woman was wearing a wide-brimmed hat with flowing cream chiffon around the brim and under her chin; its tails danced beyond her shoulders like racing silks. The man was brown-suited, high collared, in goggles and yellow driving gloves. He was laughing, hunched over a black wheel that apparently guided the thing, and he was trying to catch the trap of Reverend Elliott of Trinity Church as it bucketed down Spring Street. Bishop Elliott held the reins of his bay mare who, last year, had beaten a Peerce stallion in a match race. The mare was galloping, almost running flat out. Dangerous in town at high noon and most unlike Bishop Elliott whom Audrey knew only as a most proper gentleman. He must be on an emergency mission of mercy, she reasoned. He must be hastening to the bed of a dying man to perform the last rites....

But the race was on, and Audrey and the other pedestrians stood back. The several other carriages on Spring Street stopped in their tracks and waited, too, for the fury to pass. One called encouragement to the man—"Get her, Rails!"—and one lady waved a delicate, white-gloved hand in encouragement, but Bishop Elliott's mare was clearly the winner, three coach-lengths ahead and more with every stretching leap....

So that's what it's like to be rich every day, Audrey thought, watching, excited in spite of her impatience to carry on. No rules apply when you don't want them to. It must be hard to be good when you don't have to be; it must be impossible, given temptation enough....

He was there beside her, taking her arm, turning her body to his. Bayard Lockholm.

"Oh!" she said, suddenly shy, suddenly so happy.

He was grinning at her, that mysterious half smile. His hair was blown by a breeze and there was road dust on the ivory shoulders of his suit, so he had been as close to the race as she. His eyes were not grinning. His eyes were cold, the cold, flat gray of the sea before it sucks itself up into storm. . . .

"Did I startle you?" he said, still holding her arm, looking down at her from his height. "Frighten you? You look as though you'd seen a ghost."

"N-no," she stuttered, unable to pull her eyes from his. But he did frighten her, he frightened her in the most exciting way. . . . The heat of him! She felt it again. She wanted to roll in the heat of him, it was like the first sunshine after winter. It *pulled* her. . . . She was very cold. Her blood had stopped running in her veins, and only this man, this broad-shouldered, elegant man, *if* he laid his hands upon her, *if* he stroked her long and slow, could melt the ice that froze her heart. . . . "I'm just so happy to see you," she finally said. "Thank you for what you did."

"I haven't done anything yet," he said, and stepped closer.

There was only an inch of space between them. If she could move just a little she would be against him. Her head would fit *there*, below the knot of his tie. Her arms would encircle his waist, and his arms, his strong arms, would draw her to his mouth. . . . With a blink, the ice that had been in his eyes and chilled her to freezing was gone. Now there was play and dancing in his face, and his lips parted. *Now*, she thought. . . .

A carriage was drawing up to the curb. The strange man she thought was Mr. Smythe was in it. The carriage was coming for Bay. She didn't want him to go. . . .

"I wish we had met at a different time," he said. His hand fell away from her arm, he stepped back and bowed, and the sun faded, cloud-quick, from the gray of his eyes.

"I hope things go well for you. You will learn a lot from Ally."

"I want to learn from you," she said.

The carriage door opened. "Are you ready, Mr. Lockholm?" said the man inside.

"I am," he said. Lithe, he swung himself into the seat. "I'm sorry I cannot offer you a lift, Miss Smoke. We're on official business, it seems. Maybe next time."

She just watched him. The hand she had meant to wave lay forgotten upon her lips. She stepped to where he had stood, to feel him still.

With a sturdy trot, the carriage horse bore him away from her.

In Darling's, Audrey headed down the long aisles of cloth to the back wall and the pattern books. Two women were standing before a great, open book turned to a double page of splendid gowns.

Audrey stopped dead. She recognized them both. Mrs. Lockholm, matriarch, and Celeste Lockholm, bride-to-be. Up close, Mrs. Lockholm had an imperial air. Black gowned, garlanded in miles of pearls. Pearls in her ears, at her throat five tiers, on her bosom, twenty chains, each one-pearl longer than the one before. Close, she did not look sad or bent, as Audrey had thought, from a distance, she looked yesterday. Close, she breathed fire, was proud and hard eyed, and Audrey stepped back with a gasp she couldn't suppress. She turned up the aisle to her right where thick bolts of summer muslins in pretty flower prints half hid her from their eyes.

But if Audrey thought she was noticed, she was mistaken. Celeste, taller than Audrey, thinner than Audrey, fragile in upswept dark hair under a feathered hat of purple mist, in a long, filmy fall of lavender lace, in lavender silk shoes with two-inch heels that buttoned on a strap over her arch, Celeste had eyes only for the designs before her, and Mrs. Lockholm had her eyes on a tiny, gold-backed notebook, in which she was writing with a golden fountain pen.

"When it's done fast, it's never done right, you know that, my dear. I'll not go over it again. You could have had Worth, Worth all the way. Now you're stuck with Priscilla, and she's impossible, and if the wretched woman suggests off-white again, I'll personally murder her myself. With a hatchet."

"Mother," a sigh of a voice. "The dress is body-beige and diamanté and whitest seed pearls and it's delicious. Now stop, and choose one of these for the servants, please do."

"This one, I think. The skirt's like a tulip, it will be becoming on them all. And the petal sleeves will let them stretch their arms. Yes, this one, Celeste. And now how many yards of the cotton will we need?"

"Twenty girls with different figures is Priscilla's problem, not ours. Let's leave it to her and go have our lunch. Thorne's waiting to tell us how he did at the bank. I do hope he succeeds, Mother, and you must hope so, too. It means so much to my happiness."

"Piffle and fiddlesticks. That young man will succeed whether I pull for him or not. He has that look about him. He snagged you quick enough." Mrs. Lockholm was writing in her notebook, noting the number of the pattern, the sizes and the price. "And how is he," she said as she snapped the book shut, "how is he progressing with his grammar?"

They were moving away now, to the left, the pattern book left open to the pages. Celeste took her mother's arm and said something Audrey couldn't hear that caused Mrs. Lockholm to bark a laugh. And then, louder but only just, Celeste said, "I'm glad you chose the petal dress, Mother, it was almost the prettiest...."

They were gone.

Audrey crept out of her place and approached the pattern book. She looked at the dresses. They were ball gowns! True, they were shorter, above the ankles in the new, so-called tea-dance length, but they were ball gowns, dresses for a debutante, not for a house servant. And twenty girls were to have them? For one splendid day? It would cost hundreds of dollars to do it...maybe into the thousands....

It is something I don't understand, Audrey thought, and should not concern myself with. I'm here to find a costume for an office girl. But now she was unsure of her choices, and she pored over the patterns too long. Her time was growing short and she did not want to keep Mr. McGregor waiting. She had to buy something and the material for it; she would have to hurry and, like Mrs. Lockholm, choose one. And probably, like Mrs. Lockholm, too, Audrey would choose "almost the prettiest...."

She chose. It is a perfect office dress, she thought. I cannot be wrong. It had a high band at the neck and a neat gathered waist and a wide hem, edged top and bottom in velvet cording. The bodice was intricately tucked with tiny pleats and set off either side in velvet, as were the cuffs. It would not be an easy dress to make, but it was quietly fashionable, she thought, a constructed dress, much better than any she had had before. A woman-of-the-world dress; a dress for a woman who worked for her living. Broadcloth was suggested as the fabric. She bought in three colors, black and brown and light blue. The velvet was black on all. The purchase took all the money Mr. McGregor had loaned her, but it was, she felt, a gesture of faith in herself. In her future.

And then she ran almost all the way to the Casino, the heavy parcel's string cutting into her fingers.

Outside the windowed white-and-brass door of the Casino café, she stopped. Within there were fresh flowers and starched lime-green tablecloths—lime green, to show every stain. Within there were polished braziers over little blue flames roasting delicacies Audrey had never tasted, did not know the names of, had never seen. Within there were white-coated waiters who knew a shop girl from a lady and would treat her accordingly. Within was Bellevue Avenue and Ocean Drive, the pampered rich, at leisure. High society at its proper play.... And here was Audrey Smoke again, penniless town girl, clutching a huge brown-paper parcel tied with string in a gloveless hand. Here she stood, face flushed from running like a twelve-year-old, un-coiffed hair wisping out of its bun, scattering pins. Here she stood, *sweat* under her armpits, about to move into a cir-cle of her betters. Where she had no right to be....

She went in, her head down. She would go in, but she could not look Gilt Hill in the eye....

Through a mist of rich smells, rich colors, rich faces, Audrey searched the room for Mr. McGregor. Blessedly she spotted him, on a banquette before a wide window, as the maître d'hôtel descended upon her.

He wore a dinner jacket. He had golden curls. He was beyond fifty and corseted. His mouth was pulled down to his jawline.

"Scoot now, servants go round the back or wait out-side, there's a good girl."

Audrey stood beneath the man's lifted chin. "Mr. McGregor, please. I believe I'm expected." She had re-membered her rehearsed line from this morning. She al-most danced in place with self-congratulation because the man, instantly, bowed and smiled and extended his arms, one to touch her back, one to sign the way, and led her through the room.

She trembled, holding her parcel to her breast so as not to disturb the tables or the patrons. Her knees were weak. All faces swam indistinctly before her glazed eyes. But she crossed the café floor and stood, terrified, for the first time before a seat reserved only for her.

Mr. McGregor was chewing toast. "Ah, Cinderella. Sit down, my dear. You look as though you need to."

"Yes, sir," she said, and sat.

"Orestes," said Mr. McGregor to the man in golden curls. "This is my new assistant, Miss Audrey Smoke. Au-drey, this is Orestes. He is an institution in Newport, knows everyone and everything worth knowing, and is a fine fel-low besides, aren't you, Orestes?"

The maître d' bowed over Audrey's hand. "I am indeed a fine fellow, Miss Smoke, and I am delighted to make your acquaintance. Welcome to the Casino. Ah, here, Mr. McGregor, is your wine."

Audrey nodded, frightened to breathe; watched as a waiter presented a bottle wrapped in cloth for Mr. Mc-Gregor, watched the bottle opened and sampled and poured. Watched a glass filled for her. Watched as a plate of strange, glossy shells was set before her, a round plate with a circle of hollows especially made to hold the shells. Watched with orphan eyes.

"Ah," said Mr. McGregor, "escargot and escarole, my favorite luncheon." He dotted his lips with a great napkin and observed her. "Audrey," he said.

She looked at him, afraid to speak.

"It's going to be all right, my girl. I've decided just now that I like you. And when I decide such a thing, I never change my mind. So it's going to be all right, you see. Now eat up. Just follow me. I'll show you how...."

"Yes, Mr. McGregor. Thank you, Mr. McGregor. I—I like you, too."

"Attagirl!"

8

To work with Alabaster McGregor was to ascend into a different world entirely. The Newport that Audrey had known all her life was transposed, wonderful and strange. As the butterfly, growing wings, hides awhile within an earthbound caterpillar and then, suddenly, flies, so Newport, a fulsome Newport, spun, unfurled, before her senses. Glorious, yes. All new, yes.

And frightening, very frightening....

For even as she, stumbling and eager, began her work, Newport hummed and buzzed of John Bayard Lockholm who, so many said, had killed his wife. Killed her, they whispered, with his baby in her womb, and, they added, *almost* got away with it. *Would have* got away with it, except for the courage of a little servant girl who could not rest, who would not run, until she had done her duty....

Might still get away with it, unless justice was done....

Audrey rarely saw him. And when she did, he was stopping only to confer, briefly, with Mr. McGregor. Once, looking down from the second-floor newsroom, she saw him in the street, in a small coach, with his mother. The horse was a fine gray with polished hooves that glistened on the cobblestones, and Mrs. Lockholm's gown matched the horse, dark dappled moiré and jet lace. Alabaster McGregor went out to Bayard Lockholm that day. He talked with the matriarch, too. Audrey thought that long ago Mrs. Lockholm must have been as beautiful as her daughter....

Audrey never saw Celeste around the *Daily Whirl*. Or Thorne. And she never saw Bayard Lockholm with a woman she could think him romantically interested in....

She wished she would.

One or a dozen, she would have known then that she was forgotten—or never remembered—and begun to heal. She thought that seeing him only once with a woman of his own kind would stop her dreams, stop her heart from hurting, stop her hiding secrets from her mother in the mirror....

She asked Mr. McGregor, "Who will Bayard Lockholm marry now, do you think? Is there a lady in his heart?"

Alabaster looked at her with his depthless eyes. "What do you think your chances are?" His face was as pale and thrusting as a shark's.

She was flustered and humiliated. "Don't be mean, Mr. McGregor, don't tease me. I know Mr. Lockholm is far above me. I—I just see him so alone now, now when he needs love near...." Then she attacked again the typewriter she was beginning to master and said, without meeting those eyes, "You know everything else, Mr. McGregor, I thought you would know that, too," meaning to sting....

A couple of times the hulking Mr. Smythe was with Bayard Lockholm, a quiet shadow. The two did not converse when they passed McGregor's and Audrey's desks—hers was pushed side to side against his: "I don't like anyone in front of me ever, in anything," Alabaster explained—and Bayard always went first, leading the way back to the last desk, partitioned by itself. The two would sit and talk in low voices. And then Mr. Smythe would leave alone, nodding to no one. The detective from Providence came only twice that Audrey saw; still, she constantly heard of him. He was questioning Newporters...Bayard's friends...and Bayard's enemies.

Audrey asked Mr. McGregor, "Does Mr. Lockholm have enemies, true enemies, who would speak against him to Mr. Smythe?"

And again that gaunt, unsmiling face, the knife-edge eyes. "In the midst of a smile, the public bares its teeth, my girl. And the man who puts you up for the club is the one with a black ball hidden in his fist.... Remember Phineas Brown?"

"But that was Mr. Lockholm's great-grandfather. Not Bayard. And that was a long time ago, a myth now."

Alabaster shrugged. "Is it? Now get along. Finish typing my column. I love to see myself in print...."

At home Audrey hoped to make peace with her father. Not capitulation, but a kind of peace; a tolerance and Audrey's acceptance of what she could not change. But Lawrence Smoke avoided her in the week before his wedding. She rose at six; he rose at eight. She returned home after long days and her father would have already eaten, the dishes washed and put away...and he would not be there. Late, after midnight, she would awaken to his booted step upon the stairs, across the kitchen, down the passage to his room. He would not look in to see if she was safe, tucked in, as once he had.

And Audrey noticed subtle changes in the position of the kitchen things. So she knew Dolly Dowd was in her mother's place while she was away. Dolly Dowd came to the Smoke house and made the supper and ate with Audrey's father, getting used to her new home. And then Lawrence walked Dolly back to the rooms over Grimsby's Tavern. They would have a drink or two in the saloon with his new friends—her old ones—and then they would climb the stairs to Dolly's bed.

And the laughter would begin....

Lawrence would rise and head home—for propriety's sake, now that he was making Dolly Dowd an honest woman?—tramping from the Long Wharf to Bridge Street, hoping his daughter would be out of his way, in her bed, out of his sight....

Alone in the little house, for the first time Audrey listened to its creak and heard the soft ghost-runs of mice feet in the walls.

Before bed, each night, she talked to her mother while she brushed out her hair before the cheval glass, sitting on the foot of her bunk, legs crossed Indian-style under her nightshirt. She told Josephine about Dolly. "She is formidable, Mama. She is autumn haired, russet as maple leaves in October, and her complexion is fine. There is fire in her cheeks, whether of boldness or shame or a combination, and her eyes are soft, yet they question. And when he is

with her in his room the bedsprings squeak and she laughs
low and long.... He is going to marry her, Mama. For her,
he has forgotten you and me. Is it all right with you,
Mama? Do you understand? She has a terrible reputation...."

Somewhere in Audrey's heart, sympathy for her father,
just a tendril, curled. She took it for the soul of Josephine,
tracing an answer.

By the time Audrey finished her work on Friday evening, it was dusk. She walked to the harbor and along the
strand and then followed Cliff Walk to a height where she
sat, her skirts a cushion, and sought the whales.

She did not climb to WaterWalk; she could go to
WaterWalk no more. Bayard might suspect her of hoping
for him.

Here, by the sea, he was Bayard again, the Bayard of that
night, and so it would have to be: she would not give up the
sea for him, for anything! The sea was too dear.... But
Bayard Lockholm had done enough for her, more than
enough, and she did not want to make him fear that she was
coming, again, to snivel on his jacket in the night.

Worse than the threat of Bayard Lockholm was the fear
that Thorne and Celeste might see her at sea's edge and
think she was mooning, pathetic and alone, for him, her
once betrothed....

How long ago Thorne seemed....

Audrey could not see over the promontory that was
WaterWalk; could not see where the lawns of Whale's
Turning rolled to their seawall and then opened to a wild-
ness that fell down to the sea, down to the foaming, rock-
excited waves, down to a thin tongue of pier. That was
good. If she could not see them, they could not see her....
And Thorne and Celeste might be docking *The Rose* now
after a long sail. It was a good day for sailing; warm, with
a soft, steady wind out of the west, over the ocean; a sail-
or's wind to send a boat wherever it wanted to go....
Thorne and Celeste might be docking. They would be tired
and happy, and scrabbling onto the pier. They would climb,
breathless, and then, with a start, they would see Audrey,

quiet as a sea hawk in its cleft. And they would think she was hunting in their wake....

Please no.

Let them be married quickly, she thought. Their wedding was two weeks away and then, surely, they would enjoy an extended honeymoon. Let them marry, and then perhaps Audrey could climb again to her favorite spot and watch in twilight, where the water bent into the bay, a whale making rainbows as it played....

At length, Audrey left. It was dark, the harbor lights spangles. She wound her way through the streets, at her ease, in no hurry to come, in an empty night, to a silent home.

She passed Mrs. Olsson's bakeshop and saw the woman inside. Mrs. Olsson was positioning a two-tier cake in the window, a wedding cake set upon a round plate of brilliant blue to approximate Rhode Island Sound. Around the base of the first tier, on the blue glaze of the plate, swans swam, egg-white and sugar swans, their wings aloft to signify happiness. And on the top tier a man and woman, tiny dolls, stood in a circle of icing lilies of the valley and wedding bells. The dolls were in formal dress; the man in white morning suit, the woman in a pouf of white lace with a tiny lace bouquet.

Audrey stopped to admire it. It was to have been her wedding cake, and now it was her father's. She felt no loss, but she smiled at the confection. It was pretty; it would please any bride.

Mrs. Olsson saw her, beckoned her in. Audrey entered the shop, smiling. She was not ashamed any longer of her lost wedding. It had been a different person who had giggled and ordered this wedding cake....

"She'll love it, Mrs. Olsson," Audrey said. "It's a work of art."

Mrs. Olsson was admiring it, too. "Yes, I'm the Rembrandt of cakes, I think. And it will taste good, too. It's butter cream inside, and I dropped a little ring into the batter, for a lucky someone to find in her slice.... How are you, Audrey?"

"I'm fine. I've started working on the newspaper with Mr. McGregor, the editor. I'm learning so much. My days are full."

"That's why you look so well. Your dress is handsome. Did you sew it up yourself?"

Audrey turned around to show it off. It was the only one completed of the three she'd planned. It was the brown one, and she liked it, too, though Mr. McGregor said it made her look like a mouse. "All night, the first day I started. Mr. McGregor said I would have to look the part if I was to have the job. It was harder than I thought it would be, but dresses always are.... Has Miss Dowd seen her cake yet? Has my father?"

Mrs. Olsson had the round face and figure of someone who enjoyed her bakery work. When she worked, she wore a shapeless dress covered by a large white apron. She took off the apron now and shook off powdered sugar. "Tomorrow your father is picking it up. She wanted to be surprised, she said. Here, I have something for you—your deposit."

"Oh, that was yours, Mrs. Olsson. I've forgotten it."

"No, your father paid for the cake in full. Wait just a minute." Mrs. Olsson crossed the shop to a door in the rear, folding her apron. Then she was back, an envelope in her hand. "Two dollars and fifty cents you gave me, and there you are. And...I made this for you, too. Just a froufrou, but it's for you. It's so you'll remember me when you want another wedding cake, as you will when the time is right."

Mrs. Olsson moved behind her bakery case and bent below Audrey's sight. Then she was in front of Audrey again, a white whale in her hand, an egg-white and sugar whale, its flukes lifted, a hard-sugar spout of spray rising from its head. She set it in Audrey's hand. "It's not to eat, it's to dream on."

"Oh, Mrs. Olsson.... How did you know?" Was Mrs. Olsson a witch or a sorceress who could see dreams?

Mrs. Olsson was shaping cardboard into a little box. "But you're always talking about the whales, Audrey. Ever since you were a little girl. You used to come here with your grandfather and I called you 'the little whaling girl.' You don't remember that?''

Audrey shook her head. "It seems like magic, though. I—I've just come from Cliff Walk, looking for the whales. There weren't any in the bay at sunset. And now I have one."

Mrs. Olsson put waxed paper in the box and took the whale from Audrey's palm and set it in. Then she closed the lid and tied the box with string. "There," she said. "Be happy, darling. There's a great big world out there."

"Thank you, Mrs. Olsson. Thank you so very much."

"See you tomorrow, Audrey. Maybe you'll get the slice with the ring."

The slice with the ring....

But Audrey wasn't going to her father's wedding. Or the party after. Her father hadn't told her where the party was to be, and as for the wedding, he hadn't invited her.

THE UPSTAIRS DOOR was closed, the rooms dark. Audrey climbed the stairs feeling, despite Mrs. Olsson's kindness, very old and alone.

In her room she got the gas lamp going and freed the whale from its box and set it in her window, on the ledge where the westerly sun would catch it. Then, turning, she saw an envelope on her bed pillow. She opened it, turned away from the cheval glass.

It was a note, written in a bad hand on turquoise paper rimmed in gold. It asked her to the wedding of her father to Dolores Dowd at the Congregational Church at eleven in the morning on Saturday, the fifteenth of June, and to the "celabration" after in Grimsby's Tavern on the Long Wharf. It was signed "hopefully, Dolly."

So that was how it was to be. Nothing from her father. No semblance of understanding for her feelings, no gesture of reconciliation.

She sat for a moment, staring out her window at the lamppost outside. She would have to make her supper now....

Rap, rap, rap.

She didn't take it in at first. She sat, having heard it, as though it were a memory.

But then it came again. Rap, rap, rap.

Thorne's signal.

Thorne's signal—but how could that be? And what could he want? Oh, was it possible he had broken with the beautiful Celeste and was coming back, repentant, hoping to take up with Audrey again? To go back to before...to before his betrayal?

Rap, rap, rap.

Thank God her father wasn't there. But what should she do? She did not want to see Thorne. If she could have erased him from her life as chalk from a blackboard, and then washed the blackboard shiny and blank, that is what she would have done. But now, what to do? Sit like a ninny while, alone in her home, she waited for him to tire and leave? But he would know she was home; he would have seen the little light in her room, soft at the window. He would know she was hiding from him...in shame...in fear? He might climb the stairs and try the upper door. It was not bolted....

Rap, rap, rap.

She went to the first door, swung it open, slipped down the steps in the dark. "So little and so mean...."

"Yes," she said, the timbered door still between them.

"Aud." His voice was mellow and cajoling, inches from her ear. "Aud, please, could I speak with you a moment? It's awfully important."

She opened it to him.

He stood just beyond, as he used to stand. Hair deeper than the Newport night, skin as bronze as the gates of the mansions on Ocean Drive, with that serious cast to his face, which she had thought in the erstwhile time, had meant the intensity of his longing for her....

"Yes," she said. And then Audrey saw his companion, a step or two behind. A tall woman with hair just as brilliantly ebony, cloaked in ruby velvet with diamonds at her throat. Her hands were gloved and held to her breast as though in supplication. Her complexion was as cool and soft as star haze.

"Good evening, Miss Lockholm," Audrey said.

"Aud, we had to come—" He was nervous, she saw that now. She had never seen Thorne uncomfortable before. She waited.

"It's this terrible thing about Virginia."

"Yes," Audrey said. There was no feeling. No surprise, no curiosity. "What is it, Thorne."

"Could we come in?"

"Father's sleeping," she lied without even thinking about it. The lie came to her lips from the nothing-feeling inside.

Celeste spoke, a sigh in the night. "Then may we sit in my carriage, Miss Smoke? What we have to say is very personal to us and very private."

Audrey closed the door behind herself and followed them without a word.

Away from the street lamp, under the shadowy overhang of a hickory tree, was a covered coach and the dappled gray that Audrey had seen before, looking down from the second floor of the newsroom onto the street, when unseen she had gazed at Bayard Lockholm and his mother talking with Mr. McGregor. She climbed in, swept her skirts close so as not to take up much room. The leather that enveloped her was warm, still, from someone's body heat. It was a soft leather, thin suede. Audrey stroked it with a wondering hand. The night was cool but fine, the wind just strong enough to make the leaves above her murmur an unknown tongue. In the distance, by the water, she could hear, too, a tavern piano, fast and saucy and loud, but faint here on Bridge Street on Saturday night.

Thorne began, leaning on his knees to put his face close to hers. Celeste Lockholm, at Audrey's side, looked straight ahead.

"It's about the investigation into the death of Celeste's brother's wife. Detective Smythe is questioning everyone about everyone, and he will come to you...about me. I gave

Mrs. Lockholm some sailing lessons last year, I don't know if you remember—"

Remember? She had never known the names and the faces of the heiresses of Gilt Hill and Ochre Point that Thorne squired for money in Narragansett Bay. She had never given them a thought, except how, by their knowing him, his ferry business might succeed.

"And now I'm marrying into the family..." He paused to drop his eyes from hers. "Well, I've come to ask you not to speak against me, Aud. I only knew Virginia Lockholm in the most formal way, and it is a delicate time for Celeste and me now." He reached over and took his intended's hand and held it. "Celeste and I are very much in love, but we know our situation. I—I'm not worthy of her, we both know that—"

"Oh, Thorne," from Celeste, sweet as baby's breath.

"I know nothing about Virginia Lockholm, Aud."

"I know that, Thorne," she said.

He looked at her again then, a naked pleading in his eyes, eyes she had never seen plead before. "Then will you tell Detective Smythe that when he asks? It would mean so much to us, so much to all the family."

"And I know, Miss Smoke," Celeste said, soft as the leather under Audrey's palm, "that you are a friend of my brother's. He's been through so much. If you could help us in this way, we would be in your debt."

"Please rest easy, then," Audrey said. "I won't speak badly of you, Thorne. I wish you both all happiness.... May I go now? I have so much to do."

Thorne released Celeste's hand and took Audrey's. He squeezed it and kissed her knuckles and dropped it back on her lap. "Thanks, Aud. I told Celeste you were a brick." His eyes were dancing now, glad now. He was the Thorne she remembered, a confident Thorne, slightly preening....

Audrey nodded and, somehow, she was out of the carriage, feet firm on the street; her street, in the center of town. Where she belonged.

There was no driver. Thorne took the reins and the gray tossed its head, pulled against the tightening of the bit.

"Thank you, Miss Smoke...." It hovered around Audrey like perfume as she stood and watched the carriage's yellow spokes spin like silent wheels of fortune, rolling uptown.

Back in her room the little egg-white whale lay powdered to sugar dust on the floor. The wind from the sea, the sailor's wind, must have gusted in, upset the whale and sent it crashing.

The next morning's sun found Audrey already up and dressed and packed, one big cloth bag. Her father had not come home last night; he would not come to the Smoke house again, Audrey thought, until he brought Dolly Dowd home to stay.

She knew Mr. Kirchner and Sal would pass her house about seven. They came, every day including Sunday, once in the morning and once at sunset. Audrey went down to the street to wait. When she saw the cart, she flagged it down. Sal wore her Sunday hat, a boater with a red-plaid band, holes cut in the brim for her ears.

"Will you give me a ride, Mr. Kirchner, please?"

"Don' see why not." He reined in. Sal yawned, showing long, yellow teeth and a large-white tongue. "Where you goin' this fine day? Not a funeral again, is it? But wasn't that a day."

"To Mildred Falk's, sir. My father's getting married today, and I'm going to visit with Miss Falk awhile. To let the new Mrs. Smoke get used to her new home, without an old daughter around."

"Well ain' you the sweetest thing ever was. Let me take that bag—" He hoisted it into the foot space in front of the bench where he sat. "You can boost yourself up, I reckon."

"Yes, sir. Thank you very much."

"No trouble. We're gettin' used to you ridin' wid us, ain' we, Sal? Heee-uppp, girl."

Audrey liked Mr. Kirchner. He never asked personal questions. He was kind to all things. He worked every day but never seemed to grow older; seemed to have been born

just as old as he was today. And so, too, Sal. The cart horse
was no more gray of muzzle and splayed of hocks now than
when Audrey first tottled out of her mother's arms to pet
"the horsie" with the great clown face.

"Does Sal ever get tired pulling corn and watermelon and
baskets of cabbage, Mr. Kirchner? Do you?"

"Well, I'll tellya, I asked her once. 'Sal,' I says, 'do ya
wanna quit? You already done a fair lot of work in your
time. How'dya like to sit under an apple tree all day instead and just open your mouth?' And she said to me, no
hesitation mindya, she said to me real quick, 'Nope,
thankya just the same, Mr. K. I got used to haulin' young.
I don' even notice the load anymore. I reckon I'm like you,
boss. I like walkin' around and watchin' the world go by....'
So there's your answer, Audrey."

He let Audrey off on Sunshine Street, close to the cemetery.

"Give Mildred my best," he said, handing down Audrey's bag. "Used to be a girlfriend o' mine, didcha know?
Way back. But she fancied Hiram Ader who ended up wid
the Sutter girl.... Well, so long now.... Heee-uppp, Sal."

Mildred Falk rented Audrey a spacious room. Its two
large windows overlooked the cemetery where her mother
was buried. The wallpaper was tiny yellow wildflowers
against a blue-dotted cream background. And the bed was
a wide four-poster with a white chenille spread. She charged
Audrey two dollars a week, and went on with her dressing.
Mildred was going to Lawrence Smoke's wedding for "Josephine's sake," she said. She added, almost girlish,
"Anyway, I wouldn't miss it. I adore weddings. They make
me feel young again."

Most amazing to Audrey, who had thought of Mildred
Falk as a silly old woman, easily hysterical, was that she
had not acted surprised at Audrey's coming, had asked no
questions why, had not welcomed her effusively or grudg-
ingly given in to Audrey's need. She had understood on
sight Audrey's delicate position and awkward situation.
Why, she's just being wonderful, Audrey thought. Mildred
Falk would have been a good wife and mother. It just

hadn't worked out right for the dear woman. For her, either....

In the new room Audrey was nervous, conscious of the clock on the mantle ticking the time to her father's second wedding day. So fast, so slow.... She tried to think that it might have been her day, but those thoughts did not seem real. She did not feel like a spurned bride as Mildred Falk must have, three times left by different men. Audrey did not know Miss Falk's story. It was old conversation by the time Audrey was told it, and Audrey hadn't cared. Mildred Falk had been, to the child Audrey, just another faded spinster with an ever-narrowing life and a head full of shallow ideas. But she must have been somehow exceptional to have lured three men to the marriage commitment.... Even Mr. Kirchner, just now, remembered his passion for Mildred Falk vividly enough to speak of it. Miss Falk must have had, too, some lack as a woman, which, discovered late, caused all three men to change their minds in the final hour. What could it have been? And did Audrey have the same?

Audrey stood at a window looking down at the cemetery, thinking she would go, at eleven, and sit at the foot of her mother's grave while her father pledged himself to another. Loud she heard, though she tried to shut it out, the inexorable ticking of the clock. Ping, ping, ping, ping.... On and on forever. How high was the count—now—no now—no—and what was the number of time, measured in those hard little pings since the world first began to turn...? Ping, ping, ping, ping.... Making bright hair white and strong hands frail. Making a hot, desiring heart a cold and rigid thing.... Ping, ping, ping, ping....

Bayard Lockholm was walking in the cemetery.

Two stories up, across Farewell Street at the corner of Sunshine, Audrey recognized his hatless head bent to the wind, the brown hair falling over his forehead like a boy's. He was solitary and seemed uncertain of his direction. He moved up one path, then retraced his steps and began another way. He moved beyond her view.

Was, then, Virginia Lockholm over there, covered by summer grass and a simple stone like Josephine had? Or was there, somewhere she couldn't see, a mausoleum of dazzling granite, great blocks, columned and arcaded like a Grecian temple, with the Lockholm crest—three waves in chips of tourmaline below a platinum sailing ship—set large into the architrave to remind all who passed that *royalty* lay in rest . . . ?

He should have a dog, Audrey thought; a faithful hound quiet and separate like himself, to keep him company and give him ease. With a dog he could relax, perhaps even be foolish—kick over an anthill, climb a tree, laugh at nothing—and no one would frown and no one would tell. With a hound he could walk for miles, silent or talkative as he chose, well dressed or shaggy, and have an agreeable companion. Someone never disappointed, someone always content, just to be with him, rambling unconcernedly by his side. . . .

Unthinking, Audrey ran to him.

BAYARD LOCKHOLM WAS nowhere in sight.

In the cemetery, Audrey had time to reflect, and uncertainty gripped her—what, after all, had she to say to him, here, that she would not say to him in the office of the *Daily Whirl*—but a sense of urgency impelled her, a dread. She did not name it, could not define it, but she knew it was important she find him and speak to him again, alone...if only this once, this last time. And she had to find him now, before it was too late. . . .

There was a gatekeeper, but Audrey avoided him. He might wonder who she was, seeking the grave of Virginia Lockholm just after Bayard Lockholm had passed. So she wandered, under a full blue sky, hot already in June, but the heat eased from the breezes off the sea. She hurried past her mother's grave; she would come back to it, but first she had to find him and tell him she believed; believed in his innocence. She had to tell him she knew he would not harm anyone he loved, not for anything, no matter what the people whispered....

She looked for grand burial buildings, but there were none. The graves were much alike, all topped with simple stones. The grass on some was sunburned already, unshaded. The mounds of some were flattening with the passage of time and the settling of the earth. A few were fresh and grassless. Most of the stones were of slate and slanting, tilted back so that a great eye above could look down and read them if it chose and, perhaps, pause to remember a good deed done or kindness in a heart. On some the name and dates had worn thin. On others the name and inscriptions were cut very deep and were filling with moss, the moss deepest green, soft and creeping, obliterating memory. Very few of the graves wore flowers. On one, someone had planted flowering ivy. It was budding now despite the dry; she thought it was honeysuckle, soon to smell sweet. On another, one of Wicke's wreaths, gone brittle, was breaking up. On two were fresh flowers: long lilies tied with yellow ribbon on a grave just filled in, unmarked; and on the second a single rose dropping its petals, dying.

Where the path dipped and circled, the other side of a spreading beech, she saw him. He was before a grave as simple as the rest, as flowerless as the least....

Audrey began to run.

She saw him look up at the sound of her sandals slapping on the gravel like gunshots in the quiet. His brows were drawn tight over his eyes, his face was unpleasant.

The path dipped and Audrey was running faster, hurtling downhill. Breathless, she stopped herself with her hands against the trunk of the tree and turned to him. "I—I just wanted to tell you...have to tell you..." she said.

"Tell me what?" He is astonished to see me, she thought. He thinks me a terrible disturber of his peace. Rude, breaking in at this most private moment....

She would have to tell him now or never be able to. If she did not tell him now she would hold it forever inside her, shriveled and as heavy as sod. "I—I know you didn't do it," she said. "I know you didn't harm her, but only loved her, always and ever. I—I just ..." she was mumbling, losing her conviction, the urgency of a moment ago gone at the sight of his angry face. "I just wanted you to know...." She gasped to catch her breath, sought his eyes with hers. Would he understand?

He was laughing. Laughing at her. A mirthless laugh. His hands were deep in his trouser pockets, as she had seen him before when he had paced back and forth on WaterWalk and said, "Let's see, we'll get out of this, and worse." But he was not gentle now....

"You fool," he said. "What do you mean coming here—here!—to tell me this?"

She was leaning against the tree trunk, her breath coming in great heaves. She looked at him and thought how doglike must her eyes be now, filled with devotion and hurt and the knowledge that she was not good enough, could never be *good enough*.... There would always be something missing, something essential, something without which ...

She gestured behind her head. "I—I saw you at my window across Farewell Street. And I felt I had to come, I may never have the chance again. I wanted you to know before others say it, too, and make my words less, joined with theirs. There was never any doubt for me, I know your goodness. I—I never even had to think about it. I—I just wanted to—"

The bad smile was gone, but his eyes were disinterested.

"Thank you," he said in the impersonal way she had gotten used to in a week, hearing it above her head addressed to Mr. McGregor, hearing it across the room into his telephone.... He turned his head away. Tired of her, she thought. Wanting her gone, she thought.

"Yes," she said.

She turned to leave, to walk the swell of curve away from him, his eyes boring into her back to hasten her going or, worse, his instantly forgetting she was ever there....

His hand on her wrist was a death grip.

"She bored me," he said, and Audrey did not recognize his voice; it was harsh and savage. "She bored me early on.

Do you hear me? Two weeks into the marriage, three, four.... By Istanbul—ha!—exotic Istanbul, I was thoroughly bored, and knew I always would be."

He yanked Audrey around to face him. She did not like his face now. It was hard and cold, the eyes bled of their blue, the eyes only gray now as barren rock, as his cheeks were gray, and his lips. "What has marriage to do with love, anyway?"

She tried to pull her arm free, but he held her, hurting.

"I picked her from a flock of girls just like her, all perfectly wonderful girls with perfectly fetching ways. My mother said I must marry, it was time. She wanted to see her grandchild, wanted to know the Lockholm line was safe. Mother wasn't well, she said. She was a widow, and I owed her a peaceful grave. I must marry, Mother said—"

"Please," said Audrey. "I—I..."

His eyes were as bleak as a dungeon and his voice was a devil's rasp. "You don't want to hear this? You want to think me perfect? Well, I'm not perfect. You want to go on with your little-girl dreams that Bay Lockholm never gets angry, never lashes out, never strikes back?" He grabbed her other arm, jerked her closer. She was almost against his chest. "Well, I do," he said. "Given provocation, I strike back."

He freed her with a push.

"You're a fool, Audrey Smoke. You don't know your man. You think I live like a god because I have a large house and a clean shirt. You think I'm happy, think that money, lots of money, is all that happiness requires. God save me, there is more to it, my lost little beauty. Much more to it." His eyes raked her face, her body, his eyes in sudden storm.

She had not foreseen this, running to him. She had not wanted this, seeking him out alone. She had not meant or wanted to give him pain. She had only wanted to tell him, without baring her heart, without him thinking that she hoped for his friendship, that she loved him not because of who he was, rich John Bayard Lockholm III, lord of

Whale's Turning, but for what he was: a man of worth, the best man she had ever known....

He was calmer now, his hands deep again in his pockets. He was pacing now, but he was still angry, still speaking in a dull, hard tone, as gray as his rock-cold face. "You're foolish and you're ignorant. You were in love and were left. You think everyone left is as devastated as you are. Well, *I wasn't*. I wasn't devastated. I was sorry for her, sorry for the child I might have had. But I was not devastated. She was a silly, spoiled creature, and I was, in some part of my soul, relieved."

He was finally silent. When he spoke again it was as though he had never been fierce, had never lost control. "There is room here for two more," he said. He pointed out the places on the ground with a black-booted foot. "My mother will go here, alongside Father. And I will go here, I suppose, alongside Virginia.... No one seriously thinks I killed her, do they?"

He glanced sideways at Audrey who stood where he had thrown her, twisting her wrists with her hands. His voice was mild now, all passion gone, and his face was regaining its color.

He hadn't heard, then. No one had told him. Alabaster McGregor, who knew better than almost everyone, had not told him. His sister Celeste had not, nor Thorne, soon to be his brother-in-law. His mother had not told him...and surely they all knew. And Mr. Smythe, who had sat in the back of the *Daily Whirl* with Bayard Lockholm for hours on several days...had he, the investigator, not told him, either?

The coachman that night had come forward to say Bayard had been seen. The coachman, now retired, had sworn he saw Bayard Lockholm, under the moon, with his hands at Virginia's throat....

Audrey had not told him. She, who thought herself his friend, had kept quiet, too, thinking it was not her business to tell, leaving the hard chore to someone else, to someone closer, to anyone else....

Audrey lowered her head. It would probably cost her the job at the newspaper and it would certainly end her dreams, but he had been kind to her when she needed kindness, and she would be truthful with him now when he needed truth.

"They are saying you quarreled with her, a terrible quarrel over her spending, the night she died."

He shrugged. "That is true. She was profligate. She bought five times more than we needed. Left to herself she would have brought even my fortune to ruin."

"They say when you left her the last time you were in a rage."

"Also true. I can be enraged, as you've seen."

"They say when you left, you threatened her life. She was in tears of despair."

"Not true. I said I meant to divorce her whatever the cost. When I left she was screaming and throwing her bills at me, demanding I pick them up and pay them without another word."

"They say you sailed in your yacht, the *Catbird Seat*, down the bay."

"It was the smaller boat, *The Canary*."

Audrey stood beside the beech tree, rubbing her wrists. He sank down at the tree's base, his knees cocked up. "Go on," he said.

"They say you spent the evening at a saloon with a woman of bad reputation, a woman who, for pay, took off her clothes in front of men. A woman who later married a man whose fortune is larger than yours."

"Ah, the beautiful Tory VanVoorst. Well, so I did. I sat at Burty VanVoorst's table at his invitation. Victoria joined us later. It was the first time I'd ever laid eyes on her, and I didn't know she was going to strip that night. But she did, while singing a song I completely forget. I liked her—still do. So would you. She was happy that night, he was happy. And I...I was looking for happiness. We had a good time. They were already, by then, very much in love."

"They say you snuck back to the house you were building, knowing your wife was in the unlighted house, sorting through furniture with only a candle to see by. They say you crept through the unfinished walls, stealthily climbed the stairs . . .''

"Yes, yes, go on, Audrey, what do they say?"

She looked at him, miserable. "They say you pushed her, when a shadow was over the moon."

He reached up, gentle now. He took her hand and eased her down on the grass beside him.

"Well, I didn't," he said.

"I know," she said.

His eyes were haunted. They were bleak, beautiful eyes. "I came in at the dock," he said, "tied up the boat, and looked at my house by moonlight. Almost as soon as I arrived, she fell. It was so dark I couldn't tell, witnessing it, that it was Virginia who was falling. I thought at first it was a burglar who thought of using the window as a drop. Who, stretched out to see what lay below, somehow lost his balance. . . . She fell silently, straight out and down. It seemed to me she fell in slow motion, that it took forever for her to plummet that small space. . . . And then when she landed I felt the vibration of the ground."

"Don't tell me," she said. "Don't relive it." She trembled, wanting to hold his hand.

"I ran as hard as I could, as fast—running, I was sure it was her. I bent over her, smoothed away her hair. I had some matches. I struck one over her face. . . . It was not a pretty sight. Then I ran to the front of the driveway, hoping the coach would be there. It was, and Bascomb was there, standing by the horse's head. I shall never forget Bascomb's staring at me then. His face so old, his eyes all white. . . .''

Bay leaned his head back against the bark of the tree trunk and closed his eyes as though he were very, very tired. He's known all along what they were saying, she thought. He just wanted it confirmed. . . .

His fingers were tracing wavy lines on her arm. Her heart danced at his touch.

"For the first time," he said, and gave a little laugh, "I was not invited to a dinner party at the Benson-Ward's. Last night. My mother and sister went without me." His eyes were still closed, his fingers still lightly caressed her forearm. "Imagine. There is nothing more tedious than a Benson-Ward dinner party, Audrey, but not to be invited when everyone else was... I've been convicted, then, in the court of public opinion?"

She was careful to keep her voice as soft as his. "Oh no," she said, "I wouldn't say that. Everyone is just having fun at your expense. The maid has come back telling stories—"

"Fanni St. Flour."

"And then your friend, Mrs. VanVoorst, with whom you are accused of consorting, hired the maid for the season. They say it was to still her tongue, to control her."

He opened his eyes, followed the outline of her lips with a finger. She sighed and hoped he would never stop. "There must be a curse on the Lockholms after all," he said. "Virginia... and now me.... And poor Celeste, marrying the first man who asked her—" He sat up. "Never do that, Audrey Smoke. Never, never, marry the first man who asks you."

She was so close. She could watch his chest rise and fall. She tried to match the rhythm of it to her own heart. "I won't," she said and grinned a silly, self-conscious grin, appreciating his little joke.

She was so happy. She had never been this happy. If she never moved, perhaps the world would cease to turn and this moment, this one moment, would last and last and... Her father would be marrying now, maybe repeating the vows just now, as she sat at the side of Bayard Lockholm. Her father might be kissing his new bride now. Or they could be toasting each other and all the company in Grimsby's Tavern. Or dancing a wedding polka. Or cutting the wedding cake, Dolly carefully saving the swans until later, in the bedroom, when they were alone together, their clothes loose....

And someone would bite into the slice with the ring inside, which presaged good fortune....

His words broke her reverie.

"They are going to dig her up," he said. He was getting to his feet. "I signed the permission yesterday. We should, I think, not be here like this."

Their moment was over.

Instantly she was on her feet, brushing grass from her skirt, wondering how to say goodbye. "Please don't lose heart, Mr. Lockholm," she said. "Things will turn out all right. People just like to talk. It amuses them."

He was looking at her as though she were a stranger. His muscles were tense, like a leopard wanting to spring. "I wonder how your mouth tastes," he said. "I have wondered that, it seems, for a long while.... If you'll excuse me, I'm expecting the excavation crew. I don't think you should be here when they arrive."

She turned to go, confused. Had she heard right? Had he said something intimate, something—

"Audrey."

She turned back, almost afraid to, afraid he'd take back his wonder at her mouth.

"Don't call me Mr. Lockholm," he said. "My friends call me Bay."

She went then, walking away fast up the curve, which, when she breasted it, hid her from him. She framed his name silently with her lips over and over; to say his name was to open her mouth to his....

She ran, past a crew of muscular blacks with shovels and spades on their shoulders. She ran to another grave, to tell her mother....

WHEN MILDRED FALK RETURNED from the wedding of Lawrence Smoke to Dolores Dowd, she brought a piece of wedding cake for Audrey. Audrey thanked her but did not ask Mrs. Falk about the day, and Mildred Falk volunteered no information. Alone in her new room, Audrey broke up the cake in its napkins, looking for a ring. But the slice held only candied cherry and pistachio nuts and crumbling almond cream....

9

IN THE TWO WEEKS that followed the Saturday on which she had once expected to be married, Audrey Smoke worked with Alabaster McGregor reporting the ever-widening investigation of John Bayard Lockholm in the sudden death of his wife.

Her days were spent typing the editor's notes, typing his column, typing news items, running his errands. She did not see, correspond or hear from her father. She saw Bay Lockholm only infrequently. He came in, spoke at his desk in the back of the room to Mr. McGregor, attended to letters that were typed for him by a man who worked downstairs alongside the printing press. He did not speak to her at all, and she kept her head bent over her work when he passed.

In the evenings at Mrs. Falk's, Audrey ate supper in her room, from a tray she fixed herself. She sat at a window, and under a good light she finished the other two dresses, the material for which she had bought at McGregor's insistence.

Now it was Sunday, June 30, and Audrey was going, with Alabaster McGregor, to the marriage of Celeste Lockholm to Thorne Cockburn.

"Oh, please," she had said when he told her, "I don't think I ought, Mr. McGregor. You see—"

He stopped her with a raised hand and eyelids that drooped with condescension. "I know your sorry little story, my dear, and I don't give a fig," he said. "You are my assistant and I require you to be just that, functioning at my pleasure, always at my right hand for my need. Enough. That's all there is to it. You will meet me at the steps of Trinity Church at fifteen minutes before four,

Sunday afternoon. That's fifteen minutes to, not twelve or ten or three. Have a notepad and pencils in your purse...a pretty purse, something small and jeweled if you have it, and try to wear something that is not so—'' he was standing and he sniffed from his height ''—not quite so pedestrian as the barely adequate ensembles you garb yourself to work in.... No wonder nothing exciting happens to you, no wonder this Thorne fellow strayed. You don't look exciting, my dear girl. You should follow Mrs. Peerce's example, now there's an exciting woman. Or—dare I say it—the style of Miss Lockholm, Mrs. Cockburn-to-be. You look decidedly dowdy if you really want to know. Now I, on Sunday, I will be resplendent in morning coat with tails and top hat of robin's egg blue, very nice, thank you very much. So do not shame me. Now shall we go on? If you cry I will fire you, Miss Smoke. This is a warning you will hear from me only once. I will not, I absolutely refuse, to work with a woman who cries. Tears are as disgusting as a man exposing himself. Now have you got that into your empty, rattling head?''

''My head is not empty, it does not rattle, I am not going to cry. It will be a great embarrassment to me, Mr. McGregor, as you, who know everything, know very well. But if my job depends upon it, I will meet you on Sunday in the best dress I own, which will be below your expectations I am sure, and I will do my best to be of use to you.''

''Ah, the cub makes progress.... Now where were we, at long last?''

DETECTIVE SMYTHE had come to her as she was leaving the *Daily Whirl* on Wednesday evening, but he had not kept her long.

She said she was sure Thorne had not known the late Virginia Lockholm except in the most formal way as her sailing instructor. Detective Smythe had asked, gently, if Audrey thought she would have known if her fiancé had been on friendlier terms with Virginia Lockholm than his position would dictate. Audrey said she could not be sure of that, of course, but she had no reason to assume the worst and many reasons to think the best of Thorne who was, she emphasized, in her opinion as good a man as any.

Detective Smythe asked her if she was still in love with the man Celeste Lockholm was going to marry.

"No, sir," she said. "Last year Thorne and I were both young and inexperienced and congenial to each other. That passed for love in my mind and perhaps in his, for a time. But when he truly fell in love he knew the difference and so, I hope, will I."

And that had been that.

And now Audrey stood trembling in front of the mirror on the door of her room at Mildred Falk's, missing the cheval glass she had left behind, missing the dusky depths that had been, for her, her mother's eyes.

She was wearing her wedding dress, the pretty white shiny cotton with round neck and cap sleeves and a flirty ruffle at the hem. Her hair was full down her back, free and glittering, so clean it stood away from her head, crackling with electricity, when she brushed it. She had made a circlet of hydrangea to wear in her hair, and she had borrowed a purse of silvery chain mail from Mrs. Falk, just big enough for a small pad of paper and two pencils. Mildred Falk had given her a tin of rouge, and Audrey had rubbed it, primrose pink, just a finger touch, on her lips and then, ever so daringly, high on her cheeks along the bone.

Mr. McGregor was wrong, Audrey thought. She was not dowdy. She was not as elegant as Celeste named for the heavens and not as splendid as Mrs. Percival Peerce, who had been pointed out to her several times by Mr. McGregor in the Casino, and who was the reigning beauty of Newport as well as its social mistress. But she was, in her own way, she thought, beautiful, too. Audrey was brilliant noon, blinding gold, unshadowed. Celeste was cool summer night, and Mrs. Peerce was a breathtaking rose-and-silver dawn. Audrey's face was fresh and held no secrets. The other women knew how to hide their souls, knew how to lure and to beguile....

Well. There was nothing for it and, after all, who would she be trying to impress? He who had said to call him Bay,

as his friends did? He had seen her at her worst, snivelling
and bedraggled and naively drunken on champagne....

She did not want to be late. She left the room, sneering
at her simple sandals.

ONLY PRINCESSES had weddings like this. Only princesses
swathed a church in drapes of creamiest ivory taffeta,
swagging the loops, two layers deep, from post to post high
and low the length of the interior. Only princesses secured
the celebratory drapery at each post with crossed long-
stemmed roses, one of red, one of pink, the stems hand-
painted gold.

Only princesses lay down a carpet of white satin to walk
upon. And hired four harpists for the church corners to
play a solemn melody.

Only princesses filled the church with four hundred
friends and well-wishers, each, even to the children, the
precious of a nation. Only princesses had a wedding coach
of scarlet and gold, pulled by four palominos, golden
horses with flaxen manes and deep red harnesses and
matching plumes. Only the coach of a princess would be
escorted by golden dogs, red leashed; collies bearing gold-
en chests around their necks on loose red collars, the chests
filled with wedding favors, round coins of gold struck with
a likeness in profile of the bride and groom.

Audrey stood beside Alabaster McGregor, overwhelmed, overcome. She was glad of his protective presence, in wonder at the way Mrs. Astor, *the* Mrs. Astor,
turned out of her path to speak with him, asking him to a
boating party in July. She trembled when Alabaster introduced Mrs. Peerce to her, calling the lady "Dove."

Mrs. Peerce, so beautiful in cream and gray, collared and
cuffed in ostrich dyed to match, her hair an angel's halo of
wind and ice, said to her, "Ally's column has always been
clever and entertaining, Miss Smoke. Before it only lacked
beauty. Now he has, it seems, achieved perfection. Congratulations, Ally, dear. Miss Smoke, this is my husband,
Percy...."

"Hullo," said a man with a tired, lined face that must once have been fine. He tipped his top hat, leaning hard on a black cane with an ivory head. "When you get married, young woman, try to do it on such a glorious day as this. What do you say?"

Audrey blushed and promised, twisting inside, feeling inane, thinking how nice everyone was, how elegant, how...

"And this is my daughter, Nicola, who is marrying Rolf here. Miss Smoke, Lord Pomeroy, the marquess of Denton."

Mrs. Peerce's daughter was a wild beauty, her hair as red as pomegranate seeds tight with juice, cheeks the color of her hair, and great brown eyes that burned unladylike; an explorer's eyes, a conqueror's eyes. She almost took Audrey's breath away, she was so round, so white, so jeweled in emeralds that glittered in the rays of the afternoon sun like a fish flashing skyward in a spume of sea spray.

"I'm told you swim, Miss Smoke," were Nicola's first words. "Do you find the skirts and long legs of your bathing clothes a burden?"

A silent cry for help rose in Audrey's stomach. She smiled, helpless. But Nicola was waiting for her answer, and Nicola's eyes were rating her, taking her measure.

Audrey swallowed. "Yes, I do," she said. "I tie down the skirt as much as I can and wear the dress as close to the body as possible."

"How good," said Nicola, and her emeralds shimmered.

"Delighted to make your acquaintance," said Lord Pomeroy. He was handsome, with the build of a strong man, light haired and light skinned like Nicola, but without her hot color. He was, rather, warm and relaxed, but in his way there was the same intensity. He greeted Audrey with a full-lipped mouth that smiled easily and blue eyes that were satisfied with all they knew of the world.

Audrey did not know how to respond to a lord. She wondered if she should curtsy or lift her hand to be kissed. Alabaster McGregor was giving her no help, but he did not

bow so Audrey only extended her hand to the first royal she
had ever seen out of a picture book, and said, "It is an
honor to meet you, sir." Her hand was gripped firmly and
released, and then the Peerces were by, moving to talk to a
man and a woman they called dear "Clarissa and Tripp."

Audrey, who had never been farther from Newport than
Providence, thought this is foreign travel.

Alabaster McGregor gave her verbal notes to write as he
stood on the steps of Trinity Church, resplendent in his
morning coat and trousers of soft blue, in between his chats
with Newport's summer elite. "Dove, in her colors. . . .
Clarissa Rails in a most becoming plum, surviving despite
arriving, severely windblown, with her husband in his motorcar. . . . Zack Pink escorting one of the Misses Wetmore
looking well in saffron stripe. . . ."

And then, to applause, the wedding coach arrived. Mrs.
Edmunda Lockholm, the matriarch, was the first out,
handed down by a footman in rose and gold. Three young
boys in golden breeches removed the small casks from the
necks of the dogs and handed around the coins. Audrey,
awed at the little treasure chest proffered, slipped a coin
into her purse, afraid to look at it too long. To think,
Thorne's profile set in gold alongside his bride's. No, she
couldn't think. She simply beheld the spectacle and shivered. It was all beyond her dreaming. . . .

Thorne, his eyes a storm of pride, his hair never so curled
and gleaming, in softest gray formal dress sat in the regal
red carriage like a princeling about to be crowned. Celeste
Lockholm, veiled in layers of lace, sat quietly beside him,
almost hidden.

And then Bay Lockholm was down, dressed like Thorne
in gray tails and gray top hat. He escorted his mother inside.

The invited followed them in and took their places.

Audrey, felled by the grandeur, followed Alabaster
McGregor on feet that seemed wooden. Within, the air was
quivering with tremolos from the harps. Audrey watched
Bay Lockholm leave his mother and retrace his way up the
satin aisle. She saw Thorne far down the church before the

pulpit. She heard the slow, grand notes of an organ begin the wedding march, blending with the harp strings.

The procession of the wedding attendants, so many, was a blur to her, a blur of flowers and ribbons and pastel silks. A pretty boy and girl, in matching white satin, scattered fresh rose petals from baskets on the whitened aisle. A little boy in a white-powdered wig of parliamentary curls and a courtier's suit carried a tasseled white pillow with the two wedding rings like a crown upon it. Audrey sat beside Alabaster McGregor, dazzled and mute, and waited, as they all did, breathless for the bride to come.

Celeste descended the aisle on her brother's arm, slowly, in measured step. Her dark hair gleamed blue black against the whites of church and taffeta silk hangings. Her gown was of thinnest net, a net of ivory threads knotted a thousand times and then a thousand times again with smallest slivers of diamond and seeds of pearl, the net woven to thin, nude-colored silk the shade of her complexion. The whole so thin, so close to her body that the gown twitched and changed and blinded the eye with every reach of her long-boned thighs as she approached and passed and the organ boomed and swelled....

Sometime during the ceremony Alabaster McGregor put his head close to Audrey's and spoke. She was not sure exactly when, it reverberated over and over in her mind until it seemed she had been hearing it for hours in the chords of the music before she recognized the meaning. "You've done your part, Audrey, you can leave whenever you wish. Just don't lose those notes of mine...."

She would have liked to run right then, but she knew no one could traverse that white-satined, rose-petaled aisle before the bride. She waited, excused, superfluous, in the way now that the celebrations were to begin.

When the veil of layered laces was thrown back from her pavé diamond tiara, Celeste was, to Audrey, all that beauty defined. And Thorne, smiling broadly, a married man, his teeth as white as his shirtfront, his hair as dark as his bride's, almost mingling with it he held Celeste so close, Thorne was a stranger to her, a dark and handsome stranger who had never been poor, had never struggled, had never dreamed a little dream of ferry boats and a hard-working wife....

Audrey was conscious of her little never-wedding dress, unequal to the day. She was contemptuous of her crown of hydrangea, snipped free for the asking from a bush in Mildred Falk's backyard. She was glad she would be escaping, glad she was out of the pew, into the shoe-smudged satin aisle, moments from freedom. She exited Trinity Church to a hail of rice, flung in handfuls from the coach boys in golden breeches, flung from the treasure chests, which had held, before, the wedding favors, the rice raining white and stinging over bride and groom and guests. There was a turbulence of voices, everyone crowding around everyone, the bride and the groom in the center of a beautiful tangle trying to gain their scarlet-and-golden carriage where the horses, alerted, tossed their manes, and the dogs, excited, leaped against their leashes.

Audrey slithered around backs, seeking space to get away. Someone took her hand. It startled her; frightened her. Who would be touching her, she the uninvited, she the paid scribe of society's great moment, she the lowly, the unknown, the unwanted, the unfit...?

"Will you be my date today?"

She looked up into his eyes, as blue gray as the sea, as gray as the flukes of a baby humpback splashing where the sound turned toward the coast of Newport town....

She didn't answer; couldn't answer. And yet she gripped his hand as the gull grips a spar in storm.

He had the faintest of smiles. There was worry deep in his face. He drew her away from the push and the laughter. "Will you?" he said.

Dumb, her eyes searched his for something, anything, that said, You please me, I like you, I wonder how your mouth tastes.... She thought, but could not say, I am too poor for you, Bay Lockholm. I am untitled, mongrel-born. I have no sweep of throat sweetened by rubies. I have no brocade or perfumes or sleek blooded animals. I have no castle like yours, no famous name, no marbled furniture, no creamed meat fresh from the sea....

"My dress," she said. "It isn't good enough."

"Damn your dress," he said. "Will you come?"

"But you can't ask me. I would shame you." But her head was nodding and her eyes were saying yes; she could not stop her eyes from saying yes, yes, yes....

He smiled then, and she could see herself reflected in his eyes. There was a space between them, the length of his arm. His hand still holding hers drew her close against the soft gray fabric of his coat. He whispered into her hair, "Haven't you been reading the papers? I am already shamed. Haven't you heard? I murdered my wife."

There was such a terror in her breast. She was afraid of this world that Thorne had conquered so easily. She had never sought it, never turned its way except to gape with tourist eyes and marvel and admire. And she was afraid of Bay Lockholm....

He was safer as a dream.

Her mother had told her and she had known it was true: he was not for her, his kind was not for her....

And what was wrong with him, anyway? What was wrong with this scion of a cursed fortune that no lady of his world walked proudly at his side? What was wrong with him that he would condescend to escort Audrey Smoke, daughter of a carpenter, to his sister's wedding feast? How many others had he asked? By how many others had he been spurned? What did the eligible beauties of Gilt Hill know that Audrey, simple town-girl Audrey in her rag of a cotton dress and eleven dollars in a stocking in her dresser, did not know? "Haven't you heard? I murdered my wife...."

"I will go with you anywhere," she said. "I would go with you to jail."

"It's called prison," he said. "Let's go. Today may give you a taste of it. Today you can flutter in a gilded cage, and see how you like it."

It was the black carriage he handed her into, the black barouche with the dappled gray. "Mother's gone back to the cottage already. And I'll find you a dress—all right, Drew, carry on—there are dozens of dresses in the armoires of Virginia's bedroom, dresses she ordered and never wore. You can choose what you like. How's that?''

Audrey looked down at her skirt, shiny and simple, and remembered in a haze of wedding glitter and rustle, the fine gowns of the ladies. To have one! No, but to wear one! To walk upon that jewel-lush lawn, before a mansion of almond stone. To see the sea from there! To waltz on marble cracked out of a mountain she would never see, borne by ships across an ocean, carved by artisans who labored only for kings. To stand, elegant as all, among the ladies of America's golden bastion. To walk at Bay's side, as his chosen, his fairest.... Would they think her a princess, a visiting princess from afar? Would they envy the blush of her bosom, the fragility of her waist wrapped in a couturier's silk?

Ah, no.

They knew who she was. And what she wasn't. They had seen her already on the tower steps of the church, scribbling her gossip at Mr. McGregor's command. They had noted her cotton frock, merely ruffled, her face and figure unadorned. They had seen her surprised, alien eyes, her unfinished manner.... They knew. She was no artful imposter like Thorne, who had edged into their company and studied and practiced and learned and won, gloriously, triumphantly, his special place....

She bit her lip and looked at Bay beside her, touching her shoulder with his, Bay casually holding her hand upon his trousered thigh. "This is all so new to me," she said.

"Thank God," he said. "I wouldn't want you spoiled and heartless."

"You could have asked anyone else," she said.

The worry had left his eyes. He was grinning at her, looking very young. "I could have," he said, "but I didn't."

"I won't know how to act."

"Don't be silly. Be yourself. That's all I ever do."

"I don't know anyone."

He laughed. "You know the groom, I should think, very well. You've met my sister. You know Ally. You know me. And you'll meet the others. Don't worry, little wild girl of the rocks, nobody bites."

Wild girl of the rocks.... Was that how he saw her?

Audrey watched the great houses of Bellevue Avenue slip by, the majestic trees. Newport looked more beautiful from inside a carriage, much more beautiful on one's way to a party at Gilt Hill. Newport was a paradise when Bay Lockholm held your hand and promised you a dress to wear, a dress like nothing you had ever worn before....

She had never seen the house called Whale's Turning from the front. Great shrubs veiled it from Gilt Hill Drive, thick bushes the height of her head. Great gates opened to it, bronze gates of loops and curls to bar what was not wanted. The gates were spread wide now, thrown back in welcome. The gateman bowed them through. There was a paved way then, under white beech trees bedecked with tiny baskets of two rosebuds each, tied with pink-striped, breeze-stirred bows to hidden branches high and low. The horse's hooves on the track were soft and private, padded as the beats of her heart.

Beyond the trees, the driveway divided lawns of thick, close-cropped grass now blue, now green, and Audrey saw Whale's Turning, massive before her. It was a minipalace of sand-colored stone, three stories high, three wings wide, each window carved above, porched below with terraces of stone and sculptured balusters. Double-doored, double-windowed, five-chimneyed, red-slate roofed, it reared huge against the blue of sky and white of sea behind. She heard the ocean crashing waves, smelled sea salt in the air, saw the great reach of the porte cochere, ivy smothered already, eight columned to span the curve of the circling driveway. The rounded approach to the house was lighted, though it was just coming dusk, with great pink globes on green wrought-iron pedestals tall as trees, multibranched. There was a fountain in the center of the driveway, a fountain of Grecian marble held up by a Grecian god, his arms and shoulders naked in the stone. The fountain bubbled and fell back upon itself, and as Audrey first saw it, a cardinal was dipping in its beak to drink. The bird lifted its head as the carriage neared, caught Audrey's eyes, and in silent scarlet alarm sailed up and beyond....

"Do you like it?"

She had forgotten him, forgotten everything, captured by the majesty of this ... cathedral of a house.

She turned to him. "It is a home for the gods," she said.

"No," he said. "Come, we want to get you dressed before too many arrive."

He lifted her down from the barouche. And for a moment it was she today who, seeking Bay down that long length of satin, had walked on rose petals and vowed her troth. He would keep her in his arms now and sweep her over the marble threshold, and she would not have to walk, alone, up this step and this one and this, toward that woman, crablike, stout, huddling upon a cane, gowned throat to toe in navy, her bosom aflood in pearls. The woman who stood, beyond another abyss of stone-cold steps, in the great hall of her palace waiting to greet the wedding guests....

"Mother," Bay was saying, "I want you to meet my guest today, Miss Audrey Smoke of Newport."

Her eyes were gray like her son's, but not alive like the sea. Mrs. Lockholm's eyes were tame and dulled by the wrinkles of her eyelids, heavy lids that tried to mask the assessing in her gaze.

"My dear," she said in a throaty voice, "do I know your family? Have we met before?" Her hand, soft and loose, purple veins standing high upon the skin, took Audrey's; held it. Her nails were long and hard, painted the color of long-ago dried roses.

"My father had the privilege of building some of the cabinets in this house, Mrs. Lockholm. My father is a fine carpenter in Newport, his name is Lawrence Smoke."

That was all it took. Audrey saw the withdrawal in the woman's eyes. Saw the mask slide firmly into place and lock. "Welcome to Whale's Turning," the matriarch said,

dropping Audrey's hand. "Just through the lower loggia
you'll find the east lawn."

And then Bay steered Audrey past his mother, who
turned, without another word, to face again the entrance
steps, fearsome in her solitary majesty, waiting for better
company....

The blood was high in Audrey's cheeks. She hardly
minded Mrs. Lockholm's snub; she was too excited. She
looked around at Whale's Turning's great hall, greedy to
see everything at once yet wanting to linger upon each thing
alone. There was so much to see, to pause before, so much
beyond yet to behold. So much to touch and remember.
There was too much to it; she would never recall it all, as it
was, as it really was.... The soaring walls of whitest stone,
carved and embellished with raised garlands of intricate
design, the expanse of space, the pilasters that rose to
heaven almost and held up a ceiling of gold, gold everywhere, looped and wreathed and bursting into monumen-
tal flowers and domes from which great brass chandeliers
fell a canyon's length and still were high, high above her
head. And there, set above the red-carpeted staircase, above
the steps of coffee-colored marble flanked by railing black
and brass; there, above the staircase, and there, above every
arch, the crest of the Lockholms set into plaques of pink-
splashed marble: the platinum profile of a sailing ship upon
three sea waves in chips of tourmaline....

Audrey felt giddy. She wanted to sing, to shout. She
wanted to throw off her clothes and run, naked, barbar-
ian, into all the rooms of this beautiful place and sing with
the voice of a coloratura....

Bay was leading her to the staircase. "Hurry," he said,
"we don't have forever, come on."

She skipped at his side, turning around and around as she
ran up the steps, drunk on the beauty of Bayard Lockholm's mansion. No, we don't have forever, her mind was
singing, but we have now, and now for me is more than
enough, more than enough....

At the first landing, where the staircase divided into two,
there were rooms at either end, private studies, one male,

one female. The wall spanning the length of the landing lifted to twenty feet and more and was a great stained-glass mural, a kaleidoscope skylight to color the beams of a rising sun. And below it, at eye level, seen dimly, now at dusk, through a mist of glass-sprayed light, there was a portrait of a woman in a soft dress whose skirt billowed in bouquets of tiny flowers.

Audrey halted before it. Virginia?

But Bay was pulling her on, to the next flight up to the second floor. She lifted his hand and kissed it, not knowing why, not even thinking, not caring what was proper, what was called for, what ought or ought not to be done.

And then they were in a tapestried hall, running along smooth, brown-stoned floors, Persian carpeted, great vased with long-stalked flowers.

Before a double stand of doors, French paned, curtained behind with silken folds the color of champagne, he stopped her. "Here we are," he said. "M'lady—" The handles of the door were ivory. Bay pushed them open with a gesture; stepped aside. "Hurry, anything will do, you know. Just hurry. I'll stand guard out here."

The doors closed behind her and she was in a room larger than the entire suite of rooms over the carpentry shop in Bridge Street. She felt small—"so little and so mean," Thorne had said—in this sumptuous room of peach and beige. The walls were silk fabric, embossed peach on golden beige. The floor-to-ceiling double windows were swathed in hangings of the same, heavy and thick, swagged and looped, and hemmed by matching fringe. The draperies were caught and held away from the white-curtained windows and over the bed by towering canopies of wood, ivoried by artifice, arched into carved crowns. The carpet was a field of pastel flowers, rose and peach, on a gray background. The furniture was again of ivoried wood, carved and curved and curled, and the mirrors and screens were heavier yet and gold....

Hurry, he had said.

And how long had she been standing, a step inside the French-paned doors, seeing herself, a miniature, in the great gold frame above the dresser so far away across the room?

Did she dare cross that carpet, dense as the flowers it depicted, to open the scrolled doors of another woman's armoires? Could she search among gowns designed for the tragic-fated mistress of this room and pull out a blue and shove it back into its place, a white, this logan green, and then, coming to it, find the one, a tea gown of body-blush coral and rusty-red chiffon, a gown that bloomed against the shoulders it bared, a gown that clung to her body like grape skin and coiled round her limbs like tendrils of honeysuckle...?

There had never been a woman as beautiful as she.

She turned slowly before her golden reflection, lifted her arms to the champagne boudoir. She was very rich and she was exquisitely beautiful. She flung her back garden wreath of hydrangeas upon the silken chaise. She combed her golden hair with an ivory comb. She kicked off her grubby sandals and rose two inches in slippers of coral velvet straps. And there was a man beyond her door, a man who *adored* her, and he was waiting to take her to a ball....

She wouldn't take a last look at what she was leaving behind. She wouldn't stop walking to the doors and opening them and closing them behind her, because if she did the dream would dissolve, the way bubbles after their ascent through the wine died in contact with everyday air....

He was still there, pulling smoke from a cigar. "And about time, too," he said when she pulled the doors to behind her and leaned on them for strength.

"What do you think?" she said.

"You'll be the envy of everyone. If we had time, I'd burden you with jewels." But it was said so lightly. He wasn't dumbfounded at her just-burst-from-a-shell beauty, her finally free elegance, her...

He was walking her quickly. "Once we get down the stairs, turn right. You'll see the loggia and the lawn, just go straight through. This way we won't have to greet Mother again if she's still in the hall. She's fine, really, she just takes getting used to. Likes men more than women is her problem—"

"Just *what* do you think you're doing?"

Mrs. Lockholm was standing at the foot of the staircase, staring up at Audrey and Bay hurrying down; Audrey, lifting the chiffon above the coral shoes, watching it float like mist around her hands.... Audrey saw the older woman's revulsion of her, heard the anger; felt Bay tense at her side.

Mr. and Mrs. Peerce were standing with Mrs. Lockholm—Percy and Dove—to whom Audrey had been introduced at the church. They moved away as Mrs. Lockholm spoke, staring up as Audrey halted, half down the staircase, half up. Bay kept descending, but Audrey couldn't move. She sensed behind her, in the air—or was it only her imagination?—a ghostly giggle from the portrait on the landing.

"Just who do you think you are! You little thief! You turn yourself around, miss, and get yourself out of a Lockholm gown! How dare you!"

"Mother, I gave her the dress—"

"Upstairs, tramp, or I'll have the police on you so fast you won't know what's hit you."

"This is my house, Mother. I won't have this behavior from you."

Audrey turned up the stairs, blinded by tears she did not want the older woman to see, deafened by a muffled roar in her head. She stumbled up the stairs, there were so many and the landing was so wide and she mustn't, mustn't, damage a Lockholm gown.... Her cheeks were aflame with shame, her heart broken with humiliation, her dream smashed before the dreaming.

There was no chance for Audrey now. She was the cause of a quarrel between Bay and his mother on this ever-to-be-remembered day. Celeste's wedding would be blotted forever after with the terrible sin of Audrey Smoke who had come, a poor girl from the town, and tried to pass herself off as a lady on the arm of Bayard Lockholm, wearing one of his late wife's gowns.

What had made her think she could? Had she been
swayed by how easy it had been for Thorne?

Past the portrait, past the blur of haloed light, up the
second landing—would it never end?—finally the hallway,
long and spacious and high-ceilinged, where every flower
mocked and every twist of mystical Persian pattern whirled
and leaped and tried to suck her down. Past delicate chairs
and marble-topped long tables, all whispering smugly as she
stumbled, "We belong, we belong and you don't...."

"Go now...."

Even the ivory handles on the French-paned doors
seemed to want to deny her entrance, or was it just her
hand, moist with perspiration, that made her fumble? And
once inside—blessedly inside—avoiding the great mirror,
slipping out of the beautiful dress with her eyes squeezed
closed because she did not want to see herself again, so
beautiful, in Virginia Lockholm's gown.... And then, in
cotton slip, hanging the lovely thing where it had hung so
long, unworn; where it would wait forever for one who
would not, could not from the grave, come and take it
down and wear it to a party....

Music wafted from the lawn to the boudoir windows,
harps and a violin, and the rise of laughter.

Audrey put on again her hated dress. She looked for
something to dry her eyes, wash her face. There was a
bathroom through a door masked as just more silken wall.
It was as large as her bedroom at home—of course, she
expected it now. Its walls and floor were of marble, pink
and cream. The great tub was shaped like two swans nest-
ing, and the fixtures, two sets of fixtures, were golden swan
heads. Opposite the tub was a wall of pale wood cabinets
and drawers and shelves, with ivory handles carved into
wings. Lawrence Smoke must have built that wall, never
thinking his daughter would behold his work.... The floor
was cool under her stockinged feet, free of the elegant
shoes. At the veinless white marble basin, trembling, she
washed her face. In her purse she found the tin of rouge,
rubbed it into her cheeks and forehead to bring color back,
slicked it on her lips darker than before.

Then out of the bathroom and over, savagely, to the great dresser and the golden mirror. She combed her hair, reset the wreath of hydrangea so that it lay upon her forehead, her dark blue eyes deepening the azure of the blossoms. Into her sandals, smoothing her skirt—

"Audrey?"

His voice at the doors. And, too, the voice of Mrs. Lockholm, too soft for Audrey to understand the words, but intense enough so that Audrey knew the matriarch of Whale's Turning was still speaking her mind.

Audrey crossed the room, spoke through the doors. "I'm just coming out," she said. She bent and brushed the shoes with her hands, the velvet straps so soft, the dancing heels that had made her stand tall as a lady of privilege. She shut the armoire door.

She crossed the room, raised her chin, and swung open both doors.

Mrs. Lockholm was retreating down the hall in a sweep of navy blue, her back to Audrey, her curled gray head stiff as granite, her cane, with every step, bayonetting the carpet as though it were Audrey's bleeding heart.

Bay's hands were on Audrey's shoulders, his thumbs lightly tracing the outline of her jaw. "I'm sorry, little one. Today's not the day to beard the lioness. You're beautiful as you are. Shall we go now?"

"Go? Go where? You must stay here with your guests...."

"Child. Glorious child. My arm?" There was a softness in his face, a soft light in his eyes.

She took his arm, the gray cloth soft, held it close. Without a word they walked together down the hall. The carpet was quiet now, and the flowers; the furnishings no longer murmured in astral tongues, "Go away, town girl, go back where you belong...." They descended the main staircase, Audrey seeing nothing, just walking beside John Bayard Lockholm wherever he would lead....

The east lawn was a riot of color. A parquet wood floor had been set upon the grass for dancing, and pink tables with white bows surrounded the dance floor. Tall peppermint-striped spears, set into the lawn, blazed with oil flame. Along the north edge of the lawn preened a long canopy of Arabic silk, red and gold like the wedding carriage, tasseled like the wedding pillow that bore the rings. Its pink tables proffered a banquet of strange, rich foods. Young women in gowns better than Audrey's, in emerald-green "tulip" gowns that Mrs. Lockholm had selected that day in Darlings' Drapers and Dry Goods, offered glasses of champagne on golden trays. The harpists, their burnished instruments set at angles to one another to form a golden star, four women in dresses of like design but different color, peach and pink and apricot and yellow, played celestial music. The violinist wandered, a handsome Latin man in ruffled shirt. The bride and the groom were dancing, a beautiful couple, dark heads close, framed against an orange-and-scarlet twilight sky.

"What do you say we eat," said Bay, leading Audrey into the company. "As far as I know, it's what you do best."

Audrey was straining to see, through the flower-clusters of wedding guests, the sea where it turned into the sound, the curve of gray and tossing white where, sometimes, the whales lazed and cast their bubble nets for sand lances and spumed their fountains to the sky.

"Yes," Audrey said, "and could we sit on the seawall and watch the night come?"

"Hello, Bay. Such a pretty day. . . . Who's this?"

"Clarissa Rails, this is Audrey Smoke."

She wore plum taffeta, edged in silver, and a wide-brimmed hat of partridge feathers. She was blond and plump; very pretty. Diamonds glittered upon her ears, at her throat, upon her gloved fingers that were holding now, in a white napkin with the Lockholm crest, a thin wooden skewer of several shrimp. "I don't believe we've met," she said, her eyelashes sweeping up and down at Audrey's dress.

"Your misfortune, Clarissa," said Bay before Audrey could answer, "but the season is just beginning. Where's Tripp?"

Clarissa Rails shook her head and wrinkled her nose. "He'll be round in a minute. He's got to oil the auto. Did you ever? It just drinks oil, he keeps all these little cans in the trunk and won't let any of the servants touch... What does your husband think of the new motorcars, Mrs. Smoke?"

Bay handed Audrey a glass of champagne from a servant's tray. Handed one to the woman planted before Audrey.

"I have no husband, Mrs. Rails."

Bay clinked his glass against theirs. "Miss Smoke has done me the honor of being my guest today, Clarissa.... To the bride and groom." He sipped from his glass.

Mrs. Rails continued to stare at Audrey. "Are you one of those women who dances for her livelihood that Bayard likes so well?"

"I—I work for the *Daily Whirl*. I'm assistant to Mr. McGregor."

"And you, Clarissa, have been believing malicious gossip." It was Alabaster, leaning over Audrey's shoulder. "It's permissible to listen, Clarissa dear, even advisable, I say, but to believe it—you, of all people, should know better."

"Why Ally McGregor, I'm sure I don't know what you mean." She moved away, nibbling shrimp.

"That'll keep her worried for a week," said Alabaster McGregor. "Sometimes, you know, Audrey, you must fight back. Fight or die. It's an old adage and never truer than today."

"I have no weapons, Mr. McGregor." *Are you one of those women who dances that Bayard likes so well?*

"Goose. You have Bayard here and you have me. I'd say you are invincible."

Audrey felt a rush of gratitude. "Thank you, Mr. McGregor. I knew this would be a foreign land, but I didn't expect a battlefield."

McGregor was saying, "Although why Bayard asked you, dressed like that—"

Audrey trembled. So it was obvious. So people did notice, were noticing.... But Bay was laughing, an easy, natural laugh, and he clamped a hand on Alabaster's robin's-egg-blue arm. "Now don't you start. We've just been through Mother's swords and my girl is shell-shocked enough."

"But my God, Bay, why didn't you get the pathetic thing a dress? I've bought her three already—isn't it, dear?—three simply to work in."

And then Audrey was laughing. It was all right now, wonderfully all right. So she didn't have a proper dress. But she was here, here with Bay and Mr. McGregor. They liked her; had protected her. She would learn to fight, fight back....

"It's not you, Audrey," said Bay. "It's myself. I've been under fire, and now you're getting some of the brunt of it. You see now, it's not all creamed lobster and sunsets here on the hill."

She smiled up at Bay and took Alabaster's arm at her other side. "Oh yes, it is," she said. "I can see it, going fast. Come on!"

And they closed upon the wedding table and had their plates heaped by the serving men.

"I'm off," said Alabaster, "catch you later," and he disappeared around two of Celeste's wedding attendants to find Edmunda Lockholm; to ferret out *exactly* what had happened between the mother and the son when Bay Lockholm had presented Miss Audrey Smoke in her two-dollar dress. Leapin' Lizzie, he wished he could print it....

Bay led Audrey to the seawall. The sky was darkening now, just lingering strands of gray and pink. He raised his arm and one of the serving girls was there, setting full champagne glasses, so cold there was frost around the bowls, on the fieldstone.

"Before I eat I must dance once with my sister. Will you wait here for me, protect my plate?"

She nodded. She did not want him to go and leave her alone, perched on a wall like Humpty-Dumpty, but she nodded and smiled, and prayed the night would blacken quickly and so hide her, out of reach of the glow of the oil torches.

There were others along the wall, others also in fading light, just discernible. Mrs. Percival Peerce was there, Dove Peerce, with two women Audrey didn't recognize, and her husband. They were at a table under a stunted apple tree, and they were talking about Audrey.

One of the women was saying, in a voice that carried easily to Audrey's ears. "Edmunda is livid. Just hopping. Of course she's been knocked down over and over. First Celeste compromising herself with that beach boy—"compromising herself? Audrey listened. How compromised?"—and then Celeste rabid to marry him.... After poor Virginia last year—"

"And now the investigation of Bay," said the second woman, unidentified. "It's too horrid."

"It's not only the investigation," said the first. "They're sure he did it. They just need the proof. Edmunda won't face that at all, of course."

"And then, without a word, bringing a nobody from the town on his sister's wedding day—"

"Marrying another nobody," said the other.

"Actually," said the first, "giving her one of Virginia's dresses to wear—"

"You see she had nothing decent of her own—"

"Unbelievable, Dove, my dear, but true as jonquils. Why, Edmunda threatened to take her own life, she told me so. Threatened to make an announcement and cancel the party if Bay didn't make the hussy take off the gown—"

"Bay called her bluff and made her cry."

"Well, say something, Dove Peerce, don't just listen as though you're not as shocked as we are."

At the sound of Mrs. Peerce's voice, Audrey shuddered. Please don't be against me, too, she prayed, though how could she not be....

"I met the young woman with Ally before the ceremony," Dove said.

"What was she like?"

"Tartish?"

"Oh no." It was the deep voice of Percival Peerce. "Nice girl, pretty, out of her element, of course, but quite nice, I thought. What did you think, dear?"

And Dove, Newport's mistress of the bon mot, said with a shrug and a sigh, "The trouble is, I think, she's having gilt feelings."

It took Dove's table a moment or two to get it, but then they erupted in giggles.

"Gilt feelings! Oh, Dove, you are a wonder."

"Oscar Wilde would envy—"

Even Percy guffawed.

And Audrey, listening, fearing, felt ice around her heart, an iceberg in her stomach chilling her, causing her to shake, because it was true, is true, she thought. I'm not in love with Bay Lockholm at all. I'm only having gilt feelings.

10

FOR THE NEXT FEW DAYS, the night of Thorne and Celeste's wedding haunted Audrey. She had eaten, she had danced, Bay had driven her home to Mrs. Falk's in the coach with the dapple gray. He had not kissed her. He said to her, in parting, "You eat better than you dance, you know. But it doesn't matter: I'm not much with a tango, either."

The entire evening Mrs. Lockholm had maintained a distance from her; so had Thorne, so had his bride. So, for that matter, had most of the guests, though Bay told her it was himself the guests were avoiding, because of his scandal. She had been content; she was not ready to join Gilt Hill, would never be ready or able. She was a poor girl, and the glitter of that existence only blinded her to what was hers and possible for her....

And yet she lusted for the man, she lusted for the house, she lusted for that bedroom and that oiled-hinged armoire. She dreamed of herself in "Lockholm" gowns, mistress of that lawn, that view, best view of the whales where they feasted at sunset, where the ocean turned and softened in the sound.

She did not see Bayard Lockholm until Friday, and when she did see him he beckoned her to the back of the newsroom, to his desk behind the partition.

"Will you walk with me this evening?" he said. "We could go along the shore, wander Cliff Walk, climb WaterWalk.... There are things I must say to you in private—hard things."

Was he to fire her, then? Had his mother insisted he not set eyes again on the town girl he had thrust, unwelcome, unworthy, into the mansion called Whale's Turning? Or was he going away? Alabaster McGregor had hinted to Audrey that Bay might take a trip until the investigation was over and the scandal subdued. Ireland, Mr. McGregor had said, and Scotland, heather and heaths and the dragon of Loch Ness. . . .

"Yes, I'd like to," she said, doom in her eyes.

"Then let's meet on the Long Wharf at six-thirty. If Ally asks you to work late, tell him you can't, you have an appointment with me."

She nodded, returned to her desk. Did Mr. McGregor know? Was that why he was being kind to her this week, knowing she was leaving, knowing he wouldn't have to put up with her misspelling "brougham" again or not knowing that Mrs. Astor's gown on Sunday had been a shade of blue called "teal"?

When she came to the wharf, Bay was waiting for her by the boats. His trousers were cream-colored linen, the sleeves of his open-throated shirt were rolled to his elbows, and the hair on his arms was a raw, pale gold. His muscles were long and smooth; for the first time, it seemed, she was aware of the beauty of the masculine body, taut and clean limbed and powerful. His hair drifted, boyish brown, upon his forehead, and his mouth, when he saw her, smiled welcome, which she felt in her loins as a dangerous heat. . . .

He took her hand. "This won't be easy for me," he said.

She said nothing. She walked with him, at peace. Let him say goodbye; it was better so; she agreed with Mrs. Lockholm. It was best for Audrey Smoke to get on with her real life, to put her dreams, her fire-and-rainbow dreams, to rest.

"The results have come back from the exhumation," he said.

Audrey caught her breath. She had forgotten that Virginia's body, a year in the grave, had been uprooted, defiled, *cut into*. . . . For days she had remembered only the portrait, misted by sunlight through colored glass, vague and ghostly, the portrait of Virginia as she had been only a year ago, *as she had been when she died*, staring at the strange woman, the *outsider*, the new woman who walked at Bay Lockholm's side....

"They have found evidence of struggle, bruising at the throat, scratches on the shoulders and breast. Some of this, they think now, was not the result of her fall. The bruises seem to be finger marks, pressure of thumbs and such—"

How could he be so calm? How could she? They walked along the shore, Audrey warm despite a swift wind, warm from the clasp of his hand, the nearness of him.

"And a worker has come forward," he went on in that reasonable tone of voice, as though he were discussing the troubles of someone he did not know, had never met. "One of the craftsman working on the interior of the house. All the workers were questioned by Detective Smythe, and this man—he says there were signs of a disturbance in the attic room after...after Virginia fell. Signs of a struggle or fight. He stored his wood stains in that room, it seems, under a tarpaulin next to the wall joists, to keep them out of harm's way. Early the morning after, he reported to work as always and continued on, knowing nothing of...of Virginia's tragedy till hours later. I don't know if you recall, but that day at noon the men were sent home. We did not begin work on the house again until some weeks later...."

Audrey shook her head; gripped his hand. Audrey had known nothing of Virginia Lockholm, had never been aware of her existence until it was over; until Audrey had stood, the only mourner and a stranger, in the bowels of Trinity Church before her closed coffin, blanketing the mahogany lid in tiers and tiers of roses....

"The workman has told Detective Smythe that he wondered, at the time, that his cans had been disturbed. Not knocked over, but pushed under some furniture, willy-nilly, and the tarpaulin lifted and thrown somewhere else. He'd had to root for his cans of stain and was irritated. He is the kind of craftsman who is careful and respectful of his tools. So he looked around, he said, to see if he could determine which of the other workers might have usurped his storage space.... There was a snuffed candle, half burned off, he remembers, set somewhere, and the furniture in general had been pushed around. He noticed, too, a splintering on the beam next to the unfinished window, as though someone had torn at it. But as his equipment wasn't harmed, he'd let it go and said nothing, thinking some of the men must have had a bit of an after-hours party. And then when he heard about...about the accident, he forgot it all completely. Only Detective Smythe recalling the incident to his mind brought the memory back. This workman thinks I must have been in the room that night because I had the only key. He remembers now, he says, locking the door at my request, and laying the key back in my hand as he left for the day. I suppose I did do so, fulfilling some request of Virginia's. I honestly don't remember. Still, I must have done, thinking nothing of it, and passing the key along to her. Or I added it to the house ring, which Virginia took whenever she wanted, playing with her decorating plans. At any rate, I stand, at least, indirectly accused by the workman. 'Circumstantially implicated' is, I believe, how Detective Smythe refers to it.''

"What was the workman's name?" Audrey said, so softly she wondered if Bay heard, if he would answer. He wouldn't have to because she knew...she knew.... Who would it be, after all, except—

"Yes," Bay said, "your father. Fusty, particular Lawrence Smoke, a man who works alone, minds his own business, and does an artist's work. A man of impeccable integrity...."

They could have walked across the heart of Newport Island, a shorter way, to the eastern side. They could have begun their climb along Cliff Walk at the end of Newport Beach. But he walked her the long way, on the western side, the side she most often used, past Hammett's Wharf and Lee's. They were approaching King's Park; soon Goat Island would slide behind. Beyond Fort Adams she would be able to see the sound unhindered; she would scan the curves of coast where the sand lances fed, she would seek the humpbacks browsing, watchful of the ships....

"And Bascomb came to me yesterday," Bay continued, as though this were the kind of thing he always talked about, as though he were not breaking her heart, as though his own heart were not torn deep and wide.

"The coachman," she said, "now retired."

"Yes," he said. "The coachman that night. He was Virginia's favorite. He was old and didn't mind waiting for her wherever she took him, because he could sleep. He retired immediately after. Lives in Narragansett now and gardens. A kindly man, Bascomb."

"And what did he say to you?" One voice had been raised against him, one finger. And now the voice was an opera chorus and the finger was a fist, with claws....

"He asked whether he could feel free to answer Detective Smythe's questions. He did not want to trouble me, embarrass me, wound the family."

"No," said Audrey.

The Dumplings were opposite them now, tiny islands across the channel of the bay, and Fort Wetherill. Castle Hill, on their side, lay ahead.

Bay smiled down at her. "You make it easier," he said.

She leaned against his shoulder. Mrs. Peerce is wrong, she thought. It isn't only the gilt and the glitter. They turn my head but not my heart. It's him. The grandeur and the luxury, that's his aura, he can't help having it and I can't help marveling at it. But if he was poor, I would love him.... *Guilty*, I would love him....

"Bascomb says he remembers waking and going to the corner of the lawn to see.... A shadow floated out of the front. He thinks it was me. He saw me, he says, bent over the body of Virginia, my hands at her throat. He scurried back to his post—horrified—thinking himself in the midst of a dream. And then I ran to him.... He did not question me. Did not question his memory...until now."

"I know," she said. She had heard it from Mr. Mc-Gregor a week ago.

She said, "And you told him to tell the detective everything he knew."

"Yes," Bay said.

"Yes," she said. "Is there more?"

"More from the maid. She insists I threatened to kill Virginia, insists it was Virginia who wanted to divorce me after the child was born. She says Virginia was impatient for the baby to come. Then she would have entitlement to part of my fortune. Then she would be secure. I was not a good husband, not loving, not generous—"

"I do not believe that," she said.

"It's true," he said. "Her beauty was not enough to keep my interest. I've told you that."

"But you would not hurt her. I know that."

"Perhaps we all, in our special ways, hurt one another. One at a time, each to each."

"No," she said.

They had rounded Brenton Point, beyond the public fishing pier. Hazard's Beach lay ahead, and Gooseberry's and Bailey's, and then they would have come to one end of Cliff Walk, and the climb would start.

Audrey looked seaward for the whales.

He was saying, reasonably, conversationally, "Detective Smythe has told me to put my affairs in order. I can expect to be arrested very soon. Bail may be possible, but I will be confined to Newport. Society is closed to me for the present. I'm glad Celeste has gone. They'll be gone three or four months at least, and I shouldn't want them to return until after the trial is over.... Mother has yet to be told."

"There has been an unusual amount of whales in the bay this year," she said. "More than anyone can remember so close to shore. It must be the crop of sand lances. There must be a bumper crop of sand lances this year."

"It's cool, too, for July," he said. "And the fishermen report high winds offshore, exceptionally high winds. Good fishing, but more dangerous than usual."

"And there is talk of hurricane. Down the coast, off Florida—more threat of hurricane than's ever been. I think it is just that we are tracking the weather more closely these days, keeping better records."

"Keeping better watch," he said.

They walked, trying to tire, sloughing through the sand. They did not tire. She wished they could walk, water walk, hand in hand, all the way to Portugal, and from there to Rome, to Tibet, or to Borneo or Sumatra in the Java Sea....

They were, at last, climbing Cliff Walk. Below Whale's Turning, below the rock on WaterWalk where they were climbing to, Audrey saw the whales. A cow and a calf. And a little away, aloof, adrift, a large bull lazing mountainously on the lace of the waves. So close. Nearly upon the rocks....

Above her on the steep, he turned and waited. There was resolution in the line of his jaw, and his hands on his hips were planted firmly. Breeze lifted a lock of his wayward hair. He was very beautiful.

She was climbing hard, hands on her knees to keep her balance as she leaned into the ascent and scrambled over the boulders and the stones.

He is going to tell me now, she thought. "Go," he will say.... I can no longer work with him, no longer dream at him from a distance. He will thank me politely, he will be kind, offer me a reference, perhaps, but there will be no indecision in his eyes. "We have already hired another," he will say. "Mr. McGregor prefers the other to you, and so does my mother and so do I." I will ask him to kiss me. "Before I go, see how my mouth tastes," I will say. But he will shake his head, disturbed at my boldness. He will extend his hand, but I will be unable to take it. I will turn and run, run down, and never see him more....

She paused below him, swiped a hand at her tangled hair. Up the slope, his shirt was white and fluttering, his head surrounded by pinkening blue sky.

"I have not much to offer," he said as she reached him. "A soiled reputation, a ruinous public trial, perhaps, to come.... I need someone to love me now, someone to hold my hand through the sleepless nights...someone on my side. Audrey—"

And even then she did not see it coming, did not know what he was saying, what he was asking....

He seemed to sense that. He smiled, and closed the distance between them with a step. He smoothed away a stray gold curl, cold upon her cheek. "Audrey."

"Yes," she said and, not knowing what she did, she lifted her mouth to him.

His arms around her were the sweetest warmth she had ever felt. Sweet warmth ... and a strange excitement deep within her loins that weakened her bones. Around her heart flowed a scorching heat, a blissful fire, narcotic and exhilarating both. For he was—at last!—kissing her. At last, his mouth, sweet warm, slow heat, was taking possession of hers, pulling her *into* him, and burning, burning, sweet as sunrise, hot as desert sun. She folded into him, *changed* as he held her, into a woman.... At last! Time was stopped and the world had ceased to turn....

The strength of him, the hot weight of his chest and thighs upon her, the lean rippling of his back beneath her hands; only the breath in his mouth kept her conscious; only his hands, seeking her body through her dress, kept her from reeling down the cliff side, floating to the sky....

"Audrey," he said, his mouth against her throat. She shuddered, yielding....

He released her, she who did not want to be released. He lifted her, brought her face against his face, then kissed her nose lightly and stood her down. Soft with love, drunk with him, she sought his eyes. Now she would know that he loved her, too!

But there was too much to see in his eyes. Too much turbulence and mystery. There was passion, oh yes, the passion of a man. But *sadness*, too. A sorrow.... Oh, what did it mean? Was it Virginia he wished he was kissing? Or was it only that she, Audrey, was not, after all, as he had hoped she would be?

His voice when he spoke was almost angry. She did not understand....

"Will you marry me, then?" he said. "Will you take me as I am, socially besmirched, about to be put on trial for the murder of my wife? I am friendless, needy, desperate—do you mind? Will you marry me right away without fanfare, without the folderol of parties and coaches and four hundred wedding guests? Will you marry me knowing that my mother despises you and that my sister fears you, and that I may go to prison for a lifetime or be hanged?''

He did not stay for his answer. He climbed on. She saw him before her, shirt flapping in the wind like a sail untended to, his hair blowing straight back, his trousers flattening against the muscles in his legs.

Oh, Bay.

Still weak, still heated, she followed.

There would be no celebration for them, then, as there had been for Thorne and Celeste. There would be no flower-trimmed trees, no lovely serving girls, no harps, no wandering violin. No coin with their likeness in profile handed out proudly by boys in satin breeches, no gold-and-scarlet carriage, no beautiful wedding gown. There would be no party after. No honeymoon. Bay would stay in Newport and wait to be arrested. And she would stay with him and wait, too....

She would come to Whale's Turning to be married and she would stay. The silken boudoir would be hers. The armoire and its contents would be hers, all hers. There would be servants to make the bed, *their* bed. There would be servants to cook and clean. But there would be no parties. No parties until Bayard Lockholm was cleared, irrevocably cleared, of his first wife's death.

No parties ever if he hanged....

His mother would be there, the mistress of the house. His mother who despised her. But perhaps his mother would be kind after Audrey was Mrs. Lockholm, too; perhaps his mother would teach her how to be a lady. Audrey would do as Mrs. Lockholm bade her, and they would become good friends....

They had come to WaterWalk, to the rock before Whale's Turning's seawall; their rock. Bay leaned against it. She came to him, he put his arm around her shoulders and drew her close. She slipped an arm around his waist. Under his clothes he was too thin; exhausted from worry, she thought.

Together they looked upon the whales.

He will kiss me again, she thought. He will tell me he loves me. Loves me as I have loved him since that first night. He will say, taking my chin, "I have been driven mad loving you," and he will kiss me hard....

"I will not be a good husband," he said. He took a cigar from his trouser pocket, released her and turned away from the wind to light it.

"I don't care," she said, stung. "I will not be a good wife."

"Whatever do you mean?"

"I do not know the ways of the rich—your ways. I shall be awful, make mistakes, say the wrong thing."

"Say the wrong thing to whom? We will be pariahs, Audrey, not darlings of the season."

"I see," she said. "Then it will be all right, won't it? We will love each other and be happy, and since no one will see us you won't ever be ashamed of me. It will be all right."

He was drawing deeply on his cigar, watching the bull whale surface from a long dive. The whale was coming up headfirst, shooting out of the deep from nowhere, in silence, without a ripple of disturbance, like a black catapult. Mouth open, all his body flying out of the water almost to the flukes.

"Then your answer is yes," Bay said with teeth that clenched his cigar. "You accept my offer of matrimony, even though I may be a killer, even though I may have killed one wife and may even get away with it."

The whale was in full breach. Forty feet of leviathan, fifty tons, virtually hanging above the sea. Giant black fins, the undersides white, spread like wings for balance or propulsion or joy, Audrey didn't know, but the great creature was climbing the wind, sea froth spraying off its belly like lava spewing down the shoulders of an erupting volcano, walking on the ocean's breast, tilting backward like an acrobat to hold the moment, and then, gaily, laughing to himself, crashing mountainously back into the blue and white and gray.... The spray flung high, so high it touched their faces. The hole in the ocean was an abyss, and then all was calm, and soft, and gently lapping.... And mother and calf, watching, too, rolled on their sides in their watery hammocks, unimpressed.

She was afraid to trust her voice. She nodded, her head against his sleeve. But why did he put it so?

She wanted to say, Yes! Yes! She wanted to shout and skip and dance. She wanted to say, I have loved you so much it must leap, always, from my eyes when I look at you. She wanted to say, Tell me you love me, too. Tell me how happy you are. She wanted to say, Kiss me, kiss me as before!

But he did not speak of love.

He moved out of her grip. He said, "Mother will be angry. But all right, it will have to be.... Shall we go now and tell her? You will stay to dinner and we will work out the arrangements."

She watched him, blowing smoke from his cigar. He was looking beyond the whales now, he was looking away as far as he could to where the ocean snatched at the gray-blue sky, caught it, and ripped it off the lip of the world.

Whatever he was thinking, it was not of her....

EDMUNDA WYSONG LOCKHOLM sat, with nothing she wanted to do, in an overstuffed armchair in her curved-wall bedroom, looking through the lace at a window toward the sea. Evening was falling; dinner would be announced in an hour, and she was very tired.

At an angle, she could see her son beyond the seawall on WaterWalk with that vulgar hussy from the town. They were standing close together watching a whale breach, and he was smoothing the tart's hair—tawny hair, the color of a lion—he was smoothing it with one hand and smoking a cigar with the other.

No taste, she thought. Bayard, like so many men, had not proper taste in women. He would never have looked at Virginia Stotesbury in the beginning if it hadn't been for her. My fault, that business with Virginia. Flesh of my flesh, blood of my blood—my fault.

Edmunda Lockholm sighed, a slow, deep sigh that held in it much more than she wanted. There was sorrow in the sighing, and a little despair. There was a realization of herself as a failure: failed woman, failed wife, failed mother. There was nostalgia in the sighing, a longing for sweet William, ten years dead; dead too young at fifty-five, she a widow too young at fifty-four. There was frustration and misery, in the sighing, for her present life.

She was a bad woman, she knew. A flawed woman. She had sinned great sins. And God had punished her, was still punishing her, was still taking away the ones she loved. Taking them from her one by one. Taking them or destroying them. . . .

Jeoffry. First Jeoffry; first and always Jeoffry.

And then William, dear sweet William.

Virginia.

Celeste. . . . Celeste, with her harlot's heart. *Buying* that beach boy. Sleeping with him—wham!—right out of the box. Getting herself pregnant; forcing the marriage. . . .

Celeste had ruined herself for pride. Ruined herself because Rolf gave to another the heart she had sought, the ring he had bought—ah, men. She and Celeste worked so long and so hard on Lord Pomeroy. And they had won him. Had him in their net, gaffed and ready to fillet. Had him! Then lost him to that crazy Nicola. What could any man see in Nicola? She was a bull in the drawing room, a fright at a ball, a vulture at a tea . . . Ah, Rolf, Lord Pomeroy, lost and Celeste devastated, maybe never to recover. . . . As she, Edmunda, had lost Jeoffry and never recovered; lost him twice for good measure and then William, too, God not satisfied. . . .

Virginia.

Celeste.

And now Bayard . . . last of the Lockholm line. Well, he would not be the last. He would marry again, have sons—

Mrs. Lockholm nodded, seeing her son turn to the house, taking the cretin's hand. She would send him away if she could. Take him as she had taken Celeste, to the marriage fair. But she couldn't; not now. He wasn't legally able to leave. No, now he must prepare to defend himself in a court of law.

Infamy. Bayard was no murderer. Virginia was a silly, stupid girl. She had thrown herself out the window in rage, in pique, and John Bayard Lockholm III had had nothing to do with it—nothing, thank you very much, as Ally McGregor always said.

Bay, her baby boy, on trial for murder. The past repeated. It was just like Jeoffry—

No, not quite like Jeoffry....

"Of course I have to get rich on my own, Eddy," he'd said. "Dad's going to stake me, it won't be for long. Everybody's getting crazy rich out West in the goldfields. Crazy rich, don't you see?"

Yes, she'd seen. She'd been nineteen in 1850, and he had given her a ring. A row of tiny pearls on a band of gold; pearls had been her jewels ever since....

"I'll be back in a year. Less, probably. A year from now I'll replace those pearls with diamonds as big as your eyes. Say you'll wait, Eddy. Promise you'll be true...."

Five years she waited, waited true. Waited through weeks and months of no letters, no word, writing faithfully every day to Mr. Jeoffry Eckkles, Hotel Esplanade, San Francisco, California; Please Hold. Once in a great while a letter came her way. Little news. Ever little news, always love. "Soon," he wrote. Never a specific time, only "soon." And each time the waiting was longer and longer. "Soon I'll send for you, my darling, my life.... I've found a vein...lost a vein...the strike may be tomorrow; tomorrow, the gold strike of the century!"

She waited, learning to tat, practicing her piano, traveling to Europe with her parents. They had not pressured her. They were happy in her company, not desperate for her to marry. Her father was a businessman with sons; she was her mother's only daughter and best companion.

The friends around her married. Edmunda waited.

And then came the word. Jeoffry was gone forever, killed in a mine cave-in; his hands, at the end, upon nuggets of California gold.... Mr. Eckkles told her. He was going West to see to his son's affairs. She must not come, Mr. Eckkles said. San Francisco was no place for a lady. And there was no body to bury, nothing of Jeoffry left to mourn or to see....

But he had known, Mr. Eckkles. Known the truth. He was just trying to shield her and shield his son. Mr. Eckkles had known for years, while Edmunda sewed lace on bed sheets and pillowcases and, every night before bed, wrote her letter. Mr. Eckkles had known that Jeoffry had fallen in with wrong companions. Overdrawn his allowance. Begun to cheat or steal mine patents of gold seekers more industrious or luckier than himself. Perhaps Mr. Eckkles had not known, then, that his son had found a mine worth killing for.... He had been caught, convicted and sentenced to life imprisonment. He was not hanged because the murdered mine owner had been a vagabond Mexican, and Jeoffry Eckkles had been raised a gentleman.

But Edmunda Wysong had not known and was not told. She wore black for a year. Mourned; grew thin and pale. On Fifth Avenue, William Lockholm, son of John Bayard Lockholm, Jr., fell in love with her. She was so fragile, so sad, so lovely, he said. To be loved by her, he said, was his fervent, most fervent, wish.

Her new suitor was perfectly proper and very rich. Her parents said yes. She was twenty-four, with nothing to look forward to except regret. She said yes. They were married a year later, in late November, 1857.

It had been nice, nicer than she'd thought, being Mrs. William Lockholm. William was a gentle man, not a businessman, not really very social, shy at soirees. He had wanted, in his youth, to be an opera singer. He spent his days playing: horse races, dog shows, theater matinees. He spent his evenings with her, ardent and attentive. She would play the piano and he would sing. Two days before their second wedding anniversary, John Bayard III was born.

The first eighteen months of Bay's life had been Edmunda's happiest. For long periods of time she forgot she did not love, had never loved, her husband. Life was untroubled, festive and full. She and William partied more. Made friends. They moved into a bigger mansion on Fifth. She redecorated. Summers they stayed at Ocean House, the grandest hotel in Newport, on Bellevue Avenue. She even began to dread less the nights William came to her bed; every other night he came, rigorously scheduled, and took his husband's pleasure—sometimes quickly, sometimes not.... The nights he came he stayed, snoring beside her after, naked, his pajamas on his slippers in a silken heap.

And then the letter came.

The letter that was to prove Edmunda Wysong Lockholm a bad woman. It came to her mother's house, a registered letter addressed to Edmunda Wysong, "Personal and Private." Her mother—not curious?—had the letter forwarded to the Fifth Avenue address at once. "Eddy," it said, "I'm back. All was a lie. I'm back from the grave.... May I come to you?"

Of course she met him, met him at the Plaza in a golden gown—wasn't gold his color? Met him in a private suite.

Just like Celeste.... No, not exactly....

He was the same. Handsomer for the eleven years away. Older and stronger, mature from the life he'd led. But he was the same Jeoffry. "I couldn't tell you the truth," he said. "I was ruined by men craftier than I. I was set up and framed and sent to prison. I couldn't ask you to wait, I had to let you go, for your sake."

She hated him. She loved him and she hated him.

"And now," she said. "What do we do now? Do I divorce my husband? I will if you want me to. I'll give up my home, my child—"

"I am married, too," he said.

"To whom?" she asked, wondering, How did this follow from the story that he's told?

"She is a Mexican woman. Her husband was my partner in a mine. He died—I married the widow. It seemed, at the time, the honorable thing for me to do."

Edmunda learned the truth later on, after their affair was in white heat, after she betrayed her wedding vows, after she let herself be seduced back into her schoolgirl passion.

He had not been framed. He had partnered himself to a Mexican and killed him and married the woman....

Esmeralda Diego, a peasant, one of a dozen from a fruit-picker's litter. Pretty at fourteen, a madonna at seventeen, an obese old woman at twenty-five.

And then he'd gone to prison and been pardoned through the quiet efforts of his father. He was a black-guard. Bankrupt, he had deserted Esmeralda, come back to New York. He was raising money for gold exploration in Africa. But he was in no hurry to go. Not with Edmunda's body his for the taking. Not with her checkbook access to her husband's fortune....

Still, he must have loved me a little, Mrs. Lockholm thought, watching her son walking on the lawn of Whale's Turning, trailed by the dreadful town girl. He stayed ten years.

A decade. And in all that time William Lockholm never said a word, never asked a question, never by any innu-endo or double entendre ever intimated to his wife that he knew...and was angry or sad. William never ceased being kindly, being gentle, being loving and generous to a fault: except that he did not, not once, cross the threshold of her bedroom. For ten years, while his wife played strumpet, from her thirtieth year to her fortieth, William Lockholm was celibate.

And then Jeoffry left her again. "I'm going, Eddy," he said one day. "Going as I came, in a flash. I won't be back. I want you to know, though, I wouldn't have missed lov-ing you for the fortunes of Rockefeller and Morgan com-bined. I've had what I came back for long ago. It was you I didn't want to leave."

"And now you do?"

"Esme's found me, Eddy. She's Latin—she's not gen-teel. I'm going home to her before I get us all killed."

"Good luck, Jeoff. And yes, don't come back...."

In the decade she had siphoned a million dollars from her husband's purse. She knew why Jeoffry was really going. He had money enough now, and investors, and he had tired of her.

That night Edmunda Lockholm thought of suicide. She laid out the sleeping tablets in long rows of tens. She went to bed with the shades up and the curtains pulled wide so that moonlight would illumine her bed. She wore her prettiest gown, black satin, gray lace.

And that night William came to her bedroom again, scuffing in his slippers, dropping his pajamas in a pile....

She never asked him how he knew, what he knew, how long he had known. How could she? Their life resumed as it had been, and Celeste was born, eleven years younger than her brother. Edmunda Lockholm came to menopause and the time of hot flashes as soon as she weaned Celeste from her breast. She was grateful to her husband for forgiving her—if he did; for not shaming her with divorce and public exposure. Pathetically grateful....

She was grateful, too, that she had used a courtesan's trick for that decade, taught her by her maid, her coconspirator. For ten years Edmunda tucked a square of colored silk into her womb when she expected her lover; spread the silken pocket deep within. She had several cut and hemmed and attached to a long flesh-colored string so she could, as she cleaned herself, purge herself of Jeoffry's bastard seeds.

She fell desperately in love with "sweet William" then. They had fourteen more happy years before he died, died singing as he loved to sing, pulling her on a sled up Fifth Avenue in the snow....

When he turned to her in that last instant, what had he wanted to say...?

Mrs. Lockholm's reverie was broken. Her son was escorting his tootsie up the steps of the lower loggia—was bringing town dirt into the house again!

Edmunda Lockholm rose, knees creaking, took up her cane. Well, she would see about this, put an end to this immediately. Bay was not to let that mutt into the house. Two whores were more than enough for the house of Lockholm....

There was a tightness in her chest she attributed to the emotions wrought by memory. She was dizzy and faint of breath. This is what comes of pining for yesterday, she thought. It is not healthy to prefer what used to be to what is now. It is dangerous to loathe the future, waiting for me downstairs: a grimy girl with hands first on Virginia's gowns and now breaking and entering on the arm of my only son. There ought to be a law...

Before the mirror, she was pale. She steadied herself against the bureau, patted her hair, held a palm against her heart. Ba-RUUMP, ba-RUUMP: it was skidding and slamming in her chest, loud as drums. I'll be all right, she thought. I'm just aroused by this bad girl. I'll go now...fast put things right....

THERE WERE NOT MANY lights blazing in the house, but the gold, the burnished gold, seemed to make its own light. The mansion glowed everywhere, high, around and under.

Audrey's sandals, sliding on marble, soft on Eastern carpets, followed Bay Lockholm across the mosaic-muraled floor of the lower loggia, the great porch open to the air, vaulted like a cathedral, its lofty ceiling muraled, too, columned like a Grecian temple. She followed dumb and trembling. She would never be used to all this!

A man in livery approached, the gold-and-cream-colored livery of the staff of Whale's Turning.

"Fisher."

The butler bowed.

"Please tell my mother I would like to visit with her in the music room, if she will. I have a guest with me, Miss Audrey Smoke, who will be staying for dinner. Will it be just ourselves, or has Mother invited friends?"

"Your mother has extended no invitations of her own, sir. Shall I bring you a whiskey and soda?"

"Thank you, Fisher. And bring the same for my guest."

"Very good, sir." The butler turned to leave.

"Oh, Fisher."

"Yes, sir."

"I'm curious. What is the menu for tonight?"

The butler was in his late fifties, white haired, handsome. His eyebrows were thick and dark over brown eyes that smiled at the question as though it were a joke. "Why, turbot, sir. Caught this morning by yourself, cook said. Turbot and a vegetable compote, I believe, leek soup to lead."

"That's so, Fisher. I had completely forgotten."

Fisher bowed. "It is unlike you, if I may say so, sir."

Bay led Audrey toward a vast room of silvered walls and golden-wood furniture upholstered in red, gold-threaded brocade. "Imagine, Audrey, I forgot my own turbot. Well, let's make ourselves comfortable."

Comfortable. As though she could be comfortable in this palace. Bayard was mad, she was mad. This was all wrong, a dream never meant to be actual....

Audrey looked around at a room a hundred feet long—at least—and fifty feet wide. A room with a great fireplace, its mantel built of stone the color of cloud, carved like the altar of a church, with spires—six spires—to set off panels of naked cherubs; a mantel that soared, leapt, to that distant ceiling.... The walls were the silvery blue of a Newport summer dawn, pilastered in white, pedestaled in gold. The windows, great Palladian windows from floor to gold-notched ceiling cornice, the windows were wide and curved and billowing with heavy drapes of rose-and-coral satin twisted over gold. The black piano, concert grand, shiny as patent leather, was so dwarfed by the reach and expanse of the room that for a while Audrey did not see it, so small in its windowed bay, and she wondered why this room was "the music room" and not a ballroom with furniture set in because they would not be dancing to an orchestra tonight....

Audrey heard the grande dame's footsteps and the cane, loud on marble, heard the deliberate setting of the cane point. *Thud.* Heard the softer snick snick of shoe heels following. Slow, the sounds approached. Ominous, they closed; barring retreat.

And then, dark, bibbed in pearls, Edmunda Lockholm stood in the center of the double doorway, her cane so close to her it blended with her gown. Leaning heavily upon it, the older woman peered into the room in a menacing, head-lowered, thrust-forward stance.

"Bayard," Mrs. Lockholm spoke from the doorway. "What does this mean?"

Bay rose as she appeared. Audrey struggled to her feet, too, behind him, awkwardly, not knowing if she did right or wrong.... Must she always stand then when his mother appeared, or was this a special occasion, a particular formality when a promised woman was announced to her fiancé's family?

"Mother, please come join us." Bay sat. Audrey sat, smoothing her work skirt behind.

Audrey watched with fascinated eyes as the woman traversed the herringboned oak to where Audrey and Bay sat on a love seat of gold and rose. Mrs. Lockholm stalked toward them, *thud*, *snick snick*, neared unsmiling; the pearls, the bodice of pearls, breathed rapidly upon her bosom.

She sat opposite them, dropped heavily onto the three-seat sofa, a sofa that matched their love seat, camel backed, soft rose brocade, the frame arched and gold dusted.

"Well," Mrs. Lockholm said.

Audrey knew that couldn't be right. One said "How do you do" and "Nice to see you again," or "How are you, my dear, and did you enjoy the wedding fete?" One did not say "Well," and sit and stare with hard eyes, both palms cupping a black wood cane with an onyx head, and wait for an explanation of a guest's presence....

Into the silence Fisher came.

He set on the table between them a tray of glasses and a porcelain bucket overflowing with ice, so cold the porcelain sweated and gleamed. Audrey watched an ice-tear roll down the face of a shepherd girl, fall upon a glazed lamb, trace the curve of the bowl.

When she looked up, Fisher had gone and Bay was talking, telling his mother that he had decided, suddenly, to marry. Telling his mother that he knew it was unexpected and not looked for so soon after Celeste, but she was not to worry about ornate schemes and meticulous plans; he and Audrey would marry in this room, a simple ceremony, unannounced, as soon as possible. They would not be taking a honeymoon, as he was town-bound by the instructions of Detective Smythe. One simple hour, and life at Whale's Turning would continue on, much as it had before, as it was meant to, with a new mistress in the house....

Audrey looked, just once, upon the face of Mrs. Lockholm. It was blood blushed, excited: the eyes, blue like Bay's, but slitted, slashes of blue boring into Audrey, keen as a parrot's talons. Mrs. Lockholm's breast was heaving, the pearls afloat like sea lace on the edges of a wave bubbling up the shore, whispering down....

Audrey closed her eyes. She wished Bay would stop. She wished he would change his mind, see how impossible it was, she was. How unwanted. It didn't matter. Audrey would be content to have known him, to work sometimes in his sight. To help him as she could. She did not need to share his life, his home, his relatives....

And still Mrs. Lockholm did not speak.

Bay ended. "Be happy for us, Mother. You'll like Audrey, she'll like you. You'll have a companion again. Celeste will have a sister."

He drank off his whiskey. Audrey stared at hers, ice melting in the glass. There was a glass for Mrs. Lockholm, too, that sat, perspiring, waiting for fingertips to smudge its condensation.

Mrs. Lockholm leaned back upon her cushions. "It is not possible, Bayard," she said. "I will not give permission."

"Mother," said Bay. "That's unkind of you, unworthy. I don't require your permission. What I'm seeking is your blessing. Be happy for us, help us to succeed."

"There is one curse on you already, son of a Lockholm. Do you want to add your mother's to it?"

Bay met her eyes; stood. "If I must, Mother.... We'll leave you now. Audrey and I have much to do. Will you be joining us for dinner?"

"I won't live in the house with this rabble," Mrs. Lockholm said. "This workman's daughter, this...dress thief. Look at her—hair not done, face smudged with your kisses,

I suppose . . . I will kill myself, throw myself out the window like Virginia. . . . Or is it possible—'' and her eyes smoldered cold blue ''—that you would help me in that, as they say you did your first wife?''

Bay said nothing. He stood, looking down on his mother, then turned and offered Audrey his hand. Audrey took it, rose, too, looked, too, at Mrs. Lockholm who was staring, mouth slack, eyes finally wide and warm, at her son.

And then Mrs. Lockholm was gasping, her face suffused with red, streaking white with strain. A pulse battered at her temple, an angry purpling pulse. She struggled to speak and twisted in her seat, trying to rise.

She almost gained her feet—Audrey thought the woman was reaching for her, lunging for her; Audrey drew back against Bay's shoulder.

But Mrs. Lockholm was falling.

She dropped to her knees, eyes dilated, unblinking. She smashed into the delicate gold table. Shattered glass. Sprayed ice and whiskey and sodas. Twitching, growling, choking, she stretched a high-veined hand for her cane; rolled clear of the splintered table. . . .

Lay quiet.

''Oh my God.'' Bay was on his knees beside his mother. Fisher was there, then gone. Audrey huddled and shook. What should she do? *What should she do?*

LATER, MUCH LATER, Audrey sat at the curved white table in the middle of Virginia's bedroom, her elbows on the gray marble tabletop, staring into a three-sided dressing mirror. She was alone, her dinner of turbot and vegetables and cold soup completely finished down to the two biscuits—they had been eaten first—and the blueberry tart. The tray lay now, aslant, on the elaborately carved chaise, silver serving domes upturned. She had not rung for the maid when she was finished as Bay had told her to, apologizing for leaving her to dine alone.

The courage for that would come.

Now she was sitting and thinking. Now she was changing; she tried to catch all the changes coursing through herself in the mirror, but this was not her mirror, not the mirror with her mother's eyes, and all Audrey saw was herself already restructured, remade; caterpillar no more, already timid butterfly. She sat before the mirror, still afraid to try her wings, terrified at the splendor, thinking and planning what she was going to do....

She would sleep in this room tonight, Bay had said; this room would be her room soon, he said. They were to have separate bedrooms. His was next-door; joined to hers by a door beyond the bath. She had not seen it. Even the bath was hers. He had his own. But he could come to her, unglimpsed by others, unheard, through the bath; come to her bed. And she could go to his, garbed as she chose in lightest silk negligee or only in moonlight from windows undraped against the night. Married, they would be lovers, and she would know what it meant to burst inside with passion as hot as lava tumbling....

This room would be hers, though built for another, decorated by the other, the color scheme decided to enhance another's skin and hair....

Audrey had stood, forgotten, a long time tonight in front of the portrait of Virginia Stotesbury Lockholm that hung at eye level on the landing of the staircase, under the mural of colored glass. The woman in the portrait was older than Audrey. Her face was sharper in outline and framed by dark, sausage-curled hair. She was beautiful, Audrey supposed; there was a feline cast to her face and a swell of bosom that the dress caressed, and her dark eyes followed something beyond the picture and made them glow. But there was no mystery in those eyes or in her smile. And her fingers, spread upon a tufted cushion of delicately faded red, were idle, only draped prettily upon a folded fan. Her dress was sumptuous, white taffeta with blue field flowers, curved low in the bodice, a blue velvet sash at the waist. The whole appearance was very composed. There was no tragedy in Virginia's face, no hint why she, who should have been so happy, newly wed, so content as a mother-to-be, had chosen, instead, to plunge without a scream from the golden cavern that was to be her summer home....

And nothing in the painted surface hinted why Bay Lockholm had loved her, chosen her, married her, swearing to leave off all others for her sake, as long as they both should live.

Would Bay have Audrey's likeness painted in oils? Would Audrey's picture replace Virginia's and hang on the landing of Whale's Turning for all to admire?

And what would her picture tell?

There was nothing in Virginia's portrait to show why, in Trinity Church, her coffin lay unattended except by a flower girl, a humble stranger who would, in a year, succeed to Virginia's place and take her husband, take her bedroom, take her name: Mrs. John Bayard Lockholm III.

Audrey would sleep in Virginia's bedroom tonight. Bay would see her at breakfast tomorrow, he said. Was there anything from her lodging required for her one-night's stay? Oh no, she had said, how could there be? And yet...she missed her cheval glass, missed her little bed. But those missed things were at Bridge Street, in Smoke House where her father disported with his new bride. Only her diary—and she could not ask for that—was in Mildred Falk's rented upstairs bedroom at the corner of Sunshine and Farewell.

Hours earlier, Dr. Lake had come.

Mrs. Lockholm had suffered a stroke, he said, a heart attack and a stroke. She was in a coma now. She would awake partially paralyzed, her speech impaired—if she woke. Time would tell, Dr. Lake said. Time, not he, was the healer. Time and the woman herself. Much depended on Mrs. Lockholm. Did she want to wake? Would she make the necessary effort to recover? She had been carried upstairs in the elevator by Bay and Fisher making a cradle of their arms. She was put to bed in her room. It was a long oval room, a room blue and green and white like the sound that crashed outside her boudoir's great windows. She was to rest, Dr. Lake said. Rest for a week, a month, the season. She was to have no excitement. There would be flowers, always fresh flowers, and poems read aloud, even while she slept. She might recover, could, in time, become perfectly well. But for a long while Mrs. Lockholm would attend no more parties, would hostess no teas. She would lie in her bed and take her medicine and watch the wind float the linen at her windows. And they would all see what tomorrow would bring...when she woke, if she awoke....

And Audrey Smoke would be mistress of Whale's Turning.

Bay had said, in haste, "We must marry now as soon as possible. Without fanfare of any sort. I need you. Tomorrow Priscilla will come and measure you for a dress. I will get the license and post the banns on Monday. We will move you in during the week, and on Saturday, I think, a week from tomorrow, you will belong to me and I to you."

It was necessary that everything be done as quickly as possible. Mrs. Lockholm would get used to Audrey, would come to trust her, would tell her about the house and how Lockholm houses were run. Through the convalescence, Audrey and Mrs. Lockholm would be friends. And when Celeste returned, everything would be as it should. Bay's indictment and trial, if it came to that, over and done with. Bay's marriage to Audrey an established thing....

Audrey faced her reflection. She would do it, she vowed. She would learn the ways of the rich and master the arts of a lady. She would devote herself to clearing Bay's name and restoring Bay's position with his friends. She would become a wife of whom Bay Lockholm would be proud.

And she must begin by ringing for the maid to clear her supper tray.

Audrey pushed back her chair and stood. There was a telephone beside the bed, tall and white and edged in gold. There were buttons under the raised dial. Buttons, but no names. Which? She had never used a telephone.

She picked up the receiver. A dull tone sounded in her ear. She pushed the last button. Short harsh sounds, and then the sounds stopped and Audrey heard Fisher's voice, sleepy and alarmed. "Hello. Yes, I'm here. Yes?"

"I—I am upstairs in Virginia Lockholm's bedroom. Could—could someone pick up my supper tray?"

There was a silence.

"Hello?" she said.

"I'll come," the voice said, and the line went dead in Audrey's ear.

Trembling, she set the receiver into its hook. What had been wrong, what had she done wrong? Had she asked the wrong servant or... A small clock on the bedside pointed its hands at midnight. Perhaps she had waited too long to call....

She took the tray, placed the pieces correctly and hastened to the double doors, set the tray outside on the floor in the hall. The hall was wide and high and long—unending—and dark and deathly quiet. She retreated back into the room. She wished Bay was with her....

She began to undress, small and frightened in an overwhelming room. More than anything in the world, she wanted her mama....

11

THE HORN OF THE STEAMSHIP sounded in the fog.

Celeste Lockholm Cockburn, in the honeymoon state-room, was slowly unbuttoning her peplumed bodice. She said to her new husband watching her undress, "Open the window, please. Perhaps fog around the bed will help to-night."

Thorne Cockburn was naked, at his ease on white linen cushions in a rattan armchair. The great tribute to his mas-culinity was ripe, a thick stalk arched toward her, soon to be spewing seed. Silently he rose, proud of himself. He was always proud of himself, she thought; proud of his physi-cality, proud of his prowess, proud of his stamina, and al-ways bewildered that he could not bring her to response.

But oh, how he tried, and she liked his trying. It made up for so much....

Obediently, Thorne opened the round window, rimmed and crossed with brass. Soft, damp air swirled in. It licked around Celeste's breasts, filled her mouth. Thorne sat again, in the same position, leg square-angled on knee, el-bows propped on the chair arms, his head resting—avid black eyes, eyes darker onyx than hers, hotter than hers—on the steeple of his fingers.

"Go on, my darling," he said.

She let the bodice slide to the floor. Her skirt buttoned down the front, bone buttons in a row from her waist to her ankles. One by one she loosed them until, past the hip, the skirt fell. She stepped free of it, in corselet and panties, garter belt and stockings and ribbon-tied, black shoes. She turned her back to him and began to unlace her stays. Thorne was panting slightly, and Celeste wondered if he was teasing her as she was teasing him, or if his ardor blazed so high because he could behold, without her seeing, the bag of money on the bed. A quarter of a million dollars. Even in one- and five-thousand-dollar bills, it made a heavy bundle, and a potent aphrodisiac. For she had promised it to him if and when he brought her to ecstasy. It had become their constant bed partner; her lariat, his collar.

She glanced over her shoulder and a little strap, yellow ribbon sewn through eyelet lace, tumbled and lay like a bracelet upon her upper arm.

Ah, he was staring at her, fascinated.

He was a handsome man, too handsome to be worth a damn, her mother had said. But her mother knew nothing of men, and her mother was wrong. Thorne Cockburn was worth quite a lot. He was ambitious, not a laggard; he would succeed. The bank loan had been granted. And why not, with the Lockholm name as guarantee? His ferry business would begin, assured of success, for all her friends would use her husband's service, first as a favor to her and then because the ferries were needed; they offered convenient, pleasant travel, much easier than sending a coach and driver down to the last stop of the train. And Thorne wore clothes very well and knew how to charm women—she would be envied her handsome husband. And he was crazy in love with her....

Not like Rolf.

Rolf had been used to all she had and knew, and more. Rolf had known, perhaps loved, her kind of woman before. He had not, for all Celeste's skills and schemes, been dazzled. Rolf had not needed her, had not hardened in his belly when he held her in his arms, had not been grateful to be chosen as Thorne was. Rolf had accepted her largess, her beauty, as his due; Rolf had thought *she* was the lucky one....

Celeste turned to Thorne again and opened the corselet, baring her breasts and throat and shoulders to the light of the low candles, white candles, Thorne had set around their bed.

The candle flames flickered and blurred from the window's breeze. Thorne stirred in his chair.

"Hurry," he whispered.

The undergarment traced down her arms, glided free behind her.

"Shall I leave on the necklace?"

He pointed to his chest and loins, unfashionably golden, strikingly well made. "The rubies have scratched me here...and here...but leave them on—they'll kiss me yet."

She unhooked her stockings, let them fall. Sat on the bed to untie her shoes.

"I can't wait," he said.

"You must," she said.

The fog was thick in the room now. It hung above the bed and around Thorne's head like wraiths drawn by curiosity and lust. It cooled Celeste's body, hardened the roses that tipped her breasts.

She slipped a stocking from one foot, then the other. They slithered, small and fine, to the carpet white as Arctic bear, soft as fur. She stood, bare feet inches from candle flame, and freed the garter belt. Lost it beyond the bed. She was naked now, except for the diamond star pins in her hair and the heavy rubies, red black, around her throat.

"Hurry," Thorne whispered.

"No," she said.

She reached above her head to the elaborate curls Joanna had been an hour creating. She pulled a pin free, moved to the dresser, laid the diamond in its special box. In the mirror she watched him watch her; watched him, shadowy in the candle-dark, to see if his eyes strayed to the pillowcase she had stuffed with more money than he could imagine possessing and then tied with a green-striped ribbon—green for greed—in a gaudy bow.

But his eyes never left her body, never ceased boring into her buttocks, the small of her spine, the mirror image of her breasts, stiffened by fog-fingers.

"You are whiter than the fog," he said. "More beautiful than angels."

She pulled another pin and her hair fell, heavy, black as a rain cloud. With an atomizer, she sprayed her body with perfume.

"All right, my husband," she said, turning away from the mirror at last, "try to earn your money."

She stepped over the candle saucers, lay down on the bed open to its sheets. One hand held the neck of the money bag, the other lay, palm up, behind her head.

The ship's horn moaned again, long and close. The fog wraiths shivered and danced.

Thorne crossed to her, sleek as an archer's bow, gold as an icon, his maleness firm as stone.

"I'm going to get you tonight if it takes till dawn," he said.

"How long," she said into the dark, knowing he wouldn't, wishing he were Rolf, Lord Pomeroy, "how long did it take Virginia?"

AUDREY WOKE AT SUNRISE to high wind blowing through the open floor-to-ceiling windows, not draped last night, left slightly ajar. Gauze curtain panels bulged and floated with wind-shaped strangers, ethereal, evanescent. The specters whirled through the room, flattening the curtains at the opposite windows on their way out. The day was gray, cloud low, but gold was blazing through; a hot, waxing red gold that stretched and pierced . . .

She knew instantly where she was. She was adrift in an ornate bed as great as a raft—her bed, *their* bed-to-be—just steps away from Bay in the next room. Perhaps he was waking, too, perhaps he was excited, too, as she was excited, wind-woke, and bathed in a rising gold.

She would go to him, tap on his door beyond the bath. Her bath! But for a moment she stood looking out, bewitched.

Before her, all around her, foam-throated waves, thick and dark as whale, climbed to grab the clouds and charged—a cavalry of water—then crashed in spume that splattered the face of the spreading sun. They rolled back in heaves and reared again and approached as walls, then cracked against the rocks again, asunder. And rolled back, solid again, to surge again, to stand and fall again, and again and again and again....

She hurried through the bathroom, tapped at Bay's door, wanting to share this first morning with him, this first hour....

There was no answer.

Was he sleeping still, exhausted by last night's drama, or was he up and downstairs, already breakfasting on the lower loggia, perhaps, as impatient for her as she was anxious for him? Or was he at his mother's bed, bereaved, at a loss, even now making the funeral arrangements?

And would they still marry if Edmunda Lockholm died?

Audrey tapped again, less certain. Perhaps it was not good manners, the both of them still chaste, for her to be battering on his door in her shimmy....

The door opened. A young woman stood there, plump and plain, in a yellow uniform and white apron. "Yes, ma'am," she said.

"Bay," said Audrey, not knowing what to say, trying to see beyond the girl's shoulders into his room. It was wood paneled and dark red and smelled of leather. Smaller than she would have thought. It was a bachelor's room, with a simple fireplace, brass fender, sporting things, a small black-wood bed—

"He's with his mother now, ma'am. Mrs. Lockholm's awake and Dr. Lake is there, too."

Audrey stepped back into the bathroom, conscious of the marble floor cool under her bare feet, conscious that she had no fine lingerie, belatedly aware that she had been caught pounding on Bay Lockholm's bedroom door in her undergarments.

"My name is Sawyer," the maid was saying. "Mr. Lockholm said I was to look after you." She reached into her apron pocket and handed Audrey an envelope. "This is for you. Shall I bring your breakfast in or would you prefer it downstairs?"

"Has—has Bay eaten?"

"I dunna know, ma'am."

Audrey walked back into the cream-and-fawn bedroom; Sawyer followed. What should she say to the maid? She thought she ought to say something....

She said what she might have said to Bay. "Look how the curtains turn and change in the wind. When I awoke I thought for a moment I was surrounded by ghosts."

Sawyer eyed the curtains. "Last night nobody pulled the drapes to, ma'am. And them window-doors were left open all night. That's what causes it. If the breeze disturbs you, I'll close all up." She crossed to a window to do so.

"Oh no," said Audrey. "I love the view, the fresh air. Please leave it."

"Yes, ma'am. There'd only be one spook in here anyways likely to bother you. This was Mrs. Lockholm's room, Mr. Lockholm's wife that was... She died last year, all of a sudden.... Will this be your room now?"

"I don't know," Audrey said, watching the curtain veils float. "It—it was a window she fell from, wasn't it? I—I heard it was a servant's window on the third floor...."

"Yes, ma'am. The room right above this one. 'Twas finished after, with the rest of the house as ordered, but it's never been used. He leaves it empty, closed up. Madam says the window ought to be kept clean, at least—it's one that looks out over the sea—but the mister says just leave it.... Maybe you'll be changin' that?"

"Out of respect," said Audrey, watching the curtains sway.

"Yes, ma'am. About your breakfast."

Audrey was overpoweringly hungry. But she wanted Bay; wanted, so much, to talk to Bay.... "Let me see what he says," she said, tearing open the envelope.

Why don't you breakfast and dress and meet me on the west lawn at eleven. Mother has rallied, but is not herself. We have much to do. B

"I—I think I'll have my breakfast in here, if I may."

"Yes, ma'am." The maid turned to leave.

"Sawyer?"

The maid turned back.

"I'm awfully hungry." Audrey tried a timid smile.

Sawyer was impassive. "I'll tell cook," she said and left, closing the double doors softly behind her.

Audrey looked again at Bay's note. It was the first time he had written to her. She wished they had been words of love. She folded the note, tucked it into her purse. She would paste it into her diary as soon as she could.

She felt absurdly lonely. She noticed that the curtains were hanging properly now, unstirred.

Even the wind had deserted her.

IN THE AFTERNOON Bay and Audrey drove to Mildred Falk's in a large coach, with two stable servants in the driver's box.

Along the way he told her that his mother was conscious but suddenly senile. Dr. Lake said this might be only a temporary legacy of the stroke, they must be patient. Mrs. Lockholm did not remember last night, could not take in that her son was going to marry; she insisted he already was, to Virginia. Bay thought it was better to let her believe that. "Less family fuss," he said, squeezing Audrey's hand. By the time Edmunda Lockholm was herself again, Audrey would be Bay's wife; there would be nothing his mother could do but accept. And Bay had talked already to his lawyer, Astin Forbes; he and Audrey would marry as soon as legally possible, on Wednesday. There would be no formal announcement until later. Bay would let his mother handle that, when she was able. There would be no party, no honeymoon. And there would be, after all, no time for Priscilla to make Audrey a bridal dress.

"Wear the gown you chose the day of Celeste's wedding," Bay said. "You looked wonderfully well in it."

"But your mother protested so," she said, "and it isn't white."

"Well, they are all your gowns now if you want them, whether Mother approves or not, and as for white, there'll be no one to remark on its color but myself, and I'll know better, so there." And he kissed her lightly, as though that were enough.

"Who will stand up for us?" she asked, watching the canopy of tree boughs over their carriage, watching Newport from a Lockholm coach. Was what she was feeling how Thorne had felt, his first or second ride? Audrey felt a guest, an unworthy guest of this luxury.... No, Thorne probably relaxed at once and settled in to stay, home at last, above the crowd....

"I've asked Ally and Mrs. Elliott, the reverend's wife. They have accepted."

Audrey sat mute.

And what of her? She had not been consulted about her own wedding, not its date nor her gown nor her attendants. Not the officiating minister... Well, did it matter very much? Who was there to give her away—not her father. He had indirectly accused Bay Lockholm of wifemurder—uxoricide, Detective Smythe and Alabaster McGregor called it, trying to take away the sting of simple words. Lawrence Smoke's testimony was already taken down and sworn to and filed in official papers. Who was there to be her maid of honor? Not Katya Greenfield, her growing-up friend. Katya had married Tony Scotti and moved to California.... Rosemary Maddley? She had been an employer, not a real friend. But maybe they could be friends now; Mrs. Maddley adored the rich.... Audrey would ask her, this very day. There should be someone on my side, she thought. At least one person in the bride's pew.

"And where will we marry, Bay? Has that been decided, too?"

From Bellevue Avenue, the carriage turned toward the bay, bluer than the hydrangeas, the boat sails blindingly white in the sun. Audrey thought of the Lockholm crest on Virginia's coffin: a platinum sailing ship above three waves in chips of tourmaline. When the time came, that crest would be cut into Audrey's coffin—like a brand, like ownership—set into a mahogany lid shined deeper than Lawrence Smoke could gloss, and Lawrence Smoke was famous in Newport for his neat's-foot-and-linseed-oil hand-rubbed polishings.

"I thought the music room," said Bay. "Would that suit you?"

"I want to be married by the rock where we met," she said. "I don't care if it's raining. I want to be married on WaterWalk, and see forever and hear the crashing of the sea." And maybe the whales would come, she thought but did not say. Maybe the whales would be there for my side, my unmonied family....

"All right," he said and patted her hand distractedly, as though it were not the most romantic idea he had ever heard, as though he didn't care where, as though he were thinking, instead, of how he would answer on the witness stand when the prosecutor purred, "And now tell us, Mr. Lockholm, why did you kill your wife? Was it to free you to marry the second Mrs. Lockholm whom you married so quickly, so privately there in your house by the sea, and who did not wear, as the world now knows, white on her wedding day?"

And someone in the courtroom would whisper, maybe Mr. McGregor, loud enough to be heard by all, "She wore a dress of the first wife's, a Lockholm gown, of body-blush coral and rusty-red chiffon. It clung to her figure like a grape skin, and made me think of Virginia's blood gone dry."

Someone else would exclaim, "You were there? I heard not a soul was invited."

Mr. McGregor would lower the lids of his ice-eyes and say, "Ah yes, I was one of only two. The other witness was the reverend's wife. Poor thing, she was in such shock she never said a word...."

MILDRED FALK DID NOT express surprise that Audrey was leaving. She did not ask where Audrey had slept the night before. She sat in her parlor crocheting daisy patterns into a shawl while Audrey packed her few things, hastily gathered, into two boxes. The stable men carried the boxes down. Mildred Falk stood when Audrey came to say goodbye. She accepted a white envelope from Bay Lock-holm as though munificence happened to her often. She asked to speak to Audrey alone.

Bay left them to wait in the coach.

"It was the slice of cake done it, Audrey, that slice I brung you from your dad's wedding day, and all I hope is that this fine man you're marrying ain't what they say he is.... But if he gives you any trouble, any trouble at all, you can come here to me, girl, night or day, rain or shine. Don't forget that. Now you go be happy, and don't forget your old friends. And look in on your father and Dolly. He's your blood, all the kin you got left, and nobody's perfect. Least of all you, least of all me. And don't go gettin' above yourself. You may be marryin' rich, but you ain' bone-rich, and there's a difference. I'm only saying these things cause your mother's gone and can't, and somebody ought to. I'll be thinkin' of you, from time to time, up there on that hill all alone. You be on your guard, Audrey Smoke. Keep watchin' out behind you and don't let 'im sneak up on you in your sleep. Now go on, he's waitin', and may you live happily ever after."

"Miss Falk—"

"Hush now. And don't cry. Ladies never cry in public, that's what a private room is for—oh, you'll learn these things quick enough—not even when their husbands die or they get abandoned at the very altar. Ladies cope, and smile and smile. Into the grave they go, smilin'. That's a lady's lot, my dear. So you get on with it, and don't you never mind the things that hurt...."

From Mildred Falk's, the carriage rolled to Bridge Street so that Audrey could take away from Smoke house the two things most important to her, the cheval glass wherein her mother lurked and the little rocking chair her father had made when she was small; Audrey's chair, pink lacquered and painted with magical birds.

Jumping down from the carriage before her father's door, Audrey heard the rhythmic raspings of a saw and remembered the smell of sawdust, as sweet and warm as oatmeal in the mouth. She threw open the door to the shop and saw her father, as she had seen him always, it seemed, deep in a dark corner, sloped over the light of an oil lamp at noon, working his wood.

And, surprise, he was smiling as he worked, and he was humming a tune, a happy melody she'd not heard before and did not know. It would be a bawdy song, she thought, a tavern song he'd learned from Dolly....

"Hello, Father," she said.

Lawrence Smoke gave one more strong push and pull and paused; an edge of oak dropped quietly into a hill of yellow dust. He ran his fingers over the just-cut butt of wood that remained under his hand; looked at her with eyes shadowed in the dim.

"Have you come home, then?" her father greeted her. "An' do you bring with you good fortune or ill?"

Behind her, Bay filled the doorway, his arm at her waist.

"Mr. Smoke," said Bay. "I've come to ask you for your daughter's hand."

Lawrence Smoke spat down into the golden pile of sawdust. "The day she left my bed an' board she left her fealty to me an' mine to her. I give no permission an' I take no responsibility for that one.... Have you come to thumb your nose at me, Audrey Alice, is that it, then? Have you been curryin' favor with your betters? Have you given yourself to a man who buried his first not a year ago...?"

"Father."

Lawrence Smoke picked up his saw again, cleaned a line of wood dust from the row of teeth with thumb and finger. His overalls were clean again, as they used to be in the time of Josephine. His face was clean shaven. There was no old oil on his hands.

"May I have my cheval glass, mother's mirror, the one you gave me? May I have my little rocker? I love them so."

Her father beheld her from across the room, his fire-flecked eyes narrow with an old decision. "Take 'em, girl. Take 'em now. An' anything else you mean to take." He swung his head to the wood before him, raised a new board, set it upon the other. The saw was already balanced in his hand. He laid its face against the place he wanted and, like a violinist, began to bow upon his instrument.

In a tumult of yellow dust, the saw sang a workman's song.

Audrey advanced into the shop a step, then two. "Father," she said, "please give me your blessing. Love me again."

But her father didn't answer, didn't look up. Perhaps he couldn't hear with the razz of the saw beneath his thrust-out chin and the motion of his muscles working...working....

The stable boys carried down the mirror and the chair. Audrey and Bay waited out on the sidewalk. If Dolly Dowd Smoke was in the rooms upstairs, she did not look out.

Audrey asked to be dropped at Gardenflowers; she would walk from there to the *Daily Whirl*.

"You can't keep working, married to me," Bay said.

"I should like to say goodbye then, and finish what work I can."

"I'll pick you up at six," he said. "If I'm not there promptly, I won't be there at all and you'll have to walk."

Didn't he want to hold her and talk of love? Didn't he realize how big the step she was taking, taking alone, uncounseled, unbefriended? He was in love with her as she was desperately in love with him...wasn't he?

"Will you kiss me goodbye?" she said.

"No, I don't think so," he said. "Not yet in public. I will kiss you tonight when nobody's looking. How'd that be?"

She was out of the coach, earthbound again. The coach wheeled away.

When no one was looking, he might kiss her. Would it always be like that; he removed, correct, paying no particular attention to his wife in public? Was this, too, the way of the rich?

Two women on the sidewalk looked at Audrey in her brown-and-black working-woman's dress, then followed Bay's carriage with their eyes.

Audrey watched the coach, too, a fine coach, the aristocratic lines of it marred by her rocking chair and mirror lashed to the back, almost comical. My dowry, she thought. This was not how the rich married—in haste, to a town girl. She had been given no splendid ring to tell the world she was promised, no heirloom from the Lockholm vaults to embellish her throat. I shall not even have a wedding dress, she thought. There will not be, for me, happy friends and fat gift boxes to unwrap with squeals of joy. Not for me Thorne's proud day, swathed in luxurious display. Well, it doesn't matter. I am to marry the man of my dreams. I shall be, forever and ever, Mrs. Bayard Lockholm. . . . I will buy a bouquet from Mrs. Maddley. That, at least, I will have. White roses if she has them, madly expensive. I will buy them and charge it to Bay. . . . Cut them in the bud, Mrs. Maddley, on Wednesday at dawn, while the dew is still on their faces. And deliver them to me at Whale's Turning before nine. A dozen, I think, with green fern for color, and tie them, please, in your heaviest double-sided white satin ribbon in a great, great bow. . . .

One of the women who had been watching the carriage crossed to Audrey. She was tall and thin and her clothes were good. "I made her dress, you know, his wife's wedding dress. And his sister's, just married last week to a local boy. You just never know, do you?"

Audrey started, alarmed. What meant this strange woman's confidential manner? This must be Priscilla, the dressmaker. And did she know who Audrey was? Did she know Audrey was to be wed to Bay Lockholm in such a hurry there would be no time to make a wedding dress?

"Know what?" Audrey said with dry throat.

"About people."

The woman was appraising Audrey's frock. "Lockholm used to be a grand old name in Newport, one of the best. Last year at this time, no one would have believed a word against them. But there must be something to that 'curse on the Lockholms' business, after all. He murdered that woman he married, you know, and he'll hang for it, as sure as I'm standing here in front of you. And his sister just married riffraff. Well, it'll all come out in the wash, I suppose. . . . Have you known the family long?"

Audrey was terrified. "I—I work for the newspaper, the *Daily Whirl*," she said. She thought, Why don't I say we are to be married. What am I afraid of?

"Kind of him to give you a ride, wasn't it?"

"Yes," said Audrey. She lifted her skirt to get away. To get anywhere away. "Excuse me," she said.

"Surely," said Priscilla, still measuring her. "But you be careful, honey. Men like that, even if he is your employer—well, it doesn't do to get too familiar."

"No," Audrey said, "no...."

"Next thing you know, he'll be chasing you, asking you home to tea. God knows no woman in his set will have him. You should have seen his wife before the wedding, I never saw a happier bride-to-be."

"Was—was her dress beautiful?" *Why* did she have to ask that?

Priscilla's nose and eyelids dipped. "It was the most beautiful dress. I'll never forget—it was a month of work, days and nights. Pounds of satin, pounds of pearls. The train alone... She was buried in that dress, you know. Like a pharaoh's wife. Buried with a fortune. Of course the casket was closed—they couldn't make her presentable—but her bridal gown was her shroud.... Ah, well, the rich. They steal from the poor and then throw it all away. They don't care."

"I must go," said Audrey. Her knees were weak with trembling. She wanted to ask, Why are you telling me this? Do you know about Bay and me? And how do you know such things? She wanted to say, I won't be buried in a fortune of a wedding dress, never fear, Miss Dressmaker. I'm marrying in a Lockholm gown; it's old and rusty red...but never worn.... Did you make that one, too? That one, too, was *hers* once. Both the man and the dress were hers....

"Good day," she said, and ran to the door of Gardenflowers.

Rosemary Maddley was behind the counter, polishing eucalyptus leaves. She had been watching Audrey, too, watching her being handed down from a black barouche by the master of Whale's Turning.

"Well hello," she said. "What have you been up to? Wasn't that Bayard Lockholm I just saw you with? And weren't you terrified he'd *touch* you? Do you remember, Audrey, *we* did his poor wife's funeral?"

"I—I'm getting married, Mrs. Maddley. I shall want a bouquet."

Rosemary Maddley lifted her eyeglasses. "You are a quick worker, Audrey Smoke. Quicker than I would have thought. When's the happy day and who's the lucky man?"

But Audrey was gone again, out the glass door and into the street where the Reverend Graf Elliott's fine mare, in a hurry again, almost ran her down.

"Some people," said Rosemary Maddley to the sheaves of eucalyptus. "Unsettled nerves, that's all there is to that. Poor thing."

"WELL," ALABASTER MCGREGOR greeted her, "I've heard of quick promotion but this is precedent setting. I was almost getting used to you, too, almost, though not quite, beginning to like you. But—" he feathered his fingers to prevent her speaking "—I shall live without you very well. I've never liked sharing my secrets, and I shall protest if Bay seeks to replace you. Secretaries are all I've ever needed or wanted, male secretaries, distant from me by a floor. I put in for a raise for myself, a generous raise, I don't mind admitting, which was readily granted, and now I congratulate you."

His eyes were keen, appraising her differently. "I never thought you'd make such a fine finish, my girl. You were in my mind a dark horse, though your slowness from the gate marked you a distance runner.... But, really, the race isn't over yet, is it? Now, shall we get on with our work?"

"Sir..."

"Oh yes, I know it all, my dear. All that has transpired between you and Bayard and Edmunda Lockholm. They don't call me king of the scoops for nothing, thank you very much."

"Mr. McGregor—"

"Oh yes, I knew there was something else. You can't call me Mr. McGregor anymore, you'll have to call me Alabaster or Ally, as you prefer. Though I will continue to call you Audrey, no matter how high your pretty little bootstraps lift you."

"Mr. McGregor—"

"Yes, you cunning little social climber, you?" He tapped a pencil upon a pile of paper.

"Mr. McGregor, will you help me?"

He had been standing. He sat. "In what way, dear girl? Forget spelling. You'll never be any good at that."

Audrey sat, too, facing him, wanting to draw close, wanting a friend. She was afraid to trust him; she needed to trust him. She lowered her head and clutched her hands.

"I want to be a good wife to Bay—"

"Oh yawn," said Alabaster McGregor. "Just kiss him often and let him have his way. That's the trick, I'm told."

"Please don't tease."

"Well, then, out with it. I haven't time to dish advice about the wedding night, if that's what you're after. You'll get through it somehow, the little darlings all do. I'm much more interested in the *Daily Whirl* than I'll ever be in you, Cinderella, so do get on."

Tears were visible now, muddling her vision, making her nose run. She swiped at them angrily. "I do not know how to be a lady." She said it almost defiantly, meeting his eyes. "Help me," she said.

Behind the bluff, the posturing, there fired in his ash-colored eyes something that heated the ice of their centers. Whether angelic or diabolic, she did not know.

"Umm," McGregor said, fluttering the pencil, eyeing her up and down. "Yes, the same old problem. Luster comes only after long gloss, and you're not even shined up yet. You're in for a devil of a time, aren't you, especially with Celeste not here to help you, even if she would, which I doubt, and poor Edmunda—and then there's Bayard's arrest—"

"Arrest."

"As we speak. Didn't you know? My dear, he doesn't tell you anything. Astin Forbes is probably posting his bond now, if the judge allows it, which, granting Bayard's position in life, I predict he will. So your dear fiancé will be home for dinner, don't worry that the roast will overcook. But he faces trial, of course, a sensational trial.... I can hardly wait. When the rich are naughty, the world wants to know all about it, and Alabaster McGregor's on the beat here to do it. I've taught you that much at least in your time here, haven't I?"

She was listening so hard her tears, unminded, had dried away. She blew her nose, nodded. "Yes, sir," she said. She heard the presses rolling on the floor below, felt them through her feet, from her chair, synchronously throbbing like the heart of a mob....

McGregor rolled on, too. "And you, clever girl to marry up so high, as the second Mrs. John Bayard Lockholm III will not only be newsworthy, ah, but infamous. Hot stuff. Everyone will be watching you, wondering if you and Bay had known each other before he killed Virginia.... Did you? You'll probably be thought a fast tart who caught a millionaire when his guard was down." He shrugged. "That's what I think, at any rate."

"Mr. McGregor, you know Bay did not kill Virginia. You know I did not know him before this year, and I am not a tart, you know that, too. You couldn't think things like that."

Alabaster smoothed his bald head with liver-spotted hands. "Oh, couldn't I," he said. "But perhaps I won't. We'll see. As I think, so does Newport, most of it anyway—the ones who matter. So we'll see.... I could befriend you, make you society's darling. But what a time it would take, you're so raw. Still, it would be a tour de force if I succeeded...."

"Mr. McGregor."

"Yes, Audrey."

"You're thinking of yourself again."

"Ah, then. Let that be your first lesson. The rich always think of themselves first, just as everyone else does. By the way, I am one of them, one of Newport's local elite, of illustrious family line and considerable booty. I own forty percent of this newspaper, and I do the work I do because I must do something with my days, else I'd do very much worse with my nights. I'm not, perhaps you've guessed, a family man . . . and newspapers amuse me.''

She hadn't known. She shook her head. There was so much in this new world she didn't know, that one was never told because one was supposed to know it all already. How easy it would be to *misstep*, and thereby make a fatal mistake. . . .

"I—I'm sorry I didn't know, sir. No one told me."

"Now," he said, "someone has. To continue, in the case of the rich, foibles and frailties of character are more conspicuous, hence the desire of the rich for privacy in all things, but we do not apologize for our lot. This is what is known as the attitude of privilege. Consciously cultivate this attitude, Audrey m'girl, and in time you will come to possess a certain hauteur, without which it cannot truthfully be said that you are one of us. . . . How's that for your first great truth?''

"Yes, sir, thank you."

"*Don't* call me sir anymore, not ever. Do you hear?''

"Yes, Ally. . . . Behind your back, do they call you . . . alley cat?''

Alabaster McGregor smirked, full of himself, tipped back his chair and stretched grandly. "Indeed they do," he said, "and well they ought. Remember that, too, Jilly-come-lately. Having me as your friend is almost as good as marrying Bayard Lockholm, and there is nothing, short of bankruptcy, worse than having me as your enemy. . . . Now, fortune huntress, shall we get on with tomorrow's paper? It's going to be a real firecracker. . . .''

12

IT RAINED ON WEDNESDAY, the seventeenth of July; a slow
drizzle from black clouds that hung, a begrimed and sag-
ging canopy, over Newport's Gilt Hill. Whipped by winds
off the sound, the drops pecked disconsolately hour after
hour at stone and window, sliced interminably into the
lower loggia, and softly drowned the blue grass of the
mansion's lawns.

A little after four in the afternoon, Audrey Alice Smoke
and John Bayard Lockholm III were married in the music
room of Whale's Turning. She wore the gown of body-
blush coral and rusty-red chiffon that had been designed for
another. In lieu of a veil, she wound her tawny hair with
white ribbon. Her silver sandals were a half-size too large,
but she did not stumble. She had no jewelry of her own,
and the groom presented her with none. She wore nothing
old, nothing new, nothing borrowed or blue. The gown was
neither old nor borrowed, Audrey reasoned. Made last
year, never worn, it had been given to Audrey by Bay. It
was her gown now, and it had never been Virginia's. She
carried no bouquet, received no cards or gifts of congrat-
ulation. No friends—unless she counted Alabaster Mc-
Gregor as a friend—no family witnessed the union. At
least, no family of hers. Edmunda Lockholm was present,
catatonic in a gold side chair, eyes vague with sedation. The
matriarch was dressed in rich blue and her pearls. She sat
with good posture, hands folded, unmoving throughout the
short ceremony. When it was over, Edmunda Lockholm
clapped, as though the wedding had been a tea entertainment, and then her head fell upon her shoulder and she
snored.

Alabaster McGregor wore a gray morning suit, but Bay
was attired, less formally, in a suit of summer tan. The
Reverend Elliott, who performed the service, wore a white
lace surplice over a black pastor's frock; his wife, Judith
Elliott, wore a sensible gown of dark green that did not become her light skin and graying hair.

The staff of Whale's Turning made up the wedding au-
dience. Fisher, the butler, played the march on the grand
piano. Bay's lawyer, Astin Forbes, was part of the company, and so, too, was Detective Jeremy Smythe, sent down
from Providence to catch a murderer in Newport.

A small reception was held in the grand hall. On a moment's notice, at Audrey's request, Mrs. Olsson had baked
the cake. There had been no time for a great creation, but
the cake was very pretty; a two-tiered rich vanilla with sweet
almond icing topped by two feathered bluebirds in a cage
of wedding bells.

By six o'clock the reception things had been cleared
away, the few guests had gone, the house staff was back at
their usual work and Edmunda Lockholm was in her bed.

Audrey changed into her own handmade white cotton,
which, once upon a time, she had worked on with such
happiness, thinking it the most beautiful dress she would
ever wear. Carefully she hung away the gown in which she
had been married, and the feeling of unreality was almost
gone with the shutting of the ornate armoire doors.

"Shall I take you on a tour of the house?" Bay asked.
"You really haven't seen it yet."

"Come with me to WaterWalk," she said. "Kiss me in
the rain. I want to lean on our rock again and..." She did
not say, and find the whales if I can. He might not understand. The whales were her secret. She had stood in the
beautiful gold-and-beige boudoir last night, the casement
windows thrown wide on the seaside, and begged the whales
to come to Whale's Turning for her wedding day. She had
talked to her mother in the cheval glass last night, the mirror at last in Audrey's bedroom again, her new opulent
bedroom, vast and silken, in a corner where a screen had
stood. "If the whales came, it would be all right," her

mother had whispered from the depths of the glass. "There might be trouble, struggle even and sorrow, but if the whales came, then God blessed the union of Audrey and Bayard Lockholm...."

He was in the bedroom with her, *their* bedroom, looking out the same windows, closed now against the rain that gusted over the balustrade of the little balcony without and splashed against the casement glass. He did not answer.

"Please," she said. "It's my wedding wish." She looked at the gold ring on her finger. It was heavy on her hand, alien, a little too big. It did not really fit.

"I did not have time to buy you a proper wedding gift." He sounded angry. "Do you mind if I smoke?" He held out one of his cigars.

"Of course not," she said. "I don't mind anything you do. And you are gift enough for me. Are—are you sad, Bay? Are you sorry?"

The match flashed, bright in the darkening afternoon, wild on the end of its little stick. The cigar smoldered. He said, through smoke, "I want to see you naked. Let's go on your damn walk, get drenched. Then I'll tear that dress off you. I never want to see that dress after today. If you want clothes, order Priscilla in. When all this business is finished I'll take you to Paris, to Worth... Goddamn Virginia—her claws are in me still. It should have been you from the first, but I didn't know how to find you...."

He was against her then, his jacket rough at her upturned throat, and he was kissing her, kissing her as she had never been kissed, his tongue inside her mouth stiff and fierce and never still. He was holding her too tightly; his hands burned like a match flame on her breasts and then on her buttocks and then rushed strong and steel fingered between her thighs. And then he was lifting her in the air, his arms around her loins, locked across her back, and his head was deep between her breasts, and he was licking her like a savage....

Then, as suddenly, he set her down, held her away from him, and she watched the lust gentle out of his blue-sea eyes. She watched the pulse that was hammering in his forehead become slower, saw his face regain composure. After a while he held her again in his arms and rocked her in a slow, stationary dance; his muscles trembled as they relaxed. She heard him say, as though he were on the shore and she was under the whitecaps, far away, "We'll have an early supper here in our rooms, and then, Mrs. Lockholm, my darling, my bride, I will show you how sorry I am that we are one."

A moment before, so frightened. Now so happy. She smiled at him with a new knowledge.

"Yes," she said, "oh yes."

He found his cigar where he had thrown it, in a bloodred bowl. It was long ashed, still burning. He drew on it, exhaled. His hair was loose on his forehead, like a boy's. He opened the doors of their bedroom; took her hand.

It was as though the storm had waited for them. All day there had been the steady, gray drizzle, but as soon as they, mackintoshed and booted—Audrey in Celeste's boots and slicker, too long, and bright yellow like Bay's—braved the water-rent grass of the west lawn, the rain increased. It straightened as the wind changed, and slashed upon them, hard and ice-cold. The softened ground sucked at their feet. The branches of the weeping beech whipped out as stiff as the hair of a ship bow's wooden maiden. Color bled from nature, the waves flattened, gone black and white.

Audrey held Bay's hand and ran, laughing at the storm. She was Mrs. John Bayard Lockholm—she was! she was!—and she was going through the break in her wall, at the end of her lawn. She was turning past *their* little pier where their yacht, the *Catbird Seat*, pitched and pulled at the end of its rope. She was slipping down the cobbles of the path, ascending WaterWalk, and everything was going to be all right, after all, because she had seen, through the slur of the rain, a haze of waterspout down there in the sea. The whales were there, below the drop of rock where the world ended and the ocean ran. The whales were there; the whales had come!

She dropped Bay's hand in her hurry. She clung to the rock and her rain hat; shielded her eyes from the torrent.

She looked, and at first did not believe. She stepped back
in shock, then leaned upon the rock again—for no, this
couldn't be right, this was not what she had meant at all,
not at all! There was a crowd of whales in the bay, touching one another close as stones, long high hills in a black-
and-white storm-upturned world. Thirty, forty, fifty
humpbacks, huddled side by side, not flippering their fins
in free greeting, not rolling gracefully in wave-rocked
hammocks, not powerfully breaching into the sky in play,
not slamming their flukes as they dove, making tail prints
on the sea.... Motionless as doom, they lay like giant slugs.
As she stared, one sank, then another, rippleless into the
deep; sank to resurface, back-to-back, as grave as ghost
ships. Small ones, great ones, they loomed, hulked, below
WaterWalk, a herd. One spewed upward a sigh of wet
breath that smoked and drifted and was taken by the storm.
Another quivered, his spouting a poor dribbling,
aborted....

The wind was keening against the cliff side, a strange
song.

She shouted to be heard, "Look!" but the wind took her
voice. She turned to him, he, yellow coated, the only color
in the world, his face unclear, rain gray, running with water. Somehow he had lost his hat.

"Back," was all she heard. He took her arm to take her
away. But she resisted. She had to know what it meant,
what it signified, this massing of leviathan at her feet on her
wedding day. Evil omen, that she knew. God could not
have told her stronger if he had written it in rain on the
ocean's face. She had asked for whales, and this was what
he had sent her—a plague, a pestilence. Was all the world
in upheaval because she had married the man she loved?
Were all these whales to die because she had believed Bay
Lockholm innocent? She listened to the eerie sound in the
wind. An alien croon.... Could it be the whales whining a
dirge?

Long ago Grandfather Nally, who knew all such things,
told her that sometimes the whales sing, each to each. Sang
in a voice none could hear but the angels. But if, as some-

times rarely happened, a sailor heard the song of the whales, he would know that death was aloft and flying. The seaman could run, but it would be to no purpose. He could race to the ends of the earth, but he might just as well start planing his coffin board and writing his goodbyes, for he had heard God's summons; he had been called to judgment.

Did the whales sing for her . . . or for Bay?

Lightning fingered through the clouds, a black-and-silver lightning, silent and claw edged. High, like a skeletal hand, it stabbed and hovered, flash frozen, then faded, slowly faded . . . and flashed again, and hung. . . .

She turned away from the sea. She had courage for no more. Through the gray of the rain Whale's Turning, grand and vast and ghostly white, blazed with golden windows, lighted from within. Its red roof tiles glowed from the sky to the west; to the west, the storm was easing. She stood for just another moment, conscious of Bay pulling at her elbow, conscious of the unearthly keening of the whales, conscious of water dripping down her knees into her boots. She stood, rain driven, heart haunted, and asked the mansion if it welcomed her as its mistress . . . or was it, too, haunted by Virginia. . . .

As she was.

AUDREY WAS in her bath, luxuriating in pink bubbles and hot seawater—for Sawyer the maid had told her that the four taps that ran into her tub offered hot and cold town water plus ocean water piped in directly from the bay, heated or natural, as the bather preferred. Imagine, Audrey thought, the sea, with all its healthy properties, only a twist of the faucet away. Supper had been ordered for eight, in their bedroom; she would wear the white satin nightgown she had bought a long time ago for her wedding night. She had no covering peignoir; the nightgown alone had cost so much, but she would wear a silk shawl she'd found in one of the bedroom drawers. It was patterned in padded ivory satin roses and hemmed with a long beige fringe.

She was happy again, the storm and whales put out of her mind, only Bay and *this night* in it, when she heard the sluff-sluff of slippers sliding across the bedroom carpet, and the strong stomp of Edmunda Lockholm's cane.

Audrey held her breath, expecting at any moment to be burst in upon, ordered out of the house, screamed at. She wished she could sink like a seal under the thinning cover of pink bubbles and so hide, undiscovered, until the older woman went away. She shook more crystals into the tub to raise the bubbles higher, and kicked the water to dissolve them.

But Mrs. Lockholm did not appear, vengeful, in the bathroom doorway. The sluff-sluffing continued, slow; the stomp of the cane was a dull knock Audrey had to strain to hear.

What was Bay's mother doing. Examining the room that now was Audrey's? Poking through and sneering at Audrey's poor possessions? Tomorrow, Audrey promised herself, she would throw all she owned away and order Priscilla in....

She heard the doors of the armoire open with two snaps. Heard the rustling of fabric. Mrs. Lockholm was going through the wardrobe! Whatever for?

The water was cooling, but Audrey did not want to add more hot, afraid the sound would bring Mrs. Lockholm in. Besides, she wanted out now. She had washed her hair and her body, she was warm again, seashell pink from the heat of the bath, and she wanted to dry herself, perfume herself, comb out her long blond hair. She wanted to carefully coat her eyelashes with match soot, and ever so slightly rub rouge along the line of her cheekbones and full on her lips. She wanted to be beautiful tonight; tonight she would lose her maidenhead and learn—at last!—why Dolly Dowd laughed with pleasure when bedded by a man....

From the other room Edmunda Lockholm was talking. Her speech had been marred by her stroke; her words were disfigured. But she spoke with volume, and Audrey heard, only too well, what Mrs. Lockholm was saying.

"Are you in there, Virginia? I want to show you what that hussy has been up to. She's been into your gowns again!"

Bay was next door, only a wall away. He was the one who should handle his mother, not her, not Audrey on her wedding night....

She crept out of the tub, robed her body and hair in white towels, emblazoned with the Lockholm crest. She loosed the plug and the water gurgled; she could not hear the older woman over the sound. Dripping, she knocked on Bay's bedroom door, opened it. His clothes were strewn on the single bed. His bath door was open, too. She padded into his room, leaving damp footprints on the polished oak. He was in the shower, she could hear the water rushing and see a trail of steam. He was singing, lustily singing, something operatic and Italian.

Audrey turned away. She did not want to confront Bay's nakedness. Not yet....

Back she tiptoed to her own bath, to her bedroom doorway; looked in. Edmunda Lockholm was square on the velvet cushions of the chaise, her head and shoulders bolstered by pillows, her cane restless in a trembling hand.

She saw Audrey; narrowed her eyes for a better look.

"Why, what are you doing here?" the woman said. "Get back to the scullery where you belong. Where's Virginia?" Edmunda struggled to her feet, peered at Audrey through watery eyes. "Where are your clothes, young woman? Who are you? Whoever you are, get out!" On the wall was a button; the matriarch pushed it. "There," she said, spewing spittle. "I've called for Fisher. I may be only a woman, a sick old woman, but you'll see... I am not unprotected. Oh, *where* is Virginia?" The cane head slammed on the chaise. Her head wobbled from side to side. She was breathing quickly and spitting as she talked.

"Mrs. Lockholm, I live here now. This is my room. Bay and I were married today."

Audrey sat at the chair before her dressing mirror, made sure the towel around her body was secure, loosed the one around her head, picked up the ivory comb. She began to untangle her hair, trying to be calm, trying not to frighten the woman, trying...

"Stand up, girl," said Mrs. Lockholm in a lighter tone of voice. "Take off that towel and let me see your body."

"Mrs. Lockholm—"

"Did you really marry my Bay? He needs a good woman. I warned him off that other one. She was a sneak, town trash. I caught her stealing one of Virginia's gowns." Edmunda Lockholm sputtered a laugh. "I showed her! If you really are married to my Bay, you will have to call me 'Mother.' Virginia always did.... Will you do that, dear? I would like it so much. Tell me again, I've forgotten, what's your name?"

Any moment Bay would notice that Audrey had left open the door from his room to her bath, and the door from the bath into her bedroom. Any moment Bay would come, wondering what the matter was....

"Audrey Alice," she answered her mother-in-law. "Smoke is my family name. Now my name is like yours. Now I'm a Lockholm, too. I—I hope you recover very quickly, Mrs. Lockholm, and I hope we can be friends. I shall need all the help you can give me."

"Help? Haven't you got enough help? My word, girl, there's a staff of thirty-five at your beck and call. Stand up now and take off that towel. It's not yours, after all, it's Virginia's. This room is Virginia's." The voice was childish and petulant.

Audrey stood. She would go again to Bay. He must help her this time. Next time she would know what she should do; next time she would be all right....

There was a soft knock on the double doors.

"Come in," said Edmunda Lockholm, banging her cane head into a velvet cushion. "Come in and get this girl out of here.... Tell me, Fisher, do you see a tart in this room? Is she the one who killed Virginia? Pushed her out the window and stole her clothes and then married Virginia's husband. I—"

"Mrs. Lockholm," Fisher said with no emotion. "Dinner is served. Shall I take you down now in your chair?"

Edmunda Lockholm smiled a crooked smile. "Good night, dearie. I'll get you out of here yet, you see if I don't."

She shuffled across the room, bent, quivering, but unaided, and took Fisher's arm. The cane slammed hard on the Aubusson—sluff-sluff, STOMP....

Audrey closed the doors behind them.

IT HAD NOT been what she expected. It hurt, and she bled into the towel she lay upon, naked and excited, expecting rockets to flash as his body tilted into hers and locked and rocked and, finally, burst for him....

But she had been swept, in passion, over no rainbow. She had flown, in ecstasy, to no high mountain crest. She came into womanhood discovering no magic land of flame and song. Bay told her after, soothing her, touching her, it would get better, he hoped it would be better, as her body learned how to relax and how to respond....

The second time it was.

Bay was calmer, she was more giddy. In whispers, he told her he loved her. Tasting her, he told her of her beauty. She was not so self-conscious the second time of his naked body covering hers, of his hard loins touching, pushing, lifting away from her white hips as he swelled and pulsed inside her, and filled her womb, and overspilled....

It was a cool night after the long rain, but she left the windows open and the drapes bound back in their tasseled cords, so that while Bay truly became a husband and she his bride, she could hear, on the edge of hearing, the ocean sough beyond the rocks, and the wind leaf-rattling in the weeping beech, and she could see, in the gauze of moonlight, the curtains stir like long, pale hands silently clapping....

He fell asleep holding her in the bough of his arm.

Exhausted, she slipped into dreams of her mother held deep in the cheval glass. Virginia was caught there, too, and they were both watching Audrey and Bay, and Audrey after as she slept, forever different....

In the night Audrey awoke to the sounds of the cane in the hall outside and the strangled voice of Edmunda Lockholm as she shuffled down the corridor, crying for Virginia to come to her.

13

TORY VANVOORST SAT on the private terrace of suite 5-W of Newport's Ocean House, slicing a peach and plotting her next move.

On the glass-topped table was the already-read letter from Signore Maurice Rivalini, master jeweler of Rome. It was inconclusive, but it was forthcoming enough for Tory to drive today to Whale's Turning and make the acquaintance of the new Mrs. John Bayard Lockholm III. With any luck at all, Tory would light a fire in Audrey Lockholm and forge a friend, a fire that burned fiercely...a fire that lasted. A fire that would eat to ashes all the obstacles to Tory's grand ambition.

Shaded by a green umbrella, she surveyed all of Newport she cared about; Bellevue Avenue, Ocean Drive, Gilt Hill. Soon it would be as wholly hers as the golden peach she held in her jeweled hand, its heart being slowly cut away by a juice-wet blade. In a season or two at most, she thought, she would reign in Newport; be its queen as Dove Peerce was now. She could make it happen; she knew she could. She'd done harder. She did harder every day of her life, if the world but knew....

The bad thing about Burty was that he wouldn't retire from business. He didn't want to loaf and socially *swim* and let hired men take care of his fortune. Burty *worked*, in a tiny *cage* of an office in New York City, five days, six days, most nights a week, all year around. And you weren't supposed to work if you were as gargantuanly rich as Burty, at least not *every day*. After a while the money just grew. You invested and it grew, like coconuts, and fell into your lap when you shook the tree. But Burty said he "had to," which meant he wanted to. He *liked it*. The way Tory had

to stretch and twist for an hour every day no matter how
nice it would be to stay in bed. The way Tory had to bathe,
always, in lemon juice to keep her skin rice white—though
it could never be white enough.... She liked it, too. Liked
what she was because of what she did. Tory understood.

Because a clever girl did not lose her figure once she
captured Daddy Big Bucks. A clever girl gave value for
value. A clever girl never forgot where her status in life
came from—never, not for a moment, there disaster
lurked!—and just how lucky she was. She took Sweetums
to bed when she wanted to say thank-you, and she didn't
nag.

So Burty worked, and Tory...

"For Victoria, d'ya like it?"

"Listen, you wanna dance in my club, show me your
legs, nigger, and let's see you prance."

"I ain't no nigger! I'm white! White as you! I'm Spanish."

"Oh yeah, then who's that with ya, Pedro Jigaboo?"

She left Cajun Joey that night, outside a bar for blacks
only, and caught the night train to New York. On the way
she wrote herself a new history. A white history. She moved
into a rooming house and worked the strip clubs of Jersey.
She did what she had to do to climb, to thrive. To get into
the showy clubs of Manhattan where a long-legged beauty
could meet a star-struck stage-door Johnny. And if he was
rich enough, and she was *white enough* and very, very *enterprising*, she could waltz herself, just like a lady, into a
Fifth Avenue marriage and ... Newport....

So Tory kissed him coming and going. Minutes ago she'd
kissed Burtykins goodbye for the week; she was on her
own, her *enterprising* own, until Friday eve, with a week's
work of her own to do....

One problem, soon to be erased, was being "cottage-
less" in Newport: no matter what you did while you waited
for your mansion to be finished—and no matter how well
you did it—everyone knew you were nouveau. To look you
over, they included you a little, saying they wanted to be

nice. But at the parties that mattered, they excluded you a lot....

There had been Mrs. Astor's party on the fourth of July. Um-hmm. And Celeste Lockholm's wedding on the thirtieth of June. And other little supper parties and private dances and afternoon teas....

Well. Tory VanVoorst would show them in spades. She laughed inside at the pun only she understood. Godsend would set Newport town on its ear; Godsend would become *the* ne plus ultra as soon as it was finished. Zack Pink, the architect, had promised her: Godsend, as a Newport mansion, would never be bested.

And that great day was almost upon her. Godsend was already built, and perfect. The interiors were being finished now, the wallpapers from England, the gilt furbelow from Italy, the furniture from France.

She and Burty would move from Ocean House to their Newport mansion, and they would give their first party. It would be her launch into society. So it had to be a smashing success. *Had to be....*

Burty was more offhand. Newport would accept them, he said, there was nothing to fret about. It just took time. She was beautiful, he was rich, they were a charming and generous couple. No reason not to let the VanVoorsts in the club. "Four summers ought to do it," he said, "no strain at all. In four seasons they'll all know you and love you and be begging you to chair the tennis ball."

Oh yeah?

Well, four years was too long to wait.

Why, one could go to college a know-nothing and graduate a know-it-all in that time. One's secret could be discovered—the secret even Burty, *especially Burty* didn't know, the secret she would *kill* to keep....

She was born Alma June Brown with nothing going for her but spit—and the knowledge that she was only a quarter Negro and *white enough to pass, white featured, fine haired, very comely.* And she had inherited her great-great-grandfather's fighting spirit....

He was famous in Newport, a legend told in the dark. His name was Phineas Brown and he had cursed the whole line of the Lockholms because he had been *innocent* and in his prime: he was wrongfully condemned for murdering old Captain Lockholm; strung up and hanged from a spar of the *Quicksilver*, slave ship of the captain *who had not been murdered at all*.

A bad man, he rolled out of one of the lifeboats—covered in tarpaulin, hoisted on winches—one drunken night, raping Lillies, taken as a slave, Phineas's woman, a knife at her throat. The captain had fallen into the black waste of the sea, and only the slaves in the hold knew the story and passed it among themselves as they prayed for the deliverance of Phineas Brown.

But their prayers went unanswered.

Lillies was sold to a man in Tennessee. She put the truth into the ear of Solomon, her son by Phineas. It was a truth about white men, a truth to be remembered and passed on, in secret, *black privilege*.

Alma June's grandmother, daughter of Solomon and a white hill woman, was born in '66 when Solomon was a free man of fifty-seven and his bride an illiterate girl of fourteen. Granny Brown never married though she had a daughter. Granny Brown had been a self-proclaimed minister in New Orleans and a seer who walked in a whitewalled garden with God. Granny Brown prophesied into the ear of Alma June that the revenge on the Lockholms would come when the whales turned.... Whatever that meant.

"In the season of leviathan," quoth Granny Brown, "justice would be done...."

But Granny Brown died long ago of a thickening in the blood, and her child—put into her by a white swamp farmer who hypnotized her with a snake and took her in the name of Jesus on the dirt floor of the Tabernacle of Zion on a night of a waxing moon—Alma June's mother, Heshbon Brown, died quickly after Granny of the same.

Granny warned her daughter: the disease came from white men. "Don' do as I does, do as I say." But the warning must have come too late.

Alma June had never known her white daddy. He was a sailor from a foreign land. He had gone away while Alma June was only a bulge in her mother's belly, and Heshbon never spoke his name aloud in Alma June's time, nor ever loved a man again.

So Alma June was an only child when her mother passed to jubilation in a shanty parlor amid a chorus of hosannas. Alma June was taken to a Baptist orphanage for Negroes one day; the next she was transferred—a woman in white robes said they had made a mistake; there had been no mistake, but Alma June, even then, at six, was *enterprising*...she held her tongue—to a Catholic house in Baton Rouge. And there she stayed until she left at sixteen....

And reinvented herself.

And nobody in the world knew what happened to Alma June Brown from the day she left Samaritan House.

No one knew that Victoria "Torrid Tory" June was a name made up on an all-night train to New York.

And no one in the world knew what had become, in eighty-seven years, of the seed of Phineas Brown....

No one ever would.

If she never had a baby.

And she never would....

Because Alma June was enterprising. Alma June was a winner. She was renamed and repackaged. She was Victoria VanVoorst now, white as sheets, and she was married to the richest man in Newport.

She would have it all.

And no four years of waiting. Four weeks was more like it.

Tory consulted her calendar: four weeks from Saturday was August 10, and that date was no good because that wonderful, wild girl Nicola Peerce was marrying her English Lord Pomeroy. It would be the fete of the season—until Tory's party showed them all; much superior to Celeste Lockholm's, which was, Tory thought, too flashy and overwrought.... One shouldn't be so grand when one married a beach boy in a hurry after being jilted by royalty. And Tory's maid, Fanni—such a gossip; Tory adored Fanni St. Flour—her sly maid had told her what all the servants knew: Celeste Lockholm had not been a virgin and was probably *expecting* when she floated in white down that rose-petaled aisle. My, my....

So. Nicola Peerce and Rolf, Lord Pomeroy, were to marry on August 10. Her house party would have to be after; the opening of Godsend would close the season, and Tory VanVoorst would have splendidly *arrived*.

Besting Celeste was the easiest. A little *much*, that gold coach and gold dogs. The VanVoorsts hadn't been invited originally, but they'd gone all the same. Burtykins knew how to do it: he'd sent Celeste Lockholm a check ten days early. "You want to go, baby, we go," he said. "Not even J. P. Morgan says no to a thousand dollars." They'd been welcomed as old friends—ha!—and thanked for coming.

And now the next piece of the puzzle. Befriending Audrey Lockholm. Helping her out of her little *husband problem* and getting helped in return. Because after all, what are friends for...?

AUDREY'S FIRST BREAKFAST with her new husband was shared with his lawyer. Astin Forbes was a small man in a black suit. His high starched collar was too large for his neck; it gave him a look of fragility. He had a solemn demeanor and a healthy appetite, and Audrey found him likable. But she would have preferred to be alone with Bay so that she could ask him many things.... What was to happen now? What would she do without him in this house where she did not know how to live? When would he be back...? But she did not ask her questions. She sat quietly with a straight back and ate her melon and a kipper and slice after slice of brown-sugared toast along with Astin Forbes. Bay ate nothing. He drank black coffee, cup after cup, and smoked a cigar, in silence, too. They sat together at a little table on the lower loggia at Bay's request, served by Fisher. And they waited.

Then Detective Smythe came with two of the Newport police. Fresh-faced, they seemed as young as Audrey, and just as stiff and frightened.

They came unannounced, striding across the damp lawn from the north side of the house, swinging wide of the weeping beech, and stamping up the steps to the loggia as though they knew Bay would be just there, for the taking.

Bay and Mr. Forbes were not surprised to see them.

Of course it has been arranged, Audrey thought. This is how the rich handle trouble. Quietly, with no fuss, and at the convenience of the others involved. I must pay attention now to this, I must be calm, too...and learn. She clutched her hands together, under the table where they wouldn't show.

Detective Smythe formally arrested Bay for the murder of Virginia Lockholm on the night of June 19, 1894.

Bay did not protest. He only put down his napkin and stood. Astin Forbes did not protest. Audrey swallowed the constriction in her throat.

"One moment, gentlemen," Bay said. He walked Audrey into the great hall. He kissed her lightly but held her tight against his chest. "Stay brave," he whispered into her hair. "I'll be back as soon as I can. And don't worry about the house, it will run itself until I get back. I'll get word to you if I'm to be detained. The important thing for me is that you're here, waiting for me." He stroked her face. "Thank you for behaving well, I'm proud of you.... Goodbye for now.... Wish me luck."

Audrey nodded, framing the word with her lips, unable to get it out of her heart. Luck...luck....

Then he left her.

She ran down the hall steps to the great front door.

They were walking across the lawn, all the men, in single file as though they were a parade. Where the driveway began its circle, where the four-globed lampposts announced the final approach to Whale's Turning, a coach stood, its doors flapped open in black welcome....

She watched. They sat him between the policemen. Mr. Forbes and Detective Smythe shared the opposite seat. The coach swung round the circle toward her, under the porte cochere. She lifted her hand shoulder-high in silent greeting. Then the coach was past her door, beyond the birdbath, between the lampposts now and far away, deep down the driveway where it ran under the trees and cut a gray ribbon through blue-green grass....

She was suddenly older.

Inside, she asked Fisher to ring Priscilla the dressmaker and ask her to come as soon as she could; she would like to order some gowns. She would be in her room, she said. He could show Priscilla up when she arrived.

Audrey climbed the staircase, used to it already. Almost not seeing the soaring reach of the marble hall, almost blasé at the platinum plaques of the Lockholm crest, almost not noticing how the sun was not yet west enough to enflame the colored glass above the portrait of Virginia, eye to eye with her on the crimson-carpeted landing.

Audrey turned. "Fisher," she called.

The butler was below her, at the foot of the steps, looking up. "Yes, madam," he said.

She held herself back from running down the steps to him. She addressed him from the distance.

"Fisher, please, I should like this portrait taken down. Taken down immediately if it's possible, and stored somewhere away."

The butler hesitated. "The elder Mrs. Lockholm may be upset, madam. She is fond of that portrait. It was commissioned of Mr. Whistler while Mr. Lockholm and his first wife were in London on their honeymoon. It is, I believe, the only likeness of the late Mrs. Lockholm we have."

"Yes, Fisher, I do understand that," Audrey said. She took a deep breath. "And I do not mean to be unkind. But I want this portrait removed right away from the landing. You could ask Mother—" there, she had said it; she would always call her mother-in-law that in future, as Edmunda had requested her to do "—where she might prefer it. It could go into any of the private rooms, but I do not want Virginia's portrait publicly displayed in Whale's Turning.

Not now, Fisher. Not with Bay—you do know?—Bay has just been arrested."

The butler bowed his head. "Yes, madam," he said. "Mr. Lockholm informed me of the situation this morning. It's very grave, madam, you have all our sympathy."

"Thank you, Fisher, then you understand."

Audrey looked into Virginia's well-drawn, shallow eyes, eyes lazily interested in something beyond the picture frame....

They had been in London when the portrait was painted. On their honeymoon. It must have been Bay who entertained Virginia, out of view. Perhaps he was blowing her kisses or reading aloud their itinerary for the day. She was sure of herself, not overwhelmed at the prospects he laid tenderly before her. She was sure of his love, sure of her worth. She would agree to tea with the queen, surely, but perhaps she would say no to the pleasure of a drive to Stonehenge, just to show her power—

"Madam?"

It was Fisher, still standing in the great hall at the foot of the staircase, looking absurdly small so far away, though he stood a good six feet, as tall as Bay.

"Yes," she said. Had she missed something? Again?

"Madam, will that be all?"

She thought, he is not my enemy. He does not mind me here.... "Yes, Fisher, thank you," she said. "Thank you very much. I—I think I will go to my room now. I'll be cleaning out the cupboards and drawers, making room for my things.... Are you married, Fisher? Would you like to choose one of Virginia's gowns for your wife?"

"Oh, no, madam. I have no wife, and if I did, a gown such as you suggest would be most inappropriate for her. The late Mrs. Lockholm was about your size, a little thinner perhaps.... Madam, if I may suggest—"

"Oh yes, Fisher, please."

"You might keep the ones that please you until you form your own style, madam. It would be quite all right. The late Mrs. Lockholm never wore most of the gowns in your armoires. They were ordered after she and Mr. Lockholm returned from their honeymoon, ordered for a season in Newport she never enjoyed. They've been a year hanging, madam, but they are new gowns and very tasteful, it seems to me."

"Once Mother protested, Fisher."

He said solemnly, "That was before you were a Lockholm yourself, madam. The elder Mrs. Lockholm has not been herself since her son's first wife died. It was, of course, a sad affair for the whole family, but Mrs. Lockholm suffered most from the tragedy, I think. She was very keen for her daughter-in-law—sometimes, it seemed to me, almost preferring her to Miss Celeste. Their temperaments matched. The two Mrs. Lockholms were very close. It was the elder Mrs. Lockholm who encouraged the match from the beginning. She was always high on Miss Stotesbury.... And now, with her attack, you may find her troublesome for a while, but it isn't a personal dislike of you, Mrs. Lockholm. It is just a regret for the other."

"Thank you, Fisher. Thank you for everything."

"Yes, madam. I'll attend to the portrait right away."

"Then that will be all for now," she said.

"Very good, madam. Luncheon will be at one. Where would you like it served?"

"The lower loggia will be fine. I like the view from there. Tell me, Fisher, would it be good form to ask Priscilla if she could join me for lunch?"

"If I may, madam, it is 'luncheon.' You will no longer ever 'lunch.' And since you do not know her and she is someone whose services you employ, I suggest you invite her to, perhaps, take tea with you when her work is done. But that is as far as you can properly go."

"I will remember, Fisher. And please continue to give me such good instruction. It is exactly what I need."

"I am delighted to tutor you, madam. You are a winning pupil."

"Good day, then."

"Good day, madam."

She ran up the stairs. She'd get the hang of it yet; it just took practice, that was all. You just said the whole word.

You said *luncheon* and *draperies* and *avenue*, not *ave.*...
When Bay got back he would be proud how much she'd
learned already....

IN ONE OF THE DRAWERS of one of the chests in her room
she discovered the house plans, the architectural render-
ings for the mansion that was Whale's Turning. They were
very pretty, drawn in a fine black ink upon thick cream-
colored parchment. The furniture for each room was out-
lined as to type and painted in its color, and swatches of
material for wallpaper and window hangings had been
pasted upon each room to show their effects.

I'll frame these, Audrey thought. I'll hang the plans for
Whale's Turning under the stained glass where Virginia's
portrait used to be. They're quite handsome. Yes, they'll
look very well.

She was about to ring for Fisher to ask him to take care
of the house plans being framed and hung, but before she
could, there was a knock at the double doors of her bedroom.

It will be Edmunda, Audrey thought. She will want to
know what I have done with Bay. She will scold me, but I
won't get upset, no matter what she does or says....

But it was not the elder Mrs. Lockholm who entered. It
was Fisher, bearing a card on a salver. "You have a visitor,
madam. A Mrs. Burton VanVoorst. Are you in?"

Audrey knew the name. She had seen the woman, twice
in the Casino, pointed out to her by Alabaster McGregor.
Mrs. VanVoorst was truly beautiful, dark of hair and im-
maculate of dress. An exotic aura shimmered around her,
always. But she had already earned herself an unsavory
reputation....

She was the one who had hired Virginia's telltale maid.
She was a *fortune hunter*, it was said; she had captured the
richest, newest man in Newport. Before her marriage she
had been a *stripper*, a dance-hall girl...and, they whispered, she was the *other woman* Bay dined with on the
night Virginia jumped. The woman he laughed with over

champagne while his wife endured her last moments alone and in despair before an open window in the night. . . .

"Madam," said Fisher. "Mrs. VanVoorst is now in the reception room. What may I tell her?"

"Oh, I see, yes, I'll go down to her, Fisher."

She leaped up from the carpet where she had been crouched over the drawings. She left Fisher standing there, left a door open, and almost ran down the hall to the staircase.

She was going to meet, at last, the woman for love of whom, gossip had it, Bay Lockholm had murdered his bride. She was going to come face-to-face with the one woman in the world Bay had lusted for and had not been rich enough to get. . . .

The woman—please God, make it not so—for whom, they said, Bayard Lockholm had sold his soul. . . .

Audrey hesitated at the foot of the stairs, then forced herself to walk with measured tread across the expanse of the great hall. Her footfalls on the marble would sound her approach, and she wanted her step to be like her mother-in-law's must once have been, firm and confident, not soft and timid and scaredy-cat. . . . Across a lake of marble, down a reach of shallow steps. To the reception room at the left of the great mahogany entrance doors. Do not pause in the doorway, go in . . .

Then look.

The woman was sitting on a silk love seat of striped pink and white, under a watercolor of French women at a fair. She was reclining against the settee's back and her lace-gloved fingers were light upon a beaded bag that matched in fabric the simple summer white of her dress and parasol. Her shoes and stockings were also white, and her white straw hat, beside her, was trimmed in the same lace as her gloves.

Audrey looked at the calling card, which, unknowing—unremembering—she had taken from Fisher's tray: Mrs. Burton Regis VanVoorst.

It was deeply engraved in curled calligraphy, black on cream. And in lavender ink, a fat, hard-pressed ink, there was a word written: Urgent.

Close, the woman was smaller than Audrey had realized, seeing her from a distance in the Casino café, and dazzled by the woman's pampered beauty and luxurious dress. Mrs. VanVoorst was almost fragile, sleek and chic and young, a few years older, only, than Audrey. But there was in her face an alluring wisdom, a knowing, which Audrey envied. This was not a woman who fainted in adversity. This was not a woman to turn your back upon if you did her an injustice....

Audrey extended her hand when the woman rose.

"Will you sit with me on the loggia, Mrs. VanVoorst? It is cool there, and private."

"Thank you, Mrs. Lockholm, I will. What I have to say to you needs privacy, a special privacy."

Audrey led the way across the hall, beyond the stairs, and out upon the Italian-tiled, open-arched terrace. She sat in white wicker, flanked by great urns of blue hydrangea. Mrs. VanVoorst sat beside her and arranged the linen folds of her dress.

"Will you take some refreshment? Lemonade, perhaps, or cold tea?"

The sea was a haze of bright blue with a mist behind. A mist that fogged the curve of the horizon and veiled whatever traveled, full sailed and stately, far away. Somewhere out there was a steamship for honeymooners; revelry and passion and long sunset nights that Audrey and Bay had missed....

"Not just now, thank you," Mrs. VanVoorst replied to Audrey's offer. "I'd like to do what I must before I relax." The woman's voice was smoky and warm. There was not the practiced coolness in it that Audrey associated with the ladies of Gilt Hill. But Audrey was wiser now, and older: she waited for the chill.

She turned to the woman. "Then tell me, quickly, Mrs. VanVoorst, what it is that brought you to me?"

"Call me 'Tory' and let me call you 'Audrey.' I want to be your friend." The woman leaned close. "I have come to help you free your husband. I have information and evidence."

Free your husband. The words cut Audrey's heart. So *everyone* knew of Bay's arrest. Knew already. How fast the world spun....

"Tell me," she said.

Tory VanVoorst's eyes were green, a deep, deep green. They were big eyes in a sharp-chinned, high-boned face. "Let's be friends, Audrey Lockholm. I need a friend on Gilt Hill, and I think you do, too. I am new here, like you. I am an outsider here, like you. Together we will have more strength than standing alone."

"Tell me about Bay," Audrey said. She held the arm of the wicker, white as her hands.

Tory opened her purse and withdrew an envelope, a folded envelope with a foreign stamp. She laid it on her knees. "Bay killed Virginia for just reason, Mrs. Lockholm, that you should know first off."

Two yellow birds flew under the vault of the ceiling, one chasing the other around, then out. Audrey stiffened and said, "My husband did not kill his first wife, Mrs. VanVoorst. You cannot stay in this house and say so." How dare this *other woman*—

"Don't get angry too fast. Listen to me, please. You may not like the truth, but the truth is Bay's salvation. Throw me out if you want, but only after I have told you what you need to know, what your husband desperately needs for his defense."

Audrey sank against the back of her seat. It was a roomy sofa, cushioned in white with blue flowers. It was a seat to be calm in, to grow strong in. A place from which she could, if she tried, distinguish truth from falsehood....

The beautiful woman was speaking again. "Virginia Lockholm was unfaithful to her husband, Mrs. Lockholm. She was one of those spoiled darlings who think that the rules of the world do not apply to them. When she saw something she wanted, she took it if she could, seeing no harm—"

"How do you—how could you?—know such things, Mrs. VanVoorst?" Cold, hard; that was the way to deal with women like this. Troublemaking women. *Bad* women....

Tory did not take offense. Her eyes held Audrey's; her round, open eyes, all sultry innocence, pleading to be understood. Her deep-lashed, dark-lashed eyes, as hypnotic to men as absinthe....

"As you may know, Mrs. Lockholm, your husband and I were friends last year."

Has this woman come to tell me of Bay's infidelity with her? Audrey thought. Did Bay lie in a cabin of the *Catbird Seat* with this *whore* one night, and then after, *so in love*, tell her of this defect, an imagined defect, perhaps, of Virginia's? A defect he shared . . . but saw, in his case, as only manly exuberance, forgivable because unfelt?

Mrs. VanVoorst smiled at Audrey's thoughts plain upon her face, and shook her head. "Oh no, Mrs. Lockholm, we were not lovers, Bay and I, do not think that. You would be very wrong. I was in love with my Burty when I met your husband. He was already married to Virginia, and I'm positive he was true to his marriage vow, though he was, when I met him, no longer in love. I knew Bay only through Burty, and not well, but I knew him as the gentleman he is. He did not snub me because of my position—I was working for my living then in a nightclub: I sang for my supper and yes, I don't deny it, I removed most of my clothes as I sang. But whatever you may think, I was no harlot. It was honest work, if not respectable. Oh yes, I am a common-born woman who got lucky, with Burty. I know who I am and I'm not ashamed. But I am, too, and always was, Mrs. Lockholm, a smart cookie. I know what Burty married me for; I did not throw it away.... If I had, I tell you frankly, I would not be Mrs. Burton VanVoorst today.... May I go on?"

Audrey did not know what to say or what to think. Tory VanVoorst was an unusual woman, and there was something in her composure and directness of speech that Audrey liked—and yet the things she said were shocking.

"Just listen, Mrs. Lockholm. Hear me out. I'm your friend, you'll see."

Audrey nodded, thinking, she wants to call me "Audrey." I should let her, not stand on ceremony. I must learn to be a lady, but not a proud, vain one who hides behind her marriage title....

Tory VanVoorst inched a little closer. "The reason I hired Virginia's maid this season was to keep someone else, someone less kindly dispositioned toward your husband, from doing so. Fanni St. Flour is a true little gossip. It is one of her talents and one of her greatest pleasures, right up there with perfumes and cosmetic pots. I pay her more than anyone else would—ten dollars a month she gets from me, and she has a whole day off on Sunday, a grand concession on my part since Sunday is one of the days Burty is home. Well, I hired the girl because I wanted to help Bay Lockholm. As soon as I heard that Fanni was talking against him, I hired her and told her she was to speak against my friends only to me. Of course the harm had been done. She had already given her deposition to the police. But at least now she tattles to me, not to Detective Jeremy Smythe or to Alabaster McGregor."

The wicker settee was too big for Audrey. She could feel it getting bigger as she sat. And she was hungry. She had eaten this morning with Mr. Forbes, to keep him company, but she had tasted nothing.

"Will you have lunch with me—luncheon, I mean?" Audrey flashed crimson; immediately paled. "And do call me Audrey. I'm not used to anything so formal as 'Mrs. Lockholm.' I think it refers only to my mother-in-law."

Tory nodded. "I'd like that. I'm starving," she said.

Audrey jumped up, too fast for a lady. "I'll go tell Fisher," she said.

Tory pointed to a bell on the wicker table. "Use that, instead," she said, and set their sofa to rocking.

"Oh, yes. I—"

"I'll help you step up, Audrey. I know how to do everything, better than most of the ladies of Bellevue Avenue, except for Caroline Astor and Dove Peerce, and nobody beats them. I made it my business to learn, you see, long before I knew Burton VanVoorst existed. I'm different from you in that I always knew I'd be here. I always knew I'd climb Gilt Hill someday. It was what I was after. But you just fell into it, like a cherry into a pie.... You can use me, you see, and I can use you. We'll be fine friends."

Wondering, Audrey tinkled the bell.

Fisher came, his steps silent on the marble. Audrey saw that his black shoes were soled in rubber, cushioned so as not to annoy as he went about his rounds. She told him Mrs. VanVoorst would be joining her for luncheon; that they would eat where they were. She asked if he had reached the dressmaker.

"Miss Priscilla comes to you at two-thirty, madam, delighted to be called upon." Fisher left them, impassive and correct.

Audrey wet her lips. "Go on now," she said.

"I will," said Tory. "This will be the hardest part so I'll get it out of the way first. Bay is guilty, Audrey—let me tell you how I know.... The night she died he came to the Gray Heron; he sailed there alone in his little boat. He had been drinking, not a lot, but enough so that it showed, and he was angry at Virginia. He came to dine alone, but Burty saw him and asked him to join our table. I wasn't there then, I was still singing, down to my skivvies probably, but not through with the act...."

It was cool under the high arched mosaics of the ceiling. A wind had sprung up in the east, gaining force as Audrey waited for Tory VanVoorst to finish. She could see the haze of ocean blur and clear, the whitecaps tumbling higher, faster. If she stayed very quiet she would keep shrinking and grow colder and colder until she was the size of an ice cube, cold and inconspicuous. And maybe the ocean, then, would come and lick her away and she wouldn't have to listen anymore....

"When I joined them, I could see Bay had been talking out his troubles. The champagne they were drinking had loosened his tongue. He was angry about a bill for jewelry Virginia had presented him with. It must have been extravagant—he was terribly upset. Over dinner he grew calmer, you could see he had decided something, his turmoil was over. When he left us Burty asked him where he was going, and Bay said in the flattest voice I've ever heard, 'I'm going now to wring her goddamned neck. Remember, both of you, never marry the first one who asks you.' Then he left us. Burty thought we should go with him, stay with him, you know, make sure he got home all right. He'd had a snootful and he was sailing his boat alone.... But I was trying to land my fish. Burty hadn't promised me anything at that time, and that parting shot of Bay's gave me something to work with, that part about not marrying the first one who asks. I didn't think Bay would actually...

"Anyway, I coaxed Burty to stay with me and dance. Then, giggling, pretending I was high, I proposed to him and asked if I was the first to do it.... The next day Burty came to me, told me Virginia Lockholm had died in a terrible accident, and said I was to forget about Bay's conversation the night before. Bay hadn't known or meant what he was saying, Burty said, it was just one of those...unfortunate...things. And I did forget, Audrey, until Fanni came back to town and told the police much the same story Bay'd poured out to Burty, only from Virginia's point of view. That's when I decided to help. I had to help Bay because he had helped me.... Burty accepted my proposal, you see. It took him weeks, but that night made today possible. I owe your husband a lot, Audrey Lockholm.... And now that's the end of the bad news. Here's the good—"

Tory waved the letter with the foreign stamp. "Here's your husband's acquittal, or at least, the beginnings of it."

Still, Audrey thought, very cold and small now, that isn't proof he did it. That's coincidence—that isn't proof at all.... "I'm going now to wring her goddamned neck...."

She turned her head to the hydrangeas, lush in their great stone urns. They were as blue as Bay's eyes, in profuse bloom. They should have perfumed the little bower they made on the loggia. But they threw no scent, no scent at all, upon the air....

Still, she believed Tory VanVoorst. Hadn't Bay Lockholm said to Audrey in the graveyard, standing over Virginia Lockholm's very grave, "Don't ever marry the first one who asks you, Audrey Smoke...."

And she had smiled, thinking it a joke about her and Thorne only....

Fisher rolled out a white wrought-iron table. "Luncheon is served, madam," he said.

The meal was crabmeat and shrimp in a thick pink sauce, biscuits just out of the oven, watercress salad and lemon tarts, enough for six. But for once Audrey's appetite failed her. She drank lemonade and pulled raggedly at a biscuit and listened to Tory VanVoorst.

"Virginia Stotesbury had a lover, Audrey. Maybe more, but at least one. Fanni confirmed it to me. Virginia was mad for him, bought him gifts. Clothes and jewelry, little golden gifts. And here's the proof—"

Tory handed Audrey the long white envelope. "We must find Virginia's lover. Her infidelity is Bay's excuse. He will be found not guilty because of temporary insanity, acting in a justifiable rage—he must have caught them together. And don't you see, Audrey, that was why they fought so, earlier that night—over Maurice Rivalini's bill. Virginia was insisting Bay pay for her favors to her lover!"

The phrase "golden gifts" trembled in Audrey's mind....

It seemed so long ago, a life ago, back to that night when she had been awakened—rap, rap, rap—last June.

Unexpected, Thorne had been at her door, hot, excited, striding back and forth in the kitchen, his pirate's eyes flashing like storm flares....

He had held her that night as though he would rip her in two. He had kissed her face and throat and breasts and waist, kissed her through her wrapper, kissed her stomach, kissed her feet. He was so elated, *so desirable*. They could begin to plan in earnest now. They could marry next year.

How? How? she'd asked him, laughing with happiness herself, relieved her father was not yet home from his night at Grimsby's Tavern. How? How...?

He'd lifted her to the ceiling, twirled her around to a waltz in his head. Set her down as though she were a goblet of crystal. Thrown off his raincoat....

And a little box, tied in golden, tasseled ribbon, slipped from the raincoat pocket to the floor....

"Oh!"

She had it in a flash. Held up the box. "Oh, Thorne, for *me*?"

She remembered his face then. From the wild excitement of a moment before he looked stricken, almost mortally wounded. She thought he had not meant her to see, to know.... She thought perhaps her engagement ring was in that box, and he did not want to give it to her then, not just then.

"Am I not supposed to see?"

Unable to resist, she shook the box back and forth, wanting to hear something slide or hit or bump around...but nothing did. Whatever was in there, filled it....

When she looked up again—she was sitting on the floor, out of breath from being spun, sitting cross-legged, letting her pantalets show where her wrapper parted; she remembered she did that, and how she had giggled after, on her bed, to her mother in the mirror—when she looked up he was smiling, running rose-bronze fingers through his crow-black hair to rout the curls. He stooped beside her, there on the kitchen floor; took the box. He turned it so that the tassels faced her and said, "A little of my good fortune to you, Audrey dear. Will you marry me?"

Of course, he had asked her before that night. But this gift made it official, this gift and his good fortune: he had got his loan!

The box was square. Stamped on it in cocoa brown—no, *embossed*, she remembered running her fingers over the delicate script, lifted like icing on one of Mrs. Olsson's cakes—was a strange signature ... a foreign signature....

Was it ... as this letterhead? Maurice Rivalini of Rome, Fine Jeweler.

She had know the object inside would be gold, real gold.... Perhaps there would be a diamond, too, no matter how tiny....

Gently, she slid away the ribbon. To save it. Savoring the feel, she stroked the silken lid of the box. And then, holding her breath, she'd taken the top away and seen a cloud of cotton, white as heaven's floor. The cotton lifted and then ... the pendant revealed, a rectangle of gold as great as the box, etched with spider lines of silver. And there, off center, on the left-hand side, a ruby cut into the shape of a heart. A bright red ruby as big as a seed of pomegranate....

"Oh, Thorne."

Crouched beside her, he lifted the pendant out. He stood and in black boots paced back and forth on the wooden planking. She watched him, happiness like a child in her belly.

High above her, he said, "I didn't wait to have it inscribed. I wanted you to have it too fast. Shall I ...?" He was kneeling beside her again, she still on the floor, her arms slanted stiff behind her, her head thrown back, watching him, thinking how magnificent he was.

"I could put our initials and the date. Would you like that?" The pendant was in his closed fist. He jiggled it like a die. "What would you like, my dearest?"

But what was the date? She couldn't remember now. She had been too happy, too greedy for her prize. The date didn't matter then. She hadn't known then that Virginia Lockholm had had a lover to whom she gave "golden gifts."

She hadn't known then that Virginia Stotesbury Lockholm had died, suddenly one night, in June....

"Give it me," she said, "give it to me now. I'll have it now and wear it always. Let me put it on, please, Thorne, please!"

"Oh no."

He was away from her again, the pendant in his pocket. He was striding back and forth again. Serious. Thinking.

"It's mine," she laughed. "I want it now. Give it to me."

And just like that he'd dropped it into her lap.

"All right," he said, "but it cost me dear. Promise me you won't wear it in public until our wedding day. People may wonder where I got the money. I don't want that."

And she agreed, busy fastening the hold around her throat. She wanted to ask who was the maker, how came Thorne to a fine Italian jeweler, and how much money did such a ruby cost? But she had not asked. She put the pendant on and stared at herself in a hand mirror and told herself this was better than the tiny chip of a diamond she had pointed out to Thorne as "someday" in Vogle's window....

"Audrey... are you all right?" It was Tory VanVoorst, her head cocked attractively at an angle, a spoon of lemon custard halfway to her mouth.

To cover her lapse of attention, Audrey reached for a tart, too. "Yes, Tory, I'm all right now. I'm just shocked, you see. It's been so much. Bay and I were married only yesterday and he was taken from me today. And now I learn such things I never thought to know—"

"You must read the letter. It tells me little, but you, as the new Mrs. Lockholm, can write to Signore Rivalini again and request an accounting and a description of the jewelry ordered by your predecessor. You must do that today. Then when we hear, we will find these precious pieces of Virginia—" she paused for the drama "—and so find our man. And then, Audrey, Bay will have nothing to worry about. An acquittal is assured." Something glinted, keen, in her green, green eyes. "And don't you worry, Audrey, darling. I'll help you. All I ask in exchange is that you take me up, become my dearest friend."

"Yes," Audrey said, lemon tart sweet-and-sour together in her mouth. "Yes, of course...."

Beside her on the table, the letter from Rome was black in its creases.

14

OF ALL DOVE PEERCE'S polished attributes, the one she was proudest of was her unblemished reputation. As wife, hostess and mother, Dove Peerce stood before the world as a high example of what discipline, dedication and proper taste could achieve.

Why then, she thought to herself as she kissed Clarissa Rails good-night and teased Tripp Rails one last time about his motorcar—smelly, styleless contraption that hardly ever worked, but there was no explaining the tastes of men; Percy had whole *catalogs* devoted to the silly things—why then did she risk this dangerous liaison with the rector of Trinity Church?

It was her first disloyalty to Percy, and it would be her last: Dove never repeated herself. It was, she supposed as she slipped on thin gloves, the challenge that fired her enthusiasm.

It certainly wasn't Graf Elliott.

He was ardent enough, Lord knows—she smiled at her tiny blasphemy—but he would never do as a full-time man. God forbid; dreadful thought. A church mouse was what Graf was, poor and earnest and ordinary. He suited a woman like Judith Elliott down to the ground: theirs was truly a marriage made in heaven.

Her coach waited for her under the ivy-smothered limestone of the porte cochere of Greenscote, the Railses' summer cottage. Clarissa had done the place, inside and out, in all the shades of nature's verdancy, and done better than Dove had thought she would, bless Clarissa's budget-minded heart.

Dove's favorite coachman, Dudley, was at the reins. Escorted to the Railses' by Graf, she was going home alone back to Percy who, as usual, had been, he *said*, too ill to attend. Graf was going home alone, in his own runabout, back to Judith who rarely went out.

Or so all thought, and no one to tell them different....

No one to whisper that the Reverend Graf Elliott and Mrs. Percival Peerce would rendezvous under a weeping beech on Dove Peerce's north lawn, in half an hour. Would meet, would cleave, and enter the devil's paradise....

Though how Judith Elliott could let her husband out—like a dog to exercise—and sew cushion covers alone by gaslight, or embroider samplers or whatever it was that dull woman did, Dove would never, ever understand. That childless, humorless, colorless woman who didn't even have the sense to wonder, Graf said, when he lay beside her in the night, tormented and sleepless with lascivious thoughts of Dove's petticoats artfully lifted and arranged so as not to muss; thoughts of cool and lovely Dove opening, for him, her wing-of-angel thighs....

"Good night, darlings," Dove said to her hosts. "See you tomorrow at Bailey's, Clarissa. Prompt at ten...."

Dudley opened the carriage door.

Yes, Dove supposed, it was the nature of the affair that gave it bite and fervor. Forbidden, this indulgence kept her honed; on that thin edge of excitement that ran around the plate of boredom her life had become with poor Percy and his *hateful bowels*.

That was Graf's lure. The risk...the thrilling, thrilling risk....

Dove settled herself on watersilk the shade of her white-white hair.

"Home, Dudley. There's a good boy."

Nicola and Rolf were still dancing. Nicola and Rolf were always dancing. Or riding or laughing.... Dove sighed. She would not think of Nicola. She would think of the hour to come.... She enjoyed these assignations so.

It must be, she thought as her black Morgans trotted down Greenscote's driveway, that perfection paled when the struggle for it was over. No longer did Dove have to pull herself toward a perfect standard. These days it was simply hers, self-generated, in her bones like basic mineral. And had been, for a long long time. So, all worlds conquered, like Alexander, son of Philip of Macedon, she, honed for battle, restless for a bugle call, had looked for one more field of conquest....

And found none, except the uncharted land of sin....

And it was fun, good fun. She made a ditty, riding in the dark: "I'm mostly virtue, a little vice, I have my spouse, I have my spice."

Her left eye twitched. She pressed a finger to it to make it stop. The involuntary twitching had begun with the affair: guilt's symptom. Oh yes, she knew. Well, she would conquer that, too, in time....

The horses turned from Bowery Street onto Bellevue Avenue.

The Railses had the best gardens in Newport, Dove conceded, but they did not have Dove and Percy's weeping beech, the single best tree. At least fifty years growing, its great, espaliered boughs curved to the ground and created within their drapery a natural gazebo, private to the world. A person outside could not see within, though a person— or persons—bower-embraced inside, could spy through the greenery like a cat. Would not be taken unaware. Filigreed stone benches curved around the massive beech trunk, very inviting. There was a rattan tea table and floral cotton pillows. Soon she would lie upon those cushions like a maharani, and Graf, her harem slave, would tend first to her pleasure, and then to his....

To be discovered would be ruinous.

Although, if it really came down to it, she thought Percy would forgive her. Percy was the best of men, and he would understand: he, unable, could not really expect a woman such as Dove, radiant, desirable Dove, to do *totally* without.... But Newport would not forgive her. Her transgression made public—she shivered at the thought—her dear, dear friends would forget she existed. Her name, like bad words, would be whitewashed off the picket fences of their memories, slick-slack quick as that.

The horses slowed to a walk, turned into the driveway of Peerce House. Light in the library, Percy's room now, burned behind lace curtains. He was still up, then, waiting for her return. Or, more likely, he had fallen asleep on the chesterfield and neglected, again, to turn out the lamps. Well, she would check on him, spend a few moments relating the party. Be determinedly gay. Kiss Percy good-night. And then she would mount the stairs to her bedroom, undress...and descend by the servants' stairs to her lawn. Naked under chiffon-silk, like Diana, goddess of the trees, mistress of the chase, she would disappear into love's bower, arrange herself, and wait....

Her coach stopped before the moon-white portico. Her driver helped her out.

"Good night, Dudley. Thank you."

"Good night, Mrs. Peerce. Shall I return now for Miss Nicola?"

"No, the young ones are staying over at the Railses. Going sailing early, and fishing, I think. God knows. So tomorrow then at nine-thirty. I'm due at the beach at ten."

She moved away, cloud light up the steps. Nevvers, at the watch, opened the door for her.

And out on Bellevue Avenue, on the other side of the granite wall, Alabaster McGregor walked. He was alone, first man out of the party after Dove, and still in black evening dress—

The better to hide from you, my dear!

Under overhanging clusters of lilac he paused, positioned himself. Made himself as comfortable as possible. Though comfort is of no consequence, he reminded himself, when one is *on the beat*, out stalking *exposé* for his sweet little files at home.... The condition of his shoes, however, were another matter: he most certainly did not want to ruin his lovely British lace-ups. They'd need a hard wax and a rag-buffing tomorrow, and lots of elbow grease. And if they didn't clean up good as new, he'd just yell at Foxx until they did, that's all....

Besides, if he was right in his suspicions, all sacrifice would be worth it. Nicely worth it, thank-you very much....

Ah, he heard horse hooves; dancy, light. Alabaster prophesied: that will be Graf Elliott's mare, drawing the good reverend in his almost sulky. Alabaster spit on his palms and rubbed it in. For luck.

It was Graf Elliott's buggy, the mare fretting at being slowed, pulling on her bit. Graf was talking nonsense to the horse, soothing it.

Alabaster waited for the ecclesiastic to make an irrevocable move.

For Alabaster knew he was right. Once you suspected, you knew how to look, and where, and nothing could keep the truth invisible for long from one whose eyes had been *unveiled....*

But the runabout did not turn in. The mare was passing Peerce House, moving faster now; trotting. Alabaster heard her racer's hooves receding, on down Bellevue.

Damn, damn, damn!

He wasn't wrong, he couldn't be wrong. He had seen an exchange pass between them during the Railses' wretched dinner. He had seen *with his own shrewd eyes, thank-you very much*, Dove slip a fold of paper, blue paper, into the reverend's jacket pocket, when she bent to speak to him on her way out with the ladies. Graf, still wolfing pie, had positively glowed—hah!—when Dove told him she had called for her own man to take her home, so as to cause him no more inconvenience. Graf Elliott had had a concrete hard-on in his preacher's pants after. Alabaster'd noticed *that* right away. Because dear little Dove wouldn't need him to take her home? Sweet smiling Sally, there was an assignation going on! Coming up. It was so obvious he could draw a diagram, that's how obvious it was....

But then why was Graf not stopping, why was Graf pretending only to slow to see if darling got safely home?

Appearances.

Alabaster McGregor, with a self-satisfied sigh, settled into the hydrangeas to wait.

IN THE DOORWAY of the library, Dove Peerce contemplated her husband.

Out of his robe, in his *undershorts* only, Percival Peerce slept, slouched on the sofa, his head thrown back, his eyes almost directly under an electrically lighted lamp. He was unshaven and the grizzle on his cheeks aged him, paled his skin to a waxy yellow. His legs, his still good, firm legs, were bent at the knees and spread wide. His stomach, distended with colonic gas, bulged at his waist, glowed unsightly in the pool of lamplight. His hands were cupped around it tenderly. The hot water bottle had slipped from where he had been holding it. Precariously, it hung at his crotch like an arcane sexual toy.

Ah, my dearest, Dove thought. Whither romance when a man grew old and retreated to his library like a squirrel to its hole in winter? Where was that soft heat in her womb, that *delicious trembling* that once was when she waited in her bed for him to come to her? Where was the rush of blood that choked her heart when he came, naked and virile, came running, cock-high, his hands hot and anxious? And where was that victorious elation, that *ecstatic high*, when she knew she had won him, that he was *hers alone* for at least that moment, that night, that after-dawn, and she must try the next night and the next, and the one after that, to conquer him all over again... ? Oh, glorious battle....

Ah... it was out under the weeping beech with Graf Elliott, or in a memory book, dry pages crumbling as she turned them in her mind....

It was all unbearably sad. She loved her husband, adored him. He was the dearest, loveliest of souls. It was not Percy's fault he had grown musty; he was seriously ill. It wasn't his fault that the library—her beautiful hunter-green and black-walnut library—was rank and raggy now, unkempt and sickly sweet from unopened windows and lack of care and Percy's eternal medicines.

Life was to blame, blasted, imperfect life.

There was a cobweb in one ceiling corner, one notched, cream-colored cornice sullied. And Percy's desk was dissolute, a mess of unsorted papers and grimy lead-crystal goblets used for tonic taking, kept to pour brandy in, never washed between. He didn't want anyone in the library but himself and Nevvers. Nevvers did not scold, nor did he feather dust or straighten. Nevvers only loved, and did as he was bid. Nevvers forgave Percy all: the sloppiness, the retreat from the top of the hill, his fall, his ordinariness, his . . . mortality.

In a dirt-dull mirror Dove saw her beautiful self, in pale mauve satin sinuously draped, her thick white tresses swept in curls around amethyst pins. Her high-arched face, her tight chin line, her elongated throat, bare tonight to display, in grandeur, her clean, cool skin.

She noted the expression on her face, fine lips pulled down, a frown line of distaste between silver brows. She looked haughty . . . and hard.

Oh dear, no. Never that. *Never that.* This would have to be the end, a one last time with Graf. Percy did not deserve to be treated so . . . and she did not intend to have a peccadillo in the garden destroy the exquisite linelessness of her complexion.

She closed the library door without trying to wake her husband. Tales of the Railses' party would wait until tomorrow. Tomorrow, she would be a perfect wife again. . . .

Tomorrow and then forever after.

ALABASTER MCGREGOR must have nodded off, for he was aware that he was no longer hunched below blossoms of blue, but sitting on bare, damp ground. With a grunt of disgust, he raised himself and slapped at the back of his trousers. Foxx would have a time cleaning up his clothes. He could hear his valet now, fussing like a schoolmarm as he whacked the clothes brush on the seat of Alabaster's pants, "Sir, you are no gentleman!" Well, it would not be the first time Foxx had threatened to leave him for a better, and there was nothing for it. For now, at last, there was work to do.

Graf Elliott was walking on the grass of Peerce House, the other side of the wall.

Light-footed, stealthy-stepping, Alabaster followed.

While it would have been fun to creep so close to the trysting place so as to hear every tender word, see every inch of skin, watch every erotic *thrust*, Alabaster kept a safe distance. Better to want a nail than lose the kingdom.... If he saw what he wanted to see and heard what he wanted to hear, it would be worth a night of sleeplessness and ruined evening clothes.

Graf Elliott disappeared into the bower of the down-to-the-ground boughs of the weeping beech, and then Dove Peerce, beautiful Dove, the darling of Newport, floated upon the lawn in black chiffon suited only to a bedchamber, as though she were sleepwalking, called by a genie.

Quiet as the ghost of Phineas Brown, she slipped through green and joined her lover. There!

Alabaster, hovering now behind a privet hedge, heard the murmur of blurred voices. Timed, with his vest watch, the delectable silences. Smirked at the grunts, the little cries....

It went on for an hour. And then the tears began. First Dove, then Graf, buzzing, buzzing, buzzing, and then protestations of tears, deep and high sobbing....

Really, *what a show*.

By now Alabaster was dry of palate, damp of toes and infernally hungry. And he would have gladly paid a dollar for a comfort station.

But the delectation was still in full throttle. A lover's quarrel? Graf not up to snuff?—didn't he wish!—or, oh happy thought, could Percy have found out and threatened Dove with *scandalous divorce*? What a dear little scoop that would make for "Ally's Oops," oh my.

And still the two dawdled in the bower, as though the night was not racing to its end and dawn's gray promise not bleaching the blanket of the sky.

Oh, save me from infatuation, Alabaster prayed. What a mess it always was, how *time-consuming*, how *undignified*....

How dangerous.

He remembered with pain a summer's pining for Orestes, golden-curled Grecian icon of the Casino Café.... Younger then, both of them. Thank God he'd kept his passion closeted; untold. Orestes, new boy, danced attendance to a hot—ha!—tennis player that year; hated him by fall. The player attacked Orestes in his apartment in the Casino right before the U.S. championships were to be played . . . and wasn't that a caldron to cool down. The player got to the finals—fired up, oh yes indeed: the ball that fortnight was Orestes's "family jewels," thwack, thwack, KABOOM, he wasn't to be stopped—and won.

After that—Alabaster and others talking sense to both *bits of fluff*—there were the falsely sweet goodbyes and nevermores. And Newport none the wiser, Newport never to know that Orestes, from then on, wore a corset to hold in the ripped, ruined muscles of his belly; Newport knowing only that Orestes became, overnight, the all-business, no-time-for-play waiter, and eventually maître d' of the café.

Humph. Orestes and the other choirboys could have it. Dove Peerce and Graf Elliott could have it. Love's torch was not for Alabaster McGregor, thank-you very much. Continence: that was his meat. With continence, he could rule the world. Continence, that is, except for Foxx; Foxx a long time now. . . .

He was beyond hope for the redemption of his dinner clothes. Stretched flat behind the privet hedge, he peeped through twigs of shrub, chin on dirty hands. *Re-ally, tough duty!*

Nevertheless, this was a night of answered prayers. At last he had what he had wanted for so long: Dove Peerce, first bird of paradise, snagged forever on his talons within her gilded cage.

His to hood or let fly. His to feed or let die. . . .

Sweet smiling Sally: now to tell her.

He lifted his legs behind his back and tap danced on the air.

WAS IT KNOWING that this was the final pleasure that made it so sweet? Was it the danger of her own lawns that made it so thrilling?

This was the first time they had dared on home ground.

Always before—after that first mad Derby weekend in Louisville—it had been a little farm out of town. In a topiary garden. Always before it had been in the afternoon, surrounded by bushes pruned into amusing shapes. The long-necked giraffe was her favorite, the policeman on a horse was his. Always before, the tenants left to visit a daughter in Jamestown. Always before, it had been planned and careful....

But Graf hadn't been able to wait till next Monday, he said. He was damned—*doomed* by her charms, he said. He had to have her tonight, he'd pleaded, to live.

Well, it was over now and it had been almost grand. She was leaving him in love with her, the only way to leave a man. She was leaving relieved to have it done and finished.

He was leaving, unbelieving.

She was leaving anxious for her beauty sleep.

Ending had been easier than she'd thought. Once the mind clicks down, turns over, *redirects itself*, why the whole affair glowed gaudy, became a bauble too cheaply bright...unwanted....

Graf left first, while she, from the shelter of the tree, watched the servants' windows. Once Graf was safely out on Bellevue Avenue, he, encountered, would have a minister's excuse for being out. And she, on her own grounds, though almost naked, could explain away a restless sleeplessness on any one of her wife-and-mother's legitimate concerns.

She was safe now.

Graf was gone, off her property and out of her private life. No one would find him in a diary, no memento of her caprice remained. She would bathe, and then be cleansed of Graf forever, no more to roam. And for a long time yet she would have the pleasure of knowing that he longed for her, loved her from a proper distance.... And when Graf strayed again—as he surely would—she would be his measure of excellence. The others judged by her points...the others found lacking.

The stars were fading as Dove, black gowned, drifted, content, toward the rear of her house.

She would go in through the library. She wanted to see her husband again, accept her husband again in her bosom.

She wanted to imprint afresh on her no-longer wayward heart the man in her life, *today and forever after*. Then she would make her way upstairs as though she had come down from within—

Percy was standing beyond the window, still in only undershorts, staring out at Dove and...and the weeping beech, holding drapery as though for support. His mouth was hanging slack, in a silent roar of disbelief.

Dove lifted the length of her gown and increased her pace to him. It will be all right, she thought. I must just keep calm, I'll be able to explain it all away. I wanted succor, I'll tell him. I called Graf after I got home, worried about something Nicola did.... And if he didn't see Graf go, I was alone, worried about *him*, unable to sleep....

Percy did not move as she approached. He stood on flagstone, one foot turned awkwardly, almost on its side. His hair was in disarray. His right hand clutched a drapery of forest green. His mouth was hanging, stiff; his eyes were wide and staring...and dull.

Why didn't he step toward her? Or angry, go stomping back inside? Why didn't he close his mouth...or blink...or fix his foot?

She was running. A cold clamp was tightening in her gut. She slowed, watched her husband not moving, stone-stiff.

"Percy!"

On flagstone now herself, still several feet away from her husband, Dove stopped. Dawn was bleeding pink into the gray. The black of the sky was almost faded white, a dull white the color of Percy's tousled head.... Why didn't he reach up and pat down the offending cowlicks? It wasn't like Percy to look so cold and gray....

"Percy!"

And still the eyes didn't blink and the mouth never moved. And a shiny green beetle crawled unmolested on Percy's twisted foot.

A rope of ice twisted and climbed in Dove's stomach, tied itself around her heart and tightened. Squeezed.

"Percy, dear Percy, please speak to me...."

But she knew now he wouldn't. He couldn't. He was dead as he stood, horrified, unbelieving, the sight of his wife in her bed dress parting from her lover too much for an innocent soul.

Dove thought, as she sank into black chiffon folds, What in the world will I do about Nicola's wedding . . . ?

Alabaster McGregor, closing softly behind her, let her fall.

The screams which alerted the household were his.

15

IT WASN'T just another death that disturbed Dr. Eamon Lake: all who were born—bewildered little tykes, stained with the blood of the Lamb, all inarticulately wondering in their soft little brains, What am I doing here?—passed, in time, back to where they came from, some having answered that fundamental question, some not.

No, it was that if he had been on hand, or if the patient had done as advised, this death, this day, could have been avoided. Been indefinitely postponed, until a more convenient time.

If Percival Peerce had followed doctor's orders, he would have been alive today; would have walked his daughter down the aisle in a few weeks. In a year, perhaps, have held his grandchild; seen it christened. But no. Percival Peerce, as so many of Dr. Lake's patients, thought he knew better than doctor. Told to exercise, he didn't. Ordered off the booze, he'd continued on the brandy—so much brandy, in lieu of the medicine.

Dr. Lake shook the nib of his pen over the death certificate.... Well, Percy ol' man, you did it. One too many, once too often. Does 'em in every time. Probably he got frisky, in his cups. Tried to mount the wife again, like in the good old days. He'd been warned those days were over, but old jackasses never learn....

This wasn't Eamon Lake's fault. He'd done his job.... He couldn't stand over them all, cracking a whip, now could he?

And the suffering of the widow—that, too, sometimes saddened Dr. Lake, and never more so than now. Poor Dove Peerce. Lovely woman. Bereft and hysterical; wouldn't come out of her bath. Dr. Lake wanted to give her opium to quiet her down, knock her out, but she'd have none of it. Well, she was the one who found him, poor thing. She'd had a premonition, she said. Couldn't sleep all last night, restless as a cat. She'd called her friend, Mr. McGregor at dawn, to come to her, and then she'd gone downstairs to check on her husband....

He'd been all right, sleeping, she said, and she'd taken an early turn or two around the lawn, listening to the birds wake, watching the dawn stretch through. Percy'd come to the window and called to her....

Sometimes life was just too sad to live. But what can you do? They won't listen, these tycoons. They think they know better than anyone else about everything....

And they don't, do they?

AND SO, PERCIVAL PEERCE, in the end, got his automobile.

It was a long black Ford, the first motor-driven hearse in Newport. Dove ordered it sent by chartered train from Detroit. Burton VanVoorst, not called on to offer his services, being a stranger to Dove, nevertheless helped arrange for the special delivery. Tripp Rails sought him out because Burty often bragged he knew all the titans in American industry. And, in this case at least, he did.

Nicola, called back from the Railses', not yet having set sail, was hysterical and inconsolable. She asked her mother over and over, until Dove wished Nicola were dead, too, *dead and buried*, how it had happened.... What was father *doing* when it happened, hanging onto the drapery as though for *dear life*? And what was Mother doing, floating on the lawns like an Irish demon, a will-o'-the-wisp, that she didn't see Percy in trouble, didn't hear him call, didn't run to his aid and so *save him* . . . ?

"Explain yourself, Mother!" Nicola brayed and brayed, between glasses of brandy and soda—before luncheon, during luncheon, all day—and getting the hiccups. "Were you *rutting* with Father on the flagstones, Mother? Is that what you won't *admit, confess* to? Were you and father doing it, Mother, *standing up*? Is that what killed him?"

"Oh, Nicola...."

"Well, then, Mother, *explain yourself*...."

And Rolf, Lord Pomeroy—who should have been a help—talked of postponing the wedding until next spring. Blathered on about leaving for England immediately after the funeral services. It was the only proper thing to do, he kept pronouncing, wandering from room to room, bewildered, still in his yachting whites, foregoing luncheon but eternally cracking pumpkin seeds in wide white teeth.

Dove forbade him to even think of such action. Snapped at him not to be a dunce, insisted the wedding must go forward as planned. Forceful, she said Percy would want it that way. Percy wouldn't have died and gone to heaven, she said amid pretty tears, if he had known Rolf wasn't going to step in as head of their now-only-female household. Percy died in peace, Dove browbeat at Rolf, knowing his women were in good masculine hands. Why, the last thing Percy said to her, Dove lied into a handkerchief, the final, struggling thought, was "Promise me...the wedding." Dove, petrified, she said, hadn't understood what he meant...until now. So Rolf could not, *must not* stand on empty ceremony in Dove and Nicola's time of real need. Not if he truly loved Nicola....

Rolf thus conquered and silenced, Dove seized her opportunity and attacked Nicola's idea of *black-and-brown* bridesmaids' gowns as *completely inappropriate* now.

"And certainly, Nicola, dear, no monarch butterflies. Angels, I think, would be the better thing. Guardian angels. The idea would be they've been sent by Percy to look over you and Rolf. Celestial pastels, I think—scrumptious peach and apricot, lemon and orange. In a Grecian style, with gold braiding and dyed-to-match feather plumes in their hair in the shape of small wings. Percy, looking down, will love you for it, dear. How does that sound to you...? And we can keep the satin vests for the men and Rolf's pocket watches. They will be fitting symbols of the brevity of life and marital happiness. The vests will say, 'Enjoy your prosperity while you may.' The watches will say, 'Hurry, there is not time enough...never time enough.'"

Nicola, who rarely cried, gave in with a single hiccup. She wept by the hour and hovered by her father's bier. Overly brandy braced, at Dove's behest she filled her mouth with clove to mask her alcohol breath when the neighbors came to call.

She looked, however—Dove thought—almost stunning in her black even without the emeralds, left in the jewel vault for a happier day.

And Dove, in black lace and upswept signature white hair, jewelless except for wedding ring and engagement diamond—smaller than Nicola's, yes, but Dove believed in restraint and, for all that, not much smaller and decidedly pinker—Dove had never looked, she thought, more beautiful, more virtuous...more *perfect*. Best of all, her twitch was gone....

Alabaster McGregor, on the other hand, was beside himself with rage. He had lost the game; lost his pigeon even as he closed his claws. He would never get another chance, not in two lifetimes. Dove Peerce, caught bare haunched in the mud, had leapt away clean. It had cost her her husband, but she had beaten Ally McGregor. Her flawless reputation was unthreatened: he would not dare, in her widowhood, to speak against her.

For hold all the evidence he would, to tell would be to become a pariah. Newport would turn on him the same way they might have turned on Dove, if he ever so much as *breathed* a hint of scandal the grieving widow's way. Dove Peerce had all of Newport's sympathy and support.

Poor dear Dove, they were saying behind their fine windows. Poor dear Dove, whatever will she do? How terrible for her to lose her husband *right before her eyes* and then to face the loss of a husband for Nicola—Rolf, informed of Percy's passing while still at the Railses', had let the cat out of the bag on *that* rumor—Nicola who, if she lost her handsome Englishman of title, would surely never wed.

She would age and wither a spinster. Too headstrong, after all. Too *robust*, after all, to capture another such. Hers was regal triumph or abject failure; no in-between for Nicola Peerce.

So. If Alabaster McGregor, whom Dove Peerce had be-
friended against, as he knew, the warnings of some of the
lesser women—Clarissa Rails for one...she couldn't stand
the sight of him, and the Misses Wetmores were always so
polite to him he knew they despised him—if he now bruited
about a tale of Dove and the Reverend Elliott, who,
wouldn't you know, was performing the funeral service,
well, Alabaster McGregor could just catch a trolley out of
town, and good riddance, *thank-you very much*.

So no. His lips were sealed. Sealed like a canning jar
never to be opened. But kept, oh yes, always *kept* in the
cellar of his mind.

Though not—unfortunately—in his secret files.

Nowhere would it be recorded that Dove Peerce and Graf
Elliott had *fucked* under a weeping beech while Percival
Peerce, the good lady's husband, from his library window,
watched and died....

Dove had known she'd won. As soon as she recovered
consciousness on the library terrace flagstones she had
lifted a well-plucked eyebrow to Alabaster and said, "Well
played, Ally dear. My congratulations. But Percy has saved
me, you know. One word, and you're the one who's ruined,
dear boy. I will play the plight of my widowed state into
sainthood. See if I don't."

Angry enough to kill, Alabaster, too, was outwardly
composed. He took her hand, raised her to her feet, kissed
her wedding ring. "You have all my admiration, Mrs.
Peerce, and all my sympathy. I shall report your loss in
'Ally's Oops' most graciously. As for the rest, I don't know
what you mean. Called by you in the early hours—you
must have had a premonition...been unable to sleep—as
your dearest friend I walked from my home to your side
and found you only a moment ago, bent in bereavement
over the too-sudden loss of your husband. But for some
reason, I am almost too tired to stand. I will leave you now
and call again in the afternoon."

"You're a wicked man, Alabaster McGregor. Very
wicked, very smart."

"The only difference between us, madam, other than gender, is that you have all the luck."

"Ah, the luck of the Irish. Again."

"You, Dove? I'd never have thought it."

"Never do, Ally, dear. Goodbye for now."

Weak, she watched him go. Dear God, dear God. What had she almost wrought? She had been certifiedly mad last night, swept away by her own power, too smug in her own cleverness. Well, she had shaved too close to the razor's edge. She had, really, been off the cliff, into Alabaster's clutches—blackmail forever!—or infamy and public shame.

Percy had saved her.

Dear Percy had *died* for her. She could not bring herself to touch the cadaver looming before her, clutching its taffeta swag of forest green, its mouth agape, its eyes hard and waxen. She sank down on the flagstones, down to her knees. Kissed his feet. Rained on them with her tears. Forgive me, she prayed. Wherever you are, it was only you I ever loved. Only you I ever will....

Nevvers came then. And Rosalind, Dove's maid, helped her up to her room and the fresh, untouched-last-night bed. Dove sent Rosalind away—"Let me know when the children come," she said—and went to her bath. Before Nicola beheld her, she must cleanse her body of Graf Elliott's seed, soap the oil of Graf Elliott's palms from her breasts, scrub away his kisses inside her thighs....

As good as she was, Dove thought, she was not good enough to have the cake and eat it. And what a price she'd had to pay to find it out.

ALABASTER, FOR HIS PART, had to endure the scoldings of his valet, for the condition of his evening suit.

"Oh, Foxx," said Alabaster, world-weary. "Don't fuss at Papa...just come to bed. Hold me. I've been foiled again, by circumstance."

"Serves you right, you cat," said Foxx. "I love it when you get a licking."

16

IT WAS SUNDAY, July 28, the day of Percival Peerce's funeral, and still Bay was not home.

Yesterday, at dusk, Astin Forbes had come to Audrey and told her he was working on the release, but Judge Godfrey had postponed his decision on Bay's right to bond until the next week. Again. Audrey was not to visit Bay. She was to wait, "wait like Penelope," Astin Forbes said. "Go about your business as though not unduly worried." She was not to entertain in a grand manner—as though she would!—but she should move about in society as she wished. Certainly she should attend the funeral of Percival Peerce.

Yestereve, too, Celeste and Thorne returned to Whale's Turning. They had heard of Bay's arrest and Edmunda's stroke from Clarissa Rails—a cablegram sent to their boat. And they had heard, from the same source, of Bay's sudden wedding to Audrey.

"I do not understand why Bay did not tell me what was going on at home," Celeste said, standing in the great hall, stripping off gloves of ecru lace. Thorne stood beside her, in Panama white, his tan ruddy bronze, his black eyes questing at Audrey, asking plain as pen on paper, How did you get here, so soon, so well placed? How the *hell* did *you* get here at all...?

In thin, brown silk, run up by Priscilla in a day, in golden hair wound smooth around her head, Audrey stood before her sister- and brother-in-law, welcoming them home.

"Bay did not want to worry you, Celeste. He didn't wish to interfere with your happiness. He hoped that by the time you returned all the bad news would be behind us, and only joy remaining. I'm so sorry you cut your honeymoon short...and Bay will be grieved, too. But Mother, of course, will be happy you are home again.... Will you stay in your own room, or would you prefer to share a larger suite with Thorne?''

Celeste held her round lace hat and gloves in pale fingers. Her elegant head turned as she looked around the hall. White luggage, trunks and cases twenty strong, lined up behind the returning couple, two footmen waited to be told where to take them. Ringed by the luggage, Joanna, Celeste's maid, stood holding a jewel box of seashell and silver and a leather satchel of ladies' magazines.

Celeste stabbed a pearl-headed pin into her hat and veil, her head bent studiously over the task. At length, she raised her head. "Forgive me, Miss Smoke, I do not mean to be insolent, but your marriage to my brother was too sudden, I can't, at just this moment, take it in.... May I see my mother, please?''

Audrey stepped back without a word. Say nothing, her mind warned. Don't take offense. This is Bay's house, Bay's and mine, not Celeste's and not Edmunda Lockholm's, but Celeste feels herself mistress here...and I want her as a friend, not an enemy. Grandfather Nally told her once, when she was sniped at in school for swimming on the team, the first girl so allowed, "There are always dogs in the road, Audrey, dogs in a pack. It is better to have the dogs running with you than against...."

She remembered her grandfather's words as Celeste passed her by, heading for the staircase. Thorne followed, a subdued Thorne—Audrey wondered why—the questing still in his eyes. Joanna and the footmen moved with luggage toward the elevator.

Audrey remained as she was; where she would wait, feigning composure, until Celeste passed up the stairs and down the hall to her mother's room, Thorne trailing behind her like a lovesick boy, too devoted to question, over-anxious to please. He was surly, too. Audrey could tell by the way his shoulders strutted. But the anger was for Audrey; for Celeste there was only adoration.

She has tamed him, Audrey thought. She has made him dance to her tune. He is more handsome than ever, in his fine clothes, but less manly, less—

"What's this?"

Celeste was stopped on the landing below the mural of stained glass, looking at the floor plans that Audrey had had framed and hung in Virginia's portrait's place.

Instead of answering by yelling up, Audrey ascended the stairs, gown hem properly, daintily, lifted, thanks to Tory VanVoorst's self-styled "lessons on ladyship."

Celeste pointed at the set of seven frames that stretched the width of the stained glass. "What has happened to Whistler's portrait of Virginia?"

Audrey looked her sister-in-law in the eye. "It hangs in Edmunda's room now, Celeste. It seems to cheer her there. These are the architect's plans of Whale's Turning. I think them very fine. Do you like them?"

"Well, yes, they are handsome. Come, Thorne, we must see Mother."

Thorne Cockburn was bent over the parchments, staring at them with intent face and avid eyes. He didn't seem to hear his bride. He was tracing, with a finger, the shape of Audrey's bedroom, Virginia's bedroom that was.

"Thorne." Celeste's whisper of a voice, always a sigh, had an edge to it Audrey had not heard before, an edge of command.

But Thorne was lost, peering into the fourth frame of seven, tracing a pattern with his finger on the glass.

Impatient, Celeste touched his sleeve.

He looked up then, but not at Celeste. He glared at Audrey, and there was livid meanness in his eyes; a leaping ferocity and a naked fear.

Shocked by the force of Thorne's stare, Audrey drew back until the fourth frame was pressing into her shoulder blades.

"What—" she said. "What—"

But Thorne turned without a word and followed Celeste's lead up the final flight to the second floor. Audrey watched him retreat. The hall reached, he turned back, looked down on her.

His face was twisted with fear.

And then he was following Celeste's ecru gown as it swept, fluttering lace, out of Audrey's sight toward Edmunda's room.

Audrey leaned against the picture frame. What did Thorne mean, looking at her like that? What was there in the house plans of Whale's Turning that could make him hate her so suddenly, so...savagely?

Impossible....

She had had nothing to do with the building of Whale's Turning. Or were these pictures just an excuse for Thorne's jealousy at her invasion of his newly acquired kingdom, his triumphant assault of Gilt Hill belittled by Audrey's ascent, too.

Little Audrey whom he thought he had left behind, in the dirt....

That must be it. There was nothing else....

Wondering, she looked at the fourth frame, traced her finger where Thorne's had been, around the outline of her beige-and-golden bedroom, the bed set, off center, in the left-hand corner, drawn in the shape of a heart and painted crimson, like a ruby....

No.

No, it couldn't be....

But wait...if the black ink, *fine lines*, was silver; if the length of the room was gold, all gold as the swatch pasted in was gold; *if the bed, drawn in the shape of a heart and painted crimson was a ruby—*

The pendant.

The pendant Thorne had given her that night he came. Late. Unexpected. The night he came, excited, pacing up and down the kitchen floor, laughing, happy. The night in June he knew he'd got his loan.

The night they set their wedding date.

The night a present fell out of his pocket. A golden pendant in a beautiful box from a foreign shop...from Maurice Rivalini of Rome, Fine Jeweler.

Unconsciously trembling, Audrey looked up the second flight of stairs. There was no one there. No one was peeping, no one was stalking....

No Thorne.

No Celeste.

No Virginia....

And no Bay.

Oh, how she wanted Bayard. It had been hard enough alone in the great mansion with Edmunda wandering the dark hall...sluff-sluff, STOMP...crying always for Virginia and tapping like a ghost at Audrey's bedroom double doors.... One night she would come in, Audrey was sure of it. Whenever the elder Mrs. Lockholm shambled in the night, Audrey prayed in her bed, please, please let Bay be here to handle his mother when she braves the door, please, please!

It had been hard to eat alone at breakfast, lunch—no, luncheon—and dinner, trying to remember Tory's lessons of utensils and demeanor. It had been hard enough to pass the time, waiting for Bay to come back to her. Mornings with Tory VanVoorst helped. Afternoons, swimming off the pier. And at dusk, leaning on the rock of WaterWalk, communing with the whales....

For often they gathered now, at day's end, in the waters below Whale's Turning; in great numbers, listless, as though they were ill. And there always seemed to be, now, a hard wind blowing, sweeping landward from the open sea. A cold wind full of unspilled rain.... A dark wind. At day's end, the whales huddled among the boulders in the bay as though seeking shelter from a storm that had yet to come, had yet to pass away....

It had been hard, but it had been possible.

And now, Celeste was back and Thorne had come, and there was no Bay to protect Audrey from Thorne's wrath.... Thorne's *revenge*. Revenge for what? For Audrey being where Thorne was, *where Thorne did not want her to be*....

Why?

Because one night—*in June, in June,* one night last year in June!—he had come, unexpected, late, to Audrey's home—"so little and so mean"—and dropped a present from his pocket: a rectangle of gold with silver lines and a heart-shaped ruby, off center, on the left-hand side.... A golden replica of Virginia Lockholm's *bedroom* in Whale's Turning, made to order by the jeweler Maurice Rivalini of Rome....

Virginia had had lovers, Tory VanVoorst had said.

Virginia gave them—or *him,* perhaps there was only *him!*—presents. "Little golden gifts," Tory had said, handing Audrey the letter from Rivalini as proof....

Audrey gathered her skirts and ran up the stairs, down the hall to her room. Inside, she shut the doors. There was no lock. She pulled a gold-chased bench in front of the doors, and in the bath shot home the bolt to the door to Bay's room. Then she went to her dresser and opened a drawer.

There, hidden within the folds of a nightdress wrapped in tissue paper, was the letter to Mrs. Burton VanVoorst from Signore Rivalini.

Audrey took it out, read it again.

In reply to your letter of 13 June, dear lady, I am unable to furnish you with particulars as to the jewelry ordered of me by Mrs. John Bayard Lockholm III of America, U.S.A. I could not, in any case, duplicate an original design presented to me by another, as you can understand. To answer your question, I have executed some small pieces for the lady you mention, a few little golden gifts, and I would be happy to privately serve you, too. My work is of the highest order and my prices madly small. It may interest you that I have recently acquired some superb lapis, and my gold is always of the purest that is made. Greetings to you, beautiful lady, and to our mutual friend, the incomparable Mrs. Lockholm. Anxiously waiting to hear more from you, I remain your discreet and obedient servant,

Maurice Rivalini, Jeweler

Not conclusive, as Tory had said. But incriminating. Tory said Audrey had only to ask to know: "Bay, did Virginia ever give to you...'a little golden gift'?"

But how could Audrey do that?

Fanni St. Flour maintained that the baubles were made in Rome for discretion's sake; made for Virginia's lovers...or lover, if there was only one. Made to bind him—or them—to Virginia through greed if not through passion....

But what Mlle St. Flour said and what was so may not be the same thing, may not be the same thing at all....

Or, Tory said, Audrey could write to Signore Rivalini herself, for was she not Mrs. John Bayard Lockholm III? The jeweler did not know Audrey was the *second one*. He would tell Audrey *everything*....

Everything he knew.

Perhaps, Audrey thought—and why had she not thought it before?—perhaps Virginia, *like Celeste...like Audrey*, admired a beach boy, black of eye and wild of heart. A reckless, handsome dandy, too poor, but with muscled arms of sun gold, who ran out his sails exposing a pirate's bare bronze chest, who was so taut of waist the sea spray trickled down his belly and under the belt of his trousers loose and low...making a woman—a certain kind of woman—want to lick the sea from the sailor's loins....

Audrey went to her diary. She would find the night, and find out when, exactly, Virginia Lockholm fell.

Thorne Cockburn came to Smoke House unexpectedly, with a present in his raincoat pocket, on the night of June 6, 1984.

And Virginia Stotesbury Lockholm passed to God...

Audrey called Fisher on the telephone.

"Madam?"

"Fisher, this is Mrs. Lockholm. Could you tell me...do you remember...the date Virginia died?"

There. It wasn't so hard. She'd had a catch in her voice, but she'd done it. Direct, straightaway, no explanation....

"You do not explain why to servants, Audrey," Tory had instructed. "You speak gently in reprimand or praise, or when you want something. And, of course, you never fuss at them in public. They are more sensitive of their status than even you, poor little rich girl...."

"I do indeed, madam," said Fisher. "I shall never forget... Mrs. Lockholm left us, suddenly, on a Wednesday, the sixth of June, 1894."

"Thank you, Fisher."

And what did that prove... if anything? If *everything*....

SATURDAY NIGHT Audrey ate her dinner in her room, alone. She went to bed early, but thought a long time before she slept; thought, and wrote a letter to Rome.

All night long she was undisturbed.

Edmunda Lockholm did not walk.

Thorne Cockburn did not thunder at her door.

Though once, before she finally slept, the telephone at her bedside rang. She did not answer it. Telephones were sinister. They allowed a stranger to invade your bedroom... your dreams. A blunt, heavy instrument, a telephone was able, if one wished to use it so, to kill....

One way... or another.

IN NO JEWELS, in her former work dress of stout black cotton and braid, hair tied back in a flat black bow, Audrey sat beside her mother-in-law, in the funeral cortege. The Lockholm carriage was one of many, some one-horsed, some two, that lined the curving driveway of Peerce House behind the specially designed black auto-buggy that held the body of Percival Peerce.

Dove, in dove-gray lace, in purple veil, sat in Newport's first hearse in front of the Honduran mahogany casket, a dark-gloved hand upon a golden fitting. Nicola, pale as cloud, her wild red hair subdued, for once, under a cloche of blackest satin ribbon, sat stiff spined beside the hearse's driver, her fiancé, Rolf, Lord Pomeroy, the marquess of Denton. Rolf, in formal morning suit, black driving goggles and gloves, waited to begin the procession; held Nicola's limp hand.

On the coach seat opposite Audrey, Celeste and Thorne faced her. Audrey was conscious, surrounded by the denizens of Bellevue Avenue and Gilt Hill, all so correctly turned out, of the simplicity of her attire, but she was uncaring.

So what if the others outshone her? They always had and they always would. They cared about such things. At bottom, Audrey Smoke Lockholm did not. She wanted Bay back, wanted Bay at her side, wanted Bay free and they, together, able to live in peace. That was what was important: she and Bay....

Celeste was already pregnant.

Sawyer, now Audrey's personal maid, told her this morning, having heard it last night, at servants' supper, from Zella, maid to Edmunda, who shared a room with Joanna, the maid of Celeste. No one in the family had bothered to tell Audrey. And if Celeste did not and Edmunda would not, without Bay there was no one to tell her... except Thorne. And he could not tell a woman such personal news, that would be indelicate. Indeed, since the Cockburns' arrival last night, Thorne had had nothing to say to Audrey, though he stared at her from time to time with narrowed eyes and tightened mouth. But Audrey was determined not to take offense at whatever Thorne or Celeste or Edmunda Lockholm did. And she would not mention Celeste's condition unless and until Celeste herself revealed the happiness.

Tory VanVoorst had taught Audrey, "When in doubt, do nothing. Doing nothing is always in acceptable taste. Not necessarily the best, but always acceptable. Then, as soon as you can, consult with me."

And this Audrey intended to do. Audrey trusted Tory as her teacher even though the VanVoorsts were not accepted yet in social Newport. Tory explained it: for all Burton VanVoorst's prodigious fortune, it was too new, and business made. His marriage, too, was thought to be unfortunate. "Yes," Tory told Audrey, "I know. I have to know the truth to figure how to fight it....." Her ancestors were not known in Newport. Or New York or Philadelphia or

Boston: her lineage was, therefore, common. Her occupation and way of life before she was married were known...were scandalous. Burton Regis VanVoorst was generally judged to be a decent fellow—"though he has his detractors," Tory said—who needed tutoring only to become acceptable, but who, not having got it in time, had, unfortunately, married a woman of crimson character who would never be a lady. The VanVoorsts were too rich to be ignored and too raw to be included. Newport's answer was to treat them politely, as politely as it, routinely, handled those only passing through.

Well, the VanVoorsts had come to stay.

But they had not been invited to Percival Peerce's funeral.

"And no fat check will get us to the party this time, toots," said Burty, comforting Tory with a thin diamond bracelet he called a "service stripe."

"I know, Burtykins," Tory said, snapping the bracelet on her wrist with a happy click. "Let's spend the day in bed, instead." Tory regretted not going: she looked so well in black. And of course, not being there shouted to the world that the VanVoorsts did not belong.

But that would change. And very soon now.

Percival Peerce's funeral would be the last social event she and Burty would be denied. Nicola's wedding was coming—that was the event that mattered. That was the event that Tory, like a racer, was pointing toward.

Would get to.

See if she didn't....

In the week and a half since Audrey and Tory decided to be friends, Audrey had fallen under Tory's spell. Tory was so beautiful, so knowledgeable. So...enterprising. Nothing worried her, nothing stopped her, nothing even slowed her down. Audrey hoped someday to be like Tory: independent, confident, stellar and absolutely perfect.... A younger edition of Dove Peerce.... Someday.

Edmunda Lockholm sat heavy at Audrey's side, in navy linen and only a single strand of Lockholm pearls. Her mouth was rigid and a little crooked where, involuntarily on the left side, it lifted, and her eyes were dull. But she was as upright as a queen, hands joined upon her cane. She was sensible in her speech, though slow, and she seemed to understand very well that Audrey had married her son, that Bay had been arrested, and that her daughter, Celeste, was back from the Caribbean with the new husband. She knew that Percival Peerce had died of a heart attack and that they, as a family, were attending funeral services at Trinity Church. Beyond the physical evidence of her stroke, there was only the disconcerting confusion of Edmunda referring to Audrey, by turns, as "Virginia" or as "Virginia's killer, Bay's doxy that was" to contend with.

But Audrey was getting used even to that.

Celeste, her dark hair sheathed in black net, was magnificent in draped black crepe of ribbon weave and seeds of jet, with onyx rimmed in silver on her ears and wrist. Beside her, Thorne sat like a well-groomed hound, in black of Italian cut. The close-fitting suit gave a sleekness to his body that was sensuous and suggestive, and lent to his handsome, too-sun-stained face an exotic, foreign hauteur.

His harness becomes him too well, Audrey thought. He begins to look like a gigolo.

To the sound of a tolling church bell, the procession began, a slow and stately line. Audrey was ignored by the others in the carriage... or perhaps it was Audrey who did the ignoring, lost in private thoughts....

She must find the pendant. Find it before Bay came home; check it against the floor plan of Whale's Turning. It could be evidence. Evidence of what... *exactly*?

Which meant going home. Home to Bridge Street and her father and Dolly, a woman Audrey looked down on, as Audrey, in her turn, was snubbed by the ladies Lockholm.

Was it any different?

Long ago—it seemed—Audrey had hated Dolly Dowd. Because her father had desired the woman.

Because her father had bedded the woman with laughter. And then married her, despite Josephine, gone, years ago, all to flowers.

And because, too, Dolly Dowd was not a lady. Was not respectable. She had lived above a *tavern* and *entertained men....*

Was it so different, the ladies Lockholm sneering at Audrey? Social Newport sneering at Tory June?

She was, Audrey admitted, chewing at her lower lip, below the fine women of Gilt Hill in manners and majesty. She had not actually been intimate with Bay before their wedding, but she had certainly succumbed, still a maiden, to Bay's body in her dreams....

They were at the church. Drew, the driver, was handing her down, and her head filled with the soft thunder of the organ, added to the bell—the organ given to Trinity Church a hundred years before by Bishop Berkeley, the great English philosopher and theologian. It was a mournful ballad that sounded in the organ's great pipes; brass-golden pipes, sweet-throated pipes.

A beautiful ballad. Audrey knew it: "Danny Boy."

A tenor voice lifted, sad as oboe, clear as flute, and Audrey knew the voice, too. It was Mr. Kirchner of the vegetable wagon. Audrey had heard him, at her friend Katya Greenfield's wedding, sing a solo in the Congregational church. He rarely sang. It was an honor if he would do it. He didn't like to sing, though he had the throat of Gabriel.

"It hurts," Mr. Kirchner would say by way of explanation, by way of regret. "For days and days after, it hurts, so I don't often do it." But where it hurt or how or why was not forthcoming, and Audrey had never thought to ask him about it.

Usually when Mr. Kirchner sang, he was well paid. But Audrey knew, from Katya's own lips, that Mr. Kirchner had sung for Katya free of charge.

"Why, Katya? How did you get Mr. K. to sing for nothing?"

"I saved that old horse of his one day. She got loose—got caught in barbed wire. She spooked trying to get out. Could have killed herself, you know. But Tony and I unsnagged her, and all she lost was some patches of hair. We rode her back to Mr. K. He loves that old horse, kid. He promised me anything, and I took his voice on my wedding day.''

Katya was four months older; she called Audrey ''kid.''

Katya, gone to California. Gone forever away...until Mr. Kirchner sang and she came back, dancing into Audrey's mind vivid as tartan plaid. Katya, who thought the act of love humiliating but ... mercifully quick....

Trinity's churchyard was a graveyard. To enter through the bell tower one passed among mortality.

Edmunda Lockholm led the way for the Lockholm family, arm in arm with Celeste, their heads high. Audrey followed last, behind Thorne.

Within were dried flowers from Wicke's, basket upon basket, too many to count. Within were great wreaths, oiled ebony. Within, the Reverend Elliott stood, hung in black. High in the wineglass pulpit, he prayed, regal and ecclesiastic.

Audrey sat in a corner of the Lockholm pew and looked out the window.

It was another sunny day, beautiful in Newport. In the churchyard birds flitted upon the granite stones, lifted their tails, pecked at thrown seed. Under a tilted tombstone a large cat lay, watching the sparrows, sheathing and unsheathing its claws. The bell still tolled. Mr. Kirchner's song had ended. There was the smell of incense, cloying, heady....

And there, moving among the graves, passing the window, coming in—there was Bay!—black hat in hand, hair falling over his forehead like a boy's.

Happiness surged in Audrey's heart. Bay had come, Bay was back! She was not to be alone, adrift, at Whale's Turning after all....

Even as she saw him enter, his eyes searching—perhaps for her?—his eyes unsurprised to see his sister and brother-in-law back home again, Audrey heard Trinity Church collectively gasp. She heard the whispers, louder, more ominous, than the tolling of the funeral bell.

And then Bay was beside her. Nodding to his family. Giving his mother's cheek a kiss. He did not kiss Audrey; he barely acknowledged her.

Impulsively, she reached for his hand, to hold it. He did not take it, did not meet her eye. He did not wink or smile. As reserved as a stranger, he folded his hands together and bent his head to pray.

Audrey blushed. Why was he cold to her? Weren't the others in the family cold enough? What had Audrey done that Bay, new husband, returned from a forced separation, should be now so cold ... ?

And then Dove Peerce was walking the church aisle where once upon a time—veiled that time, too; veiled that time in white—she had walked to marry. Her bosom friend, Alabaster McGregor—faultlessly turned out—escorted her. The widow laid a tiny flower, a violet, purple as her mourning lace, at the base of the casket lid. Then she sat, in the first pew below the pulpit, cold as an icon sculpted of ice, radiant as a halo....

And the daughter, and her titled fiancé. The daughter was heart-stoppingly beautiful. In grief, the heat of her had melted, she was moon-pale. Her strength, once only exuberance, had steeled into mature composure. Nicola took her place beside her mother in the Peerce pew. Took her place as a woman of the world, as an aristocrat: American royalty....

They buried Percy where the churchyard turned, beside the tall, black iron church fence.

Audrey hadn't heard the service. She was lost in her thoughts; her fears. She wanted to talk to Bay as soon as she could, Bay who was treating her, his bride, like a stranger. But first she would go to her father's house and find the "little golden gift" that Thorne had given her, the one Thorne had made her promise never to wear in public, never to tell about ... until they were married.

Had he known even then, the night Virginia died, as he closed the chain upon Audrey's throat; had Thorne known even then that he and Audrey would never marry? Had he, even then, been helplessly, hopelessly, in love with Celeste, named for the heavens...?

The service was over. Dove had thrown dirt and a wreath, heart shaped, of white roses. Nicola had thrown dirt and roses dipped in black. There would be a gathering at Peerce House, a small buffet.

"Bay," Audrey said, "I must go to see my father. I can walk from here and then walk myself home. Will that be all right? Or I could come, after, to Peerce House. Oh, I have missed you so much, are you all right?"

The words tumbled out, unplanned, unthought. She wanted to crush him to her, wanted him to look at her with love. He was so formal, so distant....

"Yes, Audrey, we will talk," he said. "If you must go to your father, then go. We won't stay long with Dove, the wake will be subdued, I think. I'll meet you by the rock on WaterWalk. There are things I must tell you. We have decisions to make." All said calmly, lovelessly, as though he were talking to Fisher, ordering an omelet for luncheon. And then, in afterthought, he said, "Shall we take you in the carriage to your father's?"

"What have I done?" she said. "Please tell me."

"You've done nothing, Audrey, dear. It is I who have done wrong, done terribly wrong."

Terribly wrong: "I'm going now to wring her god-damned neck. Remember... never marry the first..."

"No," she said, "I do not believe it. I will never believe it."

Then she turned, slipped out the church gate, and headed for home, a familiar way that for years and years her feet had followed, foreign now that she had left her father's house, strange now that she was no longer who she used to be.... And yet, still, red brick worn down by her skipping, her hurrying, her idling, was so familiar....

17

IT WAS SUNDAY; Lawrence Smoke's shop door was closed and locked.

Audrey glanced up at the second floor. The window was open in her old room, and the window in the kitchen had new curtains drifting, sail-blue curtains, deep colored, strong like Dolly Dowd....

Audrey sighed. She would have to mount the stairs, familiar too, no longer hers. Move through the house a guest. Ask permission to search in her old room. She hoped her father and his new wife would be gone—she knew where the spare key was kept, she hoped her father would be there alone; she hoped her father and Dolly would be kind. She needed friends...even though she, child of Josephine, had resented the new woman.... Had once resented her, and Lawrence Smoke's new life.

Not anymore, though. All that had been before Audrey had found a new life and new love of her own....

"Hello, Father."

He was in his easy chair, in the corner of the kitchen, the Sunday newspaper on his lap and around his slippered feet. He had gained weight. He wore a white shirt. He was sober, at his ease. Relaxed and happy.

"Hello, Daughter," he said. "Sit down. Will you share Sunday dinner with us?"

Dolly Dowd was at the stove, stirring in a pot. She wore dark green with yellow flounce, the bodice cut square, edging great rosy breasts. The green of the dress fired her curled russet hair, long even in the heat of a Newport July. She was highly colored and handsome, theatrically handsome. Her eyes were painted, and her cheeks and mouth.

She had been talking when Audrey entered; she broke off as Audrey pushed at the door.

Upon Dolly's throat gleamed Audrey's pendant, rich and fine.

It became her. It would become any woman or...any man.

"Welcome," said Dolly. "We were hoping you'd drop by one day. How's about some lemonade?"

Audrey sat at the kitchen table. "Thank you," she said. She smoothed a fold in her skirt. "I'm glad to see you doing so well."

"An' how are you, little one?" said her father. "How is it on the hill?"

Audrey sipped from the glass Dolly set on the table. It was cold and eased the tightness in her chest. "Oh thanks, it's good."

"There's more," said Dolly. "I'm just readyin' the dumplin's for the chicken. Say you'll stay."

"Yes," said Audrey. "Yes, I'll stay. It's nice to be home again."

And it was nice.

Thorne had been wrong, she thought, looking around, noting the changes Dolly Dowd had wrought. Smoke House wasn't "little and mean." It was simple, yes, and modest of possessions. But it was clean and gaily colored—now, since Dolly—and full of Lawrence Smoke's fine work. Cabinets scrubbed a white that Dove Peerce would envy. The long table, its pine burnished by Lawrence Smoke's neat's-foot oil to a Bellevue Avenue standard. Well-made chairs, graceful chairs, strong enough to hold a man holding a woman as ample as Dolly. Field flowers in a round copper pot. Bright blue curtains floating. And a sweet smell lingering throughout; lemon and honeysuckle. A new blue-and-white sisal runner on the floor.

"The house looks brand-new, Dolly," Audrey said. "So much color. It makes Father's wood show so well—"

"House needed a woman's touch," said Lawrence Smoke.

"Yes," said Audrey, humbled. "Yes, it did."

Audrey, like her father, had never thought to change the house Josephine had made. She and her father had lived with Josephine when her mother no longer lived with them. They had kept to Josephine's ways, kept Josephine's house, left Josephine's things as Josephine had left them. At first Audrey had been too young and Lawrence had been too grieved to do otherwise. Later, neither had dared.

Dolly Dowd was good for Lawrence Smoke. Good for his bed, good for his house, good for his life.

"Dolly's even made my work improve," said Lawrence Smoke. He drank from a glass of emerald green. "An' I'm goin' to be a father again. I'm a lucky man."

Dolly pregnant, too! Dolly...Celeste....

"I saved a bottle for this day," said Lawrence Smoke. "A bottle of our weddin' champagne. Will you join us, Daughter, in our happiness?"

Tears misted in her eyes, but she sniffed them away. "I'd be honored," she said.

Dolly was already down the inside steps, down to the earthen corner of Lawrence Smoke's shop where it was always cool, where Lawrence Smoke had lain a wedding bottle to wait his daughter's blessing.

Audrey set the table. Dolly served the plates. Lawrence opened the bottle with a bang. It was so easy once the hate was gone, so easy to be friends....

There was apple cobbler for dessert, and whipped cream.

"Dolly's makin' me fat," said Lawrence Smoke.

"He's enjoyin' it, as you can see."

"*I'm* enjoying it, too, Dolly."

"A little fat is good for ya, helps the complexion," said Dolly Dowd.

"I've come for something, Dolly," Audrey said. "I wish I could give it to you as a wedding present, but it doesn't belong to me, and I have to return it."

"Durn," said Dolly. "It's this necklace, ain't it? Well, I've enjoyed the use." She reached behind her neck and freed the pendant. Elegant, it lay in its chain on her bosom. She handed it to Audrey. "It sure is a purty thing."

"I'll get you a better," said Lawrence Smoke.

"When?" said Dolly.

"Tomorrow."

"Buster, you got a date."

Audrey wrapped the trinket in a bit of her father's newspaper, tucked it into the pocket of her dress. "Thorne gave this pendant to me last year, and now I must give it back. It may be evidence that will help clear Bay of the charges against him. He's not guilty, Father. Virginia was murdered, that they say is so, but Bay didn't do it. Virginia, you see, had lovers."

"Mebbe so," muttered Lawrence Smoke, plainly unconvinced. "For your sake, Daughter, I hope so."

His daughter, he was thinking, no longer reminded him of his first wife. Perhaps it was Audrey herself who had changed; she was thinner and calmer, more composed than she used to be, and yes . . . she was older. The childish vulnerability was gone. The face was more set. There was more steel in her spine, more lift to her head. But it wasn't entirely that. If he thought hard, if he concentrated, he could see, again, the semblance of Josephine's curve of cheek, the return of Josephine's clear-eyed gaze. That was what was different: he didn't remember Josephine precisely anymore. He saw Dolly now when he thought of women. His memory held only Dolly, Dolly naked in the dark. . . . Dolly's open, red mouth, Dolly's store-bought smell, Dolly's plump white torso, pink tipped, warm. That was it: he had, at long last, gotten over Josephine. Forgotten Josephine. May she rest in peace and . . . hallelujah!

"You were saying, Daughter?"

"What you told the police, Father. It must have all been true. But it could have been another with Virginia that night. It could have been her lover. It did not have to be Bay."

"Never said it was," said Lawrence Smoke. "But what kind of woman you sayin' she was, Audrey, dilly-dallyin' around an' only just back from her honeymoon. That kind of gossip is hard to swallow without evidence. The woman was a lady, you know. She had a baby coming. Those are hard words, Audrey Alice, not to be said lightly.''

Audrey toyed with her spoon, simple pewter but as shiny as the heavy full silver of Whale's Turning. "I know, Father. And it ill becomes me, but I want it to be true. If Virginia didn't die at her own hand or fall accidentally—" She didn't finish the thought. She didn't say, *and if it wasn't Bay.* . . .

"Since it wasn't Bay," she said, and stopped, sought her father's eye. "The maid says Virginia had lovers. She bought them 'little golden gifts.' This pendant may be one of them. . . . This little thing may save Bay's life."

"Restore his reputation," said Dolly Dowd, slipping plates into a bucket to be taken down to the well and washed.

"Yes, yes."

"Well, I'll tell you one more thing, Daughter. Now I recall. This lady, I met her, you know, workin' on the house the way I did. She'd come around, see how things were goin'. A most proper lady, Audrey, don't let a maid fool you. A lovely lady, most proper. But she did pledge me to secrecy on somethin' so little I forgot it till just now."

"Oh, Father, what? What?"

"She had me make her a secret drawer."

A chill danced up Audrey's backbone. "A secret drawer?"

"Yay, in the bathroom cabinets, one of the bathroom drawers. They're all mirrored inside at the back. I don' recollect now which one 'twas, but one of 'em toward the middle, there's an ivory pin set in the bottom halfway back, it flips the end mirror up an' there's more room behind. You look, you'll find it. There may be somethin' there, somethin' hidden that'd be of use to ye."

"Oh, Father. I must go right now and look!" She was up, flushed and eager. She threw her arms around him, kissed him hard. "Oh, thank you, Father. Oh, I hope, I hope!"

"Don' stay way so long no more," said Dolly Dowd.

"No," said Audrey, "I won't." Self-consciously, she hugged Dolly, too. "May I just see my room, peek into it? And then I have to go."

"You know the way," said Lawrence Smoke.

Funny, Audrey thought, standing in her little room. Funny how a place can define you, can recreate, *resurrect*, the past. She remembered the broken sugar whale and looked for crumbs. But the floor was swept and polished and nothing of the whale remained except vivid memory. Audrey looked for dust lines marking where the cheval glass had stood; where, for years, Josephine had lived in Audrey's mind, and Josephine's eyes deep within and wise, had counseled Audrey in her imagination. There were no dust lines, only an empty space in the corner that faced the window, beyond the single bed. There was the same coverlet, the same flat pillow, plumped now, unslept upon. Where the rocking chair once sat, where the chimney turned, there was a shallow pool of sunshine, bright on an unlined floor. And yet Audrey saw the cheval glass and saw the little rocker, and saw Josephine, hovering in the mirror-dust, waiting to hear, ready to advise. And at the foot of the bed, legs folded Indian-style, Audrey saw herself in earnest conversation with the reflecting glass, one ear alert—always!—for the tap, tap, tap that would signal Thorne below.

All so long ago it may never have happened.... For there was no evidence of it now....

Bay.

She must go to Bay. She clutched the pendant in her pocket. That, at least, remained. Hard evidence....

SHE HAD BEEN walking along the strand a long time. She was striding up Cliff Walk; WaterWalk was visible above her.

And leaning against the rock was a man in a black raincoat.

Bay was there, already there and waiting for her. She waved, hastened.

The man did not wave back. His hands were thrust into his coat pockets, collar turned up against the rising wind. He smoked no cigar. He was not facing the sea. He was watching Audrey; Audrey trotting, half running, leaping the stones as she hurried. His hair, under the clouded sky, looked darker than Bay's, which was as brown as pale mink. This man's hair was black, pirate black, and curly. His cheeks were Caribbean sunned....

It wasn't Bay who awaited her upon the rocky height of WaterWalk. It was Thorne.

Oh, where was Bay? He had promised to meet her there....

She lifted her skirts to her knees, Tory's etiquette lessons forgotten, and ran up the winding cliffs like a hound.

Arrived, she caught herself upon the rock. "Where is Bay, Thorne? Has something happened?"

Thorne smirked at her. With no tenderness, he said, "He'll be along, Mrs. Lockholm. I asked to speak to you in private and your...new husband...gave permission." One leg was cocked the way he did, propped on its toe, at right angles to the leg that bore his weight.

He is feigning unconcern, she thought. But he is frightened; maybe terrified.

He is frightened, yes, she thought. But she was not afraid. They were forty feet above the breakers crashing into foam upon the rocks below, but she was not afraid. Somewhere behind them, somewhere in Whale's Turning, Bay was there. Bay was watching. Thorne would not harm her, however much he might long to.... He would not dare.

"Yes, Thorne, what is it?"

She despised him now. Or felt sorry for him now. Perhaps both emotions were the same? The man he was now, this man, she had never loved. He was shrunken. And so quickly. Once a man—so she'd thought—to risk all to be an entrepreneur, to get a start, any start, and then, brilliantly, to make his mark. Once a man driven by fierce, single-minded ambition to take a little ferry service—Sea Trains, she remembered his dream—and grow it, in time, into a fleet of ships to cruise the world....

And now he was only a well-dressed dandy, servile to the heiress he had married. Too quickly spoiled and softened. Newly short-tempered, newly faultfinding.... Newly, a rogue.

Or had she never understood...? Had Thorne always been...a little too self-indulgent?

"You know very well what I'm after, little princess." Gray cloud behind chiseled his profile, highlighted the dark of his eyes and brow. "You threw it in my face, hanging those plans where Virginia's portrait used to be."

"What is Virginia's portrait to you, Thorne? What could it possibly mean...to you?"

"I don't give a damn about the portrait, you know that. Still, I know it well. I was in that house before I married into it, Audrey—long before *you* married into it after me. I was in the house—on occasion—when I tutored the late Mrs. Lockholm in sailing, and I was often there, courting Celeste— Why, what do you think...? Are you thinking Virginia's face means more to me than it ought to?"

He was not so arrogant, when she looked closer. He was angry and very much afraid. It was the fear made him dangerous: Audrey saw that.

"They are saying now," she said, testing him, "that Virginia Lockholm, returned from her honeymoon, unhappy in her marriage, took a lover."

Pale as a burial sheet was his face.

"Give it back to me, Audrey." His voice was a menacing croon. His arms were still folded on his chest and his leg was still cocked. He still lounged like a drawing-room dandy surveying new beauties, wondering which to approach with an invitation to waltz.... But the tenseness of his stance belied his composure, and the burn in his eyes scorched her face.

"What do you mean?" she said...though she knew what he meant.

"Don't play stupid, *sister-in-law, dear*. I saw you looking yesterday, over my shoulder. I saw you recognizing...the pendant, Audrey. The floor plan of Virginia's bedroom. You must give it back to me. You must give it back to me today.''

She said nothing. She was looking at the sea. The day, already overcast, was dying, and the whales were coming in, a herd of whales, so strange, riding into the bay with the tide.

"I want that pendant, Audrey. You have no right to it. You belong to another now. I do, too. Give it to me, I demand it.''

"It was given to me in good faith . . . wasn't it?''

"You're a fool. You always were a fool—that was one of the things I wanted in you. Foolish, foolish Audrey. Did you really think such a thing was ever meant for you?''

How calm I am, she thought. Outwardly composed, like he is. Inside, roiling with nerves. "How came you to it, Thorne? It was so beautiful. It must have cost so much.''

"I found it. I stole it. I didn't buy it for you, but for myself. Free me of you, Audrey. Give it back. Live and let live. God knows it's hard enough you marrying into the same family.''

"Whose was it first?''

"No one's. Only mine.''

"I don't know where it is,'' she said.

"You are a liar,'' he said.

"The day you broke our engagement I was wearing it. I took it off, threw it somewhere and never put it on again. I left my father's house shortly after, and moved to Mildred Falk's. And then I married Bay. I do not know where the pendant is, Thorne. But I will look for it, your little golden gift. . . .''

"It was never meant for you. I was wrong to give it. But you were so taken by it, I didn't know what to do.''

"It fell from your pocket by accident that night,'' she said.

"Yes,'' he said. "Once you saw it, I couldn't refuse you. But it is mine, Audrey, and I'm taking it back.''

She was watching the whales come.

"Yes,'' she said. "It's yours, Thorne, and I'll find it for you. . . . Is that all?''

Now he uncoiled from his position. Now he stood free of the rock, balanced on both feet, close to her. "You went to your father's home today—you've just come from there.... I think you went in search of my trinket."

She didn't answer. One fist deep in the pocket of her mourning dress clutched the pendant. It mustn't move, mustn't jingle, mustn't reveal itself....

Thorne clamped his hands, heavy hands, upon her shoulders, turned her to face him. Put his face against hers, his eyes storm flashing. He said, very softly, but she heard him well, "Give it to me, Audrey. I know you have it."

"I'll find it, Thorne. I'll give it back." She struggled, trying to break free, but he held her, pressing his fingers into bone. "Let me go, Thorne. You shall have the pendant back. But I must go now, go to Bay."

"Bayard is with his mother, she has taken to her bed again. There is no one watching us, my dear. You could slip, couldn't you? So easily, you could fall. I could never get to you in time...."

The wind was picking up. The clouds were lowering.

"What are you saying?" she said.

His eyes narrowed and burned, black slits, black lashed. A muscle beat at the edge of his jaw. "Give it back to me, Audrey. It's mine and I claim it."

He was shaking her. She wrenched from his grasp, his fingers clawed down the front of her gown as she stood away.

"I haven't got it now," she said. "I've told you! I'll have to hunt it up."

Her fist was cramping, holding the pendant so tight. And her shoulders hurt where he had gripped and dug in. Slowly she relaxed her hand, withdrew it from her pocket, rubbed her shoulders. "I'm going to Bay now. I want to see him very much."

"My wife is pregnant," he said. "I shall be a father. I hope to lead a decent life. But I swear to you, Audrey, stay out of my way or you'll regret it. Get me that pendant and stay out of my way as far as you can. Because I hate you, you see. I hate you like poison."

His hands were upon her again; sea-strong hands, able to hold a sail though all the ocean beat against it.

Beyond his shoulders she saw Whale's Turning, impassive, grand. Saw Celeste, watching them, framed in a window—in the unlighted window, *the window above Audrey's bedroom, the window from which Virginia fell, in the room untouched since that terrible night last year in June.* . . . In the unwashed, uncurtained window, Celeste Cockburn stood, out of her mourning costume, in a gown so red Audrey could see its vividness despite the approaching, encroaching dusk. Celeste was pressed against the glass, hands as open as a child's either side of her face. She was staring down the length of lawn at her bridegroom holding his former fiancé in his arms.

She thinks he is beguiling me, Audrey thought. She thinks he talks of love. She has no idea he is threatening me. . . . And I can never tell her . . . or Bay. I have no evidence. . . .

And then Audrey saw Bay. At last Bay was coming. He was on the loggia, down the steps, upon the lawn. . . .

Thorne threw Audrey from him and strode for the house. He passed Bayard Lockholm without a word.

Bay was in black, too, the morning suit he had worn to Percival Peerce's funeral. He came to Audrey but did not touch her. He stood before her, his face blank, indifferent. "We have made a mistake, Audrey," he said in greeting. "Our marriage was a mistake. I see that now and so must you. I have already spoken to Astin Forbes about an annulment."

And down among the rocks the whales were gathered. Another storm had come.

18

August

"HE DISCUSSES nothing with me, Tory. He won't confide. He avoids me. Oh, he is kind. And he is sad, too—that I can see—but he is very much aloof. His days are spent with Astin, huddling, at the newspaper office. In the evening we dine as a family, with Edmunda if she is well enough, and Celeste and Thorne if they are not dining out. Nights he stays in his own bedroom . . . and I stay in mine. I do not know what I have done to lose his love, if, after all, I ever had it. Bay wants to sever us, that is all I know, and I cannot think how to defend myself. Astin says Bay is convinced he will be convicted, that he is pressing the annulment for my sake. I said I do not want it—I love Bay to the death. I cannot get myself even to cry. I just feel felled, like a Christmas spruce. Too wounded even to bleed."

"Ridiculous," said Tory VanVoorst. "You should be up and fighting."

But was it? Was it ridiculous for the heart, destroyed, to shrink to a dry seed and the wrinkles of age, suddenly, to wither a face no longer loved . . . ? For hair to gray when it had no more use for color . . . ? For a bride, abandoned, to climb the servants' stairs to an unused room and a grimed window and, opening the casement to the night, reach out to where the stars enticed . . . and fall. . . .

Tory, in turquoise crepe de chine edged in Moroccan green, sat on the lawn of Whale's Turning, under the apple tree, licking a raspberry ice.

Audrey, pale in dusty red, sat with her, picking at the tablecloth.

"You will seduce him tonight," said Tory. "I'll tell you how. But first we must plan my party."

Audrey shook her head. "I'm a know-nothing in the art of love, Tory. Bay would laugh at me. He would be disgusted."

Tory laughed. "You are a know-nothing if you think that, Audrey Lockholm. You must get him to talk to you. That's the important thing. He has forgotten, in his own troubles, that he cannot live without you. You must remind him. I will tell you this—after a man makes love, his heart is open, and a woman can snuggle in. And once you are homesteading in a man's heart, Audrey, you will always be his. Or he, at least, will think so."

"You sound so...premeditated, Tory. So...calculating."

"And so I am, Audrey, dear. All those lovely things. Premeditated, calculating and...enterprising. Don't forget, both of us started humbly, both of us have triumphed. The difference is you won the laurel with no training. I knew what I was about."

"I haven't triumphed at anything except getting on the high school swimming team."

"That's hot," said Tory.

And Audrey, despite herself, smiled. "Let's figure out your housewarming," she said. Anything, so as not to feel, so keenly, the chasm in her heart.

Anything, so as not to remember her nights....

Last night...and the night before, and yes, tonight to come. Nights she spent unable to sleep for the pounding of her heart, thudding doom, doom, doom, louder than Edmunda shuffling in the hall, louder than the boom of the sea. Nights she drifted from light sleep to bad dreams populated with nightmare-men, half beast, half human, who silently tore through the brocade walls and slithered toward her in the dark, doom, doom, doom. Nights when, in the still, behind the thin curtains, Virginia laughed.... Nights when even his body turning, walls away, woke her, and in that great, once-longed-for bed, she yearned for him, for Bay, her *husband*. Yearned for his body, long and naked and fine, hard around her, heavy upon her, lovely as a sculptor's sword. Dumb in her longing, she waited the nights away, *dying* in that part of her never meant to die....

Tory was saying, "Yes, first the party, and then your little problem. Mine's bigger, so I'll go first."

Audrey nodded, glad Tory was there. "You hired a chef."

"Cook, Audrey. I hired a cook. Remember, simpler does it. 'Cottage' for house, 'driver' for chauffeur, you're 'rich,' not 'wealthy.' And yes, I did, out of the Hotel St. Regis in New York. His name is Weatherwax, Paul Weatherwax, he's in his thirties, very handsome—he looks like an English banker though he comes from Brooklyn, and he's a perfect snoot. Of course he was French trained, and the reason he is coming with us is because Burtykins made him an offer he couldn't refuse. He's the best cook in Newport by far, and by fall he'll be the best private cook on Fifth Avenue. So that's done."

"You are a wonder, Tory."

"It only takes money, Audrey. Money...and know-how. Now. What would you think of a medieval jousting tournament as an irresistible party?"

Audrey looked up from the luncheon cloth where her fingers had pulled loose a thread in a damask rose leaf. "Oh!" she said. "Oh, Tory!"

"Exactly. The most sumptuous thing. The grounds of Godsend will become an Old-English tilting field, full of pageantry. All ladies, like damsels of old—you remember Arthur and Guinevere and the Round Table and all that?— in their colors, their scarves flying from the helmets of their knights. We're building a viewing stand for the ladies fair to cheer their heroes. We'll have suits of armor, two suits, which the opponents will wear as they war. We'll have pigs roasting on spits—Weatherwax loves to do roast pig—and, oh yes, lances! Which will be rubber, so no one gets hurt. And there'll be prizes, Audrey.... Delectable prizes like mink muffs and satin opera capes and French evening purses. All the prizes will be feminine, and every knight, you'll see, will win one prize. And here's my coup. The grand prize will be a gray Thoroughbred hunter, a champion of English bloodstock.... He's costing us thousands, and guess who will win this grand prize, Audrey?''

"Tory, do you mean the prizes will be fixed?"

"Well, not exactly," Tory said with a laugh. "Just...premeditated...and calculated. After all, Audrey, the only reason for prizes is to please people. And what's the pleasure in a prize you don't want?" Tory swung a leg, neatly crossed on the other; swung a pretty green shoe from her toes.

"Will the jousting be a contest then, or just, as they say, having a go?"

"Oh, Audrey, my dear. Of course it will be a contest. It's a jousting tourney! But a contest with a purpose. That's where I'm so smart. I'm attaining my end, which is instant social acceptance in Newport. Who wants to wait five years to be invited to Mrs. Astor's Beechwood...? Not me. That'd be the turn of the century, and I'd be almost thirty. No, no, here's the trick. I want Dove Peerce to come to my party. Dove Peerce is the key. But she won't, not ever having received me, not ever having acknowledged I exist, if you want to know the truth—''

"She's in mourning, Tory. She couldn't possibly come."

Tory caressed her hair. "Nicola's wedding has not been postponed."

"Yes," said Audrey, "but Nicola and Rolf's wedding was Percy's dying wish—''

"So the new widow said," Tory said, sly. "And who's to say differently?"

"Oh Tory. She wouldn't—''

"Make it up? Wouldn't she just! Dove Peerce wants Nicola married and a marchioness. Married as soon as possible, and off her hands. She's never really liked her daughter, you know. She thinks her a cow.''

"Oh!" Audrey forgot for a moment her pain. "Oh, Tory, how can you say such things?"

"Because it's true. Everyone knows it, silly, and my maid confirms it, which makes it gospel. Fanni's an encyclopedia of the foibles of the rich. One's maid should always be a fund of knowledge, Audrey, and I have the best. Fanni dishes with the girls of her set. On her day off, just like a reporter, she makes her rounds. And Rosalind, Dove Peerce's maid, is a talker. Rosalind is French, too, you see, so there's a connection.''

''And Fanni tells you what she hears?''

''Item by item. I *pay* her, Audrey. For each interesting tidbit I give her a dollar. And sometimes a bonus, just to keep her interested. It's the only way to really know what's out there, darling. You must start with yours.''

Audrey's ice was melting slush. She stuck in her spoon, took a bite. It was sweet and good.

''Audrey, are you listening?''

''Sawyer's not social, Tor. She's a stay-at-home. She would be shocked if I asked her to spy for me, and she wouldn't be any good at it.''

''Do you really know this, or are you just supposing?''

Sawyer was about Audrey's age, heavy hipped and round faced. Her brown hair was wrapped unbecomingly close to her head and accentuated a fleshy nose, slightly bulging eyes and acne-scarred skin. Sawyer was humorless, willing to work if asked, but uninitiating. Audrey asked Sawyer to do little, not needing much done. Audrey was used to doing for herself.

Audrey said, ''Sawyer never talks. Never says anything except 'Yes ma'am' and 'Will that be all?' She's never asked me a question about myself. But now I think, once she did tell me something about Virginia—''

''You see,'' said Tory. ''She was testing you, feeling you out. You've probably disappointed her, asking nothing at all. She sounds marvelous. Knows how to keep a secret. Keeps her mouth shut unless asked. I bet she knows volumes, and I bet she'd tell if you encouraged her. A little extra money in an apron pocket does wonders. Believe me.''

Audrey ate more of her ice. ''How have you rigged the contest, Tor? Tell me that.''

Tory adjusted the petticoat ruffles around her green shoes. ''Oh, yes. Well, you see, the idea is to get Dove Peerce. She, more than Caroline Astor, is the one I need to validate me. Sooo, rather than butter up Dove who is now officially in mourning and therefore more unapproachable than ever, I thought I'd get at Dove through Nicola. Right now, getting Nicola married to Rolf—on time—is Dove's top priority. So I thought, What does Nicola want, a lot...want enough to pressure her mother for? Horses. Nicola's mad for a good horse. And so is Rolf. He plays polo, you know, over in England. On the royals' team, partners with the Prince of Wales. Very good, I hear. Well. I couldn't do polo. Not enough interest here, too-skilled a game, too obvious. My party must appeal to the privileged multitude. Please the women first—please the men if possible. The jousting tourney succeeds magnificently on both counts. Women love a costume ball and a lawn party. Men love to show off their masculinity—to them that's fun. And since no one can lay claim to being a champion jouster, all the men, theoretically, would have an equal chance, and have a good time. See that?''

Audrey licked her spoon. "Yep.''

"Ladies don't lick spoons, Audrey. And don't say 'yep,' not even in intimate talks like this. If you slip once, you'll slip twice, and somewhere, sometime—and it's always the worst possible time—someone nosy will hear you, and you'll be tattled on as a pretender to the throne of lady-ness.''

"But I am a pretender, Tory. Everyone knows that.''

"No, they don't. And they won't, or won't *have to*, if you don't let the holes show in the soles of your party shoes. Audrey, you're accepted right now because you married into an acceptable family. It's easier for Newport, in your situation, to look the other way, to accept the second Mrs. Bayard Lockholm rather than reject her. It keeps the social order. But if you force their hand, with obvious faux pas and inferior manners—''

"All right, all right. But Bay's blacklisted now, so I must be, too.''

"That's temporary. His recent publicity has been terrible—his marriage to you is the least of it.''

Audrey sighed. "The annulment should generate excitement.''

"Quite a bit, if it happens. But we'll see that it doesn't, won't we?"

Audrey leaned back in her chair. "Bay and I—it was all a dream from the start. Never real. I don't feel married, Tor."

"Well, feel it or not, Audrey Lockholm, it's real as onions. There's no going back for you and no going back for him. Now, can I finish telling about my jousting party ploy? Or can't you concentrate on me?"

Audrey sat up straight. "Yes, of course I can. Please tell me."

"It's just this. Rolf, Lord Pomeroy, is so good a horseman he'll easily win the joust. And he'll want to. He'll want to give the gray hunter to Nicola, it will be a blissful wedding gift, don't you see? And here's the beauty part—I am not inviting Nicola and Rolf. Or the widow Peerce."

"But, Tory. That doesn't make sense."

Tory stretched, sinuous and lazy, in her chair. "Oh, yes, my pretty. The message will get to Dove, I'll see to that. Invite the VanVoorsts to Nicola's wedding, pay a call on Mrs. VanVoorst at Godsend. Party invitations will immediately ensue, then Rolf, Lord Pomeroy, will be Newport's jousting champion and Nicola will have a new horse. Do you see the brilliance?"

Stretching, self-satisfied, Tory saw a spout of water spuming in the bay. She stood to see better, a tremor snaking up her spine. There, out in blue-blue water, whales lay. A herd of whales.

"Audrey—"

Audrey stood, too, followed Tory's pointing finger with her eyes.

"Yes," Audrey said. "Isn't it strange? They gather together so often here now. They crowd down by the rocks at dusk, like avenging spirits, dark and quiet and gray. They used to play offshore sometimes, but only a few. Now there's a hundred almost, huddling. So still. As though they were waiting for something, as though the whole ocean were sick...."

Like avenging spirits....

Tory was lost in time. She was back with Granny Brown in New Orleans. Small then. *Black then*. And Granny Brown was saying in a voice that rolled like organ chords, "It may be you will see it, Alma June. It may even be you who will be God's oar, you who will roil up the waters of vengeance long foretold. For this our Lord has promised, so know this, little one, and know it well. In the season of leviathan, when the whales turn in waters blue. Doom will drown the evildoer and Phineas Brown will be avenged...."

Suddenly Tory was chill. She rubbed her arms to bring back feeling, afraid to look upon her hands, sure they had paled to gray, shadowed back to black....

Audrey was staring, too, caught, like Tory, in a sense of dread. "It is an omen," Audrey said. "Please, God, may the whales turn back."

No, not me, Tory was thinking. I am no avenging angel. No, not me. Audrey Lockholm is my friend. I may use her, but I don't wish her ill. I don't wish her husband sadness or loss.... Bay had nothing to do with my ancestor's murder, and I have nothing to do with the vengeance of Phineas Brown.

Granny Brown's words echoed in her heart. Little Granny Brown, delicate head bowed over her beautiful grandchild, making the sign of the cross on Alma June's flat breast. "Thy will be done, now and forever, amen. Say it, Alma June."

Thy will be done... NO!

Tory turned away from the sight, caught up her gloves. "I must go now," she said. She forced herself to look upon her hands, her trembling hands locked together upon the gloves, the palms scrubbing at each other as though, that way, the telltale pigment could be scoured away.... Her hands were as white as they had always been, her palms as pink. It was the gloves with which she hid her hands that were black, a black called teak, named after an East Indian wood....

Audrey walked with her friend around the side of the house. With the appearance of the whales a solemnity had come upon the frivolity of the afternoon. She did not remind Tory that she had promised to help Audrey make peace with Bay. Audrey did not want to seduce a man into loving her.

Things will work out as they should, Audrey thought. I will try my best and hope for the best—

Beavers, the VanVoorst coachman, helped Tory into her landau, gray with white trim, white wheels, white horse.

"Don't forget, Audrey dear. The invitations. You promised."

Audrey nodded. "I'll do at least a dozen a day, I won't forget."

"And Audrey—" Tory leaned over her door "—come close, I don't want Beavers to overhear."

Audrey came close, took Tory's hand.

Tory whispered, "Don't sleep alone tonight, whatever you do. Knock on his door, slip into his bed. Say you are afraid to be alone, you cannot stand it."

Audrey nodded. "All right, Tor, yes, I will. I'll try and try."

Tory sat back on figured gray satin. "And wear something simple, something simple and . . . thin."

"Yes, Tory."

"Audrey, about the whales."

"Yes?"

"They will turn when the time is right, you'll see. Don't ask me how I know, just listen, and learn to be like the whales yourself. . . . When things seem bent on your destruction, turn, Audrey, turn and find, however far away it is, the warmth and calm and quiet—and the freedom—of the open sea. Turning doesn't mean running. It means *deciding* . . . on the right way, the way that seems, sometimes, impossible. And until that right way opens up to you, huddle against the cliffs and wait. Wait, like the whales are doing, even if it kills you. Then the way will be opened, Audrey, darling, and you'll do a whale's turning. Have faith."

Spellbound, so often spellbound by Tory, Audrey listened.

"Good luck." The VanVoorst carriage rolled.

How lucky I am, Audrey thought, to have such a friend, so quickly out of nowhere, just when I needed one. Tory, at least, is a stroke of good fortune....

Dr. Lake was coming at four. He was paying his usual daily call on the matriarch Lockholm, and Audrey had asked to see him, too. She was so tired these days, and too easily depressed. It was unlike her. I need my strength for the days ahead, she thought. And I must be cheerful, for Bay's sake. Lift him up. Whatever the outcome between us....

Celeste's barouche turned in the driveway. She was alone, back from shopping or calling on friends. She rarely took Thorne with her on her social visits; Thorne spent his days down at the harbor, putting together his ferry business, it was said.

Audrey waited at the front doors for Celeste, but her sister-in-law passed her with a swish of skirt. Then Celeste stopped and said, "Your choice of friends, Audrey. Are you sure you're wise to consort with a woman like that, with her past? Especially where Bay is concerned?"

"Tory is a good friend to me, Celeste. And a good friend to Bay, too. Wait, you'll see."

"'Good.'" Celeste moved away, unpinning her picture hat. "That word isn't in Mrs. VanVoorst's vocabulary. *You'll* see."

"Celeste—"

But her sister-in-law was at the elevator, to the right of the grand stairs, stepping in.

The golden door closed and the elevator, lifting, hummed.

What would I have said, Audrey thought. Would I have asked why she doesn't invite me to accompany her on her social calls? No.... Would I have told her Thorne doesn't pine for me, never fear? No....

Audrey climbed the staircase, as she always did, avoiding the little elevator. She liked to wind her way up those wide marble and gilt steps. She liked to pause on the landing and turn in a circle, making her skirts float like Celeste's, and feel like a lady to the manor born. She liked to stand in the sun, colored blue and orange from the stained glass, and trace with a finger the lines of the floor plans of Whale's Turning....

Audrey, so tired, climbed the rest of the way to her boudoir, to wait for Dr. Lake.

SO IT WAS TRUE!

She was not sure she wanted it to be. She was so young still, and Bay was to be tried for murder, and he had asked to dissolve their union, barely begun... and now so complicated....

But Dr. Lake was saying with such heartiness, snapping his bag shut, shaking her hand, "Congratulations, Mrs. Lockholm. Now Bayard will have an heir, and you and your sister-in-law have something wonderful in common."

"When, Dr. Lake... when may I expect it?"

"Oh, heavens, Mrs. Lockholm, not for quite a while yet. You've barely got things going, you know. Say next spring, in March, perhaps, or early April. Will that do?"

"But, but it's definite... I'm going to have a baby?"

"Indeed. Look to your diet now. Lots of milk and cheese, go light on the dinner wine. And none of this fashionable starving to keep your figure. You're so young you'll bounce right back into shape, and the thing to do is to make sure the babe gets what it needs. I'm a great believer in exercise, too. Stay active. Get Bayard to take you boating, swim with the ladies at the beach. That kind of thing."

"Yes, Doctor. Thank you very much."

"May I tell your mother-in-law?" said Dr. Lake. "She'll be happy to know. Or would you rather?" He was not looking at her, he was rolling down his sleeves, setting in the cuff links, enamel fox heads with emerald eyes....

He knows, Audrey thought. He knows Edmunda Lockholm does not like me. Audrey sat on the red chaise in her bedroom. Sawyer, her maid, stood by the wardrobe, present during the examination at Audrey's request.

Audrey looked at Sawyer, Sawyer at attention, hands crossed demurely in front of her, upon a white pinafore. A plain young woman, Audrey's age, very quiet, seemingly so dull.... Audrey saw the maid's eyes flicker. Audrey looked then at Dr. Lake, plump and dignified, double chin overflowing a starched collar.

"You can tell her, Doctor," Audrey said. "I—I'm not close to my mother-in-law. She doesn't always recognize me, since her accident."

He knows, she thought. He knows everything, probably, that Edmunda Lockholm thinks. He is Edmunda's confidant. He sees her every day; hears her complaints, her secrets.... If he wanted, Dr. Lake could tell Ally McGregor a thing or two....

"But I—I would like to tell Bay myself."

"Of course, my dear young lady, of course you would, and so it shall be." Dr. Lake peered at Audrey through bespectacled eyes. "I could keep this under my hat, child, if you wish it."

"No, no. Mother should know. It may hasten her getting well."

"Yes—" Dr. Lake nodded "—yes, indeed. Now she'll have two grandchildren to look forward to. Could make a world of difference.... Well, good luck, Mrs. Lockholm. I'll be around if you need me, but I expect you won't for a couple of months unless you start feeling nauseated. And there's no reason why you should, mind. Really, having a baby is the most natural thing in the world. You, in a sense, are only along for the ride. It's nature does it all.... Well, good day."

"Thank you, Doctor. And thank you, Sawyer. I—I'd like to be alone now.... Will you let me know when my husband arrives home?"

"Yes, ma'am."

The double doors opened and closed, and Audrey was alone.

She lay quiet for a moment, a hand on her stomach. She felt nothing. Her figure was flat between the bones of her pelvis. Nothing stirred. There was no sign of life yet; no feel of weight.

And in Audrey's heart there was no maternal feeling....

Perhaps that will come as the seed inside grows, she thought. There is too much else for me to think about. I must tell Bay we cannot be annulled now. I must tell Bay how much I love him.... And I must look, right now, for Virginia's secret drawer....

She was loath to. She had put it off for days, afraid of what she would find. She did not want to be the one to go to Bay and say, "Look what I've found. Your first wife never loved you. See, here's the evidence. She was untrue to you, Bay, just look, here's a letter to her lover, never sent, who knows why...?"

She did not want to do that. But if she found something incriminating, how could she not...?

Or what if there was nothing?

Or what if there were only mementos and evidences of Bay, his love for her, his adoration...set down in tiny missives that Virginia pasted in a book?

Bay would be home soon. She must hurry.

Her father had said the drawer with the false back was in the bathroom, in the middle row of drawers built into the wall....

She was sweating and trembling. She pulled out the first. There was nothing inside. It was clean, swept clean...by Sawyer? The mirror at the back was dustless and fresh. There was no little pin set in the drawer bottom halfway back.

She opened the second. There were sponges, natural sea sponges, of different size and shape. There were pumice stones and cloth sachet bags, brightly colored satin tied with thin silk strings....

The third.

And there it was, shouting to the world, it seemed, begging to be pushed. A little ivory sliver, set at an angle in clean white wood, shining among bars of paper-covered soaps, all from England, heavily perfumed.... The mirror at this drawer's back, the mirror that hid a secret space behind, this mirror was clean, too, wiped just the other day with ammonia and water to keep it sparkling....

Audrey depressed the ivory pin.

The mirror, swinging up, pushed the bars of soaps in front of it. They skidded into their fellows. One spun, papered lime green....

Audrey bent to see what lay behind.

There was a book, a black book with a navy ribbon to mark the place left off. Audrey withdrew it, ran her hand over the gold-stamped lettering on the cover: My Diary, 1894.

It will be here, she thought. It will all be here. The last days of their honeymoon, the nights they made love. The promises he made to her.... I do not want to know!

But she kept the book, closed the mirror with two fingers that left their prints. The mirror clicked as it closed, almost a chuckle. Audrey pushed a bar of soap back over the pin and shut the drawer.

The diary was lightweight, its papers thin, edged in gold. The pages were covered with small, neat writing in ink bright and black, not yet faded, not yet tired. After all, the diary was only a year old.... And something had been written under almost every date up to Thursday, June 6, the day Virginia Lockholm died. After that the pages were blindingly white, dimly red lined, and, *of course*, blank, all blank....

Audrey carried the book to the chaise, bolstered her back with pillows, and opened where the ribbon marked the place....

I love him more than honor. We'll run away! Oh, *b*, I'll bind you to me so easily with a little golden chain. The baby is yours—that I can prove—the money is mine. You will never get away....

b....

It was ornate, the *b*, drawn in calligraphic script. It was lowercase, and there was a tail at the base of the spine, a curving tail that looked mischievous, devilish. The other words were written normally, the way Audrey and everyone else was taught. Only the *b* was fanciful, but it was obviously a *b*. It could not stand for Thorne Larcher

Cockburn; there was no *b* anywhere in that name. It was, it had to stand for ... John Bayard Lockholm III.

   Bay.
   Had to ... didn't it?
   Who else could it be ... ?

19

CELESTE. AUDREY WOULD GO to Celeste, tell her she, too, was to have a baby. Perhaps it would soften Celeste's indifference to her....

Audrey looked into the cheval glass. It is impossible, Mama, she said to the boudoir's reflection. It is impossible to stay in this great, gilded room quiet as a lady waiting for her husband to return. I am frightened and excited all at once. I want to shout, I want to run. I want a friend, a friend in this house I can confide in. A friend I can trust—

Audrey sighed. It was hard, here, to find her mother's eyes, to hear her mother's voice, wise within her. Josephine was far away from Whale's Turning. She did not know, had never in her lifetime known a mansion on Gilt Hill or the ways of rich people. Josephine was still downtown, on Bridge Street, watching, now, only Lawrence and Dolly tumbling together in their marriage bed.... And the mirror in its corner between the two long windows reflected such opulence, such stately living. The richness dulled Audrey's mother's eye, stilled a poor mother's voice....

Would Whale's Turning take Josephine from Audrey, too?

And yet if Audrey listened she could hear, faint inside her heart, her mother saying no. "No, daughter, don't go where you are not invited, where you know you are not wanted. Wait. Cling to your husband. Trust Bay, but do not trust Celeste...."

Audrey turned from the mirror, impatient. Her mother did not understand. She would go to Celeste. She would tell her secret. She would explain that Thorne had never loved her, little Audrey Smoke of Bridge Street. Thorne had been angry with her on Cliff Walk, not amorous. Audrey would say, "Let us be friends, Celeste. I would like it so...."

It was teatime, but Audrey did not want tea. Downstairs, no table had been set; the lower loggia was empty, and the music room. Celeste might be taking tea in her own room, the suite of rooms she shared with Thorne down the second-floor hall. In dusty-red slippers that matched her gown, Audrey climbed the stairs again, flowing hair as golden as the gilt upon the pillar heads. She was beyond Edmunda's room, its paneled door closed, the ivory handle locked down. For privacy...or to shut Audrey out?

Was Dr. Lake still there, holding the matriarch's hand perhaps, saying in his doctor's voice, "Be kind to your son's new bride, Edmunda. She is to be the mother of Bayard's child. Whale's Turning will have an heir and there will be, at least, a new generation of Lockholms...." And Edmunda, turning her face to an open window, where the wind lifted the folds of handwrought lace curtains, would respond, petulant, unforgiving, "But Virginia, Dr. Lake, where is Virginia? What has Bayard done with dear Virginia...and where is *Virginia's* little one...?"

To the left, down patterned India carpet, blue and silver and brown, which stretched soft and silent between high white walls and green marble urns spilling with freshly cut blue hydrangea. Once this carpet had laughed at Audrey, had screamed, "Get out! Get out! You are a town girl, you don't belong...."

I do belong, Audrey thought, as her feet passed lightly down the hall, treading on the carpet face. Here I belong and here I will stay, until death do us part....

Celeste's bedroom door. Audrey paused, hand on her heart. It raced beneath her hand. Why am I frightened, why am I such a scaredy-cat? *I'm* the mistress of this house, not Celeste, not even Edmunda. Me, Audrey Smoke Lockholm, I am first lady of Whale's Turning.

Audrey tapped upon the door. "Celeste—"

The knob turned in her hand, she was moving toward the doorway into a room of pink and cabbage rose, a room of satin flounce and taffeta ribbon, furniture French ecru,

slender legged, curved. An oblong room, shaped like a
tiara. A shadowed room: pink velvet drapery, heavy,
fringed in plaits of gold, pulled closed against the sun. A
quiet room, not seaside, quiet without the ever-soughing
sound of the sea. A warm room, too perfumed. A great
canopy bed, the posts of inlaid mother-of-pearl....

And Celeste. And Thorne. In the bed like Adam and Eve
in paradise.

He was above her, stretched like an archer's bow, naked
back sunned to brass. Paler buttocks, tight with muscle,
flexed, relaxed. Flexed, thrusted.... His chest, sun burnished, gleamed even in the shadowed room like finest
plate. He, wide shouldered, well made, leaned and lifted,
leaned and lifted upon Celeste below him, slight and silver, white thighs open, casually spread. Thorne's maleness, thick as a fireman's hose, stiff as new steel, had been
dipped in a golden dust, bespangled with twenty-four carat
fine-sieved powder. Thorne was bucking upon his wife,
showering her most private ebony hair with grains of gold
as he shook. And on his face, before it beheld Audrey
standing in the door, there was a look of adoration such as
Audrey had never seen except in pictures in books, great
painted oils of Renaissance saints.

Dumb, immobile, Audrey stared.

Thorne, aware, turned his black-curled head to look at
her. He did not interrupt his pleasure, nor utter a sound.
Only his face changed. From a man hypnotized with love
for a woman even while he enjoyed all lust with her, from
a face rapt in absolute infatuation, there came a ravaged
visage of narrow-eyed hate, as intense and openly naked as
the bodies of the lovers.

Audrey shrank away, closed the door between them. Her
knees were weak, as though she had been attacked. Not
from Thorne. Somehow she accepted his hatred of her as a
reasonable reaction to her presence in his life.

No, not from Thorne.

From Celeste....

From Celeste who had been lying as naked and uncaring
as a whore. Celeste, who had been as quiet as sculpture, as

undeterred from her activity as a flower pollinating is undisturbed by a witness. Celeste had been holding a great sheath of money in one hand—thousand-dollar bills they were—and with the other she was licking thumb and forefinger, and counting the money out loud, oblivious to Thorne's flash and heave though she was under him and engaged with him; oblivious, as though Thorne and what he was doing affected her in no way, in no place, and as though Audrey, as she watched immobilized in fascination, did not exist....

Below, faint, Audrey heard Bay's voice. He was home! She must go to him!

But she stayed where she was, leaning against the hallway wall. Perhaps, after all, Tory was right, and Dolly was right. Perhaps, after all, Josephine, who did not laugh in bed with a man, was wrong. Perhaps it was not enough to be comely and kind and loving to have a man love you, adore you for a lifetime; perhaps one had to *enchant, surprise, seduce....*

Audrey walked slowly back to her own room. I will wait, she thought. I will wait for him to come to me. And if he doesn't, after dinner, after he has had his brandy and gone to his bed, I will put on something simple and thin. I will slip into his bedroom silent as wind and tell him he is to be a father. Then I will agree to leave him, if that is what he wants. I will stand by his open window and hope the moon bares my body through my gown. My hair will be loose as leaves, and I will redden my lips. And if he insists, only if he insists, I will let him take me... and make him mine.

He was ascending the grand staircase. She stood beside her boudoir doors; heard his quick step. She waited, a hand upon the door pull. She saw his head, brown hair falling over his forehead like a boy's.

He saw her. He stopped. Great pain carved furrows in his face.

She opened her door. "Bay," she said, "come in."

Without a word, he came, pulling a cigar from his jacket pocket, peeling off the paper, snipping off the end.

She moved to close the fawn-and-golden draperies of a window. With her back to him, she said, "Do you love me, Bay?"

She turned to face him, fingers on the top button of her dress.

He was tired and worried and worn. She saw that. He sat on the chaise and lighted his cigar. "Smoke," he said, and smiled, and blew gray into the air. "My beautiful, beautiful Audrey Smoke."

She was unbuttoning her frock, letting it fall. "Please tell me," she said. "Answer me true."

"She haunts me, you know," he said. "Sometimes at night I think I hear her wailing. The room where she jumped is just above this one, did you know that? I feel responsible, you see. I feel guilty. I think in my heart the authorities are right. I killed Virginia. And now, having married you, maybe I am killing you. I didn't mean to, my wild girl of the rocks, please believe that. They say there is a curse upon the Lockholm line, Phineas Brown's revenge—"

Her chemise was slight; simple and thin. It would have to do. She was free of her slippers, she was removing her stockings.

"I am going to have a baby," she said.

"So soon?" He did not sound surprised. He sounded as weary as a hound ready to limp alone away to die in a favorite field.

"Do you love me, Bay?"

He was watching her, the cigar set down in a porcelain dish. She saw no passion in his eyes.

"I did, darling," he said, so tired. "I did."

It was terrible, the pain that twisted in her heart. *Did. Did.* Then no more. She had her answer.

"All right," she heard herself say, her voice calm and tired now, too. "All right, I'll go home. I'll set you free."

Naked now under thin silk, she crossed to him, held his head against her stomach, held it with hands that shook. Was this how Mildred Falk had felt, three times spurned?

How could Miss Falk have borne this pain three times and
lived . . . ?

Muffled, against her belly, she heard him: "I'm guilty,
you see, Audrey, darling. I am guilty as charged."

No.

The tears that leaped to her eyes blurred the peach and
gold of her room, the crystal hangings. The curtains danced
in a new, higher wind.

"Tell me," she said. "Tell me you love me as I love you.
Tell me I am the love of your life. Tell me, tell me. I know
you love me, and I know you did not kill Virginia."

His arms were around her then, tighter than the stays she
refused to wear—stays made of whale baleen, made from
whales slaughtered to slim a woman's waist. He was pulling her down upon him on the chaise, and holding her tight,
so tight.

"I love you more than life," he said. "Since that first
night, I have adored you."

There. He had said it. And where now was the joy? Why,
now, still the killing pain under her heart? Why, now, still,
the *fear*?

"And I love you, my husband. I will never leave you
now. Not ever. No matter what. We can leave here if you
want, run away, be poor—"

He was pushing the silk above her knees, beyond her
thighs, above her belly. He was licking her stomach, the
depression that had tied her to her mother in her womb. His
tongue was hot and moist, gave strength as it sapped it.

"I asked Virginia for a divorce," he was saying, his lips
against her womb. "Demanded a divorce from her. For my
sake, for my happiness. But you, my love, I meant to set
you free for yours."

The shimmy was off now, over her head and gone, into
a nowhere place where she and he were not. He was kissing
her throat, her mouth, her ears, her eyes, tongue-warm
kisses that fired her body and flamed her brain with colors
peacock-vivid, as heart stopping as sunset. He was stroking her breasts as though they were treasures being buffed;
warm hands, strong warm hands.

"Yes, I do love you, my dearest, my darling—" He was whispering into her skin and her skin was singing, thrilling to the heat of him, the feel of him, the sound . . .

Somehow, his clothes were opening. It was her hands fumbling, frenzied, pulling at knots and buttons, linen and silk falling away to that nowhere place. And then he moved and she moved and they were as raptors, plummeting, falling, falling free together, and the wind flew high over the sound. . . .

And in the hall outside, Edmunda crept and called, over and over, to Virginia.

Downstairs, the butler, Fisher, stately, stepped into the little elevator to summon, from their respective activities, the Lockholm family to their dinner. . . .

20

ALABASTER McGREGOR NURSED sweet sherry and picked at Louisiana shrimp and watercress, waiting for his luncheon companion. Mrs. Burton VanVoorst, at her behest—Victoria VanVoorst, eager aspirant for society's golden clasp, verrrry nouveau, verrrry riche. Suspiciously secretive about her past. Née June—if you believe that, stand on your head this minute—from nowhere. Was it New York she admitted to? Was it New Orleans she tried to hide? He was having her investigated, traced by a professional sleuth. Ally McGregor would come to know all that the chorus girl chose to hide, in time.... Father a truck driver, probably, something like that, and mother a serving woman.... Nothing at all to be ashamed of, unless, that is, one chose to be ashamed. Then you were vulnerable, then... Alabaster smiled tenderly at a shrimp, trucked in ice all the way from torrid little Tory's wrong-tracks hometown. Ah, yes. He bit; snapped the flesh in two, then engulfed the tail end, juiced with lemon, redolent with Tabasco. Ah, yes, that does nicely. Thank-you very much....

Of course the beauty would be late. And of course Alabaster was early, *in place* so he could watch the woman enter, see how she was received by social Newport—his set could be catty; he loved their foibles so. He would note by whom she was admired, who turned her head the other way. All grist for a journalist's mill, grinding slowly, grinding fine.... This was how he liked to spend his days; in control, *in pursuit*, observing, unobserved. Putting together the tiny slips in conduct—*the revelatory action*—that the darlings did not want him to see, did not want him to *act upon*....

Earlier this morning, in response to a call from Audrey Lockholm, Alabaster had driven to Whale's Turning and taken away from those beautiful, innocent hands, Virginia Lockholm's diary.

Ha, ha, HAH!

Audrey had said, so earnestly, "You are the only one who can help me, Ally, and help Bay. You're the investigative reporter. You know so much. Here is all Virginia's life during the year of her death. Here is her infatuation with someone not her husband, not Bay. It cannot be Bay, Ally. You do believe that, don't you . . . ?"

Oh, indeed, he'd assured her, all wolf-fang smiles. "Oh, yes, my dear, whatever you want me to say. Just give me that diary . . . there's a good little lamb . . . ."

"I don't know who it would be," Audrey had gone on, intense, anxious. "Virginia uses only the small letter *b* to refer to him. But if Virginia was . . . was killed . . . was not a suicide, it must be her lover, mustn't it? Or the lover's wife, if he had one. Maybe . . . oh, maybe a hundred things, Ally, you must find out! Whoever *b* is, he did not come to mourn at Virginia's funeral . . . or did he? Could he have? You were there. I set the flowers in place before the church service, and there was no one. There was the coffin unprotected, the body abandoned, it seemed to me, in its fine sealed box. I knew nothing at the time about Virginia. I was only the flower girl hired to place the baskets in. But it was strange that morning in Trinity Church. There was no custodian, no husband mourning, no family, Lockholm or Stotesbury—"

"Mr. and Mrs. Stotesbury fell to a virus some years before Bayard and Virginia married," Ally told her. "A syphilitic virus, I believe, quite virulent, quickly fatal. All hushed up, of course, for the daughter's sake. No fun bruiting that kind of thing about. Adam Stotesbury was enamoured of a mentally unstable female of exceptional allure and promiscuity—you don't need to know her name, she's out of the country now, poor thing. When he wouldn't leave his wife for her, she contracted the disease, purposefully—don't look so shocked, Cinderella, your education's just begun—she passed it along to him, and he, unknowing, gave it to his wife. The woman, unrepentant, then galloped off to Europe where she took the cure and married a German prince. As far as I know she is still there, living happily ever after. How much of this unfortunate family history little Virginia knew, I've no idea. She was a teenager at the time, blessedly in France at school. She had no other close family. There are some distant relatives out West, as I recall. But they did not attend Virginia's marriage or funeral. Probably thought it would take too long to make the trip East by covered wagon...."

Audrey had not smiled at his flippancy. She had listened and then gone back to her subject. A little terrier, Audrey Lockholm; not a bad thing for a woman in her position to be....

"You see, Ally," she'd said. "You know all these things. Use them, please, with this diary. Use them and find out the truth of what happened to Virginia. She speaks of her passion for the man she calls *b*. She says the child she was carrying was his. It can't be Bay, Ally. She gave her lover little golden gifts—here is a letter from a Signore Rivalini of Rome. He made jewelry for her. And Bay, when I showed him, says Virginia never gave any jewelry to him. Only the jewelry bills, Bay said. He paid, you see, Ally, for her gifts to her lover. Find him please, oh please. Find the murderer of Virginia and set Bay free."

"My darling girl," he'd purred, liver-spotted fingers sliding firmly around the black, gilt-paged book. Slipping it, even as he murmured, into his lap, into his jacket pocket. "If ever you did a clever thing, you've done it now. I'm on the case as of this moment, and every waking moment to come. Bay will be cleared, his reputation restored, you will be happy, it's as good as done...."

How he itched, now, to pore like a *dedicated monk* over those ink-filled pages. How he wanted to *know*, know the pallid, dull Virginia—pretty enough, God yes, but a dyed-in-the-wool drawing room yawn. Heavens, how had Bayard endured that blank expression day after day—night after night!—that humorless soul interested only in the weight of her hostess's dining forks or the number of Worth gowns in her upstairs armoires. Thank God women were beautiful; they were so often too silly to be borne.

He remembered, once, before Virginia and Bayard married, while they were still in that delicate, undeclared, time of courting, a garden fete at Beechwood. Wanting to know her better, he had sought Virginia Stotesbury out. She was in the side-court rose garden in a dismal flouncy print, huge skirted and bonneted to match. He remembered thinking the dear really should wear simpler frocks. She was young, but she had not the merriment or lightness of youth. Vertical lines would have emphasized her sober beauty, obscured her obvious lack of frivolity and wit, so necessary to a woman still unclaimed, unspoken for. No, Bayard had never gone off the diving board for that one that Alabaster ever saw. It was Edmunda who doted on Virginia; Edmunda, now he thought about it, had been the one in love. Virginia had been a woman's woman, a mother's perfect prospect for daughter-in-law. Interested in little. Passionate, Alabaster would have thought, about almost nothing at all. And not intellectually deep. Oh no, no. . . .

He had come upon her bent over rose heads.

"And what are you doing, you rose, yourself?" he had asked, debonair as always, gently probing—as ever.

"I'm counting Caroline's rose crop, Mr. McGregor. I'm up to four hundred seventeen, and not a blowsy bloom among them. Really, Mrs. Astor's gardener is to be congratulated." And then she had continued, unself-conscious, "four hundred eighteen, four hundred nineteen. . . ."

And *there* you had Virginia Stotesbury, he had thought, dismissing her that day with a shudder. But again . . . he tapped his jacket pocket, drummed eager fingers against the solid feel of the diary within. But again, perhaps, as had been the case before . . . once or twice . . . perhaps he had been wrong, and there were hidden gullies to the girl, nice dark crevices of spice and sin.

Alabaster hoped so.

Over by the Casino doorway, the maître d', Orestes, golden curled, corseted—still handsome, lucky dog— fanned his pile of bills of fare. It was Alabaster's "Alert" signal. Mrs. VanVoorst's coach had drawn up to the side- walk.

Dear Orestes. He was one of Alabaster's best spies-in- place. Orestes had recently discovered—uncovered—the blissfully staggering fact that Suzanna Reed Peerce, Mrs. Percival Peerce, was not conducting herself at all as she should as a new widow.

Alabaster, after his terrible failure to gain ascendancy over the woman, had had to leave Dove alone for the nonce. He meant to bide his time, be a perfect angel. At- tend Nicola and Rolf's wedding, write drippingly sweet copy...note how nobly Dove mourned.... And then make, in time, a new rapprochement. So Alabaster had not known, until Orestes had told him, that Dove Peerce, in her grief—oh yes, her grief, thank-you very much!—had gone on a rampage of unconventionality. She was over the moon, kicking over the traces, creating a scandal all her own wherever she went—and she was going everywhere, which was a right royal scandal right there.

Imagine. The doyenne of Newport. The perfect one.

Orestes said she was out to dinner almost every night, always in black—of course always in black, but black of lissome satin, black of winding silk, black sinuous as nightgown, black cut to show inches of her ivory breasts! And she was wearing her diamonds, her rubies and her pearls. She was laughing, taking champagne, dancing with Newport's single gentlemen! No one knew what to do. She was being forgiven for now, her reputation and the idea of madness through sorrow excusing her. But heads were shaking, mouths were mercilessly chattering.... Alabaster shivered with delight.

How wonderful was Dove Peerce. Alabaster wished, again, he was a normal man. How he wanted to marry her, to stroll through life with that exciting, gorgeous, *surpris-*

ing woman on his arm; at his side. What a couple they would be! Dearest Dove, his only rival, his only equal; perfect so long. And now, like a reformed drunkard, fallen off the wagon. And Alabaster—damn it all to hell!—Alabaster must tiptoe in her presence, mustn't remark one little thing. Well, he would find a way back into her good graces. Perhaps, through the ravishing and greedy Mrs. VanVoorst, even arouse Dove's jealousy. Tory VanVoorst obviously wanted him to champion her.... Why else had she called this tête-à-tête? Terrible Tory from nowhere wanted to make the run...wanted to unseat Mrs. Peerce from the precious queenship of Newport....

Oh yes, he led an interesting life, an amusing life. Thankyou for asking, thank-you so *very* much....

He finished his sherry, lifted two fingers so that, by the time Mrs. VanVoorst was threaded through the tables by Orestes, there would be champagne just poured and waiting, teeth-chillingly cold and fizzing. And there was the camellia waiting to be admired. A dewy, plump, darkleaved camellia with which Alabaster had adorned her service plate, fresh from that hardworking woman, Mrs. Herman Maddley of Gardenflowers. Rosemary, that was her name. A woman like Rosemary, easily manipulated, cheaply ensnared: she could prove useful in future. No beauty, but nice looking, with her glasses off. Yes, Rosemary Maddley was a woman with ambition to climb if ever Alabaster McGregor had seen one, though of course she did not have the money to play. She worked for hers, too bad, too bad.... As Alabaster always said to merchant wives, "Now don't despair, my precious, where there's a will, there's a way.... Only let us hope the will has lots of U.S. Steel in it, ha ha...."

Ha, ha, ha.

Alabaster stood. "You ravishment," he said, accepting Tory's extended gloved hand. "You do me such an honor, sit down, sit down. Orestes, you have outdone yourself, escorting Mrs. VanVoorst to me. Your finest deed, without a doubt. You must drink champagne with us right now.

We will celebrate this moment, this significant moment, we three.''

Orestes, a star in his part, bowed, overcome.

Tory took up her glass, noting the lush, richly scented flower at her intended place. Careful, little girl, she cautioned herself. You're in the deep water now and playing for keepsies. Bigger fish, clever fish. Careful now.... But you can do it.

So let's go get 'em....

Blushing prettily, she drank.

"OH, POOP, MOTHER, don't you know *anything*? It's all over town!''

"Hush, Nicola, marchionesses do not bark. Marchionesses do not say 'poop.'''

In white-stockinged feet, solid on a brocade footstool, Nicola barked happily on. "A joust, Mother! Have you ever heard anything so heavenly? A medieval joust!''

"The parties of people like the VanVoorsts, Nicola dear, do not interest or concern us. We have our own celebrations, of which your wedding is the next. Now do let Priscilla measure, or you'll look crooked walking down the aisle, and how would that be? Stand tall and steady, now. Do not slump.''

And why did she want to cry, sitting in Nicola's yellow bedroom, with so much yet to do...? Why did she, who took no alcohol, not even dinner wine, for days on end, want—right now—to be roaringly drunk? It was not even teatime, she had finished her Spartan luncheon less than an hour ago. What was it she had eaten? Oh yes, a caviar omelet and good coffee, coffee strong enough to drown the taste of cyanide, if she'd had any, if she'd wanted any—

"And silent,'' said Nicola. "You'd like me silent, too, wouldn't you, and obedient and comme il faut and, and...what else? Oh yes, thin.''

Dove, in new hunter-green-and-black, exhaled through

lips shined with a thin, clear wax. "You are to be a marchioness, Nicola. I would like you dignified, most of all. You will be a married woman, a royal—"

"I am dignified, Mother, you just don't notice. And, yes, I'm high-spirited, too. I'm American, don't forget that— new stuff. Dandy new blood, Rolf says.... Listen, Mother, your best friend Ally McGregor is involved, so the party is certainly acceptable. And everyone's dying to go. Caroline Astor has already ordered her Queen Guinevere gown, hasn't she, Priscilla?"

The dressmaker, chalking button points, nodded. "But not from me, she is not smart, that one. Mrs. Astor is using her New York couturier. She'll be sorry!"

"It's a costume lawn fete, Mother; we're to dress in our 'kingdom colors,' like damsels of old. The men will be as knights. They will joust for our favor, flying our scarves from their lances.... Oh, it's too exciting, you must want to go, you've always been mad for a costume party. And since you've not been staying home, and my wedding's going off on time, don't give me your 'I'm in mourning' excuse. You're not in mourning, you've become controversial since Father passed, for the first time in your life. A merry widow in capital letters. Clarissa Rails was full of it yesterday in the Casino with the Benson-Wards. Rolf and I overheard. Clarissa said you danced too long with her husband at Greenscote on Sunday, and she was right, you did. But you also danced too long with Judge Godfrey and Dr. Lake, and who knows who else.... I'm not scolding, Mother, I understand you're out of your mind with grief. And Father would want you to be happy. But if we're going to talk about what's proper—"

Dove did not look at her daughter. She looked at her daughter's reflection in a bureau mirror of silver bamboo. Yes, she had been head-over-tea-kettle lately. She missed Percy abysmally, more than she would have thought possible. She missed Graf Elliott, too, something she would not have believed. For the first time in a long time, Dove needed something. Needed someone. And there was no one to whom she could turn. No one to lean on, no one to trust. Clarissa Rails—horrors, no. Clarissa told *everything*, even her age for heaven's sake, even how much money Tripp had.... Not Graf anymore, that was entirely over. Graf had quietly asked the archbishop for a transfer. Judith was ecstatic, naturally.... Judith had never liked the party pace of Newport. Dove hoped Graf Elliott was sent to New Zealand, the only place on earth nobody ever went to... And not Nicola, self-absorbed Nicola. Nicola had never understood her mother, never tried to. Nicola was daddy's girl all the way.... And not Alabaster, that weasel. He had tried to halter her, tried to make her his puppet, able to pull her strings through vicious blackmail—tried and failed, thanks to Percy dying as he did....

Dove smiled vaguely at the room, the filtered sunlight. Idly, she stroked the cool cushioned arm of the wicker chair in which she sat. She tried to tune out Nicola, nattering, nattering. She wished she was on a little tropical island, lost to the civilized world. She wished she was almost naked and her hair was python-long. She wished she was wrapped in the arms of a handsome stranger whose name she would never need to know....

Nicola was still talking, while Priscilla tucked and pinned and pulled the wedding fabric. Beautiful fabric. Nicola—almost—beautiful in it.

Terrible Nicola. Dove was too old now, husbandless now. She could never have another child, a better....

"Ally is to be the town crier for the thing, Mother. He's so excited. He will hand deliver every invitation—they are to be scrolls, written in gold, in Old English runes, hand lettered by a professional calligrapher...Audrey Lockholm is helping with that. Alabaster will ride around to the cottages on a golden horse. They really exist, these golden horses. They come from out West—and I thought Celeste had had her grays dyed for her wedding, silly me! The Mexicans, or the Aztecs, developed them. They're called palominos, they breed true, always hair of solid gold, and their manes and tales are flaxen. They're not fast yet, of

course, they've been bred for show, not speed, but I can't
wait to see Alabaster on one. Think of it, Mother, that
fussy old bachelor all dolled up in courtier's breeches, riding to our door on a golden steed, bearing our invitation to
the joust!''

"We can't go, Nicola, and that's that. We've not been
socially introduced to the VanVoorsts, and that woman,
you know, is up to her neck in Bay Lockholm's murder
trial. Now don't be tiresome. Isn't marrying Rolf enough
excitement?''

She wanted to hurt her daughter, deny her daughter....
Why did she want to do that ...?

"Rolf and I have discussed this, Mother, we're not nin-
nies, we're adults. But we don't intend to be stodgy old
rearguard. We'll live in England some of the time, and the
smart set there, Rolf says, is very much like me—full of
catnip, though they are more pretentious, Rolf says. And
the rest of the year we'll be here with you, Mother dearest,
in New York and Newport. I'll be a marchioness, yes, all
right, but I'll still be me, whether I'm abroad or at home.
And everyone will approve of me. Rolf says the English
dote on American heiresses, particularly when they're as
rich as I am. So I'm not to worry, and you're not to worry.
My future happiness is assured.''

Priscilla pulled at a length of heavy ivory satin. "Pretty,
so pretty...I'd like a big bow here, madam.'' She patted
Nicola's rear, showing Dove the proper place. "A big flat
bow, the satin draped, lifted in front, so. It will make the
waist appear as nothing, it will subdue the hips, here—''

Nicola peered into the mirror to see. "Rolf likes my hips,
Priscilla. He says they make him dizzy. So it's all right if
they show.''

"Nicola,'' said Dove, "you're just trying to shock. Show
me, Priscilla, let's see how it looks.''

"Yes, ma'am.''

"I am not,'' said Nicola. "Ask him then, if you don't
believe me.'' She lifted her voice to shout out the windows,
"Rolfo, oh, Rolfie, come here, come here!''

"Oooh, you can't. Not in your wedding dress," said Priscilla. "That would be very bad luck."

Dove moved to the window, graceful, quick. Rolf was in the training yard, beyond the stable, riding the bay mare, Rapunzel, over a set of jumps. He hadn't heard. He was too far away. He was talking to the mare, intent on their form, the horse and him together. He was a handsome boy. He would make love like that, Dove thought, he would make love the way he rides, intense but controlled. A stickler for form and detail. He would be a good lover. He was older than Nicola. . . .

She turned back to Nicola, pink and busty in her tight satin corset. Nicola swelled with flesh; young, plump flesh, firm as muscle, flesh that resisted being pinned into a wedding gown.

"He's handsome, your Rolf," she said to her daughter. "You're a lucky girl."

Nicola was too young, Dove thought, lust had not moistened her thighs or stiffened her nipples or weakened the walls of her belly. Nicola loved, but she did not yet know what love was all about. If she was lucky, she would never know; would have no reason to ever be. . . unfaithful. . . .

Nicola was shrugging, hugging herself.

"No, no," said Priscilla. "Arms at rest, please."

"He's fun," said Nicola, "that's what I like most, Mother. He's thrilling. Just think, Kenya for our honeymoon. His idea! A month in the bush after big game, and then Scotland and the monster of Loch Ness, and grouse shooting—"

Dove lowered her eyes at the thought. "And then home to Denton, darling, and London and the queen."

"And you, Mother. You'll be waiting for us, in Rolf's house, won't you? You'll do the season with us there."

"Yes, Nicola. I'm looking forward to it, and I know Percy would want me to be with you, your first year. You'll need a guide, darling, someone to steady you. You're still too. . ."

"Wild, Mother? Is that what you're afraid to say?"

"Uninhibited, dear."

"That's what Rolf loves. I can't change that. Oh, I'll grow gentler, more mellow as I age, but—just stop right there, Priscilla, I don't want a train. They're boring and clumsy. The hem should just sweep the ground, because I'm going to dance and dance the day I marry him. Dance my fool head off, and drink champagne, and be passionately deflowered in the hay shed, next to Rapunzel. We've already planned that out."

"Yes, Miss Peerce," said Priscilla, her mouth around pins, her ears alert to everything. What a lot she'd have to tell....

"And I want to go to the VanVoorst joust, Mother. I truly do, and so does Rolf. They're giving away an English hunter, Mother, as first prize—a great gray! Rolf will win it for me, I just know he will. I want to go, I'm dying to go, and I will go, whether you go with us or not. So there."

Ah. Now that Nicola knew the contents of Percy's will, now that Nicola knew the extent of her wealth, her power. Now that Nicola was getting married and didn't need her mother's blessing any more....

Dove said, "We haven't been invited yet, ungrateful child. Why don't we wait until our invitations come and discuss it then?"

Nicola nodded, distracted by the bow Priscilla had artfully constructed and was pinning to the back of the dress. "Oh, Priscilla, it's pretty. I do like it very much. What do you think, Mother?"

"Very pretty indeed, my darling."

Dove was looking out the window again. Percival's automobile was parked beside the stable. Percival's burial car. The man was coming to take it away today, to replace with another, a gray one, much smarter, with a movable gray top. A new motorcar for Dove, in her color.

Percy would want her to have it, wouldn't he...?

She wanted to go downstairs and sit in the library again, sit in the room Percy ruined while he was ill. She was hav-

ing it redecorated, English country chintz this time, no
more of that masculine-clubby kind of thing.... But nothing had been touched yet, and the room still smelled of him.
She could almost hear him there still, see him...talk to him.
She wanted to tell him, fiercely she wanted to tell him,
"You brought it on yourself, it was all your fault, not mine.
You loved Nicola more. And I, who worked every moment of a lifetime to make you love me only, I lost out to a
freckle-faced, heavy-footed elephant of a girl who never for
an hour schemed to earn your love. Because she didn't have
to, Percy, darling. Because she had only to breathe for you
to give her your heart and half your fortune. It wasn't good
of you, Percy, it wasn't right. You brought my infidelity
upon us all yourself. And then you died to spite me, to
make me feel guilty, almost as guilty as Bay Lockholm
choking and pushing his Vir—"

Handkerchief to mouth, Dove exited her daughter's
room.

"Poor Mother," said Nicola to Priscilla. "She adored
Father, and now she's suffering so."

Priscilla fussed with the gown's new bow and kept her
thoughts to herself. "Poor Mrs. Peerce," she echoed duti-
fully.

EVEN ROLF, Lord Pomeroy, out in the training ring, heard
the shot.

Nicola was first to the library, fastest down the heart-
shaped staircase in stocking feet. Nevvers was second, in
the pantry counting out the silver pieces to be shined, called
to the side door by a tradesman's knock. Priscilla, shaking, spread the satin bow upon the bed cover, to keep it
from crushing, before she followed. Rolf had to dismount
and tie the mare to a rail, and sprint a quarter mile of lawn.

It was Nicola who hurtled through the library door to
find her mother behind the rolltop desk, holding one of
Percival's old dueling pistols.

Dove was standing, silver hair a perfect turban, not a curl
out of place. She was facing the open window where Per-

cival Peerce had stood and watched his wife—*unfaithful wife, drifting homeward, all dishabille, her lover's seed still hot upon her thighs*. Dove was staring at the curtain Percival had clutched in his death grip. She was laughing, too bright eyed, hysterical.

"I missed, Nicola," Dove said, shaking the pistol like a parasol. "I tried, by God I did, I tried and I missed! So let me take this candid opportunity to tell you that I have never liked you. Not ever, not while I was carrying you, not when you were born or growing up, not this afternoon. And that, no matter whom you're about to marry, you are not chic. You are much too fleshy to be considered chic."

And then Nevvers was there, and Rosalind, Dove's maid, and Priscilla, and Rolf, in through the open window casement.

"Yes, Nevvers," Dove said, as the butler rushed in. She replaced the pistol on its rack. "Yes, what's all the fuss? What is it?"

Nevvers collected himself. "The motorman, madam," he said, aligning his sleeve cuffs to cover his nervousness. "A Mr. Thompson, madam, here to exchange the automobile."

"Thank you, Nevvers, will you have him join me outside by the stable? Oh, and have that pistol cleaned, won't you, it needs it. Excuse me, everyone."

Beautiful, languorous, perfectly in control, Dove left the room. The sweet scent of her perfume lingered behind her, mingled with the fresh, raw smell of gunfire.

"Isn't she wonderful," one of them said.

Nicola sighed. I get it from her, she thought, my fire and my spunk, not from Father, after all. . . .

"Nevvers," Nicola said, "please attend to the pistol. Priscilla, let's finish our work. Rolf, I shall see you at tea."

"Nick, you're a marvel. You do me so proud. For this one moment, I must win you that gray!"

Rolf blew her a kiss, on his way out to play again.

Nicola smiled as she ascended the stairs, back to her bedroom, tagged by a silent Priscilla. Rolf could play, but she had work to do. Yes, her mother *was* magnificent. Ah, how Nicola admired her.... If she could love Rolf as exquisitely as her mother had loved her father. If she and Rolf could be as happy, as perfect, as perfectly in love....

It was something to shoot for.

Nicola smiled at her pun, her first witticism worthy of her mother.

21

THE TRIAL HAD OPENED, in Providence. The *Daily Whirl* did not mention the fact, Alabaster McGregor making all editorial decisions now; Alabaster McGregor leaving to other papers the juiciest scandal in his town.

"It's early days yet, Audrey," he said into the telephone. "They're still choosing a jury. Nothing really to say, nothing vital to report. The whole thing can still be aborted . . . pray for a miracle, dear girl. Pray we find solid evidence of the other man."

"Have you read all the diary, Ally?"

Audrey was in her bedroom; she had Tory's invitations to print. It would keep her occupied by day while Bay was gone, while Bay sat at a great, scarred table flanked by lawyers, watched by the curious, condemned by the quick to judge. "I do not want you there," he'd said. "Not now. Now is not important. Once the trial proper opens, I will want you close, I will want to see you there for me. We'll lunch together. We'll hold hands. We'll take a room in a hotel close to the courthouse. We'll make love. . . ."

She did not want to go to Providence. She did not want to cling to him in a room rented by the day, the week, to strangers. She did not want to spend their last days in an alien place, in a room that would not remember them amid anonymous furnishings, between travelers' linen, rumpled and washed a hundred times for a hundred different salesmen and their doxies. . . . She did not want to sit, expressionless, while lawyers rustled papers and exclaimed for the world to hear that her husband was a murderer. She had to think. . . . She had to act. Was there anything she would not do to save him?

No.

In a moment. As soon as she could, she would take up the pendant and match it against the floor plan of Virginia's bedroom on the landing of the staircase. And if it fitted, what would it prove? If it was a perfect golden miniature, after all, there was no name to link Thorne to it, no word but her own how *she* had come to possess it....

"Dear girl, are you listening?"

"I'm sorry, Ally, my mind drifted. You were saying..."

"I'm saying that I agree with you, you are a clever girl. There was a lover. She seems quite thrilled with him, too. She calls him, time and again, her 'black-sexed lion.' Imagine! I never would have thought it, but demure Virginia had decidedly hot knickers. Oh, very hot indeed."

"Who, Ally? Do you know who?"

"Ah, the nub of the matter."

His voice was light, flyaway, like the flip of his slender liver-spotted hands. But that is just his way, she thought, he is on our side. Of course Alabaster McGregor was on Bay's side. Why wouldn't he be...?

"But you don't know who yet," she said, uneasy with the heavy weight against her ear, uncomfortable speaking into a flared flower of a mouthpiece. It was the telephone that frightened her, not Alabaster. It was the telephone she did not trust....

"Well, there's *b* for Burton Regis VanVoorst," she heard him say, as though he were lounging beside her, having invaded her bedroom, invisible but loud.... "But I've had a chat with Victoria—I'm so glad you like her, Audrey, because I like her, too. I may take her on, my new patron. Isn't she fun?"

"Yes, Ally. What did Tory say?"

"It seems that last June she was monopolizing much of—to use her expression—'Burtykin's' free time. But she admits she's not sure. VanVoorst was a rake in his single days, a man of sumptuous appetites and vitality. Well, what else is new, I said, of course, dear Burton still is. And yes, she says, she thought it was just barely possible. So she asked him about it. He says absolutely no. Never looked the woman's way. Never interested. He considers himself a man of character—don't we all, my dear?—says he never, even in his wildest youth, ever looked at a married woman, and the thought of cuckolding a friend is absolutely anathema to him. What a fellow. Sterling as they come. I'm putting him up for my club.''

"He's not the type," Audrey said, "to be seduced by 'little golden gifts.' ''

"Yes, there's that, too, of course. Burt VanVoorst gives to women, he doesn't take.''

"Then you're still uncertain, Ally, the puzzle's not solved.''

Audrey knew how to solve it. The pendant and its chain lay on a thin saucer on her bed pillow, palest yellow porcelain rimmed in a lifted gold. Unsurprising to her now, the rich plate. Accepted now. Now she understood that everything that was, could be well made or ill made. The tiniest saucer. The grandest house. A love affair.... But she needed more than understanding.... She needed a *name*, she needed *proof incontrovertible*....

Audibly, she sighed.

"Don't worry, boss's wife. Alabaster McGregor, Newport's top investigator, is on the job.''

"Alabaster. Bay sits in court today. They are naming jurors to the case.''

"And I gallop to the rescue. Au revoir, madam.''

"Goodbye, Ally.''

And with the replacing of the telephone receiver, it was time. Time for her to rise and prove her mettle, prove she was worth marrying, worth loving, worth growing old with, worth mourning over if it came to that....

She picked up the chain and pendant, held them in her fist. At first the gold was cold, but quickly the metal warmed to her own heat. Capricious metal, taking on the properties of wherever it found itself. Fickle metal, warming to anyone who held it. Embraced it. An eternal metal, used to being handed around, handed over, because it outlasted its possessors and warmed, easily, to this new hand and that one and the one after that....

She would go now, pendant in hand, and check its design with the floor plan of Virginia's bedroom, drawn to scale and stretched and framed and hanging, by her request, above the landing of the staircase.

It was not yet noon and the house was quiet. Celeste was gone, as usual, house calling and to luncheon. Would Thorne be with her? Sometimes she took him and sometimes she did not. Thorne had an office now, on the waterfront. He was having boats built, heavy ferry boats. He was planning schedules, lining up captains. Within a year Sea Trains would be a reality, all Thorne's dreams come true....

Edmunda, these hot summer days, sat out on the lawn in white wicker. Her maid, Zella, attended her; read to her. Dr. Lake visited almost every day. Edmunda, Audrey had been told, seemed most interested in watching the passersby on Cliff Walk, open to the public; whoever wished to roam that way from one end of Newport to the other. Sometimes Edmunda called out to a man she did not know. She waved and beckoned him in through the break in Whale's Turning's long stone wall. "Jeoffry, is that you? Come in...come on in, it's been so long!" None, so far, had responded. If any did, Zella was there to chase them politely away.

Once, Zella told Audrey, a woman stood where the stone wall parted. She was an ordinary woman—"not a lady, ma'am, and a foreigner"—and well past middle age. Spanish, Zella thought, or Mexican. "Black-eyed, Mrs. Lockholm. Swarthy skinned." She was stout, with thick dark hair, braided in a plait, heavily threaded with white. She was commonly dressed, said Zella, and she was with a pretty young woman, Spanish, too, or Mexican. Perhaps a daughter, though much finer, tall and slender. But like the older woman, poorly dressed. "Ragamuffins, ma'am. You know ragamuffins?"

While the young woman hung back and kept to the Cliff Walk, the older woman came forward and planted herself and stared. For a long time she stared upon the broad green lawns of Whale's Turning. For a long time she looked upon Edmunda Lockholm, in flowing afternoon dress and her always pearls. Finally the woman had turned away, limping a little, down the rocks. And Zella had relaxed. Later she asked the young Mrs. Lockholm if sir would buy his mother a dog. It would be a companion, Zella said. It would discourage the unwanted.

Bay bought an English bulldog, just a pup; all wrinkles and loose brindle skin. The puppy nosed now on the lawn, at Edmunda's feet, tearing at a slipper. Sometimes the matriarch seemed to know it was there and would ask to hold it on her lap, her dress protected by a towel. Edmunda Lockholm did not seem to mind that the puppy chewed on Lockholm pearls, growling happily, sloppy with saliva. But Zella did. Zella covered the pearls with a bib, and when that wasn't enough, she removed all jewelry, even Mrs. Lockholm's rings, before she handed the squirming, eager beastie to her mistress.

Edmunda named the bulldog "Breaker," for a wild wave—for its disposition, Bayard said. Zella was kind to it, but remarked to Audrey she had hoped for a greater creature, a grown, trained animal. A bloodhound, Zella said, or a mastiff was what she'd had in mind. A dignified dog. A protection.

"Breaker will grow very quickly, Zella," Audrey said. "And he will grow up loving Mother. That is what Bay hopes."

"Yes, ma'am," said Zella. "I guess he's better than nothin'. Thank sir for me, and for Mrs. Lockholm. But it's a handful, is Breaker, and no help a-tall."

Audrey paused now on the upper loggia and looked down upon the lawn. There was her mother-in-law, dozing in the shade of a blue umbrella. There was Zella, unconcernedly reading aloud beside her. And there was the puppy, slipper abandoned, sleeping on its side, its tight fat tummy glowing in the sun and looking, from Audrey's height and distance, like the largest of Mrs. Lockholm's precious pearls.

Then Audrey turned with a sweep of white skirt, and in stocking feet so as not to be heard by the servants, she hurried down the hall to the staircase.

The grand hall was empty. The servants in the kitchen. Fisher, somewhere, about his work.

Pendant in hand, Audrey moved down the upper branch of stair to the landing. The stained glass glistened. The floor plans seemed to quiver in the brightness of the light.

She found the bedroom, her bedroom now, in an instant. Biting a lip, she set the pendant against the place. And yes, the shape of the gold followed the contours of Virginia's boudoir, and the fine silver lines marked where the double doors stood, and the bathroom door, and the line of ocean-facing windows. And, oh yes, the faceted ruby, cut in the shape of a heart, exactly matched in scale and dimension the great long bed....

Virginia's lover had been Thorne Cockburn! Thorne, before Celeste, long before; while courting Audrey, had danced with others. Opened his mouth to others. Done more. Much more....

As Thorne, pledged to Brigit Norris, had come one day to Gardenflowers, to buy his fiancée a bouquet. Had come, had turned from Brigit at the sight of Audrey's face—

"You were the fairest flower in the shop, Aud. And you were built like a racing sloop, graceful and strong and as beautiful as a swan. Oh, you were the instant end of Brigit Norris, Aud, and there was nothing I could do about it except—"

He had bought the posies, then presented them to her, Audrey Smoke, shop girl. He hadn't then, even known her name. She had been delighted; he was handsome, modest, overcome by Audrey's charm. He had asked to call upon her that night, and she had said yes.... And a week later Brigit Norris, confronted with Thorne's rejection, threatened to drink silver slipper polish before his eyes—he said. He took the bottle away with him, and Brigit Norris, before the month was out, was gone, married a dairy farmer in Connecticut.

Audrey had felt no pity.

At the time she had only felt triumphant, already, by then, in love; captivated by a dashing Thorne who promised, if they worked hard, a good life. He a sea captain with a thriving business. She, the captain's wife.

And even then, in those early days, Thorne was cheating on Audrey as he'd cheated on Brigit. Thorne was charming Virginia Stotesbury Lockholm during their sailing lessons together, and she was writing to Italy—to Rome!—for "little golden gifts" to bind her beach boy, betrothed to another.... It was hard to grasp. He had seemed so desperately in love with her, Audrey Smoke. He had been obsessed with his work, their dream.... And then, after Virginia...had he spurned Virginia, too? After Virginia—Virginia come and gone without Audrey ever knowing!—after Virginia, there had been Celeste....

And Audrey to be told the dream was done.

Well, he was captured now. Audrey had seen him in abject, fawning adoration while, beneath him, Celeste with an expression of stone, naked and lax, held thousands of dollars, and Thorne strained and strained and broke himself upon her body trying, in vain, to make her moan....

Rap, rap, rap.

He was in the great hall, standing at the massive table, drumming his knuckles as of old: beating his tattoo of arrival upon the table face. He was in blue, light linen. His dark face was smiling under dark, mischievous curls.

The pendant was in her hand. She lifted her skirts and ran. She was fast, strong thighed from swimming. She came to her doors in a flash, was inside, the bolt thrown, and then the bolt to Bayard's door that opened into the bath.

In a second the drawer she wanted was pulled out, the soap pushed back, the pin pushed. Audrey hurled the pendant into Virginia's secret space, closed the mirrored false back, snagged the soap's paper wrapper upon the little pin to hide it. Closed the drawer, level with its fellows.

The telephone rang. Black and ominous beside her bed,
it shook with the sound of its ringing.

Audrey did not answer.

She watched it, fists clutched to her heart.

And she watched the curtains float gaily at the windows
like the ghost of poor, misled Virginia.

SOMETIME THAT AFTERNOON, the hydrangea-blue sky of
Newport thinned, shadowed, then quietly thickened, and
dropped. Without a belch of thunder, without a notice-
able rise or force of wind, the rains came: straight and
steady and heavy and gray.

Audrey, in her bolted boudoir, paid little attention. She
had grown accustomed to this season's unusual number of
storms. The sudden lowering skies. The hard, high winds.
She had even accepted the swarming of the whales among
the offshore boulders below WaterWalk. She'd had no time
to ponder an inconstant summer sun. . . .

And that afternoon she was riveted with anxious waiting. Waiting for Bay to return to her. "I will be back tonight," he'd said. "We'll have the weekend here before I
will have to stay in Providence. I will be back, my darling,
my bride, I will return to you tonight. . . ."

And then she would tell Bay of Virginia and Thorne.
Then, alone together in this room, she would show him the
pendant and the letter from Signore Rivalini of Rome. . . .

Thorne would not get her then; Thorne would not be able
to harm her. Then, the police would come. And Detective
Jeremy Smythe. They would take Thorne away. And even
if she did not have the proof incontrovertible, Thorne
would not be allowed to remain at Whale's Turning. . . .
Celeste would be devastated. Distraught. Celeste would
blame Audrey for Thorne's being taken from her. . . .

But Audrey would not think of that, either.

She would try to steady her mind to the printing of Tory
VanVoorst's invitations. Anything to get the day to pass;
anything to have Bay close, beside her. Tory had given her
a booklet of Old English runes. "Use runes for the first

letter of each word, Audrey, darling. It's all there—just
look up the letter you want and copy. Black ink on the
outside, thick and fat. Use the broadest nib. Thin gold leaf
around the inner lines. That's all there is to it. You're an
angel.... I'll do the same for you, your first party...."

Audrey set out her inks and pens, the letter opener, a silver stiletto, the stack of heavy parchment paper. Finally she
opened the book of runes and bent her head over it. The
rain, cool and heavy, was comforting. It seemed to seal
away the world. Electric light made the bedroom bright.
And it was only a few hours more. She was safe, and Bay
would soon be home. Wherever Thorne was, whatever he
was thinking, she was safe from him for now. And soon
forever....

MRS. WHITTAKER, of Bridge Street, did not sit out that day
on her porch, crocheting. Her husband, an old-time
fisherman, had warned against it. "A high old rain is
comin' in, Martha. I kin smell't. You light the whale lamp,
you stay inside."

And Mrs. Whittaker had stayed inside, by the front room
window, and lighted her lamp and gone about her business. As Mr. Whittaker had gone about his. He had warned
her off the porch, but he had gone, as usual, out in his little boat, gone rowing for bluefish, said to be feeding in
quantity in the upper bend of Narragansett Bay. "Mind
you bring home some butter with that fish now, Wallace,"
she said. "Don't forget." But he might forget; he forgot so
many things these days; getting older....

It was raining so hard now. Not much wind yet, but a
torrential rain. That was a bad sign. Mrs. Whittaker knew
all about weather on the sea. Her husband had taught her.
Though he, foolish old man in a dinghy, dreamin' always
and ever of being a whalin' captain, he never paid it much
mind. "I'm the pride of the fleet, wind, rain or sleet. So do
not worry 'bout Wallace, m'sweet!"

But she did worry. He was a stubborn old jackass; a dear
old thing.

Git yerself on home now, Wallace, she was thinking, crochet hook flashing. Fergit them bluefish, they worth nothin' in the market. Used for cat food mostly, spurned by most Cat'lics because the meat is dark. Them which ate fish on Fridays liked their flesh white, not bein' real fish lovers. Now she and Wallace, they were both very partial to a juicy side of bluefish, but they knew their onions. They were connoisseurs. Some folks—call them 'the know-nothings,' good name as any—called the blue a "trash fish." If the thing on the plate wasn't bass or sword or tuna...landlubbers wouldn't tetch it. Nuts to that. Wasn't nothin' much better with yer peas and potatas than a butter-browned side o' tasty blue.... But no dinner is worth losin' a husband over, so you git on home now, Wallace. You can even let the butter go by, it can wait. You jist come on home right now, and we'll sit in our nook and eat macaroni, and be as happy as if we had good sense....

TIME AND AGAIN Tory VanVoorst had congratulated herself on her thoroughness, on her leaving nothing, ever, to chance. And now, once again, it had paid off. *In spades.* For Tory, bad news always came *in spades....*

"Pull the blinds, will you, Fanni? Now there's wind and rain."

"A great storm, madam. It is August in Newport and such a great storm I think I never saw."

"Yes, Fanni. Pull the blinds. And go somewhere, will you? I want to be alone."

"But, madam, where am I to go? There is a storm outside—" Plump, pinafored, in black uniform and white lace cap, Fanni St. Flour was peeking through the blinds of Ocean House's best private suite. "The waves, madam. They are standing as tall as stallions. And the sails of the ships—they are being overcome by the waves. The ships in the harbor, madam, they are drowning! It is a storm to die in. I cannot go out!"

Soundlessly, the electricity died in the lamps. The room was dark, midnight-dark, at three in the afternoon.

Fanni gave a little squeak.

"Just light the candles, Fanni, don't get hysterical on me. It's only a summer storm. And then go to your room, if you don't mind. That is all I meant, and you know that. I did not mean for you to return to France on the next boat. Sometimes you're so sensible, so valuable to me, and sometimes you're so silly. I never know which you'll be. It's annoying, Fanni, and I wish you'd look to it."

"Yes, madam, I'm sure." Said with dignity; said with a hint of sass.

Fanni found matches, illuminated tall yellow candles in a golden candelabra without a word. But her fingers were shaking and she was panting as though she were, suddenly, asthmatic.

The wind, at gale force now, whistled and moaned at the windows and tore at the corners of Ocean House.

"Leave me, Fanni. Go and rest. I shall lie down myself, I think."

Tory was trembling more than her maid, but she did not want Fanni St. Flour to see it. Not from the storm, a hiccup of Mother Nature. No; Tory was trembling for her life, a continual storm more turbulent than any tidal wave or hurricane—

She had to read the letter from her man in Louisiana. The one who reported to her whenever anyone asked *anyone* about Alma June, the little nigger-stripper who could sing and dance; whatever happened to her.... The man who wrote right away, *marked Personal*, whenever anyone asked around, "Did you ever know, in New Orleans, an Alma June *Brown*...?"

"Madam, couldn't I stay with you? I'll be very quiet. I'll brush your hair...."

Tory did not want Fanni to know it was the letters—two letters; one from New Orleans and one...it looked like a wedding invitation, perhaps Nicola Peerce's?...from Newport proper—that required she be in utter solitude. She looked at her maid with what she hoped was a disarming smile.

"Why don't you go see Priscilla and see what she has designed for your costume at the party?"

Fanni brightened. "Oh, yes, madam. If you don't need me—that is a very good idea. She won't be busy now with callers, will she?"

"No, Fanni. And since she's just down the square, you can stay with her, chat with her. Maybe learn something interesting, yes? Some little tidbit we'd both like to know. Get something from the bakery, why don't you, and take tea with her. There's a good girl."

"Yes, we could watch the storm through, Mlle Priscilla and me. We will be intimate. We will talk the most intimate talk."

"There's a good girl. A very good girl." Tory gave the maid her change purse.

Fanni flurried into a raincoat, took the strongest black umbrella. And after a hasty curtsy, Fanni fled.

Tory locked the door behind her, tore open the letter from New Orleans. With her back against the door for support, should she need it, she read....

Ah. It was her new *friend* Mr. Alabaster McGregor, who had been making inquiries. He had traced her to New York City; yes, with a little effort and the proper connections, that would be easy enough. Harder, he had found a thread back to New Orleans. She must look to that. Find out how he had managed it, and snip that thread forever. Her man in Louisiana, highly placed—*invaluable man!*—had led McGregor to the false identifications he had set in place for her there. Those documents would lead McGregor astray; they would lead him to a little town in Kentucky where the courthouse burned, all town records destroyed up to 1844. Her made-up past was set in that unfortunate whistle-stop. Without records to prove different, there was nothing more to follow, nothing further to be ferreted out.... Ally McGregor would run Victoria VanVoorst to ground in Minersville, Kentucky, a place she'd never been. He would find she was a poor miner's daughter. A *white* miner's daughter, of course, but he wouldn't even notice that, taking her color for granted. He would think Minersville was what she covered up in shame. And he would be content; he would look no further....

Tory slowly smiled as she folded the letter and replaced it in its envelope. This was all for the best. Now Ally McGregor would think he knew her secrets, think he knew her pathetic past. He would throw hints around, about coal probably, to see how she responded. She would act brought-up-short; she would fuel the lie. And Alabaster would be pleased, thinking he had her circled....

Setting up such a false trail, finding and paying the man in Louisiana, had been costly—still was costly—but what a bargain. If Ally McGregor was convinced the shabby little story of Tory's childhood was genuine, it would be the buy of a lifetime.

Tory tore up the letter, small and fine. Burned the pieces in the drawing room fireplace. Stamped on the ashes with a well-shod heel.

The wind was howling like a rabid dog now, and down the hall she heard doors slam and the raised voices of men, and an infant crying. She washed her hands in a basin bronzed in India, dried them with a thick cotton towel. Creamed them with an ointment from France. And then she sat again, before the drawn windows, under a seven-branched candelabra of Venetian gold. She opened the invitation to Mr. and Mrs. Burton Regis VanVoorst to attend the wedding of Nicola Reed Peerce of Newport and New York to Rolf Alfred Constantine, Lord Pomeroy, the marquess of Denton.

Tory was, for the moment, content. The invitation was not enough, but it was the beginning, the crack in an opening door. Dove Peerce would still have to call on Tory in person, take tea with her. They would talk of houses and husbands... and of parties to come. Tory folded her manicured hands upon the creamy, engraved wedding card, lay her head back on a paisley shawl and closed her eyes. She daydreamed what she would say to the most desirable hostess in Newport....

While all around her the hotel shuddered, and a hurricane, a mighty tempest, slammed straight and wide and angry into America's first city by the sea.

ALABASTER MCGREGOR CURSED as the telephone went dead. Here he was, trapped in his rooms over the Casino, because of that blasted old woman, his valet, Foxx. And Audrey Lockholm *needed* him, poor girl. Needed him right now, some emergency.... But what could he do? There was a *hurricane* out there, and he was *at least* two miles from Gilt Hill....

Foxx, hysterical at the storm, had called him home.

"The roof is going, the *entire ceiling*, Ally." Foxx forgot the proprieties when he was upset. Alabaster was always having to reprimand him, saying "sir" with lowered lids and injured expression. But it was difficult to enforce discipline upon a person you sometimes slept with.... Yet Foxx had never, in Alabaster's memory, been as hysterical as this.

"Everything will be ruined, completely, totally—you must come home this instant, you must, you must! HELP!" And Foxx's voice, flying higher than what's-her-name breaking Ally's heart with her sad little ballad, "If the Waters Could Speak as They Flow."

Well, sometimes, you know, it's just first come, first served, and that's all there is to it.

Because at the sound of his lover's wail, Alabaster McGregor, who never in his life had run from danger, had left his post at the newspaper. To be fair, he had already closed the paper down. All seven of the employees, even the incomparable Mrs. Gottschalk, had put down their tools—in Mrs. Gottschalk's case, her broom—when the wind began to shake the coaches in the street. Below stairs in the machine room, they'd bolted for the door like piglets after Farmer Gray's cornhusk gravy. Really, when you came to think about it, the underclasses were *so* timid, so emphatically without *derring-do*. Which proved—thank-you very much—that class was more than simple circumstance and complex money. There was a difference in the blood, a definite—why, it was as plain as the nose on Clarissa Rails's dear face, which she should have done something about long ago. . . .

But such self-congratulation was beside the point. Here he was, Alabaster McGregor, the most trusted man in Newport in Audrey Lockholm's innocent blue eyes, and she had just *called him at home on his private telephone*, babbling something about "breaking the code," and to come to her, right away. Right away. "Proof incontrovertible," she'd said. Meaning she'd found out *who* was the lover of Virginia; maybe even the *murderer* of Virginia. Yes, of course, he'd stir his stumps for that. . . .

But the storm—a tempest!—was raging. At full blast. He couldn't go out now, it would mean his life! He must hire a photographer for the *Daily Whirl* full-time; he *must* have a picture of Newport under sea siege, a whole front page. And the telephone lines were gone, down for a lifetime for all he knew. So even though little Audrey had called in desperation, he was only a mortal man, not a god, and he wasn't able, *just now* to go. . . .

She would have to wait.

"Foxx?"

"Yes, sir."

"There's no electricity. We've pushed the furniture into the dry and rolled up the rugs. You've poured us each a brandy, it's four in the afternoon, and I am unable to get to my work."

"Yes, sir."

"Then, why don't we snuggle here on the window bench, watch the storm do its stuff, and take advantage of the dark?"

"Look, Ally, the storm flag is flying in the harbor, and the ocean's over the wharves! The trees are breaking. The whole town will be destroyed."

"Listen, you wanton. I pay you. Now you pet me."

"Sir, we are in the midst of another biblical flood—the end, again, of Sodom and Gomorrah. Perhaps we should light tapers and pray for our souls."

Alabaster settled himself at the window. He loosened his ascot, his vest, his shirt.... Wrong biblical allusions—that was another limitation of the poor-at-heel. They were improperly educated. Thank God some of the huddling masses could read and had a penny to buy his newspaper....

He breathed deep and tried to quiet his excitement at the storm and the broken telephone call.

Through the window, slashing gray *waves* at the window, through the rattle and whistle of a whipping wind, Alabaster watched the hurricane shatter into Newport and shake it like a dog. He watched...and felt Foxx's soft, rhythmic hand. This was exciting: a sudden, natural catastrophe, an utterly *stolen* afternoon....

Sometimes even boss's wives and first-rate breaking gossip had to wait until Alabaster McGregor was ready. After all, he was important, too. He had a life, too.

And things that needed tending to. Things that couldn't wait.

"Ah, Foxx, you do like me, after all, I can tell...."

Tomorrow, first thing, he'd see Audrey Lockholm. He'd ride over to Whale's Turning on the new palomino mare. He'd wear the courtier's suit Tory had had done up for him....

Tory VanVoorst, former Louisiana white trash....

What a pity her secret wasn't grander, more *inflammatory*. Who cared that the little jewel box had been *illegitimate*. Who cared that her mother had drunk herself to death? Finding out had been expensive, and it was strictly *no news*.... We all kill ourselves in the end...one way or the other. And as long as we're quiet about it, no one gives a fig how. He was very disappointed in Victoria VanVoorst's "secret life." He had hoped for something much more *somber*....

"Foxx. Shall we go to London in November? The weather will be just like this, every day, but the tourists will have all gone home. I'll take you to Christie's and buy you a pinkie ring."

"What's happening outside now, sir?"

"Tripp Rails's gas buggy just skittered into the Maddley's flower shop. He'll have a bill to settle, oh my. And the waves have destroyed the fish mart. It's utterly gone.... There's a woman down in the street, no one to help her."

"I've got to see."

"Another moment, Foxx, just another moment, please. The storm will last for hours. Just give me another fifteen seconds...there's a good boy. There, there.... Oh my God—"

In the bedroom behind them, another piece of roof gave way.

OVER NARRAGANSETT BAY the wind increased to scream force.

Wallace Whittaker was lashed to his boat seat, hunched on the floor of his dinghy, surrounded by whales. A mob of whales, noses pointed landward. Their backs broke some of the brunt of the wind, and their bodies made a channel for his little boat to ride in.

It wouldn't be bad to die like this, he thought. It would be painless and quick, and there was a kind of grandeur in it—

Martha would miss him, though.

WORD OF THE HURRICANE over Newport was slow in reaching the Providence, Rhode Island, courthouse, and Judge Godfrey was slower in ending the session for the day. There was wind and rain in Providence, too, but it was not a severe storm in his opinion. And when Judge Godfrey sat in his robes, it was his opinion that counted.

But finally, the clock hands in Courtroom 2 stood at five, and rather than ask the assembled to stay on another hour to pass on another juror or two, Judge Godfrey banged the gavel and adjourned his court until Monday morning at nine.

Astin Forbes was in no hurry to depart. The rain was heavy and a coach ride home would be interminably slow, miserably cold and wet.

"What do you say? Shall we both stay in town tonight, Bayard? We could dine in and sleep at the hotel."

They were waiting under the courthouse portico for the carriage.

Bayard considered Astin's suggestion; it was the sensible thing to do. Newport was forty miles and more away and the rain showed no sign of letting up. But he had promised Audrey he would return to her this night, and he wanted to. Very much. There was an urgency in his wanting he did not understand. All day, while the sky had been dull and gradually darker, when he should have been intent upon the men who would be his judges, his mind had drifted to his bride. . . .

And to the one before. . . .

Audrey was young, not yet twenty, almost young enough to be his daughter, and she was unprepared for the life he offered. That he could have handled. Could she . . . ? If it had not been for this misfortune, yes. They would have grown blissfully old together, he thought. They would have. . . . They were so different together from him and Virginia, so happily, blessedly *different*. . . .

Virginia. For whom life held no surprises, only minor inconveniences and sumptuous rewards. Virginia, who had so captured his mother's heart that he, knowing he should marry as his mother pressed him to, knowing it was time; weak when his mother spoke of her mortality and his duty to carry on the Lockholm line, he had allowed himself to be seduced by her, committed to her. Virginia, whom he'd married even though he knew she had not been virgin. Knew because she had asked him to take her one sweet, warm night . . . and he had, he had. . . .

And then she told him she was to have his baby, and she asked him to marry her. And he had, he had; in great part because of that male weakness in his groin that had died so quickly, been surfeited too quickly... with Virginia.

Who had lied, of course.

She confessed to him in London—in the midst of her fling with the painter, Whistler—that she had been mistaken; that she had been so tense and nervous during their courtship her body "postponed" its natural functions for a longer time than should be. It was an honest mistake, she said. She hadn't meant to be deceitful. She hoped he would forgive her.... And then in Rome she told him she had a yen for sun-browned boys; did he mind terribly? And in Madrid it was a "tight-trousered" servant she found irresistible....

And when finally they returned to New York and Newport and Virginia was pregnant, truly pregnant—Dr. Lake confirmed it—Bayard had wondered who, really, the father was... and would he ever know for certain. She had assured him she had taken care of herself; that his was the only seed she, fertile garden, would grow.

"I am not stupid, Bayard," she said. "I mean to enjoy your fortune, and I mean to have your child. You'll know. The babe will be your spitting image. Oh, you'll know all right, I'm not worried about that."

But she had been worried about something, that fatal week. She had picked fights on purpose. She had stolen five thousand dollars from his accounts. Immediately, Astin discovered the loss and told him. He had gone to Virginia angry, demanding an explanation. She screamed and cursed and threw more bills-due in his face. That night he left her, shattered in his soul. For how could he divorce the mother of his child? He had left her that night knowing he would have to live celibate, would have to protect his fortune, would have to be miserably married for another eighteen years at least, until the child to come was old enough and strong enough to understand... to cope....

He'd gotten drunk that night, growing up himself that night. Suddenly, at thirty-five, thoroughly a man of the world. Because he hadn't really minded about Virginia, about his bad choice of a wife. He just hadn't given a damn about her: that was his shame.

And then the tragedy, and his release.

And the overbearing guilt.

For he had stood, drawing on his cigar, under the moon. Stood, good and drunken.

And he had seen the great black shadow in the window of Whale's Turning. There was a low light behind, a candle burned to a stub, which intensified the shadow and gave it the mass of two. The shadow loomed and dimmed and loomed and dimmed at the window....

Was she fighting then, Virginia, for her life?

Was she deciding yes...then no...then yes...to suicide? Seeing her husband, *her unloving husband*, smoking a cigar beyond the stone wall in the dark. Watching him watch her. Him, content, away from her. Him, silent, staring up, while his wife decided...

Yes.

Then no.

Then yes.

And the shadow loomed and dimmed and loomed—

And tilted toward him. As though, he'd thought, to smother him and his estate and all he stood for. And then, finally solid, the shadow—Virginia's body!—tilted too far, and fell.

And he, *released*, he had been loath to move. *Loath to move*. He had had to force his feet across the lawn. For shame....

How long could he live with such a guilt?

And then, one day, from nowhere, there was Audrey. Beautiful, high-spirited, frightened Audrey Smoke. Innocent. Unprepared. Insecure. How he had looked forward to teaching her the good life! But it was not to be. What was real was to sit in Providence...and protect himself.

For shame.

Free—but how would he be free, even if acquitted—he would show Audrey all the world and teach her all he knew.

Convicted, he would sit in prison—before he was hanged—and write her letters. Love letters. He would tell her his delight in her and the new baby, only just engendered below her heart. Perhaps he would live to see his heir, if Astin appealed. He had been wrong about the annulment: Audrey would be rid of him soon enough...or never. However the nickel turned, heads or tails...he did not really mind. If he was forfeited, perhaps that would lift the curse from the Lockholm line. His child would have a better life, and the debt to Phineas Brown would be paid in full at last....

The carriage stood before them, door held open by Drew, under a black umbrella.

"You stay, Astin," Bay said. "I've got to get home tonight to Audrey."

"Sir," said the Lockholm coachman. "There's a great storm under way in Newport. A hurricane, they say. The roads are flooded, trees down.... The ocean is on a rampage and even some of the houses may go. It will be hard to get home, and hard, on Monday, to get back here."

Astin Forbes was already in the coach seat and wiping his shoe tops with a handkerchief. "Be sensible, Bayard, and stay in town. You can call Audrey from the hotel."

"The telephone lines are down in Newport, sir," said Drew.

"We'll drop Mr. Forbes at the Providence Hotel," said Bayard, from inside the brougham. "Then we'll go home, Drew, as fast as we can." He patted the coachman's gloved hand, which still held the door. "Sorry to work you and the horse so hard."

"Perfectly all right, sir, glad to be of service," said Drew, shutting the door carefully, turning down the latch. He was saddened at the thought of a four hours' ride—five, if the roads were muddy and branches across the road.... His supper would be late. He would be drenched to the bone and catch pneumonia sure....

Nevertheless.

He returned to the driver's seat, closed the umbrella and laid it at his feet. He pulled down the brim of his rain hat and slapped slippery-wet reins on the back of the dapple gray.

"Hee-yup, handsome," he said through gritted teeth. And sneezed.

DETECTIVE JEREMY SMYTHE WOULD have sorely liked, too, to go home to his Lizbeth and a hot English meat pie. Take off his brogans, read the newspaper, pet the dog. But there was an uneasiness in him, a wariness.

Bayard Lockholm was free on bail, but he was not a free man. He was a guilty man, Detective Smythe was sure of it. One day, Bay Lockholm sees the wide-eyed blonde. She's fresh, poor and admiring. Next day an "accident" befalls the society wife. It was a sad old story: happened all the time. Sometimes the rake even got away with it and lived happily ever after. But not when Detective Smythe was on the case....

So Bayard Lockholm had to be watched. And tonight, in the storm, would be a good time to run. Maybe the best time.... Well, better men than Bayard Lockholm had tried to skip on Jeremy Smythe: the pork pie would have to wait.

"Follow the Lockholm carriage, Rafferty. Can you go without your supper, if need be?"

"Yes, sir. No, sir."

"You'll never make detective, Sergeant."

"Yes, sir. Here's Connors to relieve me."

"Connors, have you eaten?"

"Yes, sir. Thank you."

"What did you have?"

"Sausages and potatoes, sir. Very good."

Detective Smythe nodded and slumped back in the police coach, toes soaked and squishing in his shoes. "It'll be a late night, Connors."

"I'm ready, sir."

"Good man." His stomach rumbled but Detective Smythe was content: there was excitement in his gut. He was on the sneak again, on the chase; closing in. And there was nothing—not even pork pie—that Jeremy Smythe loved better than a spectacular grab.

So flee, Mr. Lockholm, he thought as two stout horses pulled him through the wet. Go on, make your run. The bloodhound of Providence follows sniffing at your tail.

22

AUDREY FOUND the English rune just as the electricity died. It was heart stopping.

She sat in the dark, her finger on the place, unable, for a moment, to move.

She had seen it, found it, the *proof incontrovertible*. Not looking, she had found it, *found it*.

The windows were shut firm, but they trembled against the pounding of the wind. And the wind cried so loud it drowned all other sounds. The sound of her pen, pulling on the invitation, heavy vellum. The sound of her shortened breath. The sound of the ringing telephone....

As soon as she came upon the rune, *a long-tailed þ*, which wasn't a *b* at all, but the Old English character *th*...as soon as she saw the long-tailed *þ*, and saw next to it its definition, she raised blood-drained eyes to her cheval glass...and *boom*, little like that, the dark had come....

Heart stopping.

The dark was come and the telephone was ringing....

She didn't answer it. She sat in the dark and listened to the howling of the wind until it silenced even the telephone...eventually....

Then she whispered toward the mirror. "Mama, oh Mama, it is a symbol from the Old English alphabet. It represents the sound of 'this' and 'thistle.' It is not a long-tailed *b*, Mama.... It is an English rune, and it is called the *thorn*."

"Act," her mother counseled her.

Weak-kneed, Audrey went to the telephone, lighted the taper on the table beside her bed. She sat on the satin coverlet and watched the wind at the windows. Watched the dark outside roll and winced as the slashing rain cut at the window glass.

"Act," her mother repeated. "Move, Audrey, now."

Whom should she summon? Fisher, below stairs, working with the servants protecting the house from storm? No, not Fisher; he was an ineffectual weapon. Bay was unreachable, too far away. And at any rate, he would be home soon. Perhaps he was already racing to her, homeward bound. Tory? What could Tory do that Audrey could not? She could not ask Tory to brave a storm like this to come and sit beside her in the dark. And if she did, would it help?

No.

Alabaster. Alabaster McGregor had the diary. Ally was strong in mind and personality, if not in muscle. Alabaster would know what to do—

She found his number in her address book. A little book, not many names.... The telephone dial turned slowly as she pulled it round and round. Through the receiver she heard a far-off ringing.

And then the ring stopped and she heard a click and a voice—Alabaster's voice—distant seeming, too, but that would be the storm. He was, after all, not so very far away....

"Ally, this is Audrey. I have found it."

"Cinderella, what a time to call! My roof is caving in, my man is drowning. I'm about to take a bath! What is it?"

"Ally, I have found it, found the proof incontrovertible. It is the *b*. It's not a *b*—"

Boom.

And then, little like that, the connection died, and she was clicking the telephone handle and shaking the telephone itself, but there was nothing inside the heavy, black receiver but a muffled sound like a shell held to the ear that will not roar of the sea.

Oh no.

The hands of the carriage clock on the white French bureau were stopped at 4:19. How long had it been since the electricity had died...?

She left the telephone, broken, on the bed pillow. She went to a window, looked out.

It was impossible to see.

The wind was turning the world over and spinning gusts of rain in circles. The apple tree on the west lawn stood trunk black, wet black, bent as a widow, its branches tangled to one side like hair gone stiff with fright.

Beyond the lawn, the ocean roiled in caps gone black. Huge, black waves stretched as high as monuments, crashed like mausoleums. Spewed black, spit black, black as caldrons...then flashed, skeleton white. Then blasted into black again and clawed loose the ocean stones....

Whale's Turning was trembling in the storm's attack; Whale's Turning, built of marble from mountains in Tuscany. Audrey saw the servants, Fisher and the men, in yellow slickers, down at the pier, trying to save the boat. Staggering under sandbags, building a makeshift wall where the cliff side gentled down to the pier; setting in another where the seawall broke; free entrance to the lawns.

Tree branches pirouetted in funnels of wind. Free of their trunks, they were gone mad with liberty. They smashed against the walls of the mansion, they flew to the level of Audrey's eyes. They shook at her like demons. They swooped like bats.

She stepped back from the window. She wanted a cup of tea. But she would not leave the room until Bay came and Thorne Cockburn was taken away....

She could not see the whales, but she thought they would be there, in place, hunkered below WaterWalk against the feet of the cliffs.

They could turn if they wished to, she thought. They could turn back to the safety of the open sea. They could sink; sink deep below the level of the storm. They could sleep, if they wanted to, and dream until all was done.... But I think they will not go. They have come for a reason. To see or to learn or to remember, I'm not sure. But for some reason, they have been *called*, and they will not turn until the storm is past.

Rap, *rap*, *rap*, at the double doors of her boudoir.

She crossed to the makeup table, her makeshift desk. She closed the book of runes. She did not respond to the signal.

Over the surging of the wind she heard his voice, "Aud? Come on, Aud, I know you're in there. I've come to escort you down to the cellar. The storm cellar. We've all got to go. Open up."

She slid the book under her bridal bed, far under; hidden by the dust skirt.

She looked around for something with which to protect herself. She saw the letter opener, silver, stiletto. She covered it with Tory's invitations. She sat at the desk, facing the doors.

He will have to break them down to get me.

He was pounding at the doors. "Come on, Audrey, last chance. Open up now. Come on."

She folded her hands in her skirt, squeezed them between her knees. This is how the rabbit feels while the fox paws at the only way in, the only way out. . . .

Something slammed against the doors, at the weakest part, where they joined. Something heavy and solid. A shoulder . . . or an entire body honed strong from a lifetime of struggling on the sea.

"Audrey—"

I could lock myself in the bathroom, but that's worse. That's smaller . . . a true cul-de-sac. I'm better off here, even when the door breaks—

CRACK.

The door was rending around the bolt. He slammed against the thin edge where the doors met and locked. Silent now, working now, *no need for words now.* . . .

The bolt was shaking, pins loosening. The doors were giving. . . .

He was in.

He leaned against the doors, facing her, his legs, in rough-weather breeches, spread warrior-wide. The weight of his body closed the doors behind him. Well-oiled, well-made, the doors, though damaged . . . swung . . . met. . . .

Shut.

His hands, behind his back, tightened the screws his body had pulled away. Working at the bolt-broken door, twisting the little screw heads, he said, gently now, but above the screaming of the storm she could hear him clearly, "Ah, Aud, you always did make me work for whatever I got from you."

And still she sat, with her hands squeezed tight between her knees. Bay will be here soon, she thought. Thorne will not hurt me in Bay's house. He will not. . . .

Something inside her whimpered, but Thorne did not hear. *He could kill her, but he would never hear. . . .*

She stood. He was not so big when she stood.

"I'm staying here, Thorne Cockburn," she said, "here, safe in my room. I'm not going with you, I'm not going down to the cellar. So get out, it's not proper you should be here. Celeste will be very unhappy you broke down my boudoir doors."

And still he leaned against the doors, bolt-driven again. The pale wood framed him. In the storm's dark, he was darker. The candle she had lighted threw his shadow, shapeless and high, up to the ceiling. It flowed along the ceiling, the plaster-sculpted, hand-painted ceiling of ivory and pink and beige and gold, overshadowed now by Thorne encroaching. . . .

Audrey looked into her cheval glass. Almost black, it reflected Thorne. Only Thorne. Replicated him hazily, like a ghost; a booted, rough-trousered ghost. . . . He is a pirate at heart, she thought. He should be snarling at me now, with a knife between his teeth and a skull and crossbones tattooed in blood upon his lower arm. His shirt should be torn and dirty, and he should be wearing a gold ring in his ear—

"Give me the pendant, Audrey. You know that's what I'm here for."

He was still against the doors; tense, waiting.... For what? To spring? To kill ...?

He is supposed to be outside, she thought, helping Fisher and the others. No one knows he is here in this room. He excused himself to dress against the weather, and then he snuck—

"Stand straight against him," her mother said. "He is the curse Bay suffers...."

"Get out," Audrey said, "get out this instant or I will scream. Sawyer will hear me. Celeste will hear me. Celeste already suspects, Thorne—"

He sprang, was upon her, black-haired fingers around her throat.

Was this how it had been with Virginia?

He lifted Audrey by the throat. Threw her. In a tangle of white-striped silk her body collided against the stout pine base of the cheval glass. Sturdy, the mirror trembled but stood.

Thorne hulked over her, hand doubled into a fist; sun-gilded, black-haired hand raised as a club.

"The pendant, Audrey," he said, so calm. "Get it for me now."

She tried to get her feet under her, tried to rise. She was in stocking feet, the polished oak floor was slippery....

He grabbed the collar of her dress and the coil of her hair, hauled her to her feet, the dress ripping, a red haze before her eyes. She fought to get her legs under her, to stand, to face—

He flung her against the fawn-and-golden wall, beat her head against it. She was beside a window, and she felt the wind—wild and cold the wind—blowing through the casement. She heard the storm outside, trying to get in, keening a hysterical requiem in a language she did not know, but very beautiful.... Perhaps it was the song of the whales the storm-wind shouted.... There was color in her brain, flashes of orange and mustard yellow, and bolts of purple, a deep red-purple tinged with a brilliant green....

He was leaning his weight against her shoulders, bracing his body against the lengths of his outstretched arms; breaking her bones, it seemed, with the force of him.

"Get the pendant, Audrey." Black curls fell like a victory wreath on his forehead. He was not even out of breath. His eyes shone with a blue-black gleam.

He stepped back suddenly; the pressure, the weight of him momentarily gone. But only to reach out and tear again, tear at her dress, shredding the strong silk of her bodice, ripping away the sleeves. A cuff held. The torn sleeve-silk was his leash, her chain: he pulled her from the wall. In the center of the room he wound the rope of silk around her throat, twisted tight and hauled her to her knees. She fought only to breathe. Aubusson carpet rough at her cheek, the stale smell of it choked her. She rolled against the makeup table. It was delicate and slight, balanced on spindle legs. It quivered as she struggled against it, and the quill pen fell and the bottle of black ink. Tightly capped, the bottle was a weapon. It struck Audrey's ribs, rock hard. Tory's invitations fluttered before her eyes like doves, frightened by the stranger in their midst....

He was bending over her, a knee in her back, forcing her face to the side, his hand a crown of talons in her hair.

"Get it for me, Aud. Get it for me now."

"Yes," she said.

He pushed her head into the carpet then as he stood away. The pile smothered her mouth and nose.

She rose to her knees, fell back. Her bodice was gone, but her camisole still covered her breasts, though so thin, so thin....

It does not matter, she thought. He can have the pendant, it only convicts him more. What matters is that I have the proof incontrovertible, safe in Ally's hands, safe in the diary. I have only to tell Ally what it means, it means....

She staggered toward her bathroom, oblivious to a great tree branch, which, storm-torn, smashed against a window's glass and broke through into the room. She realized only that the storm had invaded Whale's Turning at last, and that its howling filled her head and that the wind, like Thorne, was throwing her around. Could kill her . . . would kill her, if it chose. . . .

Wall of mirrors in the bathroom, but dark, so dark. No candle flame in the bathroom. No candle flame now in the other room. Thank God for the darkness; her almost nakedness would not show. Still, there was shape and shadow, even here, as she bent over the drawer with a secret back. Strands of hair were in her eyes, her hands were shaking...and *he* was behind her, in the doorway, blocking out the remaining light.

"Hurry, Aud," he said *so calmly*, "they're waiting for me outside. I've got to help with the work. Save the furniture, you know, darling. Save Bayard's boat."

Her hand was inside, pushing aside the soap. Clicking the lever. Sliding under the false, mirrored-shelf back. Her fingers were damp—were they bleeding or was it only sweat?—they closed around thin, tumbled chain. The pendant, like a coin, filled her fist. She withdrew her hand, stood straight . . . threw the pendant at his face.

"Take it and be damned," she said.

Clink.

She missed him. The pendant fell into darkness somewhere on the veined marble floor.

"Find it," she said with a sneer. Beaten, she would still stand against him, again and again. . . .

"Go on, Thorne," she said, and her voice, at least, was strong. "Get down on your knees and crawl for it. You'll still hang. I don't need the pendant to prove you killed Virginia—"

No.

No, she should not have said that. She should not have taken that tiny victory over him *just now.* . . .

He was so quiet. As quiet as . . . death.

His body filled the doorway of the bathroom. Blackened it. She could see nothing but a gray haze where his curls, swept by the storm, made a dancing pattern, black on black, ever changing. . . .

And then he moved. He crouched on his knees, and she heard his hand, like a bat wing dragging over tiles, she heard his hand scan across the marble, seeking his pendant. For it was his, after all, wasn't it? she thought. It was made for him in Rome at Virginia's request, by Signore Maurice Rivalini, master jeweler....

"You are a dead woman," Thorne said in a storm-rent quiet.

Beyond, in the bedroom, glass shattered, wood creaked, the storm screamed. Objects rolled, hard and loud, unused to rolling on high-shined oak. Something high and heavy fell with a plaster crash, probably a drapery cornice, carved carefully by hand and overcautiously hung so it would never, never fall....

She heard the scratch as his hand found the chain and rectangle of gold. Heard the soft click as the pendant scraped on marble as his fingers lifted it. She felt his arms make a motion in the dark as he dropped the pendant around his neck and shook it down inside his shirt....

And then the hand, steel fingered, closed around her wrist. But Audrey held, with her other hand, a long bottle by the throat. She knew it; it was blue crystal, stoppered, and full of liquid soap for bubble bath. She swung from her heels, swung at his head....

The bottle caught his shoulder. He grunted, released her, staggered back. He wrenched the bottle from her hand. The stopper loosened and fell and splintered upon the marble. Shards skittered against her feet and the smell of soap enveloped her, sticky and sweet.

And then Thorne was swinging the bottle at her, swinging it by its long, long throat, and in a haze of faceted slivers it burst upon her head.

She tasted soap as she lost consciousness, and breathed it in, high in her nose....

Slipping into nowhere, soap consumed, she feared, now, only for her baby, new under her heart, barely begun....

She would try, for the baby's sake, to crawl away...to...

Down the hall, over the chattering of window glass and the muffling gusts of wind, Edmunda Wysong Lockholm heard Audrey scream.

Edmunda, too, had refused to leave her room, her safe room, she said, and join the female servants in the cellar. She did not care what Celeste did—Celeste was visiting the Misses Wetmore, she was told—or what "the new girl" did. She had been interrupted by the weather from her nice lounge on the lawn; that, the elder Mrs. Lockholm made clear, was inconvenience enough for one day.

"I shall be quite all right, Zella," she'd said, settling herself on her day chaise. "Now don't coax me anymore. You go on down. I'll stay here where I'm happy and watch the wind blow. I will be highly amused."

"But ma'am," said Zella, "Fisher insists."

"Fisher does not give the orders in this house, Zella. Now go. Leave me. Take the pup, and go."

"Oh, Mrs. Lockholm, I don't know—"

"Well, I do. Dis-missed!" And Edmunda picked up her blue silk volume of poetry by Donne. "What a lot of old women you servants are, you and Fisher and the rest. How William, dear sweet William—do you remember William, Zella?—how he would have laughed at you." Edmunda opened the book where a ribbon marked a favorite place.

Zella considered. Mrs. Lockholm seemed lucid. Mrs. Lockholm seemed determined. And her son, who could have persuaded her, was away. Zella did not really think Mrs. Lockholm would come to harm in her room. She did not really think Whale's Turning would crumble in the wind. And if Mrs. Lockholm insisted on being silly—the rich always insisted on their own way—well, Dr. Lake, heartened at Edmunda's improvement, told Zella, some days ago, not to baby her mistress or treat her as an invalid. "Mrs. Lockholm needs to feel in control of herself again, Zella, needs to think she is well. You understand that, don't you? It's the most important medicine she can have."

Zella was unconvinced, but voiced her agreement to Dr Lake as he expected her to. She was still, as she called it "of two minds." But now she had herself to think of: she was going straightaway down to the cellar, with or without Mrs. Lockholm, and if *Mrs. Lockholm would not come* then see you later ma'am, all right....

She shook her head, picked up sloppy little Breaker, who slobbered on her uniform front and began to gnaw a button, and went. If Mrs. Lockholm died in Zella's absence, it would not be Zella's fault; it would be Mrs. Lockholm's. Zella had done all she could; all that could have been expected of her, and more....

And now, amid the hurricane, Edmunda Lockholm heard a scream. A scream, coming from *Virginia's room*....

Was there never to be peace in a Lockholm house?

And what *could* be the matter with Virginia...? Hadn't she caused enough trouble already, jumping the way she had, and Bayard being blamed for it? What a bother. And then that town girl, wearing Virginia's gowns when she had no right, Bayard, foolish boy, telling her she could, because he liked...what had he liked about that town girl...?

Another scream.

Poor thing. Frightened of the storm. Perhaps she should stir herself, Edmunda thought; give comfort where she could. Have a chat perhaps, and watch the storm perform. They were having duck tonight for dinner. Perhaps she should warn the town girl not to wear one of Virginia's silks. Grease spotted silk; ruined it. And you couldn't rub silk to get it clean. The fibers broke when you rubbed against the grain....

Edmunda eased her legs off the chaise. She was wearing gold-embossed fox-head slippers. She admired her small feet. Size five, narrow, triple-A in the heel. High-arched aristocratic little feet. Jeoffry used to kiss her fine ankles while William, sweet William, never noticed such things. William simply dove into the heart of the matter, so to speak....

The woman, the Mexican woman, who came with her daughter along Cliff Walk and stared. Edmunda knew who she was: Esmeralda Diego Eckkles, Jeoffry's widow. The girl, then, was she Jeoffry's? Or the Mexican's, that first man? The man Jeoffry had had to kill, in self-defense. . . . Probably the girl was Jeoffry's; she was fine boned and beautiful. She looked Castilian, high born, even though the mother was a fishwife. The woman had once hoped Edmunda would help her daughter rise in the world. Of course, Edmunda never would. Jeoffry had stolen a million dollars from William, hadn't he? Edmunda should know; she had given it to him, and William had never said a word. "A stake," Jeoffry'd said. "Just give me the stake, Eddy, and I'll get rich and pay you back a hundredfold. . . ."

He had not gotten rich. He had gone away to Australia—or was it Africa?—after diamonds. He had gone away, gone back to the Mexican wetback, and been broken again. And then *she* had come—imagine the nerve—Jeoffry's widow, with a beautiful babe. Had come to Edmunda one summer in Newport, long ago, and said, "Jeoff told me about you. Jeoff said you'd help."

Jeoff. How Edmunda had laughed.

"He told you wrong, my dear," Edmunda told her. "I knew your husband only in a business way. I invested my husband's money and lost it. His widow and child are not my concern, and I'll not throw good money after bad. Good day."

And she had gone, greasy Mexican nomad, fat and shapeless, arthritic already, a dowager's hump forming on her back. She had gone, she and the babe who hadn't made a sound, who had only gazed, black eyed and openmouthed, at Edmunda's flower-filled rooms.

Long ago that was, years and years. . . .

Edmunda had not seen them since. Until last week, and this week, when the woman had appeared out on Cliff Walk beyond the wall. Esmeralda Diego Eckkles. Could she spell her own name? Probably not! She had stood on the public path and stared at Edmunda. She pushed the young girl forward, but her daughter had pulled back...and turned away. Edmunda would have liked to have seen the girl close now that she was grown. She would have sought Jeoffry in the shape of his daughter's face....

Well, they'd left. And Jeoffry's daughter could go to hell, and quick, *in a hand basket*, and so could the town girl, screaming at a touch of wind...ignorant creature. A thief, too. Edmunda had caught her in Virginia's dress, and hadn't she told her? Told her straight....

The old woman was up now. She gripped her cane and steadied herself. Set forth: sluff-sluff, stomp....

All right, Virginia, I'm coming, I'm coming.

It was dim in the hall, without the electricity. But she could see. Here was the table Bayard had bought in Paris that had once stood in the Palace at Versailles. And here was an Italian garden urn, overflowing with hydrangea, the blossoms so sweet if one waited, just a moment, and let the scent surround...

Her slippers dragged, slow, along the hallway carpet. She used the cane and a hand on the wall, the furniture, to steady herself as she crept forward. It was a long, fine hall, like a monastery tunnel, high and beautiful. Edmunda liked the hall of Whale's Turning. It suited very well....

Sluff-sluff, stomp.

The doors to Virginia's boudoir were closed. Handsome double doors, handles of ivory, gilt at the tips. Virginia had succeeded with this cottage and its accoutrements, despite Bayard's grumblings about the cost. Zachary Punt Pink, the architect, had helped her of course. Zack Pink was the best; Celeste would use him—Edmunda would insist on it—when Thorne could afford to build....

The storm seemed to be right behind the boudoir doors. Edmunda could hear the wind within, smashing things and howling.... The doors were shaking from the force. And some great heavy thing was banging against a wall—why, a storm inside a bedroom would ruin the draperies.

Whatever was Virginia thinking of? Had she left a casement open... *in this weather*?

But of course. Virginia wasn't within; it was that other one, the know-nothing, the *town girl*, what's-her-name. She'd run to the cellar with the servants, like a creature who lives in a barn...cheap little hussy. Don't think I won't tell Bayard when he comes, thought Edmunda. This nonsense has to stop. Such destruction won't be tolerated. *Not in this house*....

Edmunda rapped on the door with her cane. "Girl! Girl, are you in there?"

Over the wind, Thorne did not hear. He had the window open, and Audrey almost to the balcony without. The gale resisted him, hurled itself at him a hundred-plus miles an hour, and the curtains veiled his eyes, whipped at them, but he was gaining ground. A few feet more, and Audrey would be a sack upon the concrete balustrade. He would heave her over and be done. Done. And who to say it was not the storm that had taken her?

Rain, slashing in, made the floor a slippery slide. It slowed him, weighted her, silk skirts drenched....

Down below the men were working, stumbling under their bags of sand, stored in the cellar for such an emergency. They did not look up. Even if they did, they would not be able to see, The hurricane was at landfall, and full force. He had only to hurry—

Audrey came back to consciousness, thinking she was drowning in the sea. Waves smashed at her face, the current pulled at her legs. Water-wind slapped at her, snatched her breath....

Oh. She opened her eyes to the apparition of herself in the cheval glass, being dragged by the feet by Thorne over bird-and-flower Aubusson carpet, past the little table, upturned, a leg broken.... Her hand closed upon the letter opener, silver, *stiletto*.... She pulled it to her bosom, knowing where she was now... remembering all.

Thorne was lifting her; he slipped.

Mama.

With all her strength she swung an arm wide, plunged at him, and sank the silver shaft into his chest.

But he was slipping, slipping on the rain-slicked wood, and the blade, though in the mark—

He flung her away with a scream. She fell against, upon, *into* the mirror. It rocked and swung and spun on the slick oak floor, shattered under her into a thousand flying glass-stars.

Mama.

Thorne, wounded but unstopped, felled but *unstopped*, sat like a rag doll. Staring at her with hate, he pulled the stiletto from his chest. Dark, *blood-smothered silver now*. He hurled it across the room. It struck the double doors....

Thorne was crawling for her. She filled her hands with broken mirror glass. Screaming, she sprayed them at his face.

It did not stop him.

She found a chair leg. Tried to move the chair between him and her, tried to scramble up and out.

He had her.

He held her by an ankle. She kicked, screaming, at his face. He was upon her, slimy with blood, soaked with the storm, full still of life and hate . . . and *murder*.

Beyond, old Mrs. Lockholm rattled at the handles. Within, they did not hear.

The old woman pushed. In a lull of wind, a door opened. Edmunda pushed it wide. Then the storm blasted full again, howled round the room again, spiraled like a tornado loosed from a genie's jar. And Edmunda saw a man leap upon a woman, a woman down on her back, fighting for her life....

Virginia....

Mrs. Lockholm was in the room. She tried to cry out to stop the monstrous thing. Her cane skidded on the storm-flooded floor. Unsteady, she lost her balance. She fell, hard on her side, her feet flung out from under her, her body buffeted by wind.

Something gave as Edmunda fell, something in her chest. It hurt terribly. She was senile; sometimes she knew it. She was old, too; she admitted it, didn't mind. She was slow.

But she was not so senile that she did not know *murder* when she saw it.

The man.

He was trying to kill Virginia!

Her eyes, blurry, tear-filled eyes, still saw. *Saw* the silver blade, inches from her stunned, nonfeeling hand.

Nonfeeling, clammy, bloodless, still her hand could *move*. Did; and closed upon the letter opener...blood thick as...*cold as*...jelly on the hilt.

The man had Virginia by the throat and hair, wild golden hair, *which Virginia never had*. He was pulling her toward the Juliet balcony outside, throwing her into the storm. He had her—out there! He was *choking* her and pushing her over backwards, forcing her back...and back.... She would break in two or fall...*as she fell last year, and died....*

The casket kept closed so no one could see the remains.

Edmunda Lockholm, still of considerable bulk, bursting with righteous rage, flew, an old tigress, toward the man, storm rent, at the balustrade. She leaped, withered limbs suddenly supple, dull heart surging bright. Across the great room she charged, into the gale, into torrential rain. She attacked: the stiletto a spear in her hand.

She was at his back.

She sank her weapon deep, behind his heart. Scraped bone going in; *pushed, pushed*. And twisted the hilt back and forth as he, confounded, bucked back and turned.

The blade withdrawn she sunk it down again, and up and down again....

He shuddered, and was stopped.

He sank onto his knees, eyes rolling up in a starch-white face, as the rain flailed upon his cheeks and ran in rivulets through Indian-black hair.

Down like a dog, hands outstretched, the holes in his back already washed clean...he trembled, he swayed...then staggered to his feet, face unrecognizable, ruined by rain.

Virginia—thank God!—*Virginia* had pulled herself back from the balcony. *Virginia* was screaming and lifting her skirts, trying to *step over him!*

But he was rising, trying to—

Audrey was trying to get to the old woman, to pull her away from Thorne's wrath, his vengeance, his *murderous intent*....

Audrey fell as Thorne rose. Fell against the outer stone of Whale's Turning, against the house side of the balcony. Fell spent. She was frozen from the cold and drained of all. She waited, dumb, for Thorne to kill her. She thought of her baby, crossed her arms upon her stomach to protect it... while she could....

Thorne was turning, swaying in stiff half circles, back and forth, back—eyeing, with eyes that couldn't see, Audrey... Edmunda... Aud...

The storm struck him.

He stood. Bent. *Stopped.* He leaned upon the balustrade for strength.... And slumped, and sighed, and died.

Edmunda sank, too, beside Audrey. Audrey held the older woman in weary arms.

The storm battered them.

The rain scourged them.

The hurricane ripped the room....

Hours later, in deep darkness, in after-storm calm, Bayard found them, huddled together on the balcony like cubs, mother abandoned, in a makeshift cave.

And over the balustrade, like a sack, hung the body of Thorne Larcher Cockburn come, at last, to grief....

THE SCREEN DOOR banged.

She had been waiting at the window a long time. A forever time. She could wait a little longer.... She did not have to know the news... just yet.

Someone was coming through the kitchen. She would have to face it—

"Wallace?" she said. Her voice cracked. Her voice, in a summer's day, grown frail... and old.

"Wallace," she said, hopeless. "Is that you?"

Something dropped on the kitchen table.

"Aye," said a voice. "With a six-pound blue. And I brung the butter, Martha."

Now.

Now, she could cry....

23

TORY VANVOORST SAT on the terrace of her suite in Ocean House and contemplated her guest, Dove Peerce. Tory wore sandy summer taffeta, flounced with matching lace. Dove was in her signature gray, bordered in black. They were drinking tea.

"Of course the garden is ruined," Dove was saying, so at ease, so unembarrassed, Tory thought, in her capitulation. She is doing it for Nicola, of course, as I knew she would, and yet, why can't I see that she is doing it only to please her daughter? She is very good, this one. She wants me to think I have won the war, when, really, this is only the first skirmish.

"But then what will you do, Mrs. Peerce? The wedding is upon you." Tory sipped at scalding tea.

Dove touched the onyx of her bracelet with pale nails. "It occurred to me—" She paused. "Have you ever seen such a blue sky anywhere else? Newport is heaven. Do you find it so, Victoria?"

Ah, we parry, Tory thought, and rose to the occasion. "Newport is heaven and hell together, I find, the best of both, and I wouldn't have it any other way."

"Why, what do you mean?"

Tory shrugged prettily. "Well, the troubles, Mrs. Peerce. The scandals. Just yesterday, the hurricane. Godsend was completely spared, though it got quite wet, while you lost your fountain, that exquisite fountain, and half your lawn. And as for the Lockholms—well, it's an ill wind that blows no good, I suppose. But Bayard's yacht was sunk, and his pier destroyed, and Audrey's bedroom must be completely redone, down to the walls. Dusty red, I told her. Do it in dusty red and gold. But she's leaning toward authentic restoration, an exact replica—"

"Ah, that dreadful, dreadful man," said Dove. "Celeste's beach boy. She isn't staying in town a moment. She leaves tomorrow for Switzerland, and a long, long rest. She has to think of the baby, she said."

Tory laughed. "Celeste's beach boy! You see what I mean—the scandals. He was Virginia Lockholm's beach boy, too, and once Audrey Smoke's, before she married Bay. He must have been something, that Thorne. Fortunately, I never knew him. I might have been tempted."

Dove Peerce did not pick up on that. The old Dove would have, would have spun a bon mot for Tory to repeat, crediting Dove's wit. "Poor Edmunda," Dove said, humorless, *duller than she used to be.* "She's down with pneumonia, and they say she may not survive it."

"My maid will testify that Virginia did, indeed, have a lover."

Dove blushed. It was more and more difficult—once it had been as easy as breathing—to maintain her composure when illicit love was mentioned.

"Oh, Victoria," Dove said, "please excuse me. Since Percy left, even the mention of the word 'love' reddens my face and makes me want to weep."

"Darling," said Tory, marveling. "Don't. Don't even think of your Percival as in the same world with Thorne Cockburn. The joyous thing is that Bay's troubles are over. Audrey saved him. She found Virginia's diary—the lover was named by a strange configuration. Audrey broke the code while helping with the invitations for my joust. She's a clever girl. And I feel I can take some credit in clearing Bay of all that terrible suspicion. My taking on Virginia's former maid was a stroke of luck, too, because she's confirmed to that reptilian detective all about Virginia. I know I was criticized for hiring Fanni earlier in the season, but these days I'm feeling very virtuous about it, I don't mind telling you."

And how do you like that, Dove dear?

"Edmunda killed him, you know," said Dove, composed again, nodding yes as Tory lifted the teapot to refill the Limoges cups.

"Yes. It must have been so exciting. An old crippled woman acting as the arm of God. It just goes to show what righteous rage can do."

Dove looked at Tory over the teacup rim. She had not expected such a Biblical slant to the social climber's conversation. Victoria VanVoorst, Dove thought, was not to be underestimated. She spoke well, she thought quickly, she took risk in expressing her opinion before she had heard your own. The minx was proving interesting, maybe even *fun*. She would be a beauty in any season, certainly, and if she would learn to tone down, just a bit, the *utter magnificence* of her costumes—

"He wore a piece of jewelry that convicted him right here," Dove said.

"A pendant round his neck, yes," said Tory. "So Bay's clear now. And I'm so glad. I was one of the few who remained convinced of his innocence."

"How nice you are, Victoria. I confess I thought him guilty. I knew Virginia Stotesbury, you see. And at times I thought of killing her myself. She was a greedy woman. And too much greed, well, it pulls you down, one way or another."

For a moment they sat in silence, two women, over tea, sizing each other up. Newport was beautiful, tranquil in the sun against a cloudless royal blue sky, because the great winds had driven all the clouds away.

Workmen on Thames were tending to the street damage. Townsfolk strolled the brick sidewalks. A broken-down mare, black-and-white-spotted, wearing a sea captain's hat, pulled a vegetable wagon with a spring in her old legs. Smart-coached horses acknowledged the mare, frisked with her, unaware of the differences in their social standing. Tripp Rails's motorcar was running again, fenderless after the hurricane, but running again. In the harbor, long-rigged boats swayed. In the sound, sails bulged with

friendly breezes, heading in to port. A lean dog paced be
side the pony of a pretty boy. The Reverend Elliott and his
wife stepped out of Darling's; did not look the women's
way. Graf Elliott was leaving at the end of the season. He
had a sudden—longed-for, he said—offer from New Zea
land. But Alabaster McGregor waved up to the women on
his way back to the *Daily Whirl* from who knew where.

Alabaster, as he waved, was thinking, Ah, two little
wolves in sheeps' clothing. He thought he would contact his
source again, *his secret, hard-working source*, and ask him
to try again on Victoria VanVoorst. Keep digging, he would
say. Her past is too eventless for such an up-by-her
bootstraps beauty: there must be something more. Some
thing *really juicy*, something *well hidden*.... And if Ally
McGregor didn't ferret it out this year, there was always the
next, and the one after that. Mrs. Burton VanVoorst wasn'
going anywhere. And neither was he, patient Alabaster
McGregor who always, sooner or later, *always* got his man
thank-you very much. And Dove, poor Dove. She looked
tired. A season in London would do her good. He wouldn'
miss her....

"About the wedding reception," Tory brought Dove
Peerce back to her subject. "I offer you the grounds o
Godsend, if you'd like. The landscaping was set in last week
and, as I told you, nothing was touched, hardly a leaf wa
lost. Use it, Mrs. Peerce. Burtykins and I would be hon
ored to have your daughter's happiness bless our new
home."

There was a scrap of tea left in Dove's cup. She gazed a
it, eyes lowered, held the cup in two white hands. Clariss
Rails had offered Greenscote, but it was damaged, too. And
Caroline Astor's Beechwood; well, the Peerces and th
Astors had never been really close. Whale's Turning wa
out of the question with Edmunda close to death in her bed
and parts of the second floor a wreck, not to mention a
those whales, gathered like dark spirits below WaterWalk
which wouldn't go away.... The Benson-Wards'? Impos
sible. Grim, grim, no taste at all....

Dove looked up at Tory, at a slender, firm-fleshed beauty with ebony hair and cream-ivory skin. There must be conquistador blood in the woman, she thought, or Brazilian or Argentine. Victoria kept herself well up, in the superb condition of a show girl. It was, really, the only thing—other than a murky background—that Dove had against her.

"I would never have dared to ask," Dove said. "You're truly much too kind."

"Fiddlesticks," said Tory. "I'd be delighted. After all, Mrs. Peerce, what are friends for?"

"Dove," said Dove. "You must call me Dove—all my friends do."

Tory was careful, very careful, not to let the victory spoil her smile.

CELESTE SAILED tomorrow for Gstaad. For rejuvenation, she said. She was pregnant and did not want anything to happen to the baby, no matter her husband had been a blackguard, no matter she was a widow. "I cannot bear to be here now with you," she told Bay. She said nothing to Audrey, even when Audrey tried to hold her, she shook her off. "Please," Celeste said. "Haven't you done enough to me? Please, please."

And tall and dark and elegant of head, Celeste went to pack, her maid, Joanna, frowning behind her mistress's back at the work to be done.

"Excuse her," said Bay. It's all been such a shock. Celeste is not used to... things like this."

"You came home to me," said Audrey, sitting at his feet in his room, the room they would share, man and wife, until her bedroom, *never Virginia's again*, was restored. Their bedroom, hers and Bay's....

Celeste's room, which might have been a nursery... it would stay as it was for as long as Bay's sister wanted it. The third floor was where, properly, the nursery should be, Bay said. When Celeste came back to Whale's Turning with her little one....

Unconsciously Audrey spread her palms upon her stom
ach. It was flat, and empty. There was no life inside: sh
knew it. Thorne had killed the Lockholm heir. He ha
murdered Virginia and almost wrecked Bay's name and a
his life.... And he had taken both Bay's babies, the on
before, blissful in Virginia, and the seedling, the tiny seed
ling, which, until yesterday, had slept fragile in Audrey'
womb....

All last night, Audrey had bled. Bay, himself, ha
changed the cloths for her and held her through the nigh
"There will be no bad dreams," he said. He would not le
Sawyer near her, though Sawyer cried to be allowed.

Now Audrey's womb was white and dry and empty, he
stomach cold and flat. She sat at Bay's feet, her head upo
his knee. Dr. Lake was with Edmunda, doing what h
could. When he could do no more for the elder Mrs. Lock
holm, he would come to Audrey. She was content to wai
she knew what he would tell her....

It was pleasant, this small bachelor's room of Bay's.
reminded her of home on Bridge Street. Finer, much fine
but small and, *and cozy*. She was drinking tea laced wit
brandy. The puppy, Breaker, snored on a pillow in Bay
bed.

I would like to sit like this, Audrey thought, until th
snows come and whiten the world and silence it. I woul
like to sit here with him until the whales turn far south t
winter feed and then head north to spawn....

"You came home to me," she said again, more to he
self than to Bayard. The mirror had broken, Josephine
cheval glass. So Audrey had lost her mother, too. Jose
phine would not be back; she had stayed with Audrey a
long as she could. Her daughter was grown up now, a ma
ried woman now. Audrey was on her own. She had *a
most*, even, been a mother herself....

"Tell me you love me," Audrey said, setting her chi
against his thigh, gazing up at him with midnight-blue eye
that held neither insecurity nor fear. She may not be a lad
yet, but she was on her way. And as she was, she was goo

enough; good enough to be a Lockholm, or a Smoke. To be richer or poorer....

"I love you more than life," he said, and stroked her hair. "You are all the world to me and all its treasures. Drew and I used up three horses trying to get to you. I'm sorry I was late."

"And Detective Smythe was running behind you. He thought you meant to flee, he said."

"Thank God for Jeremy Smythe. He took care of everything, even helped with the whale pup. Its flukes got tangled in the *Catbird Seat* as she went down. Do you remember, last night I told you about it."

"Tell me again."

The fire popped gently. Breezes lifted lace at the windows. It was fine in the early evening in August at Newport, though Edmunda Lockholm lay dying. Mrs. Lockholm, who hated Audrey, had saved her. The baby hadn't survived... too vulnerable, too newly sowed....

"The whales around were singing," Bay said. "It was like the end of the world. The hurricane was roaring. Past peak by the time we arrived, but we didn't know it then. Someone gave me a knife. It was black as Hades and the waters were wild. One moment mountains, tunnels the next. I looked at your windows and saw, at the balcony, what I thought was Virginia, Virginia come again to haunt me forever. I thought I was mad. I thought of the curse of Phineas Brown. I leaped from the pier into the sea."

Audrey shivered. Held close to his leg. "And the whales were singing," she said.

"And the whales were singing, keening to the music of the wind."

"I have never heard the whales sing," she said, and kissed the cloth upon his kneecap.

"It was like no sound I ever heard," he said. "Like no sound in this world. There were strange metallic-like whines and screeches and then there were bongs like bells chiming deep underwater, or chains dancing upon sunken rock. It was, somehow, hypnotic—horrible and beautiful all at once." He began combing her hair, lifting the back of it, drawing the comb through the weight, smoothing the top with his hand.

"You jumped in," she said.

"Yes, and Jeremy Smythe followed!" Audrey heard the smile in his voice. "He thought I was going to kill myself, I guess, and he was having none of that. I like our Detective Smythe, we must have him to dinner soon."

"Yes," she said. "And then?"

He stretched his legs, crossed his feet, only in socks, at the ankles. "It's hard to recall it coherently."

She waited.

"The whales' singing kept the young one calm, though it was drowning, caught in the lines. I was sure it would kill me, so great a thing, in blackest savage water. I couldn't see, I felt. Hacked at a rope, surfaced to breathe. Then down again, and up. Smythe held the ropes for me. It took a long time."

"But at last the whale was free?" The comb was gentle in her hair, as Bay would have been gentle with the whale pup, though it meant his life.

"I thought it would splash, buck at least, when I got the last rope cut loose. But it didn't. It moved off, away from me, like a ship in the night, a shadow. Then it surfaced and blew. That was what almost finished me. Smythe hauled me back to the rocks—the pier was long gone by then. The whale was wounded from the rigging, long gashes in its side...."

"Did it go to its mother?"

"I don't know," he said. "I came then in search of you."

There was a knock at the door.

"Yes," said Bay, combing Audrey's hair. "Yes, come in. What is it?"

It was Fisher. "Please come now, sir and madam," he said. "Dr. Lake asks that you both come. It is time."

DR. LAKE WAS STANDING outside Edmunda Lockholm's room.

"She has already seen Celeste," he whispered. "And she has asked to see her son now, alone."

Audrey nodded and stepped back. Bay squeezed her hand, opened the bedroom door, closed it softly behind him.

"She hasn't long," the doctor said.

Audrey nodded again.

"She will not live to see the next Lockholm heir." Dr. Lake was referring to Audrey's pregnancy. He does not know, Audrey thought, that we will have to start again.

"You won't leave before you have seen me, will you, Dr. Lake?"

"No, Mrs. Lockholm, as soon as you see Bayard's mother, I'll have a look at you. But you're strong, in good health. I don't foresee any difficulty."

"I—I bled last night, Doctor. Bay knows. He was with me."

"A lot of blood?"

"It seemed a lot to us, perhaps not so much actually."

"Well," he said, "we'll see, we'll see. Your condition is very new. That's good. Hard to dislodge new life, if it's healthy. But we'll have a look. Don't worry until you know."

"How—how is Celeste? Is she all right?"

"That one can have ten children if she wants, but she won't. She concentrates too much on her figure."

"Oh, she is so lovely, I understand how she must feel."

"Not so lovely as you, my dear, if you'll forgive my saying so."

Audrey said nothing. He is being kind, she thought. He knows I have been through so much. . . . Then she thought, but then again, maybe he means it. I shall prefer to think he means it. Why shouldn't he mean it, after all . . . ?

Bay came out of Edmunda's door, reached for Audrey's hand. "She wants you now, Audrey, darling. She's very weak. Don't be frightened if you can't hear her. Just lean close."

Audrey nodded, but she was frightened. Mrs. Lock-holm had never liked her. Mrs. Lockholm did not even re-member—or at least had never used—Audrey's name....

She expected her mother-in-law's room to be shrouded and dark, the draperies pulled against the sea. But the green draperies were pulled back in velvet bracelets, the lace cur-tains danced against low rays of sun, and the oval room, itself, was brilliantly lighted. The great, blue-crystal chan-delier blazed in flame-shaped electric candles. Matching sconces, set around the walls upon hydrangea-blue silk, added their halos, and on the tables, the many little tables, and either side of the mirrored mantel, lamps glowed. There was a small fire in the fireplace, its summer screen of gold wood, hand painted with green ribbon and bouquets of flowers, pulled back to show the dancing flares.

Hanging over Edmunda's great bed was the portrait of Virginia, Virginia looking out into a middle distance, be-yond the frame, at something that amused her—looking at Audrey, trembling, just inside Edmunda's door.

The elder Mrs. Lockholm was lying in her bed, face framed in a frilly cap. Bolstered by pillows, the face was yellow. As Audrey approached she saw blue veins, dis-tended and crooked under the strong chin, and blue veins beating at the temples.

"Mother," Audrey said, close now. She took Edmun-da's hand. It gripped her own with strength; gripped and pulled her closer.

"My dear," breathed Edmunda.

"I—I want to thank you for the help you were to me—"

"I saved you, didn't I?" The voice was low but steady. The eyes looked up, not at Audrey. The eyes were looking in the mirror above the fireplace mantle, wherein reflected was the portrait of Virginia.

"Yes," said Audrey, "you did. I hope you are better soon." She sank upon a needlepoint cushioned chair, set beside Edmunda's bed. Mrs. Lockholm, fiercely, still held her hand.

There was silence for a moment, and Audrey heard the mantel clock beating its slow crawl into eternity. She remembered once, at Mildred Falk's, another clock, in concert with her heartbeats; her heart broken then, bewildered.... Her heartbeats would be stronger now....

Edmunda spoke, pulling Audrey's hand to bring her close. "Bay says you are bringing forth an heir. I want to see it."

"Yes," said Audrey, wondering wildly what to say. She would not tell Mrs. Lockholm the baby had been lost. She and Bay would try for another....

"Show me," said Edmunda.

"The little one has not yet been born, Mother," Audrey said.

"And I'll not live to see it, I know, I know."

Audrey started to protest.

"Hush," said Edmunda. "Show me your body, girl. Let me see the next Lockholm. Let me touch it, hold it."

Edmunda released Audrey's hand.

Audrey stood, uncertain. Then, decisive, she slipped quickly out of her dressing gown and stood naked before her mother-in-law under the blaze of lights.

The older woman's head turned slowly Audrey's way. Sunken eyes appraised her. Lifted to the mantel mirror.

"I always knew," said Edmunda Lockholm, "that you were not Virginia. I only, you see, my dear, wanted you to be."

"Yes," said Audrey, her skin chilling in the breeze, flushing from the fire. "I'm sorry, Mrs. Lockholm," she said. "But I will do my best, I'll try very hard to be a good wife to Bay—"

Edmunda Lockholm waved a hand. "I want to apologize for that," she said.

"There's no need, Mother, no need—"

"I used to look like you, firm and white like you," Mrs. Lockholm said. "I was known for my beautiful white skin."

"It's still beautiful," said Audrey.

"My legs were thinner, but my waist was not as small."

"Yes, ma'am," said Audrey.

"Turn, please. Let me see your stomach in profile."

Audrey turned. There is nothing to see, she thought. There might have been yesterday, the tiniest difference, but not today....

"It will be a girl," said Edmunda, so weary. "How nice. Girls are carried low and wide, and don't show much until late. Boys show early. You carry boys high, under your heart."

Audrey said nothing. She spread her own hands on her stomach. And there was nothing, nothing but flesh flat upon her bones.

"Come close," said Edmunda. "Let me touch her, let me hold my hand against her place."

Audrey sat on Edmunda's bed, and a strong, pale hand gripped her stomach, a thick, blue-veined hand, very hot.

The old woman held her hand on Audrey's body. Neither spoke. In a while Edmunda smiled at her. "I am blessing the coming Miss Lockholm," she said. "I am wishing her beauty and good fortune."

Audrey was crying. It was hard to bear, so much love after such indifference.

Edmunda's hand dropped away. "Thank you, my dear. Now, for goodness' sake, get dressed again. I have something to give you."

Audrey dressed, tears she couldn't stop spotting her ivory silk. "You have given me this time with you, Mrs. Lockholm, I don't want—"

"Raise me a little, dear."

Audrey did, lifting her mother-in-law, pulling a pillow deeper behind her head.

"Yes, that's better. Go to my dressing table. You'll see a box, a golden jewel box—"

"Yes," Audrey said.

"There are initials set into the lid on a brass plaque. Read them out to me."

The box was large. The letters, scripted fine, etched into brass, read ASL.

"Oh!" said Audrey, stunned. "I—I don't understand." She turned to the old woman in the bed. "What—"

Something rattled in Edmunda Lockholm's throat. "You see," said the old woman, "it is as I told you. I always knew who you were. That is the cache for my pearls. I had the initials changed when you married.... They are your pearls now, Audrey, you are the only Mrs. Lockholm now. Give them, when it's time, to the woman your son marries...when you have a son. Promise me."

"But, Mrs. Lockholm...Celeste! Celeste is your daughter—"

Edmunda Lockholm sighed. "Celeste's husband, when she finds him, will bejewel her in his family name. These are Lockholm pearls, my dear.... Bay can explain it all to you."

"I—I don't know what to say," said Audrey. "Except get better, get well, Mother. Wear these pearls for years and years to come—"

"I do not have an hour," said Edmunda. "Now tell me, come close again and tell me...what will you name your daughter on her christening day?"

Audrey had not thought of names. She crossed to the bedside, sat again on the side chair. Then, "Wysong Smoke Lockholm," she said, deciding. "For your maiden name and mine."

Mrs. Lockholm's head dipped and her eyes closed. Audrey thought she should call Dr. Lake—

"Reverse it," murmured Edmunda. She took Audrey's hand again. The grip was weaker now. "Call her Smoke Wysong Lockholm, my dear, and pray she is beautiful."

"Yes, ma'am," said Audrey. "Yes, Mother, I will."

Edmunda's hand relaxed, fell away. "Will you call my son back now. I want both of you to come with me, to take me there."

"We can't come all the way," said Audrey, overcome. "But we'll come with you as far as we can."

"Yes," whispered Edmunda. "Call Bay. I can see the gates now. It's not far at all.... It's ... very close."

Audrey ran for Bayard. He was with her then, both of them, either side of Edmunda's light-flooded bed.

"Dr. Lake has gone for Celeste, Mother," said Bay.

"She is not to come," said Mrs. Lockholm, shaking her head, her eyes closed, her fingers weak in her son's hand and in Audrey's. "Celeste and I have said goodbye. She forgives me killing the beach boy, but she is not to be here for this."

Bay smoothed the old woman's forehead, kissed her dry cheek. "Tell us, Mother, what you see. And is it beautiful?"

Edmunda's eyes were open again, wide open and sparkling. She fought to sit higher. Bay bolstered her with pillows.

"Bayard, Bayard, darling," she said, excited. "I can see the gates—all wavy.... Just like the view from my windows here. And—oh look, there is William, dear sweet William! And—"

She grasped both their hands. She was strong again, young again. She laughed a girlish laugh. "And, oh look, oh look, Bayard, there is Jeoffry, too! There's Jeoffry, too, standing just inside.... He's with William, they're holding hands, holding out their arms.... Oh Jeoffry...." Weak, she sank back, deep into her bed. "Oh, Jeoffry," Edmunda said, smiling, "I've waited for you so long...."

Audrey looked at Bay across the coverlet. He was closing, with trembling fingertips, his mother's blue-gray eyes.

"William was my father," Bay said. "I do not know who Jeoffry was, nor ever want to."

He set the jewel box in Audrey's hands and led her from the room.

24

THERE WAS SO MUCH, then, to be done. The funeral arrangements to be made, no fanfare, immediate burial. Thorne had been cremated a few days before—Detective Jeremy Smythe, alone, in official attendance. Edmunda Lockholm was buried in the Farewell Street cemetery the evening of the day she died. Celeste insisted on the next day's early train to New York to catch the ocean liner to Switzerland, no matter the scandal, no matter what people thought.

"I must go immediately," she said, "or lose my mind."

Bay gave her no argument.

And there was Tory, come to pay her respects and to tell Audrey, after condolences, that Dove Peerce had visited her in person, and that Ally would ride on the morrow on his golden horse, and present invitations to the ladies Peerce to the VanVoorst joust and ball. "Not only that," crowed Tory, beautiful in black, "but Nicola's wedding reception will inaugurate Godsend. I'm made, Audrey, darling, socially Burtykins and I are made!" And there were legal matters, Astin Forbes with papers for Bay to look over and sign, and Edmunda's will to be found, and Zella hysterical at the loss of her mistress. There was the puppy to be fed....

It was the next morning before Dr. Lake, who stayed the night, was able to examine Audrey. She hadn't minded. He would only confirm what she knew already. And that grief, she thought, could well wait, well wait....

But then the time came and she lay on Bay's bachelor bed, finally, being examined by Dr. Lake.

To ease the pain she thought of other things.

Of the hurricane and the curse of Phineas Brown. For it had come to pass, had been fulfilled.... And Bay was free now—they were all free of it at last.

The thought seemed to come as a revelation; come so clear as she closed her eyes against the intimate probings of Dr. Lake and the push and pinch of cold instruments in places of her body she had never seen....

She tried to think of other things, of happy things, the future, hers and Bay's—and, suddenly, in the dark of her eyelids, the thought came: *Captain Larcher.*

The curse had been thrown at Bay's great-grandfather's children, yes, but it had not been meant for them at all.... The Negro, unjustly hanged, had been wrong. It was not the Lockholm line that was accursed. It was Abel Larcher's; he, the captain of the *Quicksilver....* He the jury, judge and hangman....

She had lost her baby. Bay had lost his first wife, two potential heirs and a mother. Celeste had lost a husband. But misfortunes came into a life, a home, a family.... And the curse of Phineas Brown had not been meant for the Lockholms, after all....

It had been meant for Abel Larcher.

Captain Larcher, right-hand man of John Bayard Lockholm I. Captain Larcher who had hanged the Negro, Phineas Brown. Old John Bayard I was gone by then, *murdered, they said*, fatally lost at sea. It was Abel Larcher who blamed Phineas, tried him for murder, found him guilty, strung him up. Phineas, *free man*, who had smuggled himself aboard to steal back his wife, taken—illegally taken—into slavery...so Audrey had heard the story. John Bayard Lockholm I hadn't been the murderer of Phineas, he had been the *murdered* one, thrown overboard for lying with Phineas's woman: so Abel Larcher said.

Always *Abel Larcher.*

And Thorne *Larcher* Cockburn...of course, of course.

She had never thought of it before. Thorne's love of boats and sea. His desire to be a sea captain, an entrepreneur, owner of Sea Trains, ferrying the rich. As, once upon a time, *his* great-grandfather, Abel Larcher, had ferried slaves from Africa, bought with profits of Jamaican rum....

Well, the curse of Phineas Brown had been fulfilled. Thorne Larcher Cockburn lived no more. In the storm he had come to grief...while the whales sang, gathered for the retribution below WaterWalk....

As soon as Dr. Lake released her, Audrey would run to Bay and tell him. We can start free, start over, she would say. The curse has been lifted, the doom foretold fulfilled....

"This will hurt, Mrs. Lockholm," she heard the doctor say.

"All right," she said. And it did hurt. It felt like tiny teeth biting, tearing, sniping....

"Good girl, it's over."

He was swabbing her with alcohol. It stung. "Would you like to see the reason for your bleeding?"

She wanted to see nothing, only Bay.

"A wood splinter, my lovely." Dr. Lake was holding, in a tweezer, a tiny shaft of pine. "Probably from the frame of your cheval glass...all gone now. Well, time to close up shop."

He was washing his implements in a basin, drying them himself.

Audrey sat up, swung her legs over the side of the bed and let her dress fall to cover her. "But Dr. Lake," she said, "the baby...the baby..."

He was rolling down his sleeves, fitting the enamel links, fox heads with emerald eyes, into his cuffs. "Oh yes, Audrey, the baby. I don't know how to tell you—"

Ah, she thought. Just tell. Don't stand on ceremony, *please*....

"And maybe I shouldn't," he said. "But, what the heck, I'll take the chance."

"Please, Dr. Lake, just tell me, please."

He shrugged into his jacket. "Twins," he said. "Quite healthy. Doing well. Expect them in late March, in time for Easter."

"Twins?" She couldn't have heard correctly. *Quite healthy, doing well....*

"Twins, I'm afraid. Twice as much bother, but twice as much fun. Or so I was taught to say."

Twins!

"Healthy, you say, Doctor? Doing quite well?"

"Far as I can tell. There's nothing to see yet, nothing to hear, but if I know my obstetrics—twins, Audrey, I know the signs. And you, you're doing well, too. Oh, you'll be sore for a week or so, but other than that, you're right as rain, my dear...unfortunate metaphor under recent circumstances—"

She was running from the room.

"Bay!" she called.

He was not there.

She ran down the great steps, shouting for him. "Bay! Bay!"

Fisher presented himself, Fisher with a band of black around his uniform arm. "Madam, Mr. Lockholm is behind the house, out on WaterWalk, I think, waiting for you. He wants you to join him, asked that I tell you as soon as you were free—"

She was gone, running through the grand hall, familiar now, around the sweep of stair, out onto the lower loggia, under its arches, down the marble steps. She was running over soggy, muddy lawn, still damp with storm rain, sweet with the scent of flowers. She was at the wall, where it broke, and to the right, onto the rock-strewn path, barren of townsfolk now that it was torn and tangled with branch and seaweed—the sea had tossed its litter high. There was work to be done, the clearing...but she was up and over the barriers, she was at *their* rock—

And there Bay was, waiting for her, smoking a cigar. "Smoke," he said, as she ran into his arms. "I do enjoy a good smoke. And I have something to show you, love."

She wasn't listening.

"Bay," she said, "Bay, dearest darling, did you hear?" She was laughing, so excited. There was a flutter in her belly as though the babies felt the jolt of her joy in new blood and were gleeful, too, gleeful without knowing—yet—what glee was....

He held her. He kissed her. He turned her shoulders to the sea. "Look, Audrey Smoke. Look, love, the whales. They're turning, they're heading out to sea."

She looked. The bay was calm and fine. The waters *Newport blue*, rippled with lacy whitecaps.

And the whales, massive, impassive, in a long, gray line, stretched away from the cliff below WaterWalk, swam solemn in a ponderous parade, single file, out toward the ocean where it wound, wild ribbon, around the world. Great ones, little ones, a hundred, they flowed to where the sound curved beyond Audrey's sight.

Bay pointed. "There, Audrey, the one behind the white-flippered one blowing rainbows in the air—do you see?"

"Yes," she breathed, "I see." She held him.

"That's the pup I saved. It's going to make it. See, now it's rolling, see the gashes on its side?"

There were three long tears, but healing already; three gashes that formed a figure like an alphabet letter, an elongated A.

"That's your calf, Audrey. When it returns next year, we will know it. It will be a giant by then."

"Will it come back, Bay? After its trouble here, will it come back to visit?"

There was such joy in her heart, she thought she couldn't hold all the happiness.

"At season's end, the whales turn, my darling. At season's beginning, they return. That's their way. And that's why we live here, Mrs. Lockholm, so we can watch them, and have them with us for a while."

Have them, she thought. Regal visitors, until they turn again, turn back, turn away. And then we wait for them to come again, to return, glad tidings....

"The curse," she said. "It's been lifted, Bay. I can explain it all to you."

His arm was around her waist. She leaned upon his chest, felt the soft-rough of linen lapel against her cheek. A lock of his hair was disarranged on his forehead. It fell forward, windblown, like a boy's.

"Yes," he said. "I think you're right. The curse of Phineas Brown is lifted."

"And everything will be all right from now on, won't it? We're going to have, Dr. Lake just told me, twins."

"Everything is all right for now, at least," he said. "For this season."

And together, in bright morning, they watched the whales turn toward a rising sun.

The *Choice* for Bestsellers
also offers a handsome and
sturdy book rack for your
prized novels at $9.95 each.
Write to:

The Choice for Bestsellers
120 Brighton Road
P.O. Box 5092
Clifton, NJ 07015-5092
Attn: Customer Service Group